Flightless Falcon

Also by Mickey Zucker Reichert
in Victor Gollancz/Millennium

The Renshai Trilogy
THE LAST OF THE RENSHAI
THE WESTERN WIZARD
CHILD OF THE THUNDER

The Renshai Chronicles
BEYOND RAGNAROK
PRINCE OF DEMONS
CHILDREN OF WRATH

SPIRIT FOX with Jennifer Wingert

Flightless Falcon

MICKEY ZUCKER REICHERT

VICTOR GOLLANCZ
LONDON

The right of Miriam S. Zucker MD to be identified as the author
of this work has been asserted by her in accordance
with the Copyright, Designs and Patents Act 1988.

This edition first published in Great Britain in 2000 by

Victor Gollancz
An imprint of Orion Books Ltd
Orion House, 5 Upper St Martin's Lane, London WC2H 9EA

To receive information on the Millennium list, e-mail us at:
smy@orionbooks.co.uk

A CIP catalogue record for this book is available
from the British Library

Printed in Great Britain by
Clays Ltd, St Ives plc

To Carl Halpern,
Still quick-witted at 97, he finally got his wings.

And to Evelyn Migdal

Even a writer's words cannot describe the
generosity of spirit that came so naturally to
these two, their simple and never-lapsing
kindness. Both left the world a far better place.

ACKNOWLEDGMENTS

I would like to thank the following people:
Mark Moore, Sheila Gilbert, Jonathan Matson,
Jo Fletcher, Sandra Zucker, Jennifer Wingert
and, of course, the PenDragons.

Flightless Falcon

Prologue

COOL, dank air jelled the sweat on Tamison's brawny arms, and the flickering light of the mining lanterns painted shifting checkers of shadow on stone. Clutching his pick in blistered hands, he raised it for a strike. Even as he balanced his weight onto the stubby legs that well-suited his miner's lineage, a clang of metal against stone echoed through the caverns, followed by a thump and his father's curse. Tamison froze. This was his first day down in the mines, and he could not yet read the urgency or normalcy of his father's profanity.

Sutannis squeezed Tamison's shoulder, calluses scratching damp flesh.

Reassured by his older brother's touch, Tamison glanced into eyes as dark as their father's, dark like those of nearly all of the citizens of Lathary. Sweat-plastered black hair flopped across Sutannis' broad forehead, and he shook his head to indicate that nothing seemed seriously wrong. Like Tamison, he had inherited the distinctive miner's physique of his father's side: short-torsoed and -legged with a powerful upper body. In fact, Tamison found it difficult to see any of their willowy Carsean mother's influence in his brother, aside from an unflappable and patient gentleness. In contrast, his own mouse-brown hair framed a face more softly contoured than his father's and brother's coarse-featured oval, and he had inherited his mother's gray eyes.

The voice of Frandall, their uncle, boomed through the cavern. "Uland?"

Tamison's father appeared from the darkness ahead. As Uland blocked, then stepped into, the lantern light, Tamison caught a glimpse of the two other men beyond him. Though not related by blood, they seemed nearly as familiar, coworkers of his father's since before Tamison's birth. "Broke my damned pick." Uland flung the notched head to the stone, followed by the shattered remains of its haft. "Just tapped a new vein, too."

"We'll handle it," one of the men called from behind, deepening Uland's frown. Their team would get credit no matter who pieced out the silver, but Uland loved the thrill of defining a new vein. As the discoverer, he had first right to that reward.

"Hilarious," Uland called back.

Knowing what would happen next, Tamison shrugged free of his brother's hold and feigned engrossment in his own area of exploration. Since joining his father's team, he had done little but chip at stone already inspected by the more experienced miners. Even Sutannis, only three and a half years older, had uncovered flecks of metal that had led to a substantial find.

"Tamison."

Tamison froze. Screwing his face into the expression of defiance created and perfected by adolescents, he slowly turned to face his father.

Uland waited until his younger son met his gaze before speaking again. "Give me your pick. Then start back and get—"

Before Tamison could stop himself, he whined, "Why me? Why am I always the one—"

"Tamison!" Uland snapped, cheeks reddening in the torchlight. "You will not interrupt me. And you *will* do as I say."

As Uland's tone hardened and his volume increased, Tamison's blood heated. "It's not fair." The words exploded from him, again without thought or intention. In the last year, everything his father said and did seemed to bother him. Dropping his own pick, he kicked it toward Uland. The implement skidded across the rocky floor, forcing the elder a step backward to spare his booted feet. Tamison whirled, his father's dark stare like a dagger in his back.

Sutannis' voice sounded little louder than a whisper in comparison. "It's all right. You can use mine." He tapped Tamison's balled hand with the haft of his own pick. "I'll go get a new one."

Tamison's rage fled as abruptly as it had risen, replaced by nearly fathomless guilt. His toes ached from slamming against the heavy pick. He appreciated his brother's sacrifice, but it only made him feel worse: useless, unappreciative, and mean. He would trade all of his serenely exotic features for a temperament as gentle as his brother's.

"Thank you, Sutannis." His oldest son's sacrifice softened Uland as well. "But I asked Tamison to do it." He added forcefully, "And he will."

Tamison fought down another flash of anger, successfully this time. Without a word, he snatched up a lantern and started down the cavern to where they had left their extra tools and food.

His father's words chased him, "What's wrong with that boy?"

One of Uland's friends came to Tamison's defense. "He's fifteen."

Sutannis spoke next, in a low tone clearly intended not to carry, but the strange acoustics of the tunnels funneled it plainly to Tamison's ears. "Three years ago, I wasn't easy to get along with either."

Thanks, Sutannis. Tamison managed a smile as he continued past an indentation hacked out just that morning before the granite thwarted them.

Uland grunted. "You were never like him."

Frandall loosed a loud guffaw. "Maybe not, Uland, but you were. When you were his age, you told Papa you weren't going to mine. You wanted to be a minstrel, remember?"

Sutannis snorted, laughter badly suppressed.

"You're a liar!" Uland shouted.

Frandall did not let up. "You don't remember, do you?"

"Of course, I don't. It never happened."

"You could barely get those stubby fingers around a fret, and you've got a voice like a cow with quinsy. But you were going to be a minstrel, all right." Frandall chuckled, and the others joined him.

Resentment fully abated, Tamison tried not to take too much pleasure in his father's discomfort.

As usual, Frandall continued longer than he should have. "Papa stormed around for days, and you just kept on banging on that out-of-tune lute with the missing string. He was so red-faced and hot, I thought his hair would catch fire. Maybe it's a second son thing . . ."

Tamison glided out of range of the men's voices. Needing to hear, he backpedaled, just in time to miss most of his father's reply.

Uland made a dismissive sound. "Get back to work."

A moment later, steel rang irregularly against stone, and Tamison skittered toward the waiting packs. The exchange had fully calmed his irritation, making it seem childishly silly. He could not explain his outbursts any better than his father, but he found some solace in the realization that it probably bore some relation to his age. That meant it would pass, and he could gain control of emotions that sometimes seemed more suited to a five-year-old than a young man of fifteen. He only hoped the similarities between their adolescent years did not mean he would grow up with the disposition of his father.

An unfamiliar noise rumbled through the cavern, followed by a shrieked warning. The ground trembled. The air filled with a horrible tearing that drowned all other sound. *What's happening?* Thrown suddenly to his knees, Tamison scrambled back toward his team as the tunnel bucked and rolled like a ship in a gale. Stone pounded around him. A chunk slammed his shin, shocking pain through his entire leg. Lamp oil splashed his face in boiling pinpoints. Screaming, he flung himself into the blind alcove, pawing at his cheeks. The pain died as terror flared. The darkness hid the barrage of stone that thundered through his hearing, and grit stung his eyes. He pressed his back to the wall, its jagged surface bruising his spine as tons of shifting rock filled the corridor in front of him.

Then, abruptly, silence fell. Pinned against the hollow that had rescued him from being crushed, Tamison stared into impenetrable darkness and heard nothing but an unsteady ringing in his ears. Soon, even that disappeared, leaving him in tomblike solitude.

"Papa!" Tamison shouted. His cry fell like lead, strangely solid after the seemingly limitless echo of the open mines. "Sutannis!" Again, his call went nowhere. Mindless panic gripped him. He screamed repeatedly, writhing and clawing against a press of stone that left little room for movement. He struggled and screeched until his voice went raw, his fingernails ragged, and every part of him felt bruised and abraded. Frantic tears followed, soothing the burning in his eyes, though it granted him no vision. Not a thread of light penetrated the depths of his prison.

"Papa." *He'll come.* Comforted by inexplicable certainty, Tamison calmed. *Papa will find me.*

Hours passed. Tamison hunched in his crypt, wishing he could see or hear something, anything, through the crush of stone. Attempts to dig his way free had only sent cascades of rock tumbling onto him. Once a hand became hopelessly pinned, he stopped. He shouted at intervals, hoping someone might hear, and slept when exhaustion overtook him.

Tamison jarred awake, uncertain what had startled him. He could not guess how long he had slept, but shards of grit filled the corners of his eyes. His mouth felt parched, and his stomach grumbled an angry protest. *I'm going to die.* The thought caught him off guard. Once it did, he wondered why he had not thought of it sooner. Regrets followed. He hated that his last words to his father had been resentful and harsh, rued that he hadn't worked harder to become like his near-perfect older brother, and loathed himself for coveting Sutannis' skills and virtues instead of cultivating his own. His thoughts turned to his mother and sister. At least he had left them with pleasant good-byes. He sighed, then cringed at the memory. He had also delivered the usual trite vow to remain careful and come home safely. *Sorry, Mama. I wish more than anything I could keep that promise.*

Abruptly, it occurred to Tamison that, in his world of numb darkness, the only thing that could have awakened him was a sound. "Hey!" His voice emerged as a strangled croak. He cleared his throat, gathering as much saliva as he could muster into his dry, sticky mouth. "Hey!"

A muffled yell came in glorious response, "Is someone there?"

Tamison trembled with excitement. Hope blazed anew. "I'm here! Help me! Please, help!"

Another voice joined the first, "Don't move. We'll get you out of there."

Tamison bowed his head in appreciation to the gods.

The first voice: "Are you alone?"

"Yes." Tamison barely made a sound. Again, he lubricated his tongue as much as possible. "Yes! I was with Uland's team." He added, to put his father at ease, "I'm his son." Concern sparked then, "Is *he* all right?" Tamison assumed without need to question that the cave-in had buried only himself, but he now realized the others would have had to climb past the rubble.

A worrisome pause followed, then: "We're going to get you out of there."

The repetition made no sense. Assuming his rescuers had misheard him, Tamison asked louder, "My father. My brother. My uncle. Are they all right?"

Another agonizingly long hush occurred before a fresh voice replied, "They're fine. They're all fine. Worry about yourself."

Tamison loosed a pent-up breath he did not even realize he'd held. His throat felt as dry as the grit that coated him completely, and a fire seemed to have sprung up in his eyes and mouth. His limbs felt detached, and cramps racked his lower back.

The sounds of chipping and rolling stone filled the ensuing hours, pierced by an occasional cry. Tamison slipped in and out of consciousness, trusting the men who had come to save him, his fate beyond his control.

A loud, close voice calling his name jerked Tamison awake. The movement sent pain howling through him, and he grunted in anguish. Every part seemed sore, every limb kinked, and his back throbbed sharply. He tried to reply, but his tongue stuck to the floor of his mouth. He managed only a wordless noise of acknowledgment.

"I can see him," a man said.

Tamison opened his eyes to a dry blur of patchy grayness and light. He heard motion, then another man spoke, "There he is. Careful, now."

Stone thumped and scratched against stone, raising a cloud of dust that triggered a weak fit of coughing. As the rubble dislodged, Tamison found room to shift one arm. The movement soothed its cramps but incited the more biting pain of restored blood flow. He screamed, but no sound emerged from his parched throat.

"Easy. Easy, now." The unplaceably familiar voice was accompanied by a pair of enormous, work-hardened hands that eased Tamison from his prison. Though careful, the transition ignited a frenzied flurry of anguish. Blinded as much by discomfort as the brightness of the lanterns, Tamison closed his eyes and sagged into his savior's arms. "It's Uncle Lorran, Tamison. You're going to be fine."

Tamison forced a nod. Only a year younger than his brother Uland, Lorran had taken the week off to rest a bad cough. Otherwise, he would have accompanied his nephews and brothers.

"I'll take him up," Lorran said to someone else. "Keep looking for the others."

Others. The word failed to register. Tamison lay still, eyes tightly shut, gritting his teeth against each jarring footfall.

Every hacking cough of his uncle's further fueled his suffering, but he did not have the strength or will to complain.

After what felt like an eternity, fresh air channeled into Tamison's lungs, and he heard the steady rumble of voices. He opened his eyes. Sunlight glared in, forcing him to snap them closed again, but not before glimpsing the worried face of his mother above him.

"Tamison," she said, voice breathy with tears. "Oh, Tamison."

Lorran laid Tamison on grass warmed by spring sunshine, and his mother immediately wrapped her arms around him. Shadowed by her presence, he peeled apart his lids once more, his vision striped by gritty, gluelike strands. His ten-year-old sister, Sheldora, also knelt at his side.

"Water," Tamison forced out.

Anticipating, Lorran propped his nephew against one knee and pressed a flask to Tamison's lips. Pure, cold liquid filled his mouth, sweeter than fresh honey. He gulped greedily, with a sloppiness that sloshed water over feverish cheeks and burning eyes as well. He followed the flask with his head as it retreated.

"Not too much at once," Lorran insisted.

Vitality returned with the water. Attention fixed longingly on the flash just out of reach, Tamison spoke. "Where's Papa and Sutannis?"

Tamison's mother lowered her head. Sheldora looked toward the caverns. Lorran replied. "They're still looking."

The answer made no sense. Tamison rubbed filth from his eyes. "Looking for what?"

"Frandall, Uland, and the others."

Mind slowed by exhaustion and thirst, Tamison could not grasp the obvious. "I don't understand."

Lorran coughed, then looked nervously at Tamison's

mother. "They haven't . . . found . . . your father and brother yet."

"Haven't found . . . ?" Tamison reached for the flask, and Lorran surrendered it. He gulped down several more swallows before continuing. "Then how did the others know they were fine?"

"They didn't," Lorran admitted, still studying Tamison's mother. "They told you that so you wouldn't give up."

Tamison choked on a mouthful of water, hacking louder than his uncle. "Papa and Sutannis are still down there?"

Sheldora clung to their mother, who burst into a fresh round of tears.

Tamison stumbled to his feet, awkward as a colt in its second hour of life. "I have to find them."

Tamison's mother moved with him. "Be still, Tamison."

Lorran seized an arm. "You're not well enough to go anywhere."

Tamison tried to shake them off, without success. Dizziness crushed down on him in a savage dance of black-and-white spots, and he waited for the wave to pass before speaking. "I'm the only one who knows where they are."

"The mine-fore knows their assignment." Lorran pressed Tamison back to the ground. "There's nothing you can do."

A weak struggle gained Tamison nothing, and he sank back into his mother's grip. Spotting the flask beside him, he snatched it up for another drink.

Lorran allowed a few more swallows before taking it away.

Water dribbling down his chin, Tamison turned his gaze to the mouth of the mine. Great piles of rock rimmed the opening. Men meandered in and out like ants reclaiming a nest, tossing more rubble onto the stacks. The wives of his father's companions waited, one clenching her hands to bloodless fists, the other pacing rapidly. Frandall's frail wife sat with her face buried in her hands, rocking silently. They had no children.

"How long was I down there?" Tamison asked softly, fearful of the answer. He had never heard of anyone surviving longer than three days without water. Even if his father, brother, and uncle could find dribbles on walls and ceiling, the rubble would likely pin them down . . . if the rocks hadn't simply crushed them. Tamison felt lucky to have had an alcove to shield him from the bulk of the cave-in.

"Two days." Lorran finally met Tamison's gaze. He shook his head slightly, demonstrating a hopelessness he would not dare speak aloud.

"I need to help." Tamison leaned toward the caverns, immediately stopped by uncle and mother. "I have to . . ." He did not know how to finish, so he repeated, "I have to."

"You can't."

"I can't." Tamison found himself incapable of tears, though his uncle, mother, and sister shed enough for him as well. A question filled his mind and would not be banished. It seemed disrespectfully trivial to ask, but he could not escape the need to know. "Did . . . did Papa really want to be a minstrel?"

Lorran rallied a smile. "Where did you hear that?" Before Tamison could explain, his uncle continued. "He said so, but I think he was just trying to provoke *our* father." The tight grin grew more genuine. "It worked, too. But Uland loved mining. Always did."

Tamison nodded, reaching for the flask in his uncle's hand. He had heard his father's excited descriptions at the dinner table, had seen the light in his dark eyes whenever he discovered a vein. Like nearly all of his ancestors, Uland had lived to mine . . .

. . . and died for it as well.

Three years passed in an agonzing crawl as each of Tamison's days became a battle for his sanity and his family's subsistence. He still felt more like a lost child than a young man of eighteen, the default head of a household. During the first six months after the mining accident, the guild and Uncle Lorran had kept Tamison, Sheldora, and their mother in the simple comfort Uland had once provided. Then Lorran's attention turned to drink and his own family's struggles. The guild lapsed into the hardships left by the loss of its most valuable mine. Since then, Tamison's family had slid gradually into poverty, selling their keepsakes for food, wearing their clothes until threadbare, delaying repairs to the cottage. Loyal to Uland, the guild had trusted Tamison's promises that he would eventually return to the mines, allowing him to perform only the aboveground, ancillary duties reserved for apprenticed children. Every month, he attempted the caverns again. Every try, he was assailed by a savage anxiety that sent him racing for the light in a frantic skitter, his heart pounding, his thoughts in wild disarray, his breath a desperate panting.

The very thought sent panic exploding through Tamison. Now, safely seated on the bench in the center of his family's cottage, he chased wits dizzied near to madness. Entombed again in memory, he moaned and sprang to his feet.

His mother's voice wafted from the bedroom. "Tamison? Are you all right?"

Her voice shook Tamison free of his waking nightmare. His heart hammered, and he had to swallow several times to keep his answer honest. "I'm fine, Mama. Just thinking."

"Think of something else. Something happy."

Tamison wrestled up a smile. She could find the good in

anything, a trait he did not share. Saddled with the burdens
of a mother and sister, unable to perform his life's work, he
shouldered a commitment that grew heavier with each passing day. He carried bad news he had not yet delivered, worried she might grow weaker, concerned even her positive
spirits might shatter under one more calamity. "Something
happy," he repeated. "I'll try."

"How about this," his mother started, her voice stronger
than Tamison had heard it in months. "Your sister's getting
married."

"Sheldora?" The name was startled from him. He drifted
to the doorway.

Tamison's mother lay on her pallet, blankets drawn to her
neck. Her willowy features seemed positively pale, and white
streaked her hair. Her eyes lay deeply recessed, but her lips
formed a gleeful smile that somehow managed to light her
features. "Sheldora?" she mimicked. "Of course, Sheldora.
Do you have another sister I don't know about?"

"But . . ." Tamison stared. "But . . . she's only thirteen."

The smile never dimmed. "Young, but not an unheard of
age to marry. I was fourteen when your father and I—"

"Who?" Tamison interrupted, unable to imagine his sister as anything but a child. "Who is she marrying?"

The smile crept upward to touch his mother's eyes. Little
had kindled them in the past several months. "Rannoh,
Charltun's son."

Tamison bullied past shock and eased himself against the
doorframe. He processed the name until a mental picture
rose: a large-boned, well-muscled man with rough hands and
a gruff manner, the owner of an upstart tavern he named for
himself. "Mama, he's *old*."

"He's twenty-three, Tamison."

"Shel's thirteen," he reminded.

"I'm well aware of your sister's age." The grin finally

wilted. "Rannoh's older because he put off marriage to get his business started. He's dedicated and a good provider. I think that's admirable, don't you?"

Tamison cringed, swallowing hard. Though surely unintended, the guilt inspired by his mother's words pained him. *Dedicated. A good provider. Exactly what I'm not.*

When Tamison did not answer the mostly rhetorical question, his mother continued, "Making a new business work while so many established ones languish shows a keen mind. Competence. A hard-working attitude. That kind of devotion is exactly what Sheldora needs. What she *deserves.*" His mother seemed almost to be pleading, her need for him to express approval, even joy, for Sheldora's marriage oddly desperate.

Rattled by his mother's clear need, Tamison forced himself to reconsider. He did not know Rannoh well, only stories that the barkeep pursued money ruthlessly and never shied from physical conflict. A friend had spoken of troublemakers whom Rannoh had personally ejected from his tavern. Still deeply concerned, Tamison asked softly, "What if he . . . hurts . . . her?"

The mother's smile returned, more subtly; her eyes gained the serious glint her expression otherwise denied. "That's what big brothers are for."

Surely, she meant to be soothing, but her answer put the burden squarely back on Tamison. He pursed his lips. "I'm the man of the house, aren't I?"

"Yes, dear. Of course you are."

"Shouldn't Rannoh have asked me? Don't I get any say in this?"

Tamison's mother closed her eyes. For a moment, she looked as peaceful as death, her features weathered and waxlike. Then, her lips parted again. "Tamison, the days of requesting a woman's hand from her father were waning when

I married. And you have to remember, Rannoh's four and a half years older than you. It would have been . . . well, awkward."

Sheldora's only thirteen. The detail refused to budge, and Tamison remained as firmly entrenched. "So, I don't get a say."

"I'm listening. What do you want to say?"

Tamison studied his mother, jaw set. "Does it matter?"

"Of course."

"If I forbid it, does that mean Sheldora won't marry Rannoh?"

His mother's gray eyes met Tamison's, so much like his. For the first time, he noticed a deep, watery fatigue there. His own concerns for his family, the challenges he faced daily, had kept him from realizing the truth. His mother was gravely ill. Likely, she would not last the winter. Tears stung his eyes at the understanding he had so long denied. Grief, stress, and poverty had weakened her to illness, and his meager efforts had done little to lift the strain. Suddenly, he understood. She wanted Sheldora married and secure, before she died. Likely, she wished the same for him as well.

Tamison's mother dodged his question with one of her own, "*Are* you forbidding their marriage?"

Truth continued to seep, unwelcome, into Tamison's consciousness. Since the irreparable collapse of Lathary's silver mine, all of its citizens had suffered. As the economy dwindled, many of the best artisans and merchants had abandoned the city for more affluent places. Sheldora did deserve a man who could create his own prosperity in the worst of times, a hard worker and a good provider, a husband who could support her when her brother could not.

Yet she also deserved a life of fondness and warmth. He doubted the tough barman could supply her that. "Does she . . . does Sheldora . . . love him?"

The color returned to Tamison's mother's cheeks. "She says she does."

Tamison ran a hand across his scalp, tousling his mousy hair. "Is she happy about . . . this?"

"Yes."

Tamison nodded, forcing a smile of his own. "Good. Then I won't stand in their way."

A knock on the door obscured his mother's reply. Glad for the interruption, Tamison turned and trotted across the bare planks. Tripping the latch, he pulled the panel open.

Cool, night air funneled in, driving a shiver through Tamison. Linnry stood on the threshold, the oval of her face appearing even longer than usual, stretching her fine features. The black hair that fell to her shoulders lay in tangled disarray. Red lines spidered through her enormous eyes, and the lids appeared puffy and flushed. He had known her for as long as he could remember, a friend only a year younger than himself. Her father had discovered the silver mine that Uland, Sutannis, and Frandall had worked. Her mother had succumbed at her birth, and her father never remarried. His discovery of the mine had brought their small family from obscurity to wealth, but the family fortune had died with Uland and the others. As the money dwindled, so did her father's friends and contacts. A month ago, he had committed suicide. Tamison had seen little of Linnry since.

Her appearance distressed him. "Linnry?"

Linnry threw herself into Tamison's arms with unexpected fury. The force sent him stumbling backward, and he maneuvered wildly back to the door. They had not yet resorted to scarce firewood, and he dared not let the chill fully invade the newly caulked chinking.

Linnry sobbed. Fighting for balance, Tamison hooked his toes around the bottom edge of the door and kicked it shut. The clumsy maneuver worried further at his equilibrium. He struggled to remain standing, lost the battle, and toppled. Linnry fell on top of him. Her hair glided like silk across her face, smelling of lavender and night wind. Her cheek felt cold against his, but the warmth of her body raised a heat that surprised him. He had never thought of Linnry in that way before. She had always seemed more like a sister.

Climbing off Tamison, Linnry sank to the floor and wept.

Tamison clambered to his knees beside his sobbing friend and embraced her firmly. She shuddered, burying her face in the thin fabric of his shirt. He knew his mother could hear them and surely wondered about the goings on in the next room, but she kept silent, giving him as much privacy as she could in the small cottage.

For a long time, Tamison and Linnry clung to each other. He rubbed her back encouragingly but did not question. When Linnry felt ready to speak, she would. In the meantime, he tried to focus on her sorrow and not the desire her closeness stirred within him. Though almost seventeen, she had barely a trace of womanly curves, her hair feathered from generous ears, and she snuffled wildly into a shirt already soaked with her tears. None of his friends considered her pretty; but her features had, long ago, become too familiar for him to judge. They were simply Linnry. Now, the candlelight lit red highlights in her dark, fine locks; and, to him that night, she looked positively beautiful. *Mama, what thoughts have you put into my head?*

At length, Linnry whimpered out her plight. "It's my father, Tamison. He's . . . he's . . ." She broke into a griefstricken howl, accompanied by another rush of tears.

Tamison's lids narrowed in confusion. Her father was already dead and set to pyre.

Linnry gathered composure long enough to blurt, "He's gone, and I thought I could handle it alone, but I can't, and I'm all alone and . . ."

Assailed by sudden guilt, Tamison leaped to his feet, breaking the embrace. *She needed someone. She needed* me. *And I wasn't there for her.* He studied Linnry's streaky face. A clump of hair clung to her sticky forehead. The huge eyes, now accentuated by rings of scarlet distress, eclipsed her small, upturned nose. She looked like a suffering parody of a china doll, yet, to his surprise, he still found her breathtakingly beautiful. "I'm sorry, Linnry. Of course you can't handle it alone. No one could. I should have known that, and—"

"Tamison." Linnry rose and met his gaze. "I didn't let you help. I didn't let anyone—" She hovered unsteadily. "Oh, Tamison. What am I going to do?"

"What are you going to do?" The answer emerged without conscious thought. Tamison enfolded Linnry back into his embrace. Moments before, he would not have considered such an idea. Now, perhaps because of his previous conversation, it seemed the rightest thing in the universe, the very moment for which he had lived so far. "What are you going to do? You're going to marry me."

Linnry stiffened and jerked free. "What?"

Still certain of his decision despite its suddenness, Tamison became less sure of his delivery. "I mean . . . would it be all right if . . . would you consider . . . becoming my . . . wife?"

"Tamison . . ." Linnry started but did not finish. She wiped tears from her eyes.

Abruptly, the answer to that question became the most important thing in Tamison's life. He wanted, yet feared, to hear it.

"I don't . . ." Linnry sniffled. "I don't know."

Tamison's heart seemed to stop beating. "Please, Linnry. I love you." As the words emerged, he realized they had been true for far longer than he knew. The differences in their families' stations had once made the their union so unlikely, he had never seriously considered it. Now they had come to the same place. He only wished that place was not the bottom. "I'll always love you."

"I know." Linnry's tone remained devoid of doubt. "I've known it for a long time. I love you, too." She leaned closer. "But, Tamison, what about . . ." She cringed, as if loath to speak the words. ". . . our future?"

The mine-fore's words from earlier that day returned to haunt Tamison. He had spoken of it to no one yet, had let it sink to the base of his thoughts like a forgotten dream: *Tamison, you're a good man. I liked your family, and I like you. But—* Tamison had known then what had to follow, had received several gentler warnings in the past; yet the words still jolted him like a plunge into icy water. *We can't afford to keep paying you for what an apprentice would do for board. I'm sorry, Tamison. I really am. But either you work the mines, or you have to find another line of work.* Tamison had not met the mine-fore's gaze, could not. A sense of obligation to his father, or perhaps simple pity, had allowed the guild to keep him on far longer than they should have. In the long run, they had done him more disservice than favor. At eighteen, he was too old to apprentice. The skilled jobs were sewn up by family guilds. He had only one choice: to overcome his fear and return to the job his family had performed and loved for generations. Winning Linnry would give him the strength to succeed. "I will always find a way to support my family," he vowed with a sincerity that came straight from the heart. "Always, Linnry. I swear it."

Linnry studied Tamison, and a light flashed through brown eyes blurred by tears. "Yes." Her chin tilted bravely, almost fiercely, upward; she accepted his promise. "I will marry you."

From the bedroom, Tamison's mother's voice floated in a happy whisper. "I approve."

Chapter 1

THE sea breeze whipped Tamison's brown hair into a tangle, and he studied the fog that hovered over the ocean with a scrutiny that approached fanaticism. Around him, the other would-be dockhands exchanged bawdy stories or played games with dice, chips, or cards. Their booming laughter occasionally cut through the desperation that turned all else into insignificant and inseparable noise. Mist clung to Tamison's brows and lashes, and salt stung his pale eyes. Afternoon sunlight slanted through a press of fog, winding like gold filigree around the edges of every cloud. He had come to the water's edge while stars still speckled the sky, anticipating the ship's arrival at dawn.

The voice of the dock-fore drew Tamison from his daze as nothing else had managed. "No work today, boys. I'm sorry."

Tamison thrust his hands into tattered, empty pockets, cold dread seeping to his core. He stared at his feet, nails rimed with dirt, bare since his boots had disintegrated beyond repair a month ago.

"*The Tudor* went down two days ago."

The gathered dock workers broke into a din of speculation, silenced by a raising of the dock-fore's hand.

Tamison rolled his eyes to their dark and massive leader as he continued, *"Arnahan's Eagle* picked up the crew. They're all right, but her cargo's food for the fishes."

Grumbles mixed with good-natured comments about the luck of *The Tudor*'s crew. The crowd of would-be dockhands dispersed toward town as despair hammered Tamison. He pictured Linnry, whom he had already put through too much suffering. Her china-doll features had coarsened over the eleven years of their marriage, and the first wisps of gray touched her raven hair. Yet he found her even more beautiful as the years passed, enhanced by the depths of a sweet and generous soul, by the life they had created, by the rigors they had survived together.

Tamison closed his eyes, lower lip clenched between his teeth. His own words haunted him, ghosts he could never banish: "I'll always find a way to support my family."

And, so far, he had. Though thin, like their parents, all three of their offspring had survived. But four months ago, when Linnry announced her newest pregnancy, she had done so without the excitement of the others. Her breathtakingly large brown eyes seemed dulled with a worry that barely skirted betrayal. One more mouth to feed would surely prove too many.

A hand clapped to Tamison's shoulder. He whirled, battling tears, to find himself facing a gruff-looking man with grease-stained skin. "There'll be other ships, other days. Join us at Rannoh's?"

The very thought pained. Had Tamison had the money for a drink, he would spend it on food for his children. He could not accompany them even to watch the others drown their sorrows. Rannoh already thought little of the perpetually down-and-out brother-in-law who had paid back little of the money they had lent him after the last of Linnry's father's assets had dwindled to nothing. Six years ago, Tamison and Linnry had sold their family homes for necessities and now lived in a humble cottage on the poorest side of town. Tamison had spent their last coppers on dock guild dues, which had bought him only the opportunity to wait for a chance at work on any given day. He shook his head.

The worker shrugged. "A drink'll make things more tolerable."

Tamison said nothing. Nor did he watch the other man leave. He walked to the edge of the pier and looked out over the ocean swells again, prepared to stay the night, if necessary. *Arnahan's Eagle* creaked in her mooring, sails strapped securely to the mast, cargo emptied by those assigned to her days ago.

The dock-fore crouched at Tamison's side, a frown scoring his thick features. "Might as well go home, ducky. Nothing more due in for at least a fortnight."

Overcome by despair, Tamison clamped his hands over his face and wished the other man would leave.

"You're not thinking of jumping, are you?"

Surprised by the question, Tamison looked at the dock-fore. Glazed with sweat, his jowly face revealed genuine concern as it jerked toward the water.

Considering the possibility for the first time, Tamison shook his head. "Can't. Got a family."

The dock-fore ran a hand through dark hair stiff with salt, and it stood up in patches where he touched it. "You wouldn't be the first to do it. Not in these times. Even with a family."

Forced to make conversation at a time when he did not even want to think, Tamison grunted. "Hard times for everyone."

"Yeah." The other man rose, now more than a head taller than Tamison. "And I see the worst of it. Dock's the last resort of the laborer."

Tamison made a dismissing gesture. He could not speak for anyone else, but the words proved true enough for him. Too old for apprenticeships, he did not have the right connections or talents for any of the skilled trade guilds. Over the past eleven years, he had tried his hand at every unskilled occupation in Lathary, even returning to mining at twenty-three. Driven to tears by the click of pick against stone, requiring the light and air aboveground every few moments, deathly terrified by every rumble, he had been of little value. The guild's sympathy and patience proved finite. Dismissed in disgrace, Tamison had worked with road builders for more than three years until a landslide reawakened the past, sending him skittering in a blind panic. As word spread, he became branded as an unstable coward; none of the labor guilds would take him. Except the docks. Anyone who could afford the dues got in, then waited and hoped from one day to the next. "Last resort," Tamison repeated. He turned the dock-fore a pleading look. "Isn't there anything I can do today? Cleaning? Repairs? Anything?"

The dock-fore sighed. "You know the crew gets first chance at the barnacles. Lot of grateful and desperate seamen on this run, from *The Tudor*. And the shipbuilders aren't going to let an outsider take their coppers."

Tamison had already known the answers, but he had still needed to ask.

"Try back in a fortnight. I'll make sure you get something then."

"Thanks." Tamison pursed his lips. His family could not survive two weeks without food, but the dock-fore had done as much as he could do. Head low, wind cold through the patched sleeves of a gansey worn far beyond its useful lifetime, he shuffled toward town and home.

As he walked through streets light with foot traffic, past stalls, shops, and cottages, Tamison's attention remained firmly fixed in his mind. He pictured his homecoming, Linnry expectantly looking to him for spun wool, cloth, and something she could stretch into a meal. He turned his thoughts to his children. The oldest, a boy of ten, bore a striking resemblance to the long-dead uncle, Sutannis, for whom he was named. His girls, Ellith, seven, and Danara, three, still greeted their father with excited hugs and kisses. All three sported their mother's brown eyes and black hair; few of Lathary's citizens did not. Danara would be clutching one of their few luxuries, a battered and filthy doll he had found and which Linnry had lovingly patched and resewn.

Tamison discovered a smile on his face and smothered it with reality. In his mind's eye, he saw Linnry's hopes crumble, could picture her fingers stroking the bulge in her abdomen as she worried for the baby's life. Sutannis would say nothing, his pride in his father crushed to hopeless hunger. Ellith would cry, and Danara would ask the myriad questions of the innocent, unable to sleep for the pain in her gut. Tamison stopped dead in the road. *I can't go home with nothing.*

Suppressing the last shreds of dignity, he turned on one bruised, callused heel and headed toward Rannoh's.

Though an hour before dinner rush, Rannoh's seemed unusually full. The other dockworkers occupied five tables at the farthest end, their moods elevated with drink. The hunter's guild filled a table near the door, voices raised in a toast to a long and successful trip. Coins lay heaped at several elbows, stark contrast to the more frugal dock workers who could not afford to spend much for several weeks. Other patrons were scattered throughout the confines in small groups, mostly unfamiliar to Tamison.

No one seemed to notice Tamison's entrance until he

pulled an empty keg to the bar behind which Sheldora and her drink mixer worked, preparing bowls and mugs for this unexpected boon of customers. While his sister arranged product on the shelves, Tamison studied her back. Now twenty-four, she had filled into the plumply elegant form of their mother's youth. Black ringlets floated down her back, the curls her only exoticism. She wore a simple dress, at least from the back; and the ties of her apron wrapped a narrow waist and rested on ample hips.

A barmaid Tamison did not recognize flounced to his side. Loose strands of hair floated free of her tie, and sweat glinted between her nose and upper lip. "What can I get for you, sir?"

"Nothing," Tamison replied, trying not to lose his nerve. "I'm just here—"

At the sound of his voice, Sheldora whirled. "Tamison." Her expression was a neutral parody of the once-warm welcome. "You're looking . . ." She paused just a beat too long.

. . . *terrible,* he mentally supplied.

But Sheldora stuck with friendly cliché. ". . . good. I saw Linnry a few days ago at the market. She's beautiful. Women with child just . . . just . . . glow."

Tamison forced a smile. Little longer than a year ago, Sheldora would have avoided discussing Linnry's condition. Now that she had borne twins of her own, breaking nine years of barrenness, she no longer looked on every pregnancy as a taunt. Though he had sympathized with her anguish and never pushed, he rued the distance grief had created between Sheldora and her nieces and nephew. They hardly knew her and felt none of the closeness he had shared with his father's brothers as a child. And Linnry had no siblings. "With or without child, Linnry's always beautiful."

Sheldora drifted closer, resting her elbows on the bar. "How nice of you to visit." She spoke the words with little more warmth than a monotone, though she did turn him a wan smile and her eyes revealed the concern her voice lacked. "Can I get you anything?"

Tamison glanced at the barmaid, who quickly scurried toward the dockworkers. He cleared his throat, unable to meet his sister's eyes. "Some scraps to get us through a couple of weeks."

"Oh, Tamison." Though soft and gentle, Sheldora's voice cut.

Tamison focused fixedly on a beer stain.

"You know the leftovers and leavings go to the staff. It's part of their pay, and they need it, too."

Tamison traced the old spill with a fingertip. In the past, Sheldora had given him everything from fresh meals to money. He loved his little sister but hated her charity. Hated his need for it. Hated that he had to beg for it—again. Tears burned Tamison's eyes, and humiliation stole the last of his strength. He could not even manage to rise.

Apprently reading Tamison's despair, Sheldora placed a gentle hand on his head and stroked his hair. "It's all right, Tam. Everything will work out. It always does."

The platitudes accomplished nothing. Sheldora was wrong, and her pity made him feel tiny, hopeless as well as worthless.

"Tamison, look at me."

Tamison forced a slow headshake. If he raised his eyes, he would lose control.

Sheldora straightened. "Stay right here. I'll see what I can do." Her footfalls retreated. The door to the storage area opened with its telltale squeal of hinges, then banged against its jamb. The latch did not click. Sheldora's steps continued onward, beneath the sluggish creak of the door gliding back open a crack. The thump and rasp of moving crates leaked through the opening, then stopped suddenly.

Tamison did not hear Sheldora speak, but Rannoh's reply came to every ear in the tavern, loud and distinct. "What does that bloodsucker want this time?"

The rumble of conversation stopped. Tamison's blood seemed to freeze in his veins. His attention to the beer stain became even more fixed.

"Rannoh, please. He just needs a little to tide him over—"

"Tide him over? Tide him over till when? Our next handout?"

Tamison wished he could disappear. He felt certain the eyes of every patron and worker pinned him.

"He's my brother, Rannoh. He's got a family—"

A crate struck the floor. "I've got a family, too. I love them enough to work and provide for them. I shouldn't have to support his family, too."

"Rannoh . . ." Sheldora's tone turned pleading.

"I don't want to talk about it anymore," Rannoh growled. "I'm going to be late for the hunter's guild auction. All the best meat will be gone."

Tamison willed himself to move, to leave before his sister returned, but his muscles would not obey.

Sheldora had not finished. "Couldn't we give him some work here?"

"We've been over this." Rannoh's voice went flat with warning. "We're struggling to pay the crew we've got. I worked long and hard, within guild law, to find the best help at the best price. I'm not dumping competent workers to hire a slacker with no skills. And I'm certainly not going to buck the labor guilds. That could cost me my business." His boots clomped toward the common room. "I have to go!"

Tamison forced himself to stand. His limbs felt liquid.

Sheldora called desperately, "You didn't see how skinny he's gotten."

The footfalls stopped, and Rannoh's words grew more

muffled. Apparently, he had turned to face his wife. "Sweetie, I'm sorry. We've done what we can for him, but your brother's a lame horse. A falcon that can't fly."

Worthless, Tamison interpreted. When a beast of burden lost the use of a leg or a game bird broke a wing, they swiftly put the useless creature out of its misery.

"At least let me feed him a hot meal."

"I forbid it. Now, let me go, or no one will get fed." Rannoh clomped toward the door again.

The anticipation of meeting his brother-in-law galvanized Tamison. He scurried from the room as the door hinges screeched fully open, suffering the heat of dozens of judging gazes. Face low, hands blocking peripheral vision, he missed all of them.

A light evening breeze ruffled Tamison's hair and wound through the gaps in his clothing. He skittered into an alley, worried over accidentally confronting Rannoh in one of the main roads. Sinking to the dirt, he listened to passersby in the streets talking about their jobs, their families, deals at the market. *I am a flightless falcon.* His hand winched around a rotting scrap of garbage, fingers plunging into the slime. Composure wholly lost, Tamison wept.

By the time despair gave way to need, the sun had disappeared behind the horizon. A sliver of moon and an early sprinkle of stars lit silver glimmers in the cobbles of the main street. Tamison's gut gnawed at its own lining, a familiar pain he had long ago learned to ignore. It bothered him more that Linnry and the children suffered that discomfort as well. *I'll always find a way to support my family.* Tamison scrambled to his feet. Now, as always, he would keep that vow.

Tamison headed deeper into town, for the moment wanting only to put distance between himself and his brother-in-law's tavern. He cruised the familiar thoroughfares and byways, searching the closed street-market for discarded scraps of cloth, dropped coins, and bruised fruit. Empty-handed, he wandered around established shops, finding only a stale quarter loaf among the bakery's inedible garbage. He clutched the stiff brown bread like a lifeline, drawing it from the shadow of the building and into a puddle of light. There, he could see the toughness of its scale, the patches of fuzzy blue-and-white mold that spotted it at intervals. For several moments, he pinched these off, left with a ragged handful of bread with a motheaten appearance. *Barely enough for one.* Tamison stuffed it into his pocket. *My family deserves better than this.*

Tamison imagined their reaction to this meager fare: Linnry's tight smile of welcome, Sutannis' hungry stare of betrayal, Ellith's stalwart acceptance, and Danara's tears. The baby inside Linnry could not survive two weeks of this, and the others might not either.

Wandering blindly toward the opposite end of a town whose every street had grown familiar, Tamison soon found himself in the warehouse district. His mind unconsciously checked off each building's contents. He had sought work everywhere, of every type; and he could name past and present foremen until his lips went numb. He did not stop until he reached the storage facilities of the hunter's guild. Cued by their rich and rowdy presences in the bar, and by Rannoh's hurry to attend an auction now surely finished, he knew the trappers and bowmen had recently returned from a highly successful venture.

Tamison had not come here with a premeditated purpose. Yet, now that he had arrived, he studied the brick-and-mortar buildings. Crumbling turrets ringed the edge of the rooftops, ancient reminders of a time when these had served as the outermost fortifications of Lathary. In his youth, the city had spiraled steadily outward, rendering these buildings obsolete until the hunter's guild purchased them. The heavy construction helped keep the ice frozen longer, and the tunnels that had once served a myriad of defensive purposes now allowed for underground stockpiling and direct transport of goods.

The newer bastions and ramparts made these appear crude and primitive, though, to Tamison's knowledge, Lathary had not known war in at least a century. According to rumor, the ruling brotherhoods of Trifinity and of Callos had designs on one another and on Lathary. If it was true, however, it seemed not to affect the citizens at all. The brotherhoods waged their wars economically or as small-scale, quiet skirmishes unbeknownst to the populace. Yet Lathary appeared to be losing, struggling since the loss of its great silver mine. Many of its finest businesses and artisans had abandoned the withering city, and the rare users of magic shunned it altogether.

Tamison circled the main warehouse of the hunter's guild. No windows looked out from the forbidding structure, and narrow wedged rocks, thatch, and mortar had long ago plugged the spy and arrow slits. At the front, the dais used for the bidding still remained. Behind it, a massive padlock hung from the sturdy oak door, dark and forbidding in the moonlight.

Tamison froze, disappointment trickling through him. It was only then that he realized he had planned to take what his family needed, and he suffered another cold wash of despair. *I'm not even competent enough to steal.* Unable to stand any more humiliation, even from himself, he found the realization contradictorily funny. A chuckle escaped him, then a full-throated laugh. For several moments, he stood in the near-darkness, staring at a lock he could not hope to sunder, and released his tension in a loud display of self-deprecating amusement.

I must be going mad. The thought sobered Tamison enough to quell the flood of laughter. *If I'm going to become a thief, I have to start somewhere.* He sighed at a thought that morality had always managed to keep at bay, when his family's situation had seemed less desperate. *Finally, I've found an occupation where I don't have to worry about breaching some guild.* Nervously, he peered around, looking for signs of other life on the street. Seeing none, he crept toward the door.

Arriving at the oak panel without challenge, Tamison loosed an unsteady breath of pent-up air. He examined the lock, a thick iron monstrosity with a keyhole big enough to admit his smallest finger. He inserted it, finding greasy hunks of metal and fluted cogs that meant nothing to his touch. Knowing he could not hope to understand it without locksmith training, he withdrew his finger and mapped out another route of garbage checks. By now, the street orphans and beggars would have confiscated anything of value.

Frustration plagued Tamison, hot and ugly. The emotions building up inside him desperately needed an outlet: shame and inadequacy, urgency and sorrow, rage and hopelessness. Suddenly, he seized the lock in both hands and jerked with all his strength. Metal shifted in Tamison's grip, a surprise that sent him staggering backward. The lock had opened.

For a shocked moment, Tamison stared. Then, understanding struck with the power of a galloping horse. Apparently, some thief more competent than he had tampered with the lock. For days, months, perhaps decades, this canny man or woman had pilfered from the hunter's guild without their knowledge. And now, he could do the same.

Tamison shook his head clear. The longer he stood here marveling, the more likely the town guard would pass by on patrol and catch him. Tossing one last glance around the empty street, he removed the lock and tripped the latch. The click of its movement made him cringe, and the soft creak of hinges seemed more like a shout. Afraid to look again, willing observers away, he entered the warehouse, easing the door shut behind him. Pitch-blackness descended around him.

Tamison's heart pounded. He pressed his back to the door, waiting for his eyes to adjust to the darkness, for his jitters to calm enough for him to move. Gradually, he gained control of his shaking hands, but his vision did not improve. Apparently, the interior was utterly lightless. And chillingly cold.

Tamison took a step forward, groping through the blackness. His shin crashed against something painfully frigid. He tumbled over a block of ice and slammed to the floor. Shards like frozen glass stabbed into his side. He rolled to his feet, shivering. *Can't do this blind.* Carefully maneuvering around the now-revealed ice, he opened the door a crack. Moonlight funneled through, sparse but brilliant contrast to the previous total darkness. He could now make out partially melted hunks of ice, hanging carcasses and bloody parcels of meat, a lantern strung from a gimbal near the doorway, parchments for wrapping, and a floor ring that revealed a trapdoor.

Wishing for a tinderbox, Tamison dodged the scattered objects as he wandered deeper into the room. It seemed prudent to take the older meat; whatever lay stored beneath the floor seemed less likely to be missed. Grabbing the ring, he pulled. The heavy trapdoor rasped partway open, then proved too substantial for his grip. Tamison lost his hold, and the panel slammed closed.

Tamison sucked air through his teeth, face puckering, and hoped no one had heard. Bracing his feet, he tried again, this time managing to lift the trapdoor and rest it quietly open. He glanced down into the square of darkness, gripped by an abrupt and terrible fear that sent him staggering backward.

He would settle for the meat he could see, taking a bundle so small that the hunters would not miss it. He only needed enough to feed his family for a fortnight. Someday, he promised himself, he would replace what he took with money, just as he would pay back Rannoh and Sheldora.

Seizing a piece of parchment and string, Tamison searched for a promising piece of venison. He found one almost immediately, a large chunk nearly crushed between two pieces of ice. At the thought of venison roast, his stomach growled hungrily. He fought against stuffing a piece of the raw catch into his mouth. It might satisfy the rumbling for awhile, but the diseases that could result might kill him. Resisting, he crouched, placed the meat on the wrapping, folded the corners, and started to tie.

The door creaked. Still securing his find, Tamison looked up, expecting the night wind. Lantern light shone white circles across the floor, and he jerked his gaze to at least two guardsmen. He lurched to his feet, stammering.

"You were right, Calima." A broad man in a spotless uniform stepped into the warehouse. "Caught ourselves a thief."

Tamison dropped the parcel and back stepped. His heart pounded wildly, and his thoughts rushed so quickly he could not focus.

Another man entered after the first, then a third who closed the door and stood against it, barricading the way. The first approached Tamison.

Tamison retreated. "Please. My family is hungry. I just wanted enough to feed—"

"Tell it to Lord Byrran," the man growled, drawing ever closer, lowering his center of gravity as he prepared for a fight.

As ignorant of martial skills as of any other, Tamison continued to give ground.

The second man laughed. "You know what the brother-hood does to thieves?"

Tamison swallowed hard. In the heat of desperation, he had not considered the consequences of getting caught. Now, he remembered hearing of murderers executed, peace-disturbers flogged, adulterers stripped of their manhood in the public square. As a convicted thief, he would lose his dominant hand. "No," he moaned, curling the fingers of his left hand around his right wrist. Thus maimed, he would no longer have a prayer of providing for his family. *What have I done? Oh, Linnry. I'm so sorry.*

The lead man waved his partner silent without taking his gaze from Tamison. "Come without a fight, and we won't hurt you. Struggle, and we use whatever amount of force we reckon necessary."

Tamison glanced at the second man, probably Calima. The lantern lit glimmers in dark eyes that looked cruel, and he wore a lopsided half-smile. The other two seemed much gentler. Tamison forced himself to take a step toward the closest man. "I won't resist," he promised. "Be gentle, please."

Tamison took another shuffling step, then a third. Just as the guard reached out to grab him, anticipatory pain ached through his right wrist. The dark hole caught the corner of his vision. Forgetting his vow, he hurled himself for the opening.

"Hey!" the guard shouted.

Tamison tumbled through darkness as muffled curses filled the room above him. Footsteps clattered on the ladder he should have taken. Trained to the mines, he battled down instinct and fully relaxed as he struck bottom. He landed on a sticky pile that gave enough to rescue him from serious injury. Bruised, tasting blood and salt, he scrambled into a tunnel in the seconds his fall had gained him. The thump of boots scrambling down rungs echoed through the confines. A ring of light revealed the piled jerky that had broken his fall before Tamison charged beyond it.

Even worried for life and family, Tamison could not escape the claustrophobic panic that scattered his wits. Though barely winded, he gasped for every breath, imagining himself suffocating in the close darkness. Shutting his eyes in a feeble attempt to trick his vision, he felt, intuited, and smelled his way through a simple maze of tunnels. Behind him, the sounds of pursuit diminished, then disappeared. Movement came easily, his build perfect for the crawl and scuttle motions necessary to move him swiftly through the pipelike interiors. Then, abruptly, the trail curled upward and ended. His fingers struck wood, and a splinter dug painfully into flesh. Desperate for fresh air, he shoved the trapdoor open.

Light funneled into Tamison's eyes, revealing a storage room filled with foodstuffs. Then, a hand latched onto his sleeve, and he noticed two guardsmen hovering at the exit.

Tamison hurled himself backward. The darkness enveloped him again, then his shoulder jarred hard enough to flare pain through his entire arm. The weakened fabric parted with a loud tearing sound, flinging Tamison back into the tunnels.

The guard swore, his voice echoing.

"Over there." A gruff voice rebounded from rock and dirt, impossible for most to pinpoint yet easy for a miner. Pursued from at least two directions, Tamison found himself left with few options. He knew it best to remain in the catacombs until the men either cornered him or grew tired of searching. That bare thought sent him racing forward. He bit off a terrified scream, trying to calm a heart that seemed determined to hammer free of his chest.

Out! Out! Tamison followed another upward corridor, slammed through another trapdoor.

Enormous hands clasped Tamison's wrists, this time catching flesh instead of clothing. Again, he jerked in retreat. Agony ached through his arms, and he gained no ground at all. A large man with gentle eyes hauled him through the opening and dangled him several feet above a grocery floor. The stranger wore the town guard's uniform, and he kicked the door closed without relaxing his grip on Tamison. "Got him," he shouted in a booming bass.

A smaller man dashed across the room, panting. He clamped a set of leg irons onto Tamison's dangling ankles. The larger guard lowered Tamison, and the other snapped shackles to his wrists as well. Now, the massive man placed his captive on the floor.

Drained of fight, Tamison collapsed and went still.

"Sorry, Harrin." The man who had placed the restraints stood over Tamison. "Got here as fast as I could. He must move like a squirrel."

"Underground," Harrin reminded. "A rat's more like it."

Tamison curled his arms and legs beneath him. The ice, night air, and a torn tunic left him feeling chilled in every part. The iron felt achingly cold against his flesh. "Please. Cut off my hand, if you have to. Just let me go."

Harrin responded first, "I've never met a man so eager for mutilation."

Still hunched, Tamison spoke into his own chest. "It's not that. I just want this finished so my family doesn't suffer any longer than necessary." He rolled an eye upward in time to see the smaller man flinch.

"I wouldn't do that, even if I had the authority." He crouched to Tamison's level. "You have to stand before Lord Byrran. Tomorrow at the soonest." He glanced at his partner.

"Tell me where you live." Harrin also crouched. "I'll let your wife know what happened to you."

Tamison wished he could do that himself, but this was more mercy than he had expected. "Thank you," he said, hoarsely. Then, once again, he surrendered to tears.

A chill, sourceless breeze carried the odors of damp granite, mildew, vomit, and urine. Huddled into the tattered and filthy remnants of his clothing, Tamison stared at the gray-drab ceiling of his cell and wished he could sleep. He knew he would need his wits about him to convince the ruling brotherhood of the necessity of his crime. Remorse would probably serve him well also, but it proved impossible to summon. Given the opportunity to repeat this day, the only thing he would have done differently was to work more swiftly and quietly and to better hide his tracks.

Lost beneath an avalanche of worry for his family and fear for himself, gripped by hunger pains as intense as cramps, unable to escape memory that cycled through his mind in an endless loop, Tamison found sleep a desperate and distant obsession, beyond his reach. Nevertheless, he tried, hugging the bare stone floor, forcing concentration on inconsequencialities, like the cold touch of granite against his cheek. He sought patterns in the snoring that filled Lathary's prison. A steady deep rumble mingled with a troubled murmur and an erratic snorting that ended with a high-pitched whistle. An occasional whisk of movement or heavy sigh punctuated the cacophony of the prison night.

Mind filled with images of his hungry children, Tamison watched the torchlight flicker across the ceiling, marred by the reflected shadows of the bars. At length, those failed, plunging the confines into a darkness pierced only by the distant and diffuse glow of a guard's personal lantern. Exhaustion weighted every muscle and fogged Tamison's thoughts, as brutal as a full day's picking at the mines. His stomach growled, and he wished he had thought to grab a handful of the jerked venison as he passed it. Back then, survival had taken precedence.

Gradually, Tamison drifted into a light doze, aroused moments later by the pained sleep-shout of another prisoner. It pierced his budding dream in Danara's voice. His youngest daughter was hopelessly hungry. The thought shocked Tamison awake with a moan of his own. *God help those I love. 'Cause I can't do it anymore.*

A hundred sconced torches lit the judgment room like day, and the grim-faced Lord Byrran who sat upon a sturdily crafted chair wore an expression of jaded fierceness. Hair more grizzled than black formed feathery tufts above each ear and a semicircle on the back of his head. Features coarsened by five decades recessed dark eyes with a hint of moisture. A short, burly man in uniform stood at his right hand. Aside from these, and the two guards at Tamison's either side, the room contained no people and no other furnishings. Its enormous emptiness further intimidated Tamison who stood, in chains, between his escort and tried not to shake. He did manage a respectful bow.

Lord Byrran looked expectantly at the guard beside him.

The compact guard turned to face his leader. "A thief, sir. Caught in the act of stealing meat from guild storage."

The lord's gaze pinned Tamison. "Your plea?"

Tamison knew he should feel frightened, but fatigue stole all emotion. He only wanted this nightmare finished. "I did take the meat . . . or I would have." He drew breath to explain. Perhaps Lord Byrran did not know about the poverty plaguing his city. If he could find the words to describe his family's plight, perhaps he could win leniency. "But—"

Lord Byrran interrupted. "Where is this man from?"

The squat guard replied, "He's Latharyn, sir."

Byrran made a thoughtful noise.

A movement near the side door caught Tamison's attention. The guard who had captured him, Harrin, found a position in the doorway, the panel resting against his knee. Beyond him, Tamison saw other guards milling, recognizing some as men who had chased him through the warehouse tunnels. They stood in silence, apparently unnoticed by anyone but himself and understandably interested in his sentencing. Suddenly recognizing an opening, Tamison started again, "If I could just explain—"

But Lord Byrran still seemed fixed on Tamison's origins. "Doesn't look Latharyn." His scrutiny grew even more intense. "In fact, if asked, I couldn't place him."

Harrin spoke from the doorway. "His name's Tamison, son of Uland of Lathary, sir. His mother was Carsean."

Every head, including Lord Byrran's, whipped in Harrin's direction. "How do you know that?" the leader asked, gesturing for the guard to continue.

"Talked to his wife, sir. He's got three children, too. Another on the way." Harrin turned Tamison an apologetic expression. "They looked hungry."

Thank the gods they're all right. Tamison managed a weary smile of gratitude. The guard had kept his word. "Very hungry, sir. That's why I had to—"

The lord rounded on Tamison again, once more cutting off his explanation. "What do you do for a living?"

Too mentally dulled for the sudden switch, Tamison babbled for a moment before replying. "My job, sir? I–I haven't got a job, sir. That's the prob—"

"Ahh." Lord Byrran misunderstood. "A career thief."

Surprised murmurs leaked through the open door. Tamison suspected his dash around the underground tunnels had convinced them all he worked the mines.

"No. No, I'm not a—this was my first—I mean I never—" Tamison struggled against exhaustion, certain the right speech could bring tears to Byrran's eyes, could rescue himself and his family. Yet his painful lack of skills did not except oration.

"Take him to his punishment!" Lord Byrran roared. "And call the next."

Harrin headed toward the lord, and the escort tugged at Tamison's chains. Tamison stumbled to his knees as the men turned him. As he tried to rise, the guards continued moving, half-dragging, half-directing his weary steps. He thought he heard something in Harrin's voice about holes and rats before he found himself in the hallways and the main entry door banged shut behind him.

Another man in chains stood in the corridor, this one with head up and eyes glimmering with defiance. Tamison did not have long to look before the guards guided him in the opposite direction, but he envied the other's rugged composure. He might have fared better with that much energy for thought and speech.

Once out of the judgment room, the guards paused to let Tamison fully gain his footing. "This way," one said, inclining his head to a door at the end of the short hallway. They resumed their journey, allowing him to select a slower pace. Even so, they reached the door too swiftly for Tamison. He tried not to think about what lay beyond it.

The guard at Tamison's left hand knocked on the plain wooden door.

A moment later, it swung inward, deceptively thick and heavy, obviously designed to muffle sound. Beyond, the room reeked of sweat and blood, smells of terror. A wooden rack held leather rods, whips, axes, and less recognizable implements. A stone block occupied most of the middle of the room, stained brown from old blood. At the sight of it, Tamison reeled.

The guards yanked on the chains, and a dull ache throbbed through Tamison's forearms where the edges of the shackles slammed against flesh. Only then, he noticed the two men in the room. The first sat in a chair near the block, expression unreadable, stance calm, and forearms well-muscled. He studied Tamison with a detached and frightening composure. The other, the one who had opened the door, looked small in comparison. He studiously avoided Tamison's gaze, for the moment seemingly focused on a wooden box of bandages near his feet.

Tamison's heart pounded, and panic banished all thought. He had expected some quiet time in a cell to prepare for this moment. At least, he would not have to face a public crowd, or worse, his family. Logic turned his latest worry to silly impossibility. Surely, Linnry would protect their children from a sight that horrible, especially when it involved their father.

Finally, the smaller of the two men glanced in Tamison's direction. "A drink, first." It emerged more statement than question. He pulled a massive mug of foaming liquid from his box.

One of Tamison's escort locked the door while the other removed the shackles from his wrists. He rubbed at the abraded flesh, loosing flakes of dirt. He would gladly trade the proffered drink for a bath. The food value of the ale enticed, but the image of stumbling home drunk and mutilated made him too sick to accept. Just a sip would make him vomit. He shook his head. "Let's get this over with."

Clearly shocked by what must have been his first refusal,

the man fumbled around a bit with the full mug. Finally, he set it on the floor and returned his attention to the bandages.

"Dominant hand here." The larger man tapped the block, turning his attention to the guards.

Tamison placed his right hand on the stone, berating himself a moment later for the weak weariness that had turned him into a fool. The punisher could not know whether he was left- or right-handed and probably would not have cared.

The punisher jerked his head toward Tamison, obviously surprised by his quiet obedience.

Tamison lowered his head. Fighting would have only sapped what little strength remained, mentally and physically. The guards would have won the battle. "Let's get this over with," he repeated dully, bracing for the agony.

The punisher went to the rack and pulled down the ax. Its blade gleamed in the torchlight, wickedly and mercifully sharp.

Tamison closed his eyes, tensed with desperate, terrible expectation.

A harried pounding echoed through the room. Tamison cringed, at first believing himself beaten. When no pain followed, he twisted his neck toward the door. One of his escort undid the lock with a snap. The massive panel flew open to reveal a nervous-looking servant. "Stop!" he shouted, gaze zipping to the block.

Tamison snatched back his intact right hand, rubbing it with his left to convince himself it was still attached.

"What's going on?" the man who had offered the drink demanded with a hint of breathy relief.

"Lord Byrran's commuted his sentence."

"What?" the guards said, almost simultaneously.

The servant continued, "Don't cut him. He gets to keep his hand."

Dizzy, Tamison staggered back, tripped over his leg

shackles, and dropped to his knees to keep from falling. Joy slogged through the blunted mass of terror and confusion.

"Two years of lockup and labor instead."

Two years? The words almost failed to register. *Linnry. Sutannis, Ellith, and Danara. They can't last two years without me.* "But—" Uncertain whether to smile or sob, Tamison surged to his feet. The sudden movement proved too much for a body racked by hunger, exhaustion, and horrendous excitement. Buzzing stars closed over him, melting into quiet darkness.

Chapter 2

TAMISON forced himself into a mindless cycle of working to utter exhaustion, then collapsing into sleep too fast for thoughts of his family's suffering to keep him awake. Road work suited him, and he used it as an excuse for self-deception. So long as he marked time, reining in thought and memory, Sutannis would remain ten, Ellith seven, and Danara three. He could scarely imagine their lives moving on without him, could not contemplate the thought that they might forget him or that another man might replace him in their hearts. Every day, he immersed himself in work that he hoped to continue as a job after he regained his freedom. He had failed at it once, but two years of forced labor would have to tone his muscles and steel his nerves.

For the first year, Tamison kept an eye tuned to passersby as he worked, longing for a glimpse of Linnry or the children. He never saw them, not even on All Feast Day, the calendar unifying day and the only day direct visitation of prisoners was allowed. As a child and a young man, he had loved Lathary's largest holiday, the bonfires and the free food supplied by the guilds, the joy and the games, the forestalling of feuds and hard feelings. Even wanted criminals could enjoy the celebration without fear of reprisal. On that day, everyone, no matter their notoriety or failings, became untouchable.

After that first year, Tamison preferred to work even through his days of rest. Those only gave him time and focus to brood.

Tamison awakened as he did every morning: in his prison yellows and shackles, with his back aching from the cold hard floor, and every movement a painful reminder of the previous day's effort. The familiar clank of food dishes rang through the room, accompanied by the rasp of the wheeled cart as it wound between the cells. Finding his water bowl near the door, Tamison edged it toward him without bothering to rise. He splashed leftover water on his face. The sudden, icy droplets brought him fully alert and stabbed a shiver through him. He ran a hand through his hair, meeting week-old tangles and dirt. *Hope we go back to the old spot.* He pictured the lake near their prior work site, remembered the daily baths he managed there, and smiled.

The familiar thump of a bowl against the bars sounded in the cell beside Tamison's, then the cart ground to a halt in front of him. A guardsman stepped around it, keys in hand. The change from routine seized Tamison's attention at once. The guards did not need to open cages to feed them, and usually they waited long enough for their charges to eat before hauling them to work. This guardsman jabbed the key into Tamison's lock and turned it. A loud click echoed through the prison. Then, the man pulled open the door on squealing hinges. Once, those details would have eluded Tamison. Now more suspicious, he presumed the guards deliberately never oiled the locks and hinges, so they could hear if someone attempted escape.

Uncertain, Tamison waited in silence. Always before, the guard had opened his door in pairs, with chains at the ready. This time, the guardsman stepped back, empty-handed.

Tamison waited. *Is he testing me?*

"Aren't you coming out?" the man asked, at length.

Apprehension blossoming to alarm, Tamison asked, "Where am I going?"

The guard loosed a gruff chuckle. "Don't know. Wherever thieves go once they're loosed."

"Loosed?" Tamison scarcely dared to believe two years had finally passed. It seemed more like a decade. He could barely remember his life before this predictable drudgery. Then he thought of Linnry, of the children, and his past came back in extraordinary detail. Sutannis would be twelve now and hopefully beginning an apprenticeship or learning an unskilled trade. The girls would seem so grown up to Tamison, the youngest five years old. He had a new son or daughter, too. The thought brought both joy and grave sorrow. He worried that a child who had never met its father for longer than a year and a half might be unable to love him. "I'm free?"

"You're free."

Tamison took his first tentative steps toward the door.

"Wait."

Tamison forced himself to stop. *Too good for truth.* He gritted his teeth. "What?"

"You'll do better without those." The guardsman pointed to the everpresent shackles around Tamison's ankles, then knelt. A smaller key dipped into the proper hole. Metal fell away, leaving Tamison unfettered for the first time in two years. The guardsman stood. "Get out of here." He made shooing motions toward the outside door. "And stay out of trouble."

All the desperate fears Tamison had kept at bay for so

long raged around him now. For the first time, he could not dodge the significance of his family's conspicuous absences. His labor kept him outdoors. Surely, they could have found him at one of his job sites. And few, if any, of the other prisoners had gone without some visitation on All Feast Day. *They're dead. They all starved.* Terrible grief rushed down on him; had he had any proof of his suspicion, he would have collapsed. *No.*

The guardsman held open the door and waved Tamison through it. The ex-prisoner wandered out like a man spellbound by a magician. *No. Linnry was just too busy finding help and food. No time to worry about me.* He clung to that explanation. Any other might kill him. *Maybe she thought seeing me like this might scare the children. Or maybe she worried I'd feel demeaned if they saw me.* As Tamison crossed the grounds of Lord Byrran's mansion, he broke into a frenzied run. Unused to strides longer than a shackle chain, his legs succumbed to momentum. He tumbled to the dirt, flying head over heels and rolling twice before he regained his feet. He staggered several awkward steps, legs wildly unsteady. He dropped back to the familiar shuffle step of the last two years, gradually increasing his stride.

Driven near to madness by the possibilities, Tamison stopped surmising about his family. Only the truth mattered, and he would find it when he reached his own front door. One way or another, they would reunite. He would do whatever it took to win his way back into their hearts . . . and to keep his promise.

Near the gate, a pair of spear-wielding sentries whirled toward Tamison. Intimidated, he slowed back to a trot, then a walk, stopping just beyond weapon range. The guards conversed softly as they studied him, their exchange too low for Tamison's ears. Finally, one spoke, "Your name?"

"Tamison." When the guards did not immediately attack,

concern gave way to all-encompassing need. He fairly
pranced in place. "Uland's son."

"You're cleared to leave." The sentry headed toward the
gate, ratcheted the heavy clasp, and yanked on the wrought
iron panel. It opened in jerky increments.

As it moved, the other guard leaned toward Tamison and
spoke in a chummy whisper. "I'd change that name if I was
you. Take a new one, new life."

The words seemed odd to Tamison, but he did not bother
to ponder. As soon as the guard who had opened the gate
stepped aside, he charged through the gap to the main street.
He raced through thoroughfares, seeing and hearing little.
He missed the angry glares of those who leaped aside to
avoid his blind rush for home. Others stared warily at the
bulky, light-haired man in the stained prison-yellow shirt
and britches. Since he had spent his days outside, two years
of changes sped by him routinely, mostly unnoticed. If anything, the city had grown poorer. Crumbling, abandoned cottages and shops occasionally broke through his urgency to
register beyond the superficial, but he did not stop his crazed
run until he came to the crushed dirt pathway that led to his
family's hovel.

There, Tamison stopped and finally looked around him.
A dozen small cottages lined the unnamed lane, looking little
different than when he had left for the docks that fateful
morning two years earlier. The old widow sat just outside her
doorway, as usual, rocking in the ancient chair that was her
prize possession. She sewed socks, scarves, and pantaloons
that her daughter sold at a battered stand in the market. The
wife of his neighbor scrubbed clothes in the muddy hole,
more puddle than pond, while their cluster of young children
ran giggling around the road. The routine mundanity of
these sights condensed the last two years to distant dream,
lost in the light normality of morning. As he reached his cot-

tage, Tamison smiled, struck suddenly by the standard tired uncertainty of a day of work-searching, glad to hurl himself into the whirlwind welcome of his loving family.

Tamison's own cottage belied the lulling sense of sameness. The thatch roof he had lovingly maintained lay tinged with mold and partially collapsed. Mortar had crumbled, allowing the timbers to fall slightly askew. *Poor Linnry.* He imagined the children and providing for them kept her too busy for patchwork. At least, he could put their dwelling right. Clenched by a mixture of excitement and terror, Tamison jogged to his lintel, heart pounding. He considered knocking but worried he'd just add more distance than years of absence already had. Seizing the latch, he pulled.

The door slid sideways in his grip, pulled from its upper hinge. Surprised, Tamison jumped backward, releasing his grip. The wooden panel sagged, held only by two nails surrounded by water-damaged locust. Stepping forward again, he threw the door open. "Linnry?" His voice emerged with a strained character he barely recognized. It echoed in a family room that contained only a stained table and several empty kegs that had served as chairs. A rancid odor wrinkled his nose.

Tamison did not bother to close the door. "Linnry?" He headed for the two doorways at the back, glancing through first one then the other. He saw only bedraggled sleeping pallets covered with rags. *Out working.* He winced. *Or scavenging.* He turned, seeing the tracks of his prison boots in a layer of dust on the floor. He frowned. Linnry had always kept the tiny cottage immaculate. As he studied the boards, he noticed other prints, large and barefoot. Sound buzzed in his ears, and he felt as if something heavy sat on his chest. *The neighbor.* He dashed from the house and ran toward the washing hole.

Startled children ran screaming toward their cottage. The

woman looked up from her work, her two eldest sons standing protectively in front of her.

Tamison slid to a halt on damp grass. "Linnry and the
children. Do you know where they are?"

Though no older than nine, the boys closed ranks. The
mother peered over them. "Who are you?"

Tamison considered his appearance for the first time. The
guards would not trust the prisoners with sharp implements
but hated the job of shaving their charges. He wore several
days' growth of beard. His hair had grown long and dishev-
eled, and he finally remembered he still wore prison yellows.
"Tamison. Don't you recognize me?"

The neighbor studied him intently for several moments
while her boys shifted from foot to foot. "Tamison?" She
stared even longer. "How . . . are you?" She phrased the last
question with careful hesitancy, clearly not expecting a
happy answer.

Too concerned for small talk, Tamison ignored the query.
"Linnry. Sutannis, Ellith, and Danara. Do you know where
they went?"

The woman shook her head. "Lots of people moved away.
I thought . . . we thought you left for—" She broke off, looking over his clothing. Her mouth snapped shut. "I haven't
seen them, or you, since—must have been a year or so. Two,
maybe."

"Did something happen? Did you see them leave?" Tamison pressed.

The neighbor's head rolled back and forth again. "There
one day, gone the next. Never saw or heard anything
strange."

Tamison realized Harrin's wee morning hour visit to in-
form Linnry of her husband's capture could have gone un-
witnessed; the guard had seemed mercifully discreet. But
moving three children, even in the dead of night, should

have awakened someone. *Was Linnry so humiliated, so desperate others not know the shame I caused, that she managed to slip away wholly unseen and unheard?* A hot knife of guilt stabbed through Tamison's chest. Forced suddenly to face all of the agony he had put on hold for so long, he stood, utterly frozen.

Oblivious, the neighbor raised her brows in question. "Except it wasn't like either of you to leave without some sort of good-bye. Where did you go?"

Tamison struggled to move, to speak. "Thank you," he finally managed, unable to say more. He hurried back to the cottage, seeking some glimmer of understanding.

The family room contained only the wobbly table he had made and the extra kegs from Rannoh's bar. In the sleeping room he had shared with Linnry, he found nothing but a pallet of soupy, rotted straw and decaying rags. He turned his attention to the children's room next, tears blurring his vision to streaks of brown. He wiped his eyes, only to have the tears return as swiftly. His arms felt cold, empty, at a time when he should have clutched their warm small bodies against him. He forced himself to look, found four small piles of fetid bedding, and wondered at the number. Closer inspection revealed one heap moving slightly and rhythmically. "Linnry?" he whispered hopefully.

No response.

Tamison placed a hand on the figure's shoulder and shook. He felt bony sinews that did not suit a woman. The person rolled with a groan, and a reek of alcohol wafted from the movement. Bleary, dark eyes flicked open in a narrow, middle-aged face sporting a grizzled beard. The stranger leaped to his feet with a speed Tamison would not have thought possible from the inebriated. "Don't hurt me!" The man cringed toward a corner.

Tamison threw a glance behind him before he could

think. "Hurt you? Me?" He had never thought of himself as intimidating. Though he had a well-muscled torso, much more so after two years of adequate food and heavy labor, relatively short legs kept his stature on the smaller side of average. "I'm not going to hurt you."

Apparently reassured, the stranger went on the offensive. "Find you own slumber space."

Taken aback by the hostility, Tamison did not bother with sarcasm or defense. If his family no longer dwelled here, it was no longer his home. Living among the ashes and ghosts might kill him. "How long has this been your . . . slumber space."

"Year . . . so," the drunk slurred. "An' I ain't givin' it up."

Tamison felt the last of his rationality slipping away. "Do you know who lived here before you?"

"Nope. Don't care neither. My place now."

"Yes." Tamison stood, the last shards of his world crashing to the ground around him. "Your place." He swept his gaze over the room one last time, noticing a colorful object near one of the ruined pallets. He recognized it at once, the doll he had given Danara, her only and beloved possession. Galvanized, he ran to it and scooped it up. He hugged the patched and floppy toy to his chest, ignoring the ancient filth it smeared across his shirt. Its eyes were scraps of brown linen, its nose a cracked button, its mouth a bit of thread stitched into a smile. It completely lacked hair, ears, fingers, and toes; yet it still carried a hint of Danara's baby sweetness beneath the fouler odors of mold and dust.

The other man stared suspiciously.

Tamison trembled. Danara, at least, had not gone voluntarily. She would never have left this behind. "May I . . . have it?" He did not know why he asked. If the drunkard refused him, he would take it, no matter the cost.

The stranger wiped his nose on a grimy sleeve. "Ain't nothin' to me. Jus' go."

Still hugging the doll, Tamison obeyed, before the other could change his mind. He ran from the cottage he and his family had called home for a decade, onto a dirt path that barely constituted a street. Tears poured from his eyes. He kept his head down, seeking someplace safe and quiet to cry. He strode through alleyways that he once would have conscientiously avoided, squalid murky havens for thieves, drunkards, and beggars. Finding a crevice partially hidden by a shattered crate, he folded his face into his hands and sobbed.

Tamison could not have guessed how long he sat, wallowing in a misery that seemed impossible to fully comprehend. He sat through evening shadows parading slightly blacker across the darkness of the threadway. The dock-fore's long ago suggestion for suicide grew from plausible to provocative, but he could not find the strength to act on the inclination. *So long as they're alive, there's hope.* Tamison finally found comfort in the realization that no one had mentioned bodies. *So long as there's hope, I have to go on.* Buoyed by the thought, driven by need and hunger, he set out into the deepening night.

Once a warm and cozy haven, Rannoh's tavern now reminded Tamison of a crouched and massive monster silhouetted against a half-moon. Smoke trickled from the chimney in a gentle curl, revealing a cook fire in the hearth that would also keep the growing evening chill at bay. Uncertain of his welcome, Tamison hesitated on the threshold. Clutching the threadbare doll in one hand, he reached hesitantly toward the latch with the other.

Abruptly, the door lurched open. Before Tamison could skitter out of the way, two large, malodorous men burst into the gloom. A huge shoulder crashed against Tamison's cheek, staggering him. He caught the edge of the door instinctively, rescuing his balance. The man burped out a reeking apology as he and his companion headed into the night, leaving Tamison clinging to the door and staring after them. Then, he glanced inside the common room.

Smoke from the cook fire formed a light haze over more tables than Tamison remembered, some of the square-shaped ones replaced by round. The newer ones sported tablecloths dyed in chaotic patches of green, red, blue, and purple, obviously by children's hands. Tamison managed a smile. Likely, the twins had created the coverings, which made them endearing but also served a practical purpose. The patternless splotches of coloring hid food and beer stains admirably.

To his right, a bearded stranger in travel-stained leathers pointed at a copper coin floating a hand's breath above his table. The magician's audience consisted of two squint-eyed men who watched with obvious suspicion. Bizarre and broadly mistrusted in Lathary, users of magic rarely bothered with the city. Most Latharyns found their scant and limited powers paltry or worried that the magicians hid greater abilities that allowed them to control unwary victims.

To Tamison's left, a cluster of burly men sat at a corner table, off-duty night guards accustomed to the late hour. Their laughter echoed gruffly from the ceiling beams, and they seemed to take no notice of Tamison's entrance. Other patrons sat alone or in couples, scattered around the tavern. Most of these stared into their drinks, studiously avoiding the guardsmen's gazes. A wary prickle suffused Tamison, and he suffered memories of his capture. Though he recognized none of them, some might have assisted that night.

Behind the bar, Sheldora tossed a glance in Tamison's direction. Like a startled deer, she tensed. Eyes dodging his, she gestured a serving boy to her, an unfamiliar, strapping near-teen with a mop of blue-black hair.

Tamison slipped inside, easing the door quietly shut behind him. The warm, red glow of the hearth fire replaced the harsher moonlight. He continued to study his sister while she whispered in the youngster's ear. Apparently finished, she turned her back, casually wiping a bowl with a rag. The boy trotted toward Tamison.

Tamison strode farther into the common room, still clutching Danara's threadbare doll. Within two steps, he found the boy directly in his path. Dark eyes without a hint of rancor met Tamison's gray. "May I help you, sir?"

Tamison shook his head. "I just want to talk to my sister."

"I can show you to a table, sir. And serve you as I would any other."

Tamison took the path of least resistance. "All right."

Although Tamison had not previously noticed any particular discomfort, the boy visibly relaxed. He led Tamison to one of the round tables near the door. "Will this do?"

"Fine." Tamison did not sit.

The boy waited several moments, then pulled out a chair. Still, Tamison waited.

The serving boy cleared his throat. "What can I get you, sir?"

Tamison blinked. He did not have so much as a copper. "My sister, if you please." He looked toward the bar in time to see Sheldora jerk her head away.

The serving boy followed Tamison's gaze. "I'm sorry, sir," he said firmly. "If you'd like food or drink, I can bring it. But my mistress cannot meet with you."

Cannot? Or will not? Tamison did not bother to verbalize the thought. Sheldora, not he, had involved this youngster. Instead, he trained his gaze to the boy's left, tensing.

The youth instinctively shuffled leftward. He glanced over his shoulder, in the direction of Tamison's regard.

Instantly, Tamison zipped around the boy's right shoulder and sped toward the bar. The boy scrambled awkwardly after him. Sheldora stiffened, then headed as briskly toward the storage hall.

"Sheldora, wait." Tamison tried to sound cheery, rather than desperate and threatening. He doubted the off-duty guardsmen would interfere, but drink might make some of them mean if they did.

Ignoring his call, Sheldora opened the squealing door and disappeared inside. She did not waste time closing it. Tamison charged after her.

A tug on Tamison's sleeve sent him whirling to face the boy. Hardening his pale eyes, he glared, reminded of his eldest son. "Don't interfere." It was more threat than warning. "This is between me and my sister."

The serving boy pursed his lips, then nodded and released his grip. Clearly, Rannoh did not pay him enough to risk his life.

Tamison turned his attention back to the storage hall. Lit only by the dim spread of the common room's fire, it revealed blocky shadows and Sheldora's ruddy face. Her mouth opened.

"Don't scream," Tamison commanded. Though scarcely louder than a whisper, his voice contained the controlled power he had learned from sentries and prisoners. "I'd rather be executed than locked up again." Though simple truth, the meaning went far beyond the words. He could never harm Sheldora, but he wanted her to believe that, if she got him arrested, it would be for nothing less than her murder.

"Tamison, please." Sheldora's voice was a frightened squeak. "Don't do this. You'll get me in trouble."

The words were a terrible affront. "I love you. I'm not here for mayhem."

"Then go." Sheldora huddled against the crates, her fear obvious and painful to Tamison. "I'm forbidden to talk to you."

"Forbidden?" Anger flashed through Tamison. He pictured his massive brother-in-law, the fierce spark that entered his eyes whenever he blithely stepped into the wildest brawls or tossed those he considered troublemakers from his tavern. Rannoh had always seemed physically intimidating, and Tamison had worried for more than a decade about Sheldora's safety. Now, her expression displayed clear terror; she worried for her very life. Hatred for Rannoh became red hot and solid. *If he hurt her I'll—* The thought broke in midstream, unfinishable. *I'll what? I can't even feed my own children.* Defeated, Tamison sighed, his voice becoming barely audible. "Just tell me where my family is, and I'll leave forever."

Sheldora glanced nervously around her, as if worried Rannoh might pop out of one of the crates. She said nothing.

Pain knifed Tamison's heart at the thought that his sister might believe she needed to protect his wife and children from him, that he might harm them. *Has it become normal to her? Does she think all husbands hurt their wives? Even her own brother?* He tossed the doll.

Sheldora shied, and it fell soundlessly at her feet. Her mouth assumed a grim line, and she bent slowly. She hefted the doll, then lowered her head.

"My children need me, Shel." Welling tears turned the storage room to a dark blur, and they surprised Tamison. He would not have thought himself capable of more weeping. "And I need them." He sobbed out, "I need them so bad."

Sheldora took a step toward him. Then, catching herself,

she stopped. Tamison got the distinct impression she had in-tended to comfort him, but she only hugged the doll instead. "I haven't seen Linnry or the children since you . . . since you . . ." Apparently incapable of speaking the words, she amended, "Since I last saw you." Her voice quivered. She, too, fought tears.

"You don't know where they are?"

"No."

Tamison believed her. "Thank you." Afraid to cause her more distress, he turned to go.

"Tam."

He stopped. Turned back.

"You're always welcome here. Just as a . . . a . . ." She did not have to finish with "customer." "Here. You'll want to keep this." She tossed Danara's doll.

Blinded by tears, Tamison missed. It struck the floor with a soft thud. He crouched and scooped up the filthy bundle of ragged cloth. It hung limply from his fingers, a dead thing.

"At least," Sheldora said, her voice and manner finally familiar. "At least I'd get to *see* you."

Tamison nodded. Whirling, he clutched the doll to his heart and fled the tavern.

The next few days passed in a haze that condensed them to one. Tamison scrounged edible scraps from garbage and drinks from the central well. The weight he had gained in prison slowly melted, and hunger again became a constant companion. He learned to search at night, movement keep-ing the chill mostly at bay. By day, he slept in his alley crev-ice, undisturbed.

Then, in the near-pitch-darkness of midnight, luck finally discovered Tamison. At Lathary's border, he found a box of

Freetonian cheese that had, apparently, fallen from a merchant's cart. Worried that someone more desperate might relieve him of his find, he stuffed it into his pockets and waistband, popping the last piece into his mouth. Though chewy and pungent, it soothed the ache in his gut. Quietly, he glided back to his crevice, glad to have rescued himself from a few days of hunting food. Eventually, he knew, he would need to learn how to competently steal. Otherwise, he would starve.

Perched on the crate with his legs outstretched, hope rekindled in his heart and food in his mouth, Tamison felt a mild stab of guilt. He worried that his family might not be faring as well, that street orphans might go hungry while he feasted. The urge to find those children and share grew strong, but he quelled it with practicality. Most of them had more experience than he did. The ones who did not should not become dependent on a man who could not even support his own family. *Good idea, Flightless One. Destroy the lives of more children.*

His own use of a degrading nickname for himself struck Tamison as painfully odd. The boy who had been Uland's second son seemed like someone else, a lifetime ago; and the guardsman's words at the gate came back to haunt him: "I'd change that name if I was you. Take a new one, new life." Suddenly the advice seemed brilliant. *A new name. A new life.* As he ate, he considered, but his mind refused to move beyond his favorite names, those he knew too well: Sutannis, Ellith, and Danara. *Sutannis, Ellith, and Danara.* His chest ached. *Su-El-Dan.* He slurred it together. *Sueldan.* "Sueldan." It emerged from his mouth as two clear syllables, with just a hint of a third in the middle. *Until they're with me again, I'll keep their names as my own.* The symbolic gesture proved oddly soothing. *Sueldan.*

A movement caught the edge of Sueldan's vision, and he

stiffened. Someone or some thing had come close enough to prove a danger. Slowly, smoothly, he turned toward it, hiding fear behind a learned mask of predatory competence.

A dog looked back at him, its head thrust forward, nose snuffling the air. Shorthaired and mostly black, it sported patches of white on its chest and belly, its legs, and the tip of its tail. Its muzzle was long and pointed. The right ear stood up in a sharp triangle. The left flopped. Long-legged and rangy, it rose to the level of his mid-thigh, though it probably carried only half his weight. It appeared big enough to protect itself from becoming the meal of a hungry beggar yet small enough that its own need for food did not force it to man-eating. At least, Sueldan hoped the latter thought was true.

The dog whined softly.

It smells the cheese, Sueldan realized belatedly. He balled up the piece in his hand and tossed it to the animal.

The dog waited only until the food hit the gravel, then scooped it into its mouth. With three chews and a single swallow, it finished the offering, then looked at Sueldan for more. As it moved into the moonlight, he could see comical black spots decorating the white portions of its legs. For the first time in as long as he could remember, he laughed. "Go on, Dog." He waved it away. "Stay with me, and we'll both starve twice as soon."

The dog whined and rolled pitiful, begging eyes to Sueldan.

Sueldan sighed, pulled more cheese from his stash, and threw it toward the animal. Warily, it moved closer and wolfed down the food. Again, it looked askance at him.

Unaccustomed to hoarding, Sueldan held out a handful of cheese. He drew in his legs and leaned forward, offering it in his palm. "If you're going to join me, you have to trust me."

The dog eyed the bounty hungrily, then looked at Sueldan, who remained utterly still but talked in a gentle sing-song, "Come on, Dog. It's all right. I won't hurt you . . ."

The dog took a careful forward step, then a second. Still an arm's length away, it sat and whimpered.

Sueldan crooked up one eyebrow and switched to speaking an endless stream of pleasant nonsense, but otherwise did not move. He continued to proffer the cheese.

The dog cocked its head, attention locked on the food. It lowered its forelegs to the ground, bringing it slightly closer.

Sueldan did not compromise. "Here, Dog. Come, Dog. If you want it, you have to come."

In a lying position, it crept nearer, entire body tensed, eyes on Sueldan. Gradually, its nose reached the cheese, and it sniffed so hard a trickle of clear discharge emerged. Finally, it snatched a morsel from his hand and jumped backward to swallow it.

Sueldan resisted the urge to tense. "That's a good dog. Nice doggy."

Clearly comforted, the dog took less time to come the second time and retreated less. By the third time, it did not hesitate. Then, it sighed contentedly and disappeared into the shadows.

Full and tired himself, Sueldan curled into his crevice and closed his eyes. He cringed, awaiting the flood of worries and memories that always assailed him when he tried to sleep. This time, they did not come, apparently put to rest by his renaming. The children felt close, an intimate part of him. Only the night wind, wending through the alleyway, awakened him with its icy touch at intervals. Then, that surrendered to a close warmth that started at his spine and spread to encompass his body.

Contented for the first time in years, Sueldan rolled. His hand touched fur. Startled, he opened his eyes. The dog lay snuggled against him, sharing its warmth. Too tired to worry for his life, Sueldan smiled. And slept.

Chapter 3

DARKNESS enwrapped Lathary's carriage house, scant moonlight scarcely disrupting the gloom. Sueldan reveled in the intensity of the shadows, though it awakened childhood memories long forgotten. Then, night had frightened him, its blackness hiding the monsters of his imagination and the quiet loneliness giving him too much time to grieve. Once the beloved hero of his youth, the sun had now become the very essence of flight and seclusion. He glided toward the narrow window with the broken catch that he knew, from experience, would grant him access to supplies.

From the alleyway, the dog whined.

Sueldan turned, considering the volume and timbre of the sound. It had taken less than a month to train the animal to reliably signal when it sniffed out food among the leavings. He had spent much of the second month refining its understanding of edible to humans, and now it quietly ate rotted carcasses and densely moldered objects without calling his attention to them. It only notified him when it discovered something they could share. Its cry had come from the opposite side of the building. Sueldan took a hesitant step in that direction.

Something slammed over Sueldan's mouth, snapping his head backward until it struck firm flesh. A blade pricked against his throat.

Startled, Sueldan froze, thoughts scattering, heart pounding. He screamed instinctively, the sound muffled nearly to nothing by the gritty hand pressed to his lips.

"Shut up." A deep, threatening voice hissed into his ear. "Scream again, and I kill you. Understand?"

It was the voice of a seasoned assassin, or what Sueldan imagined one might sound like. He never doubted the other's sincerity. He barely nodded, worried that his movement might cause the knife to cut him.

The hand disappeared from Sueldan's mouth, smearing something slimy and foul-smelling in its wake. He choked back a cough.

"Give me your money." The thief hesitated only a moment before adding, "And your boots."

Money? Sueldan clamped down on a laugh, turning it into a snort. *Boots?* Suddenly, he understood. Two months on the streets had not yet turned his prison clothes to rags, and most of the downtrodden wore their footwear into scraps within a year. His nearness to the carriage house did not help. This thief had mistaken him for a traveler. "I have no money," Sueldan replied with quiet helpfulness.

Expertly, the man spun Sueldan. Long, black hair shimmered in the sliver of moonlight, and eyes dark as coals held a dangerous twinkle. Slitted and slightly off-kilter, they were the eyes of a killer. He blended with the shadows, his skin tone a shade darker than most of Lathary's citizens. He held a long-bladed knife in his fist. Too late, Sueldan averted his gaze. The more he saw, the more likely this man would slaughter him. "If I find so much as a half-copper, you're dead."

"I know." Sueldan pulled the two pockets of his tunic

inside out to expose the tattered linings. His only possession tumbled to the ground, a rusty knife he used to shave and to gut the mice, rats, and birds the dog caught. *Dog.* He wished he had taught the animal to defend him from human predators, but he doubted it had an attack instinct. It seemed less animal than the man in front of him. One by one, he removed his boots, shaking them upside down to show they contained nothing of value. Bits of leaf and dirt pattered to the cobbles. Finally, Sueldan met the frightening eyes once more. He offered the boots.

The thief blinked. His eyes barely reopened, black slits of intense hatred: devil's eyes.

In that moment, Sueldan knew he was going to die. Horribly. "Take them," he whispered so as not to reveal the tremor in his voice, forcing himself not to shrink behind the boots. Other prisoners had spoken of creatures like this. Obvious fear might goad him to attack.

The thief's thin lips stretched into a tight smile, and his eyes returned to normal. He flipped the knife with a deft skill that might have impressed Sueldan had his life not been at stake. The blade disappeared into the folds of his cloak. "You're more pitiful than I am." A moment later, he faded into the shadows and, soundlessly disappeared.

All of the terror Sueldan had held at bay condensed in that moment. Feeling suddenly boneless, he collapsed to the cobbles, every muscle trembling uncontrollably. *What's wrong with me?* Sueldan wondered if the thief had used some form of magic. Despite two years with criminals, he had never felt so frightened, nor reacted so violently to fear. He drew some solace from the realization that his life must still mean something to him to worry about losing it this much.

The dog charged around the building and skidded to a stop in front of Sueldan. It barked sharply at him, plunging closer as if to comfort, then leaping backward and barking again.

Where were you moments ago? Sueldan gathered control and softened his tone to gentle soothing. "It's all right, Dog. It's just me." He held out a hand.

The dog approached Sueldan stiffly, then sniffed suspiciously at the proffered hand. The overlong tail waved, tentatively at first, the white spot at its tip bobbing haltingly through the darkness. The barks turned to whines, and it approached. It licked his face, breath putrid.

Lovingly, with a firm movement, Sueldan pushed the dog away. He reclaimed his knife, then pulled on his boots. He rose, noticing for the first time that the crotch of his yellows was warm and wet. The reek of the thief's hand remained in his nostrils, sapping resolve. "Come on, Dog. Let's wash up."

Man and dog headed for the public fountain.

Three weeks later, Sueldan jarred awake to the acrid odor of fire. He sat up, dumping the dog's head from his chest. It bounded to its feet with a growl, suddenly alert, scanning the area for some sign of trouble. The sun hung high, fully lighting the alleyway that hid Sueldan's crevice. Absently, he patted the dog's head, fondling ears crusted with dirt. "Good boy."

Gradually, the reek of the fire gave way to the perfume of roasting meat. The dense rumble of myriad conversations touched Sueldan's ears, frequently punctuated by laughter or childish squeals of excitement. Only then did Sueldan realize All Feast Day had come again.

The cares of the last several years disappeared, stripped away by a mental return to the joys of youth and early adulthood. The urge to charge amid the celebrants seized Sueldan, to romp and shout, to join the games and the drinking, to watch his troubles dissolve for one day amid the dancing red flames of the bonfires. A more practical realization followed. *Free food.* His gut rumbled at the thought. For one day a year his family had been able to forget their poverty and empty stomachs. Every year, on this one day, they had feasted and pocketed as much extra as they could for the coming weeks. Excitement tingling in his chest, Sueldan headed toward the main streets and the celebrations, the dog tagging along at his heels.

Once beyond the tiny threadways that surrounded his crevice, Sueldan found the streets packed with Latharyns. Streamers floated from myriad shops, beckoning to crowds seen only on this one day every year. Excused for the day, the laborers wandered the city with their families or helped haul carts of foodstuffs through the packed roadways. Lured by a toddler slick with grease and gnawing at a drumstick, the dog left Sueldan's side, rejoining him at intervals. Finding a guild stand of baked fruit tarts and braided cinnamon sweets, Sueldan scarcely kept himself from bolting down half a dozen. Instead, he selected three, munching as he walked toward the central square where he knew he would find bread and meat.

Men of every guild, women escorting children, guards and wanted criminals mingled freely on this one day. With the jaded wisdom of a former prisoner, Sueldan suddenly understood what had escaped him in the past. He now suspected the day had more significance than just a chance to unify the calendar, celebrate, and gorge. By design and tradition, no arrests occurred on All Feast Day, and even the most notorious and sought after thieves and assassins could walk openly among the citizenry without risk. Sueldan could now see that it drew out hidden criminals, allowing the guards a fresh lead to secretly track them and ferret them out another day.

The dog came and went, remarkably at ease among the crowds, especially the children. It seemed to sense that no one could hurt it either on this day. It did, however, follow Sueldan to the town square where men from the hunter's guild roasted haunches, fowl, and fish while guardsmen carved and distributed the bounty.

Sueldan stood in line, the close aromas sending his gut into anticipatory grinding and filling his mouth with saliva. It seemed forever before a hot, greasy drumstick filled his hand and he hunkered down to eat it. The first bite was ecstasy. He closed his eyes, chewing, senses solely focused on taste and texture. The drumstick jerked in his hand. Sueldan wrenched open his eyes to find the bone clean and the dog disappearing into the crowd. "Hey!"

A dirt-smeared boy pointed after the furry figure. "Hey, mister. Dog tooked your food."

The taste of that single bite lingered in Sueldan's mouth. For a moment, desperate disappointment paralyzed him. Then, remembering the abundance, he returned to the line. Soon, he held a warm hunk of chicken, dripping juices. Finding a space, he crouched again, savoring the feast with his street senses back on alert. He had only finished half when the dog returned, whip-tail waving and expression unrepentant. It whined.

"Not a chance." Sueldan turned his back on the animal.

The dog walked around him. Eyes wide, head cocked, it looked up at him with a woeful expression.

Sueldan did not spare an instant of pity. "Find yourself another victim, Dog. You've gotten all you're going to get from me today."

The dog waited several more moments. When no food came its way, it trotted back into the crowd.

Sueldan finished his piece, licked his fingers, and tossed the bones into one of the trash fires. Returning to the line, he polished off two more servings before his gut felt stretched to bursting—and his pockets as well. Even the dog stopped accepting scraps from well-meaning adults or snatching them from unsuspecting children.

Only then, Sueldan allowed his mind to return to the agony that haunted his every waking moment, along with his dreams. The idea of approaching guardsmen brought back sour memories of his arrest. Nevertheless, he scanned the crowd for them, deliberately avoiding the few who had manhandled the prisoners, including himself. Finding a small cluster who had taken a break from serving the citizenry to eat their own share of the feast, Sueldan hesitantly edged toward them. "Excuse me."

A heavyset man with a bald pate spangled with sweat looked up from the ground. Beside him, a younger man leaning against a slanted boulder clutched a partially eaten handful of ribs, a greasy finger in his mouth. Three others turned toward Sueldan simultaneously, in various stages of repose.

"I'm sorry to bother you." Sueldan's hands began to tremble, and he moved to trap them in his pockets before remembering those were full of food. "My family has . . . um . . . disappeared. I was hoping . . . maybe . . . you could . . . help me . . ." He trailed off.

The young man studied Sueldan, including the tattered and fading prison yellows. He removed his finger from his mouth. "Say, aren't you—"

"Thief," the heavy one grunted.

The younger man nodded, straightening. "Your family disappeared while you were locked up? A year or so."

"Two," Sueldan corrected. "Someone might have kidnapped them." He dug into the folds of his yellows for Danara's doll. "I found this." His hand closed over the tattered scraps, and he pulled it free. He looked up, only to find several of the guards laughing. Shocked, he lowered his hand, sputtering, "But—"

One started seriously, "Can't understand why a family wouldn't welcome home . . ." His composure broke, and his last words emerged with a volley of guffaws, ". . . a jail-cat."

"Nothing humiliating about that," another added, fairly wheezing with laughter.

The heavyset man spoke in falsetto. "Sure, darling. I'll sit home and wait for you. What's two years of starvation to a woman in love?"

A fresh wave of mirth passed through them at Sueldan's expense.

Heat flooded Sueldan's cheeks, but he suffered their cruelty because he had no other choice. "Look, I just want help finding them. If they decide they don't want me around, fine. I just want to hear it from Linnry and the children."

The young man sauntered to Sueldan and placed a chummy arm around his shoulders. "Let me give you some advice, ducky." He leaned in conspiratorially. "Find yourself a new name. New life." He winked. "And start by getting yourself some different clothes."

Sueldan closed his mouth. *What did I expect?* Without another word, he spun free of the guardsman's hand and stormed away. Within only a few steps, rage gave way to frustration, then the grim sadness that had become all too familiar. A tear stung his eye. He wiped it away forcefully, weary of his own weak helplessness; and anger flared anew. "Damn it!" he shouted, not caring about the startled stares his cry earned him. He kicked a discarded bone, sending a gentle shower of dirt into the air. "Damn it to the ends of the world. No one deserves this."

A hand closed around Sueldan's shoulder.

Sueldan whirled, ready to vent. He faced a compact, well-muscled guardsman with rugged features who appeared to be eight or nine years younger than Sueldan himself. Soft brown eyes met his gaze, and a scribble of dark curls fell across his forehead. More fell past well-contoured cheekbones, a straight nose, and a square jaw. The medium-sized lips were set in a expression of tense sobriety.

Sueldan froze, certain he did not want to enrage this man, even on All Feast Day. "Hello?"

"Is your name Tamison?"

Sueldan hesitated, considering his reply. "Not anymore."

The guard blinked. His brows lowered gradually. "You have a wife? Some children?"

Sueldan's heart rate quickened. "Yes. Yes, I do. Do you know—?"

The guard interrupted with a jerk of his head toward a clearer area away from the road. He clearly thought they should talk in private.

Sueldan nodded, and the guard headed toward the indicated site.

Afraid of losing his only hope for finding his family, Sueldan followed directly on the man's heels. It was all he could do not to tread upon them.

The guard stopped and turned. "My—" Finding himself nearly on top of Sueldan, he back-stepped before continuing. "My name is Dallan. One night, about two years ago, I was patrolling the south central area. That's where you lived, wasn't it?"

"Yes. Yes." Sueldan only wanted the man to go on.

"I heard a scream. A woman's scream. By the time I arrived, a group of men was quietly carrying away a woman and some children. I tried to follow, but I lost them in the darkness."

Sueldan's heart ached in his chest. "A group of men?"

"Dressed in black. With hoods. They wore a red symbol."

Dallan crouched and scratched it in the dirt with a finger. It looked like a star with only four points.

Sueldan stared. He recognized the symbol but could not place it in his memory. "Who?"

Rather than straighten, Dallan waved Sueldan to his own level. "Sit."

Sueldan lowered himself to his haunches. "Who?" he repeated with more vigor.

"Callos," Dallan said.

Now, an image sprang to Sueldan's mind, a dark flag flapping from a merchant's wagon with that symbol marking its center. *Callos.* His eyes narrowed. "Why would the brotherhood of Callos want *my* wife and children?"

Dallan sucked in a deep breath, then loosed it slowly. His face bunched, and every muscle tensed. His words emerged in a crisp monotone indicative of a barely contained explosion. "The same reason they wanted my sister."

Sueldan shook his head, still confused.

"For so many years, I believed my sister died of illness. Only a few days ago, I discovered the truth. Men from Callos' brotherhood took her. And delivered her to Lord Mannkorus as a slave."

"Slave?" Sueldan sank to his knees as the enormity sank in. Linnry and the children forced to do a stranger's bidding. Ordered. Beaten. Raped. "No," he moaned. "Oh, no, no. No." He gritted his teeth until they ached, welcoming the boiling surge of anger battling to replace the too-long familiar plague of despair.

"I've got a month of leave time coming," Dallan continued. "And I'm going with you."

"With me," Sueldan repeated. Though he had never stated he would go anywhere, they both knew he had to try. "Why?"

"You'd be a fool to travel the roads alone."

Though true, the explanation did not address Sueldan's concern. He had never left Lathary, knew little of travel but the tales of highwaymen recounted by hapless merchants in Rannoh's tavern. "What do *you* get out of *my* company?"

Dallan looked away. "Do I have to get something?"

"I lost any naïveté I had in prison. No one is wholly un-selfish."

Dallan sighed. He glanced around the area, to assure that no one could overhear them, then finally met Sueldan's gaze again. "I've spent the last several months gathering informa-tion and came upon something few know." He leaned toward Sueldan, eyes skipping nervously, and lowered his voice to a whisper. "Callos was built on the ruins of an an-cient city. The long-ago folk had a religious tradition regard-ing their dead. They would bury them, sometimes bunches at a time, beneath their homes. Eventually, these graves be-came layered tombs." He stopped talking, studying the older man's reaction.

Sueldan shook his head to indicate he did not see the con-nection between these basement graves and himself.

Again Dallan looked about for anyone who might hear before hissing, "I believe that if someone could break through the old underground walls, we could create a cata-comb beneath the brotherhood's mansion. A secret entrance."

"A catacomb." Suddenly, Dallan's intentions became all too clear. Fright seeped through Sueldan's rage.

Dallan finished, "I heard you're good with tunnels . . ."

"Tunnels." Realizing he was dumbly repeating, Sueldan attempted something original. "I guess I'm all right." He said it as much to reassure himself. He would overcome any fear to rescue his family. He forced his mind to the practical. "You're certain about these layered graves?"

Dallan nodded vigorously. "Why don't you start packing—"

Sueldan rose and whistled. "Dog! Dog!"

Apparently bothered by the sudden shouting after so much whispering, Dallan also scrambled to his feet.

Several people glanced in their direction. Then, the dog wound through the press and came to Sueldan's side. Sitting, it looked expectantly at him. Sueldan turned his attention to Dallan. "I'm packed. Let's go."

Dallan managed a strained chuckle. "It's going to take me a bit longer than that, I'm afraid. Why don't we plan to meet at the north border. Sunset. In, say, three days?"

The idea of Linnry and the children suffering even one extra day pained Sueldan, but he realized Dallan's help greatly magnified his chances for success. "All right."

"And Tamison?"

"Sueldan," he corrected.

"Sueldan," Dallan repeated. He again lowered his voice to a whisper. "I don't think Lord Byrran would approve of this. I need my job. Please don't mention this to anyone, understand?"

Two men declaring war against a brotherhood. Who would even believe it? "Understood."

With a quick nod, Dallan headed back toward the cook fires. Sueldan watched him go. The dog sat at its master's feet and whined.

A cold night wind twined through Lathary's streets, turning the waters of the public fountain to liquid ice. Hidden by the nearly moonless night, Sueldan scrubbed away the grime coating his body. Even the frigid sting of the water could not erase the joy that suffused him, holding sleep fully at bay. As he twined his fingers through the too-long brown locks to his scalp, sand grated beneath his fingers. He dislodged it, rub-

bing and rinsing until his hair felt completely clean. The bite
of the wind, the queasy fullness of his gut, the worry that a
guard might pass by and chase him from the fountain, naked
and streaming water: these discomforts made him feel more
alive than he had in years. Charged with hope and mission,
he would allow nothing to distract him. Finally satisfied, he
donned his clothes, wishing they were cleaner as well.

The dog rejoined Sueldan as he headed to his alcove. He
knew he should sleep, having shorted himself a few hours to
join the festival during daylight hours, but thought descended upon him and refused to leave. Since finding Danara's doll, he had maintained the belief that his family had
not deliberately forsaken him. However, painful doubts
about his worth and legitimacy had left him uncertain in the
depths of his soul. Dallan's corroboration buoyed him. He
wished he had asked more questions: about the general pro-
clivities of Callos' brotherhood, especially Lord Mannkorus;
how he treated his slaves; how he punished men who challenged him and failed. The latter, Sueldan realized, did not
matter. He would rescue his family no matter the price to
him.

And he would not fail.

Sueldan did not remember when sleep claimed him but
the sun was climbing the sky when he awakened. Shielding
his eyes with a hand, he noticed a shadow waving against the
wall of a nearby shop. He swung his head to the caster. The
dog stood in the alleyway, tail swinging, an overripe *ginga*
between his white paws. The wrinkled red-and-amber skin
looked unappetizing, especially where the dog's teeth had
punctured it, and the brownish semisolid insides oozed
through. Still slightly nauseated from the previous day's

feast, Sueldan shook his head. "Thanks, Dog, but no thanks. You eat it."

The dog cocked his head, right ear pricked forward, the other flopped against his cheek.

"Go on." Sueldan made a flapping gesture. "It's yours. Eat it."

The dog obliged. Its mouth closed around the *ginga,* and it attempted to swallow the fruit whole, head and neck bobbing. The skin broke in its mouth, dripping out the sides, and this time it swallowed the *ginga* easily. It licked its lips, then lapped up the leavings.

"We're going to get supplies. *Real* supplies." Sueldan spoke with certainty, though he had no idea of how to do so without a bit of money. He could stretch the food he had taken at the feast perhaps three days. Past that, he could only look and covet before taking what he needed from the carriage house that night. "But first, a haircut."

Sueldan used his utility knife for a dry-shave, managing to nick himself only once. Then he turned the blade on his hair. Mousy locks tumbled to the ground, and the sun lit gold highlights he had never before noticed. He glanced at his reflection in the blade. It warped his softly-contoured features and gray eyes, barely revealing the shoulder-length cut, shaggy and uneven. It would have to do. "Let's go." Lurching to his feet, he headed toward the main street.

Though dozens of people strolled or fast-walked through Lathary's streets, they seemed deserted after the previous day's crowds. Recovering from the festival, many of the shopkeepers had just begun opening for business. The plump wife of the jeweler swept dirt from the entryway. Bones, scraps of cloth and parchment, and shards of shattered crockery lay scattered across the cobbles. Occasionally, a scrawny child would dash in to collect whatever dregs of food remained from the night's scavenging.

Finding a long bone, the dog picked it up. Apparently not hungry, it carried its prize through the streets, dropping it only to sniff more interesting leavings before hefting it again.

The town looked very different by day. Although Sueldan had walked the streets in full sunlight only the previous day, food and the crowds had preoccupied him. Now, he studied the shops, cottages, and functional buildings of the city with a curious eye. Much remained the same since his incarceration, yet the changes were jarring. A few more shops lay empty or in disrepair. The cooper had repaired his steps. The grocer had moved nearer the guild warehouses, and a goldsmith had taken his place. The baker's sons now tended his shop. A new building had appeared between Charla's bed and breakfast and a run-down cottage at a time when new construction had become a rarity. Gaily painted in three colors, it caught his attention immediately. The sign in front read: "Rifkah Carlaffsdatter—Fortune-teller."

Sueldan froze. Magic of any sort was rare in Lathary, though he had heard that other parts of the world employed it regularly. In his youth, rumors had circulated of an elderly man who detected truths and lies for Lathary's brotherhood. Sueldan had overheard his parents talking about a betrayal that had resulted in the truthkeeper's execution, but he had barely listened. As a child, politics had seemed preternaturally boring, and he had taken little more interest in the subject as an adult. The brotherhoods of the various towns and cities simply were. Seeing to his family's welfare took precedence.

Like the telekinetic Tamison had seen in Rannoh's, travelers occasionally earned drinks or meals by making people float, sending objects sailing mysteriously through the air, or reading minds in the taverns or on the streets. More often, the citizenry gave them a wide berth. It surprised Sueldan to find one proclaiming herself to the world so boldly.

Only as Sueldan drifted to the door did it occur to him how useful a fortune-teller could prove to him. *Just when I needed one, here she is.* He shivered at a weirdness that went beyond eerie coincidence to the supernatural. *Maybe that's part of her magic, to appear near those who most need her.* Logic slew the thought. *I could have used her more before despair turned me into this, while my family suffers.* Sueldan studied his stained and rumpled clothes. *And even more before I got myself in trouble.* Further realization made his original thought seem foolish. *Who couldn't use knowledge of the future at any time in his life? I should have thought of this before.* Irritated that his nocturnal lifestyle had previously blinded him to noticing this shop, he tripped the latch. He could have spared himself and his family a lot of pain.

The door swung open to reveal a plain-appearing room with none of the gaudiness of the sign. A young woman barely out of her teens flicked a feather duster over a plank wall near a door that apparently led to living quarters. The shop contained only a square table fashioned from gray wood and covered with a white cloth, and four matching chairs.

The woman smiled and bowed from a slender waist, in Carsean style. Dark-blonde ringlets cascaded around a long face pretty with youth. Blue eyes regarded Sueldan mildly, and the broad lips seemed out of place amid otherwise fine features. She wore a dress dyed in random patches of color except at the skirts. These perched in layers, each of a different hue and longer than the one above. "Good day, sir. What can I do for you?"

The dog padded through the open door to sit in front of Sueldan.

Her smile widened. "Oh, what an . . . interesting . . . animal." She crouched to its level and switched to baby talk. "Come, widdle one. Come, an' I'll pet ooo."

The dog hesitated only a moment before trotting toward the woman.

Sueldan stepped from the doorway into the room, pulling the panel shut behind him. "He's not very friendly." He looked up to see the dog on its back, wriggling happily as the woman scratched its underside. He laughed. "Usually."

"Sweet widdle puppy," she cooed. "Ooo wike oor belly sqwatched?"

Sueldan glanced around the room again, though he had seen everything. "I'd never noticed this place before. How long have you been here?"

"Abou' ha—," she started in baby talk, then broke off. Now it was her turn to laugh. "About half a year."

As she turned her attention to Sueldan, the dog rolled to its feet. "Slow business, though. I'd heard times were hard here. Also magic wasn't common. It seemed like the perfect place for a beginning fortune-teller, but your people don't seem to like me much." She seemed genuinely distressed by her words.

The dog shook its head, ears flapping with a sound like applause.

They don't like me either. Sueldan kept that thought to himself. "Magic's not common. It's mostly looked upon as . . . well . . . silly. Too limited to be useful." Not wishing to offend her, he added, "Not that I necessarily agree."

The woman rose from her crouch, then suddenly seemed to realize her rudeness. "By the way, I'm Rifkah." She extended her hands, palms up, in a neutral greeting accepted in most countries. He liked her Carsean accent, so reminiscent of his mother's.

"People tend to mistrust what they don't understand."

"Indeed." Rifkah bobbled her fingers. "It's customary to return a greeting. And a name."

"Yes." Sueldan covered boorishness born of social isolation with a teasing singsong. "You're a magician. You tell me my name." As tradition demanded, he laid his palms lightly on hers.

"It doesn't work that way—" Rifkah started, then stopped. "Sueldan." She reclaimed her hands.

Astounded, Sueldan remained in place. "I thought it didn't work that way."

"It doesn't." Rifkah's manner turned brusque. "But you, apparently, named yourself."

"That's right!" An excited tingle thrummed through Sueldan's chest. "Can you help—?"

"And you aren't planning to pay me for my services. Are you?"

"Wh–what?" Sueldan stammered. Until that moment, he had not considered payment; he had not required money on the streets. In fact, having nothing had rescued him from thieves more than once. "No. I was going to pay."

The blue eyes regarded him coldly through slitted lids. "Really." It was more statement than question.

"Really." Sueldan wiped suddenly wet palms on his britches. He had never heard of anyone harmed by magic, but he knew as little about it as the other citizens of Lathary. There were the rumors of hidden powers, and she had just read his mind. "I don't have any now, but I would have paid you over time."

"Would you?"

"Yes!" Desperate, Sueldan would have promised and delivered the world for information about his family and how to save them. "Here." He offered his hands again, assuming her talent worked by touch. "Read how much I need you. The lives of innocent children ride on your reply. I'll get anything you want. I swear it."

Rifkah shook her head. "You'll never learn, will you, Sueldan?"

Tears welled in Sueldan's eyes, and a lump formed in his throat. He could not answer, did not want to hear her judgment. If a woman who could see through to his soul found him worthless, he could no longer blame his misfortunes on circumstance.

"If you can't even repay debts owed to family, how could I expect . . ." Apparently noticing Sueldan's distress, Rifkah trailed off without finishing. "Please don't cry."

For reasons Sueldan did not understand, he could not stand Rifkah's pity. "I'm not crying." He wiped his eyes with the back of his sleeve.

The dog nuzzled its master's other hand comfortingly. Even it could tell he was lying.

Barely regaining control of his wavering voice, Sueldan pleaded, "Please. Ask me for anything. I *will* get it for you. I'll put it ahead of everything except rescuing my family. Check. If I don't mean each word, then throw me out of here."

Rifkah sighed. Her hands moved, but only to the gentle flare of her hips. "I'm a fortune-teller, not a truthseeker. My powers don't work that way."

"You knew my name," Sueldan reminded.

"Because the naming was a remarkably significant part of your past. I can see the highlights of people's pasts and futures. The present . . ." Rifkah shrugged. "I see as anyone else."

Sueldan sought the loophole. "I could come back tomorrow."

"With money?"

Sueldan shook his head impatiently. "I mean I could come back, then this would be the past. And you could read my sincerity."

Rifkah strolled toward the door, transparently attempting to escort Sueldan in the same direction. "It doesn't work that way. I don't read every intricate detail, and . . ." Her tone hardened again. ". . . and why am I explaining this to you? You haven't paid me." She tripped the latch and flung open the door. "If you're so sincere about getting payment, then get it before you return."

"I will," Sueldan promised. "How much?"

"Five silvers."

Sueldan swallowed. It was enough to buy a month of modest food and lodging. "I will. Whatever it takes. For my family." The words emerged easily. He edged toward the door.

Apparently touched by the sorrow in Sueldan's voice, Rifkah relented, "I'll tell you this much now: You're about to undertake a mission that's definitely more than you can handle. You need to get yourself some help."

"Thank you." Gratitude forced out the words, even before Sueldan could consider hers. "Thank you so very much." He started toward the doorway, then noticed that Rifkah's attention had shifted from him to something outside. The dog growled.

Sueldan followed their gazes to a trio of guards marching deliberately and obviously toward them. Gasping, he withdrew behind the jamb, possibilities racing through his mind. *Did someone catch me stealing from the carriage house?* His hands trembled. This time, he doubted he would get another reprieve. *What if they caught Dallan?* Heart pounding, he cringed farther into the room. "Close the door," he hissed.

"No." Rifkah raised herself to her full height. "I won't let them intimidate me."

You won't let them intimidate you? It suddenly occurred to Sueldan that the guards would have no way of knowing he had come here. *Of course, they came for her.* Heart beating wildly, he eased back between Rifkah and the guards. The dog took a stolid position beside him.

The guards stopped a respectful distance from the door, more, Sueldan guessed, to appease the dog than Rifkah or himself. He recognized only one, a squat, scar-faced man named Burk who had occasionally handled him on the work squad. Another was well-muscled with a large gut and gray-flecked hair, the third of average build and coloring.

Burk returned Sueldan's gaze, first with suspicion, then with wide-eyed recognition. Oblivious to this exchange, the older guard said, "Rifkah Carlaffsdatter, we have some questions to ask you." He glanced at the man and dog. "May we come in?"

Sueldan felt Rifkah stiffen behind him, but her voice carried no trace of discomfort. "Certainly." She beckoned.

Sueldan froze a moment, knowing the wisest course of action was to slip out as the guards entered. They did not want him. Yet, the thought of leaving Rifkah to face three guards alone terrified him, especially after she had granted him free advice. He could not help picturing Linnry in Rifkah's place. Against his better judgment, Sueldan stepped aside, deeper into the room. The dog followed his movement, its good ear attentive.

Smelling of grease, sweat, and steel, the guards entered, swords bumping against their thighs. The last in, Burk closed the door behind him, then remained leaning casually against it.

Rifkah brushed between the other two guards, pausing momentarily, looking for all the world like a proper hostess. "Let me get you all some tea."

"That won't be necessary." The youngest, the nondescript guard, placed himself between Rifkah and the door to her quarters. "This won't take long."

"Nevertheless—" Rifkah dodged the guard and made a sudden dash for her quarters.

The guard spun for an easy grab.

Still thinking of Linnry, Sueldan hurled himself at the guard. One hand met the man's ear. His shoulder struck a muscled bulk as solid as whalebone, sending a shock of pain through his torso. Deflected, Sueldan tumbled into a heap. He winched his fingers into the guardsman's hair, as much an instinctive attempt to save his balance as intention. The guard dropped to one knee, deliberately rolling. The maneuver cost him several strands of hair but broke Sueldan's grip. A knee crashed into Sueldan's gut, jarring the breath from his lungs. For a stunned moment, he lay there, desperately gasping, consciousness swimming.

Meaty hands winched around Sueldan's neck, hauling him to his feet. "You stupid bastard! I'm going to kill you!"

Darkness seized Sueldan's vision, accompanied by a swarm of white spots. An intense buzzing filled his ears, punctuated by the dog's sharp and continuous barking. A trickle of air wheezed through his windpipe, and his diaphragm shuddered back to life.

"What are you, crazy? That's—" Burk's voice filtered through the dense fog of hovering senselessness. "Just let him go."

The younger guard's voice sounded thunderous in comparison. "The bastard hurt me. He made us lose the witch."

As the world came back into focus, Sueldan blinked rapidly.

The heavyset man spoke next. "Release him, Kristov." His tone held unexpected menace, nearly as penetrating as the dog's barks. "If you'd have chased her instead of wrestling with him, we'd have had her."

"Wrestling?" Kristov grumbled. He shoved Sueldan away with a suddenness that sent him stumbling. Already dizzy, he collapsed, throwing his hands in front of his face to fend a blow that never came. Something brushed beneath his arm.

He started to rise, then found the dog's face in his, the tongue flicking frantically over his features.

That mobilized Sueldan. He scurried to his feet, into a defensive crouch, then glanced at Burk. The guard had always seemed professional, handling prisoners with a businesslike competence.

Expression somber, Burk jerked his head toward the outer door, loosing a trickle of sweat from his brow. "Get out of here before we charge you with obstructing the dealings of the brotherhood."

Before the guards could change their minds, Sueldan sprinted through the doorway, into streets now filled with the normal bustle of city daylight.

Sueldan's sudden, rapid appearance sent one woman skittering. Another jerked away, dropping a shopping basket that spilled an assortment of roots and pungent herbs. A man glared but continued on his way. Though desperate to flee, Sueldan stopped to assist the woman he had startled. Quickly, he snatched up the fallen bounty while passersby detoured around them. At length, having found every one he could, he approached the woman where she crouched over the basket and offered her his gatherings. For a moment, her cool, dark eyes studied him. Then, apparently deciding he looked clean enough, she held out the basket. Sueldan dropped his load into it. "I'm terribly sorry."

In reply, she made a noncommittal noise. At that moment, the dog trotted up, an onion helpfully clutched in its jaws, its tail waving.

The woman screwed up her face. "Keep that one." Without further acknowledgment, she continued down the roadway.

"Good boy." Sueldan accepted the onion and patted the dog's head. The encounter allowed most of the panic to drain away, leaving him worried and confused. Placing the

onion in his pocket, he slipped into the nearest alley, surprised to realize he now felt safer in the dark, anonymous
world of thieves and cutthroats. "Now all I have to do is
teach you to attack, rather than bark, when men are . . . killing me."

The dog whined.

Sueldan patted it absently. He half-sat against a rain barrel and stared at the side of the fortune-teller's shop/cottage,
shaking his head. "Poor Rifkah." He had no idea why the
guards of the brotherhood wanted her, but he imagined
them tearing apart her belongings while she hid, shaking and
terrified, among them. He had done all he could, yet he
wished he could rescue her. Her words returned to him now:
*You're about to undertake a mission that's definitely more than you
can handle. You need to get yourself some help.* In the wake of his
helplessness against the guardsmen, those words rang frighteningly true. *I can't afford to fail.* He sighed. *Thank goodness I've
got Dallan to assist me.* The urge to return to his alcove grew
strong, but he remained in place. He wanted to see whether
or not the guards caught Rifkah and how they handled her.

Something grabbed Sueldan's ankle.

He jumped with a squeal of surprise, whirling to face Rifkah hidden in the shadows of the rain barrel.

"Quiet, you fool," she whispered. "They'll hear you."

Charged with new urgency, Sueldan did not bother with
an answer. Grasping Rifkah's hand, he half-pulled, half-
dragged her through a series of twisting threadways. Deeper
and deeper into his haunts he led her until he found himself
doubling back over ground they had already covered. Only
then, tired and aching, he yanked her down behind a mound
of discarded rubbish to talk. The dog sat nearby, watching.

Trusting the animal to alert him to the presence of strangers, Sueldan finally turned his attention to the fortune-teller.
"Why were you hiding so close? Why didn't you run?"

Rifkah rearranged her tangled curls with a hand. "Why didn't *you* run?"

"I was waiting to make sure you were all right."

Rifkah's brows rose.

Sueldan waited expectantly a moment before realizing her gesture was also her answer. "You were watching out for me?"

Rifkah nodded.

Dumbfounded, Sueldan stared. A long time had passed since anyone had worried about his welfare.

"You saved my life. I'd be a damn poor excuse for a woman if I didn't at least make sure you didn't die for your generosity."

Sueldan doubted Rifkah knew how close he had come to doing just that. "I–I only did what was right. What anyone would have done."

Rifkah snorted. "Don't belittle your courage. You saved me. That's more than any of those three cowardly minions of your dim-witted so-called brotherhood would have done."

Sueldan flinched, glancing around them, though the dog had given no indication that anyone had approached within earshot. "Watch your tongue, woman. Insurrection is a capital crime."

"Fine," Rifkah grumbled, removing the hand from her hair. Curls slipped over her forehead and into one eye. "But only because you have to live here. I'm leaving. It's too damn bad I can't read my own fortune. I'd have known better than to come to this wretched city in the first place."

Without thought, Sueldan brushed the hair from Rifkah's eye. Memories of Linnry surged back to the fore, the touch of her silken hair, the gentle music of her laugh. "Don't you think you're overreacting? You shouldn't condemn an entire government just for wanting to talk to you.

And I hardly saved your life; I only rescued you from a few questions."

Rifkah planted her hands on her hips. "They weren't going to question me. They were going to imprison me."

His own time in the dungeons still fresh, Sueldan swallowed. "How do you know—?"

Rifkah turned Sueldan a withering look.

He broke off. "Oh. Your magic."

"My magic," Rifkah confirmed. "Which is also why they wanted to imprison me. Pure prejudice. Nothing more." She contradicted herself almost immediately, revealing another, though not better, motive. "Lord Dinar didn't get the reading he wanted yesterday. He expected me to say that times would get better in Lathary, that he would get richer. Soon. But I'm not going to lie." She huffed out an angry sigh. "Stupid men commanding stupider soldiers. And those guards—" She pursed her lips around the word, emitting it like a curse. "All muscle and no insight. Get through life on their ability to bully and never learn to think."

Sueldan let her rave without interrupting. In his own intense experience, he found guards as varied in temperament as any other profession. It bothered him more to discover that the brotherhood's aversion to magicians apparently stemmed, not from magic per say, but from readings that did not jibe with their desires.

"Couple of them came around last week. They wanted me to pay money I didn't even have to keep my shop safe." Rifkah repeated, "Safe. Safe from what? The only thing that ever bothered me was them. And your brotherhood—" She loosed a dismissive grunt. "They know what I am. If they had any sense at all, they'd have sent guards who didn't know they planned anything more than a questioning."

Sueldan smiled, trying to lighten the mood. "Well, I'd

rather not damn their incompetence. Without it, you'd have wound up in prison."

Rifkah finally managed a smile. "You're right. So, I guess you'll want that free reading now."

"No," Sueldan replied, hoping he had not just out-clevered himself. "I'm going to pay you for that. But, since you clearly plan to leave Lathary, I was hoping you'd accompany me on that mission that's 'definitely more than I can handle.' "

Rifkah's blue eyes widened, and she examined Sueldan for a long moment, during which he wondered if she were using her magic. Her grin broadened. "You'll still get your free reading. Probably more than one. But you'll now get it when it matters most. Very clever."

"Indeed." Sueldan winked. "That's why I'll never become a member of the brotherhood."

"The only reason, I'm sure." Rifkah shifted to a more comfortable position. "Fine, I'll go with you. But only because I've always wanted a homely dog for a companion."

Sueldan adopted a widemouthed expression of offense. "You'd better be talking about the dog."

"Whatever makes you happy." Rifkah made a chirping noise that gained the animal's attention, then tapped her leg to indicate it should come to her.

The dog padded to the fortune-teller's side. She fondled its ears.

Sueldan watched the exchange, the dog sitting in happy stillness, the young hand moving around and over the fuzzy neck and head. Ten years from now, she could be his eldest daughter, Ellith. Guilt fluttered through his belly. "This could be very dangerous," he finally said.

Rifkah did not look up from the dog. "I believe I'm the one who told *you* that."

"I just want to make sure you don't get yourself killed

because you feel you owe me for keeping you out of prison. I've been there."

"I know." Rifkah reminded, still concentrating on the dog.

"I just mean, it's not as bad as dying."

"I'm not going to die. And neither are you. We're going to rescue your family."

Joy surged through Sueldan, sending his heart into wild pounding. "You know that? For sure?"

Rifkah laughed. "The future is never certain. Never." She met his gaze with blue eyes older than her years. "But I trust your determination, Sueldan. And it's time you did, too."

"Why?" Sueldan could not help responding, wondering how anyone who knew his past could place her life even partially into his hands.

"That question," Rifkah replied, "you'll have to answer for yourself."

Chapter 4

THE last pink streaks of nightfall etched Lathary's dark sky when Sueldan returned to the city streets. Further conversation with Rifkah revealed that she had wasted no time crawling through the window of her quarters to escape. Like Sueldan, she had no supplies to sustain her on the trip to Callos, no clean clothes, and only the few half-coppers she had had in her pockets when the guards arrived. She had refused his offer to slip back into her cottage and purloin anything else she might wish, admitting her clothing did not seem worth the danger and that the meager coinage she carried was all her money in the world, the reason she had so vigorously insisted on payment. Business in Lathary had not gone well.

Leaving the dog with Rifkah, Sueldan walked solemnly through the familiar alleys and roadways, toward the shadowy bulk of Rannoh's tavern. At least this time he would not arrive empty-handed; Rifkah had given him four of her seven half-coppers. It would not cover the month of travel-food they needed, but it might demonstrate good faith to his sister. He would have preferred to buy anywhere else but knew he would stretch their money farthest with Sheldora. She also deserved to know that she would not see him again

for a lengthy period of time, if ever. He wanted to say good-
bye.

The trip to the tavern seemed to span an eternity. The
pink faded from the sky, leaving it a uniform black interrupted only by an array of stars like stab holes in a strip of
velvet. The moon lay hidden behind a towering temple. At
length, Sueldan realized he was the cause of the unusually
long journey. His walk had slowed to a shuffle-footed crawl.
With a sigh of resignation, he quickened his pace.

Noise from the tavern filtered into the nearby roadway,
bursts of laughter and loudly uttered curses. Above it all, an
oddly familiar voice kept up a fast-paced, soothing patter.
Sueldan paused for a moment, trying to identify the speaker
by sound, without success. Again recognizing his own delaying tactics, he tripped open the heavy door.

The welcome odors of food and ale wafted over Sueldan
in a rush that brought with it some of the best and worst
memories of his life. Patrons scattered around the bar and
tables, with a cluster surrounding one particular corner. As
the unidentified but recognized voice emerged from the center of that area, Sueldan headed curiously toward it.

At length, Sueldan managed to peer through a gap in the
crowd at a dark-skinned Latharyn who shuffled a trio of *allanut* shell halves with remarkably light-fingered dexterity. The
fast-paced talking emanated from him and consisted mostly
of repetitive strings of "come on there, goodman," "find the
ha' copper," and "only players win." Sueldan stared as he
drifted toward a table, trying to recall where he had seen the
speaker before. He found himself at once attracted and re-
pelled; the friendly speech and quick movements drew his
attention, but not all seemed pure about this man. The rest
of his audience, however, seemed fully charmed, rushing to
place handfuls of coins on the table in front of the shells.

Still perplexed as much by the familiarity as the situation,

Sueldan deliberately chose a seat at the end of the bar that gave him a sideways scrutiny of the darker man's hands. He watched, entranced, as the not-quite stranger lifted the shell behind the stack of coins to reveal nothing beneath it. Noise erupted from the players, some laughing and pointing, others grumbling in irritation. The man then lifted another shell to reveal a half-copper no more remarkable than the ones in Sueldan's pocket. The shuffling routine began again, the man's happy voice exhorting every man in the tavern to play. His eyes, however, shifted suspiciously to Sueldan. Brown, they held a sparkle that seemed to change from joyful to threatening in an instant.

Abruptly, memory awakened. Sueldan had looked into those eyes before, in a dark alleyway with a knife blade pricking his throat. His every muscle tensed. Bile climbed into his throat. He swallowed hard and looked away, only to find himself facing Rannoh. Discomfort turned to terror.

"What do *you* want?" the brother-in-law demanded, his tone rife with frigid anger.

"I–I only . . . I mean . . . I . . ." Sueldan found himself incapable of coherent speech. Usually Rannoh spent his time securing supplies or working in the back on problems and paperwork. Sueldan had expected a chance to talk to his sister alone.

"Eloquent as ever, I see." The coarse black hair lay in neat waves over a peaked forehead, and deep sockets bracketed hard, dark eyes. "It's a wonder the scribes and storytellers haven't competed for your talents."

Does he demean Sheldora like this, too? As well as terrify her? Anger gave Sueldan back function of his tongue. He returned his attention to the con man, who gathered his marks' coinage and prepared for another round. "Leave me alone, Rannoh. I'm a paying customer." Sueldan jingled the coins in his pocket.

Rannoh grunted harshly. "You got money, you should pay off some of your debts. Start with the forty silvers I've lost to that serpent-tongued scam-man tonight. I've given you more than that in food."

Sueldan gained a new appreciation for the dark man with the shells. Separating Rannoh from hard-earned money seemed more like magic than anything Rifkah had performed. In the light of day, without a weapon, the stranger did not look at all menacing. Sueldan continued to watch, surprised to find himself as fooled as the customers. Following the correct shell appeared simple, yet time after time the half-copper materialized where he least expected it.

Rannoh stood for several moments in silence, gaze flicking from Sueldan to the stranger. "So," he finally said. "What is it you came to buy?"

This time, Sueldan did not bother to glance at his brother-in-law. He watched as a man he knew from the docks placed a small wager on the obvious shell. This time, the half-copper appeared beneath the chosen *allanut*. Amid a spattering of applause, the dark man scooted back the dock worker's wager, matching coins of his own, and half again the bet. Immediately, several new patrons and others who had abandoned the game returned. The exchange convinced Sueldan that the con man had complete control of the half-copper's location. "I want to speak with my sister."

"She's not available." Rannoh leaned against the table, and it listed toward him. "Whatever you want, you can tell me."

Sueldan sucked in a deep breath through his nose, then released it through his mouth. He turned to face Rannoh. "I came to say 'good-bye.'"

One brow rose.

"And to purchase supplies for my trip."

"Where are you going?" Rannoh asked hopefully.

Sueldan suspected the greater the distance he named, the happier it would make Rannoh. "Away from Lathary. I expect to be gone a while." He added mischievously, "Depends on how long my supplies hold out."

Rannoh grunted. He pursed his lips in a thoughtful hush that Sueldan suspected hid a war of indecision. He had placed the miserly tavern keeper in a precarious position, pitting his greed against his wish to be rid of a pest.

I should have done this a long time ago. Sueldan savored his brother-in-law's discomfort, only to find it stemmed from a different struggle.

"He's cheating."

The words seemed incongruous with the situation. "What?"

"He's cheating," Rannoh repeated, his gaze sliding to the shell game.

"Undoubtedly."

"You show me how, and the supplies are yours. Free."

The last word startled Sueldan. "Free?"

"Free," Rannoh acknowledged. "A month of free rations."

Excitement thrilled through Sueldan, but he suppressed a smile. The idea of allowing Rannoh to see how much he needed that food grated. Anyone else he would have thanked profusely. "I think I've got it figured out."

"Already?" The word contained more gruff intention than surprise, which further irritated Sueldan. Clearly, Rannoh believed his brother-in-law had engaged in similar scams.

Sueldan pitched his voice even lower. "He slips the coin out while he's shuffling, then returns—"

Rannoh forestalled his brother-in-law with a raised hand. "I said *show* me how."

"Show you?" Sueldan shrugged, a comma of chestnut

hair slipping into gray eyes. "I don't have the practice or quickness to do it exactly, but if you could get me some shells . . ." He glanced at Rannoh around the errant locks, only to find him shaking his head with slow deliberateness.

"*Show* me." Rannoh inclined his head toward the dark stranger.

All of Sueldan's terror returned. He swallowed hard, the pressure of a remembered knife blade making his breathing labored. He recalled the depthless insanity that had appeared in the man's eyes, the grim and horrible certainty of bloody death. "My life is worth more than your supplies."

Rannoh loosed a soft, contradictory snort that worried at Sueldan's already meager sense of self-worth. "Without supplies, your life is over."

Sueldan rose. "I'll buy my supplies elsewhere."

Rannoh rolled his eyes at the threat. "What do you have in your pocket, a few coppers? A loaf of bread and a sliver of cheese? That won't get you far."

Sueldan clenched his jaw, turning toward the opening door. Need had already forced him to accept too much of Rannoh's verbal abuse. "Tell my sister I said good-bye."

Rannoh's youngest assistant entered the tavern, followed by six members of the town guard in off-duty clothing.

The barkeep gave the men a subtle nod, then addressed Sueldan with a tone remarkably gentled. "Hey, I'm sorry, Tamison. *Two* months of supplies and plenty of protection. The guards want him as bad as I do. Once he's lost his best hand, he won't be so dangerous. And the few days he spends in prison until then will give you plenty of time to leave town."

Teeth still gritted, Sueldan sat. He had little choice but to cooperate. He and Rifkah needed the food, and he had more than enough reason to hate the dark stranger. "All right," he finally said.

Rannoh smiled. "We'll tell you when we need you."

Sueldan's gaze sank to his hands. He bobbed his head once.

Rannoh headed toward the off-duty guards as if to tend to their orders. Sueldan glanced surreptitiously at the schemer, who continued his shell game with only a wary peek at the newcomers. It was not uncommon for guardsmen to spend their downtime here. Rannoh chatted with them a bit longer than taking orders required, but soon he disappeared toward the food preparation area. The dark stranger returned to his game, apparently put at ease by the guardsmen's seeming disinterest in him. He looked over at Sueldan more frequently, obviously more concerned with one so close sitting quietly in a tavern without food or drink.

A barmaid brought dinner and drink to the guardsmen, who ate with a rowdy enthusiasm that well-suited the tavern. Sueldan wished Rannoh would supply him with a complimentary meal as well, not only because of his hunger but to soothe the awkwardness that kept the stranger's attention always partially turned in his direction. But that meal never came. Finally, as the resentment against his brother-in-law grew almost unbearable, a trio of guardsmen worked their way near enough to show obvious interest in the game.

The con man seemed to pay no particular attention to the guardsmen or their obvious weaponry, but Sueldan noted that the man's interest in him waned and his movements grew slightly stiffer. Sueldan even managed to see the dark stranger flick a palmed coin beneath one of the shells, confirming his suspicions.

Rannoh drifted back to Sueldan's side. "Ready?" he whispered.

Sueldan did not address the question, instead explained the details. "While the bet is being placed, the coin isn't under any of the shells. He puts it where he wants to as he picks them up."

Rannoh gave Sueldan his first direct gaze. Brown eyes glimmered with excitement. "You're sure?"

Sueldan disliked the expression nearly as much as the murderous glare the con man had turned on him in the alley. The dark man might deserve his punishment, but it seemed cruel to take pleasure in another's mutilation. His left hand drifted to his right wrist, and he rubbed it absently. "I'm sure."

Rannoh threaded his way casually to the guardsmen and spoke with one before removing his empty plate. Sueldan watched that guard join his fellows in front of the scam and consult with them briefly. The two remaining at the table stood raggedly and headed toward opposite sides of the room, one with a slightly drunken stagger.

Sueldan's heart started to pound. He thrust a hand in his pocket to hide his nervousness, mindlessly stirring Rifkah's coins. They seemed ridiculously minuscule compared to the silvers and full coppers he had watched the con man casually add to his pouch throughout the evening. *He deserves to lose his hand for slaughtering innocents for money.* Yet, Sueldan realized, the man had not killed him, had not even robbed him. He had no proof but an assassin's gleam in the other's eye and unproven suspicion that he had murdered anyone. Sueldan shook off the thought. Whatever the man's actions in Lathary's back alleys, he was definitely robbing people here.

The shells stopped moving, and the con man sat back. A plump merchant in silk-trimmed linens tipped a small stack of silvers toward the middle shell. Before the dark stranger could move, two of the guards lunged toward him, weapons rattling from their sheaths.

Someone screamed. Men near the table scattered. One slammed into a table, spilling mugs and bowls to the floor.

These rang against the cobbles, splashing dregs of mead and wine like bloodstains. The con man flung himself backward, chair clattering to the floor. He ducked and rolled, only to find himself pinned by four sword-wielding guardsmen, two in front and one from either side. The last no longer appeared the slightest bit tipsy.

The con man froze, manner turning outraged, though Sueldan clearly read fear in the dark eyes. *Is this the same man who threatened me?* It seemed impossible. It was the eyes he had recognized, the rest of him seeming to blend into a bland nondescriptness. "What's the meaning of this?"

Rannoh waved Sueldan over.

The con man's gaze whipped to Sueldan, and a hint of the dangerous stare returned. Sueldan read more there than the other possibly could have said without words: *I knew you were up to something. I should have killed you when I had the chance.*

"We think you're cheating these good people out of their money," one of the guardsmen explained, gaze never leaving his prisoner.

Sueldan approached, suddenly wishing himself anywhere else.

"You're overstepping your bounds," the con man hissed. "Having quick hands doesn't make me a cheat. I didn't force any of these 'good people' to bet they could follow my motions."

As Sueldan came nearer, one of the guardsmen clamped a hand to his shoulder. "This man here says he can prove you're cheating."

All eyes went abruptly to Sueldan who felt as if his heart would punch its way out of his chest. He glared at Rannoh, hoping the tavern keeper could read his mood as well as he had guessed the con man's. *This wasn't part of our deal.* Hand still in his pocket, he clenched the half-coppers nervously as the guard steered him to the table.

Sueldan looked at the con man. His nostrils flared, his eyes contained raw fear, and a bead of sweat trickled from his forehead. His steely confidence had shattered. Sueldan took a deep breath, grasping for some courage of his own. He seized the middle shell, the one with the bet in front of it, and tossed it over to reveal no coin. He turned his head toward Rannoh.

His brother-in-law rubbed his hands together, a slight smile playing over otherwise serious features. Fresh hatred sparked for the man who had diminished him in his sister's eyes, who had intimidated her and branded him a flightless falcon. Sueldan tossed over the rightmost shell to reveal nothing beneath it either.

Sueldan studied the thief, helpless between the guardsmen's swords. He would suffer the penalty of his lesser crimes. Murder meant an immediate death sentence; and, witnessed or not, Sueldan felt certain this stranger had killed his share. The dark eyes met his directly, pleading. Sueldan suspected he had looked even more pitiful when the dagger had pressed against his throat. And, he had to admit, the other had shown him mercy.

Sueldan reached for the third shell, then stopped, other hand still winched around one of Rifkah's half-coppers. Instead, he rubbed nonexistent sweat from his own brow. Taking his right hand from his pocket, he used it to tip the last shell, clumsily tossing the half-copper it contained to the tabletop. The coin rolled on its edge for a moment, then rocked in imperfect loops, finally settling flat against the wood.

The swords slipped downward, no longer menacing the con man. Rannoh's mouth fell open, and he turned his head stiffly from the coin to Sueldan. The dark man's face sprouted a wicked grin, and he came suddenly back to life.

"Is it a crime for him to pick the wrong shell?" He jabbed a finger in the general direction of the merchant.

"No," one guard admitted. The others resheathed their swords, giving Rannoh glances that ranged from bewildered to irritated. "Sorry we troubled you." They stepped away from the con man, gathered their things, and swiftly left the tavern.

The show apparently finished, the other patrons returned to their drinks, while the barmaids scurried to clean up the mess and replace spilled food and drinks. The con man rose and gathered his coins, including the half-copper that Sueldan had added to his collection.

Rannoh rounded on his brother-in-law, his features scarlet and his dark eyes nearly black. "You bastard! You—"

The con man interrupted. "Dinner, please, barkeep. And two mugs of your best mead. He pointed toward a table near the door. "There, please. This table doesn't seem comfortable anymore."

Rannoh's glare left Sueldan's just long enough to read the somber expression on the con man's face.

"I believe you owe at least that much for the trouble you put an honest man through."

The color faded from Rannoh's face as he studied his other patrons. Many watched with raised brows how he atoned for his "mistake." For an instant, Sueldan felt certain his brother-in-law would attack them both. Then, apparently putting the reputation of self and establishment over vengeance, he headed toward the food preparation area, grumbling something unintelligible except for the occasional curse.

The con man made a brisk gesture that suggested Sueldan precede him. Sueldan obliged, though the skin on his back crawled. It made no sense for the stranger to stab him now, yet something about the man made him worry about the possibility. It took self-control to keep from skittering to a chair at the indicated table; and even so, he got there too quickly. Trying to look calm, he sat. The con man rearranged his seat to allow a full view of common room and door. "Why'd you do it?"

It took Sueldan an instant to realize he had been addressed. "I—I didn't—I mean I—" He gathered his thoughts. "A man so bad off he had to rob *me* clearly needed help." Sueldan tried not to contemplate the real reasons: gratefulness that the other had not killed him in the alley and vengefulness against Rannoh. They seemed selfish and inappropriate.

"So that *was* you in the alley."

Sueldan nodded, the question answering his uncertainty as well. He met the other's stare. "Why does a con man as clever as you need to rob strangers in alleys? Pulling the right scam should fix you for life."

"Yeah." The dark man's gaze went distant, with a glimmer of something Sueldan could not identify. He looked suddenly older, wiser. "Every man has his demons." He changed the subject swiftly. "You saved my life. I'm going to give you what my life is worth and something more valuable." He slapped two silver coins on the table, a pittance compared to what he had taken in that night, yet a small fortune to Sueldan. It would buy that first month of rations that Rannoh had promised, two weeks each for Rifkah and himself. The dog would have to scavenge. Reaching into the deepest recesses of an inner pocket, the con man emerged with a small pouch and dropped it almost reverently beside the money. "Keep this till you need it. It'll get you out of a tight spot sometime."

"A tight spot? How?" Sueldan turned his attention from the pouch to find the chair beside him unoccupied. The door clicked closed, leaving him alone at the table. Only then,

Sueldan realized he had never asked the man his name, nor given his own. He shivered at the thought of those deadly eyes and wondered if it might not prove just as well.

Sueldan placed the silver in his pocket and opened the pouch. The strong, cloying odor of an unfamiliar herb assailed his nostrils, and he saw bits of dried greenery that closely resembled hay. *A tight spot.* Sueldan shrugged, placing the pouch into his pocket with the half-coppers. Rifkah likely had experience with herbs. Perhaps she could identify the contents.

Rannoh appeared with a bowl of stew and two full mugs. "Here," he snarled. "This should make up for—" Apparently noticing Sueldan was alone, he stopped. "Where'd that cheating blackguard go?"

Suspecting the stranger had ordered the food for Sueldan, not himself, he shrugged.

Rannoh leaned close. "Why'd you do it, Tamison?"

You wouldn't understand. "Do what?" Sueldan said with exaggerated innocence.

Rannoh straightened. "Eat it and get out of here," he snarled. "If I see either of you here again, I'll have you thrown out."

Sueldan did not reply. He was too busy shoveling warm stew into his mouth.

Chapter 5

SUELDAN returned to his crevice in the glow of the false dawn, greeted by a dog whose tail wagged so hard it carried the hindquarters with it. The skinny body folded nearly in half as the dog struggled to get all of himself petted simultaneously. Sueldan complied absently, seeking Rifkah in the gloom. At length, he found her, sitting quietly amid the cobbles, her multicolored skirts flared around her like a flower, her hands outstretched, and her eyes closed.

Alarmed, Sueldan rushed to her side. "Are you well?"

Rifkah opened one eye, rolling its gaze toward him. "Fine. Almost done." The lid glided closed again.

Sueldan shrugged, dropping to his haunches to accommodate the dog. He slung the sack of rations from his shoulder, placing it on the ground between himself and the fortuneteller. The dog snuffled the air, then thrust its nose into the side of the sack.

"No." Sueldan shoved the dog away, only to have it return instantly. "No!" he said louder, giving the beast a sharper, more sudden push.

Tail curled between its legs, only the tip twitching hopefully, the dog retreated. Soulful dark eyes looked up at Sueldan.

"Good dog." Sueldan gave the animal an affectionate rub, followed by several pats of approval. The tail zipped back up, waving methodically. Sueldan continued to attend to the dog, but his glance strayed to the bag. It had felt wonderfully heavy on his shoulder, but he worried it would not please Rifkah. He had considered waiting until after the shops opened to purchase supplies but did not want to return empty-handed. Besides, they would need to sleep as much as possible during the day prior to the start of their journey. So he had bargained at a nearby inn instead, pleased with the quantity, if not the variety. The owner had thrown in the evening's leftovers in addition to travel rations.

At length, Rifkah opened her eyes and looked at Sueldan, who returned her stare.

"What were you doing? Something magical?"

"No. Nothing magical, just relaxing." Rifkah uncurled her legs, stretching each one delicately. "Any luck with your brother-in-law?"

"Yes, but not the luck you're thinking of." Sueldan winced. "Or maybe it is. I forget you've got magic."

"And you've got fists." Rifkah rose. " That doesn't mean you're hitting all the time."

The dog headed toward the sack again, nose leading.

"No." Though soft, Sueldan's word emerged forcefully enough to capture the dog's attention. It sat.

"For me to read a person, he has to be a willing participant."

Sueldan found a contradiction, and his brows rose. "You read those guards."

A grin eased onto Rifkah's young features. "They were

nervous and very determined. They practically radiated their orders. That's willing, as far as I'm concerned."

"Oh." Sueldan shifted, uneasy. "So if I was determined enough—"

"You are," Rifkah comforted. "And I could read you, too, without your consent, at least the part about getting your family back. But I wouldn't without your permission."

Sueldan patted the dog. "Why not?"

"I like you." Rifkah looked down at the sack. "Oh! Did you get all this with what I gave you?" She knelt to open it.

Warmth suffused Sueldan, and he could not help smiling. "Yes," he said, the answer essentially truth. Her half-copper had won him the silvers.

Rifkah peeked inside, her words muffled by the contents. "Then you're the real magician. There has to be a month's worth of food in here."

"Plus dinner for you," Sueldan added. "I've already eaten."

Rifkah made a noise of shocked approval that further gladdened Sueldan's heart. She released the sack and looked at him. "You're amazing. So that's how you kept your family alive for so many years with nothing."

The statement, meant as praise, had the opposite effect. Sueldan's chest squeezed nearly shut, making breathing difficult. He changed the subject with inappropriate abruptness. "I got something else. Do you know much about herbs?"

"Some." Rifkah carefully closed the sack. "Let me see."

Sueldan passed over the pouch the con man had given him.

Accepting it, Rifkah opened it and peered inside. She took a cautious sniff, then turned a hard glare on Sueldan. "Where did you get this?"

Bothered by the edge in Rifkah's voice, Sueldan replied

vaguely. "A man gave it to me. Said it would help me out of a tight spot."

Rifkah continued to study Sueldan, eyes narrowed with suspicion.

"What is it?" Sueldan asked.

"You really don't know?"

"If I did, would I be asking you to tell me?"

Rifkah's scrutiny did not change.

"What?"

Rifkah finally cast her glance to the pouch again. "Forgive me for doubting. It's a very expensive drug. Not the sort of thing someone just gives away."

Sueldan wished he had explained more. He tried for humor, "Did I forget to mention I saved the man's life?"

"Yes, you did forget." Rifkah's expression did not soften. "But it doesn't help. It's not the kind of drug you give someone who saved your life either."

Tired of condemnation that seemed to come from nowhere, Sueldan pressed. "Instead of making me feel like a worse criminal then I already am, why don't you tell me what kind of drug it is?"

Rifkah cleared her throat. "It's the kind of drug that rules men's lives. A drug of abuse. A highly addictive one. Just this much could make you a slave for eternity."

"A slave?" Surprised, Sueldan could not think of anything original to say.

"You know what an addiction is?" Rifkah held out the pouch.

"Yes." Sueldan remembered his Uncle Lorran's desperate tie to mead and wine, even as it turned him bitter and mean-spirited. "Of course. Yes." He took back the pouch, mashing it between his fingers. "This little bit?"

"Would hook about one in three for life."

"Why would . . ." Sueldan gazed at the gift, cynicism

stealing over him. All of his goodwill toward the giver evaporated in sudden realization. *He's a dealer. Gets people hooked, then sells to them. I'd be his slave for life.* Irritated, he could not help adding unlikely details, even ones that contradicted his previous thought. *Probably left that food for me because he feared Rannoh would poison it.*

"Good question." Rifkah continued to study Sueldan expectantly. "Why *would* someone give you such a thing in gratitude?" Her tone remained colored with suspicion.

Sueldan sighed. "Do you think I could afford a habit like this? Emotionally or monetarily?" He jerked back his arm, prepared to throw the pouch as far as he could.

Rifkah clamped a hand over Sueldan's before he could fling it away. "Don't. Keep it. I don't like the idea, but if we got desperate enough, we could sell it."

Sueldan blinked, lowering his hand, hers still wrapped warmly around it. "Isn't it contraband?"

Rifkah reclaimed her hand. "Of course it's contraband. That's why it's worth so much. Have to sell it on the black market."

Now it was Sueldan's turn to stare. "That would be illegal."

"So's stealing, O Great Thief of Lathary," Rifkah reminded.

Shame reddened Sueldan's cheeks. "I only stole to feed my family." He raised the pouch still clutched in his fist. "This stuff could hurt someone."

Rifkah rolled her eyes. "I'm not suggesting we go into the business of dealing it. I'm just saying that if we got desperate, it might prove wiser to sell it to someone who already needs it than to leave it lying on the ground where some child might happen on it. All right?"

The dog shoved its pointy muzzle into Sueldan's empty palm, demanding attention. He scratched its lopsided ears.

Rifkah had an undeniable point. "All right." He stuffed the pouch into his tunic pocket.

Rifkah had already turned her attention back to the food. "When do you want to leave?"

Glad to switch the conversation to the practical, Sueldan ran his hands along the dog's short fur, concentrating on the animal's favorite spot at the base of its tail. "Tonight. After we meet up with Dallan."

Rifkah turned to Sueldan again. "Who?"

"Dallan. Our companion."

Rifkah gave Sueldan that same demanding stare. Her eyes, so like his mother's, seemed a welcome change from the usual sea of brown.

"Didn't I mention Dallan?"

"I'd remember if you did." Rifkah smiled. "You can use all the help you can get. Tell me about this Dallan."

Sueldan suddenly realized he had little to say. He had only met the guardsman once himself. "He's a young man, maybe a couple or three years older than you, whose sister's in a similar situation to my family. He's the one who told me where to find them."

"Is he nice?"

"Nice? He seemed so."

The dog's broad tail flew back and forth.

"Can he use a sword?" Rifkah gave Sueldan another long scrutiny, clearly to remind him that he carried no weapons and had no more experience than most commoners with them.

Sueldan laughed. "I'd certainly hope so. He's a—" Cringing, he broke off.

"A what?" Rifkah prodded.

"A . . ." Sueldan swallowed, prepared for another tirade. ". . . guardsman?"

The blue eyes turned icy cold. "A guardsman? A witless servant of the brotherhood?"

"He didn't seem—"

"No," Rifkah said, with finality. "I refuse to travel with a Latharyn guardsman."

"You said I needed companions," Sueldan reminded. "You promised me."

"Yes, I did." Rifkah admitted, her tone now grudging. "But I didn't promise you could bring guardsmen."

Sueldan ignored the outburst, continuing his point. "And I promised him."

Rifkah folded her arms across her chest, scowling. It had been his mother's way of showing disapproval as well, distinctly Carsean.

"It's not like he's one of the ones who came to get you."

"Doesn't matter."

"We may very well need his sword arm," Sueldan continued. "And we have a common purpose."

Rifkah glared.

"His sister is innocent."

Rifkah snapped her fingers at the dog, who pranced to her side. "All right, bring him. But don't expect me to be happy about it." She wandered off a few steps, the dog trailing, then grumbled. "If we're lucky, he'll get himself killed."

Sueldan shook his head, worried the journey might prove as trying as the rescue. "Luck," he replied as softly, "is apparently a matter of opinion.

To Sueldan's surprise, Dallan's resistance that evening proved every bit as strong as Rifkah's. The young man paced the boundaries of the city with a broad, heavy tread. "I told you not to tell *anyone* else. Didn't I tell you that—explicitly?"

"Well, yes," Sueldan admitted. "But—"

"But what?" Dallan interrupted, not allowing Sueldan the chance to finish that very answer. "You decided to blurt the whole thing to the first woman you meet?"

Sueldan had spent too much of that day defending himself. A good day's sleep made him stronger, but no less frustrated. "I didn't tell her anything. She's a fortune-teller. She read it herself."

Dallan clamped large, callused hands to his face. "A witch? The woman's a witch, too?"

Too? Sueldan tensed. "I think she prefers 'fortune-teller.' "

"I'm not traveling with someone who knows things about me I don't want her to know."

Still suspicious from the con man's so-called gift that had turned out to be a dangerous drug, Sueldan narrowed his eyes. "Like what?"

The guard pinned Sueldan with brown eyes no longer soft. "Like our mission."

"She already knows about that," Sueldan supplied facetiously.

Dallan's glare darkened further. "Like private things people don't get to know until they've proved I can *trust* them." Another directed bard. "She could invade me anytime. It's just . . . creepy."

Sueldan glanced behind Dallan, toward Rifkah, though she hid too far away to catch even the distant whispers of their conversation. Trees swayed, leaves casting dancing shadows across the moon. "It's not like that. She can't read people without their consent. And she says she reads futures, too. We're going into something unknown and dangerous. She could help."

"I don't want her help," Dallan growled. "Ditch her, or do this without me."

Sueldan's thoughts raged. Desperately, he sifted through them, trying to find the one argument that might rescue their union. Need drove him to leave Lathary as soon as possible, and arguments with companions had become nothing more than annoyance and delay. Righteous anger sifted in, dispelling confusion. A long time had passed since Sueldan had considered his own self-worth. "Fine. Good luck. Maybe we'll see you in Callos." Turning on his heel, he headed toward Rifkah.

"Fool," Dallan called after Sueldan. "You'll die without me."

Sueldan stopped but did not turn. It occurred to him that Dallan needed him at least as much as he needed a warrior. Without the miner's son, Dallan would never get through the catacombs. "Then I'll die. But it won't be for pettiness."

Dallan gave no answer.

Sueldan knew he had to hand the guard an out or risk losing him to pride. "We *do* need you. I wish you'd reconsider."

"All right," Dallan said gruffly, as if making a tremendous sacrifice. "But I'm not letting her inflict that magic stuff on me."

"Suit yourself." Sueldan finally turned, careful to hide his grin. He felt certain Rifkah and Dallan would reconcile once they got to know one another. "Let's go."

Two and a half weeks of overland travel brought Sueldan and his companions closer to the river, but nowhere near the end of their bickering. Sueldan had little patience for their arguments. Rifkah's hatred of all Latharyn guardsmen, and Dallan in particular, seemed nothing more than prejudice. Dallan's dislike for Rifkah, at least, had a basis in upbringing and concern for privacy, but it seemed no more tolerable.

Their angry silences bothered Sueldan the least, but it sparked too easily into name-calling and squabbling over matters neither of them could control nor compromise over.

Dawn colored the sky in rings that flowed from the sun like pond ripples frozen in time. Jagged patches of purple and pink appeared briefly through the leaves, the beauty lost on companions fighting a battle impossible to win. Sueldan came to a sudden stop, too tired to continue. Rifkah had managed to stretch the rations an additional four days, but if the meager bits of hard bread and jerky they had eaten that morning were any clue, they would have to sleep hungry.

Rifkah also halted. "So you're saying the brotherhood selectively chooses imbeciles as guardians based on the size of their muscles?"

"No," Dallan corrected with the usual edge to his tone. "I'm saying that muscles and brains have no relationship whatsoever." As he passed his companions, he turned.

"Exactly. So, the brotherhood must deliberately select the *stupid* strong."

Dallan loosed a strangled noise of frustration and outrage. "You're such a —" He broke off with another noise.

"Can't come up with anything?" Rifkah smirked and gestured at Sueldan. "Thus proving my point, eh?"

"Leave me out of it," Sueldan grumbled, trying to remind himself that he had chosen companions less than a decade older than his son.

The dog whined, pawing at him with a spotted foot.

"It's all right, Dog. I'm hungry, too."

"Maybe I'm just being polite," Dallan started, then looked at Sueldan. "If you're hungry, we'll eat. The way you two have been pecking at your food, I was beginning to think you never got hungry."

Rifkah snorted, tossing her dark blonde ringlets. "Ever

heard of rationing, genius?" She glanced apologetically at Sueldan. "I didn't want to tell you before. We're out."

"Out of food?" Dallan's brows rose in increments. "Why didn't you say something? I'd have shared."

Sueldan had watched Dallan's pack dwindle and knew he had only a few more days' worth for himself.

Having generously offered, Dallan glared at Rifkah. "For one who thinks *I'm* stupid, you sure didn't plan ahead."

"If your obnoxious colleagues hadn't chased me out of my own home, I'd have had my things. It wouldn't have been a problem."

"If you hadn't fed a third of your food to a dog—"

"If it came to a choice between you and the dog—"

Sueldan had had enough. "Stop it! Both of you. Thanks for the offer, Dallan, but there's no sense in you starving for our poor preparations."

"Poverty," Rifkah corrected with a scowl.

"Stop it!" Sueldan shouted again. "I can handle sleeping hungry. I'm practically an expert at it. But I shouldn't have to sleep irritable as well."

"Look," Dallan said. "I said I'd share my food, and I will. We'll all get to Rivertown a few days' hungry, but we can get rations there. I just wish you'd said something back at Porins. Or even in Lathary."

Sueldan sighed heavily. "Poverty doesn't buy a lot of food."

Rifkah nudged Sueldan. "We'll get by."

Sueldan knew she meant that Rivertown might have a black market where they could sell the drug. He lowered his head and nodded.

"I'll buy," Dallan said.

"Thank you." Sueldan smiled grimly, appreciating the offer but doubting Dallan's guard salary would last long supporting three. "But, as Rifkah said, we'll get by."

Rifkah pursed her lips, making them appear even larger. "Maybe I could read fortunes on the two of you. Give us an idea whether it's even worth continuing."

No matter what, I'm continuing. Sueldan nodded vigorously. "A great idea."

All of Dallan's graciousness disappeared. "Stay away from me, you witch. No one mucks around my head with magic."

"Afraid I'll find it empty?" Rifkah banished all of the newfound camaraderie.

In reply, Dallan made a brisk motion to ward off evil.

The response confused Sueldan. While Latharyns tended to find little purpose for magic and the users of it, no one he knew had ever considered it specifically sinful. *Just my luck. Both companions with unreasonable obsessions.* As always, he played peacemaker. "I'd appreciate a reading. We're in this together, so it should give us a good idea of what we can all expect." He glanced sidelong at Dallan, who dismissed him with a wave. Sueldan accepted that as a positive sign. At least, Dallan would not try to interfere. He offered his hands to Rifkah.

The fortune-teller paused to flick one last glare at Dallan before turning her attention to Sueldan. She gave her sandy locks a dismissive toss, but her eyes lingered longer than the gesture demanded.

The oddity sent Sueldan's attention to the guard. He sat on a deadfall, muscles defined against the fabric of his tunic, his dark curls trickling over his forehead, and his jaw set. The dog took a position beside him, nudging his hand with its head. Then, Rifkah's fingers closed around Sueldan's, drawing his thoughts back to the reading. She looked into his eyes. In a moment, her hands winched open, and Sueldan lowered his to his sides. She did not speak.

Sueldan met Rifkah's gaze, trying to find something in the pale eyes that might explain her sudden hush.

Dallan did not prove as patient. "So?" he demanded, giving the dog a mild shove.

Rifkah whipped her head toward the guard, curls flying. "I thought you didn't believe in magic."

"I believe in it just fine," Dallan shot back. "I just don't like it."

Tail waving, the dog returned to Dallan's side.

"Get away from me, you dumb dog." Dallan's tone emerged too gentle for the animal to comprehend, followed by a harder push that worked little better.

Sueldan cleared his throat. "I'd like to know what you found, too."

"Well." Rifkah fidgeted, clearly more comfortable exchanging barbs with Dallan than with describing her findings. "The future's a lot harder to interpret. There're always several possibilities, and I can't read myself. The more your lot's tied in with mine, the more vague and muddled the images."

Sueldan raised his brows in encouragement. At least, he now understood how a woman who could read the future still wound up in Lathary.

"There'll be hardships," Rifkah admitted. "Some serious. But I believe your honest determination could carry you through them."

"Could?" Dallan repeated, giving the dog another push that seemed more like a pat to Sueldan.

Sueldan smiled. Dallan liked the animal more than he would ever admit. He wondered if the same held true of the guard's feelings for Rifkah.

"Could," Rifkah repeated. "Didn't you hear me say the future's never certain?"

"Yes," Dallan admitted. "I just thought you felt a need to state the blatantly obvious."

Rifkah's hands went to her hips. "What are you trying to say?"

Dallan ignored the dog who continued to thrust its nose repeatedly into his hand. "I'm trying to say that any fool could have made that prediction."

"By 'any fool,' do you mean . . . *you?*"

Sueldan threw up his hands in exasperation. "Look! My 'honest determination' could 'carry us through' a lot easier if you two would stop fighting all the time! I can barely think, let alone feel determined. Unless that determination is supposed to come from boundless aggravation."

All eyes whipped to Sueldan, including the dog's. It trotted to him, whining softly.

Rifkah looked at her shuffling feet for a moment, then at Dallan. "Thank you for offering food. It was very gracious of you." Her words sounded more stiff than appreciative, but Dallan responded in kind.

"You're welcome."

The undergrowth rustled. Dallan spun, hand whipping to his hilt.

Before Sueldan could localize the sound, a man's voice wafted from the direction they all now faced. "So that's what all the shouting is about? Food?"

Dallan spoke through clenched teeth. "Show yourself."

"As you wish." More stems rattled, then branches parted to reveal the olive-skinned con man Sueldan had now happened upon for the third time. He wore travel leathers spotted with bits of foliage, and a twig was laced into his fine, black hair. He tossed a cloth sack to the ground in front of the guardsman.

Dallan took a careful step back. "Who are you?" He allowed his gaze to roll briefly to the offering. "What is that?"

"Food," the man explained. "Enough to get you to River-town, I think."

Dallan's voice grew thick with suspicion. "Why would you give us food . . . *stranger?*"

The con man tossed Sueldan a tight-lipped smile. "I owe your friend a debt I only partially paid."

Dallan gave Sueldan a wary look before returning his attention fully to the stranger.

"Is he the one who . . .?" Rifkah started.

Sueldan nodded.

Rifkah addressed her next words to the dark man. "Your gifts are not appreciated."

The man shrugged. "Suit yourself." He raised his hands, keeping them well away from the sword, knife, and less recognizable gear at his belt.

Dallan did not extend the same courtesy, fist still on his hilt.

"Are you following me?" Sueldan blurted.

The thief jerked his head back, as if affronted. "Absolutely not. I just happened to be traveling the same road."

"Where are you going, then?" Sueldan demanded.

"I believe that's my own business." Without further discussion, the con man headed farther up the forest path.

Dallan's hand fell from his hilt, and he shouted, "Wait!"

The con man stopped, turning.

"Two swords together are safer than one."

"Thank you," the man replied. "But no. I'm sure you'd make fine companions, but I'd rather travel alone." He swung back around and soon disappeared amid the trees.

"All right," Dallan said softly, still watching the place where the con man had gone. " Tell me what's wrong with this traveler."

Sueldan glanced at Rifkah, who shook her head in warning. "I've run into him twice before. Both times in unsavory circumstances. I just don't trust him."

"Which," Rifkah added, without her usual heat, "is why you shouldn't invite people into the group without consulting with us first."

Dallan snorted, still without turning. "You mean like how Sueldan let *you* in?"

"I was with him first," Rifkah insisted.

"And I love you both." Sueldan attempted to dispel the tension. "But I don't trust him." He jerked a thumb toward the road.

Dallan finally spun to face his companions. "That's why I wanted him with us. Easier to watch him. And I meant what I said about two sword arms. People do get robbed on the road."

Sueldan shook his head. "I'm not afraid of highwaymen. We've got nothing to steal."

"Robbers tend to get mean when they think you're wasting their time." Dallan patted his sword. "I don't want to fight the whole band by myself."

"You wouldn't," Sueldan said more emphatically than he felt. He would assist, but he would have to do so without a weapon. "But I do understand your point about having a possible enemy travel with us rather than trailing us in secret."

Dallan shrugged off his pack, unrolling the blanket from the rest of his belongings. "I don't think he's an enemy. And I'd have heard him if he'd been trailing us."

Out of supplies, Sueldan dropped to the ground near Dallan. "We started at the same place, traveled for weeks, and are still in the same place. By definition, he's following us."

"But not closely enough to be trailing us deliberately." For once, Rifkah agreed with Dallan. "I'd have sensed him by magic."

"And I'd have heard him sooner," Dallan added.

Sueldan did not agree, but neither did he argue. He doubted it would gain him anything. For the moment, he preferred to bask in his companions' rare consensus. He could believe meeting the same stranger twice a coincidence. Three times pushed him to the limit of credibility. *He's not following us, he's following me. The question is "why?"*

Dallan opened the sack the con man had left them. "It's food, all right. Hardtack." He wiped his hands on his tunic. "I really don't think there's much tampering he could have done, but I'm willing to leave it and share my rations if you feel strongly about it."

Sueldan deferred to Rifkah's judgment.

The fortune-teller considered a moment, then looked at Sueldan. "Why don't you plan on eating it."

"All . . . right," Sueldan said, questioning with his tone.

"Then let me read you."

Sueldan believed he understood. He gave over his hands.

Rifkah clutched them shortly, then nodded. "I don't believe the food will hurt us."

Dallan whipped his head to the others. "You mean you can tell the result of near-future actions?"

"Sometimes."

"That's . . . useful!" Dallan realized aloud. "That's really useful."

Rifkah rolled her eyes and drew the sack into her lap. "I've only been trying to convince you of that the whole trip so far."

The two studied one another, as if for the first time. It startled Sueldan to realize how nice a couple they could have made under other circumstances. Rifkah's lighter Carsean features fit well with Dallan's dark ruggedness. Sueldan shook away the thought, certain it came from memories of his own family.

Dallan grunted something unintelligible, then started in on his own rations. Though she had proclaimed the food safe, Rifkah tossed the first piece of spiced meat to the dog, who gobbled it ravenously, then danced to Rifkah, tail waving and eyes expectant. She passed Sueldan a handful of mixed dried foodstuffs, including fruits, meat, and flat bread. After four days of strict rationing, it seemed like a feast. Sueldan gobbled it down nearly as quickly as the dog, in silence, his mind still grappling with the problem of the trailing con man. He could not force himself to believe so many meetings simple happenstance.

Sueldan's concerns continued to trouble him to the next day. Rifkah and Dallan slept easily in the warm, close clearing they had discovered just beyond sight of the road. The dog lay near Dallan, head resting on his boot. When Sueldan sat up, the animal's eyes snapped open. Its tail thumped the ground.

"Quiet," Sueldan whispered.

The direct address sent the dog surging to its feet. Dallan rolled, and Sueldan cringed. But the guardsman returned to sleep as the dog sneezed and happily circled its master.

"Stay," Sueldan hissed, pointing to his companions. "Watch."

The tail slid between the dog's legs, though the end still twitched. Sueldan had worked on the watch command since the journey began, and the dog seemed to understand. After the first few days, it stopped barking at every passerby or creature, except those who blundered too near their camp.

The dog slunk back to their companions, and Sueldan headed for the road. As he pushed through a tall bank of weeds, he found the dog suddenly at his side, tail waving and head held high.

"No, Dog." Sueldan jabbed a finger toward Rifkah and Dallan. "Watch."

The dog's head drooped, and the tail folded back across its belly. It took two steps, then looked back at Sueldan.

"Watch." Sueldan kept his hand in place, finger extended. "Stay there."

This time, the dog obeyed without looking back. Sueldan turned his attention to the road, seeking footprints in the hard, dark earth that might match the con man's boots. But even beneath the harsh glare of sunlight, such details eluded him. The trail lay baked into pits and crevices left in muddier times. A few tracks disturbed the lighter coating of dust, too shallow to define minutiae. He had little choice but to go forward and hope to blunder randomly into the man he sought . . . and no one else. *This might just be the stupidest thing I've done yet.* Sueldan knew he should turn back, but he did not. Curiosity proved stronger than rationality, especially when he quantified the danger. It seemed unlikely that highwaymen would bother a lone traveler wearing rags in clear daylight.

Guessing the con man would also prefer nighttime travel, Sueldan looked for a disturbance in the roadside weeds where the man might have left the road to pitch a camp. A light breeze rattled the leaves overhead and bowed the weeds in an airy dance. It carried the mixed aroma of musk and greenery. The sun beamed, a warm comfort on arms that had chilled through the night. Secrecy had an advantage that Sueldan had never considered. They slept during the most comfortable temperatures, obviating the need for blankets or fires. During night's coldest hours, activity kept them reasonably warm. The dog had taken to curling up with Dallan as they slept, perhaps because the guardsman generated the

most body heat, a situation the younger man did not seem
to appreciate.

Sueldan took a zigzagging route across the roadway, examining both sides of the trail for subtle signs that someone
had broken through the lining brush. At length, he discovered what he sought, a crushed area crisscrossed with twigs
and broken stems as if someone had tried to hide the damage. Heart quickening, Sueldan stepped over the spot, glancing about for more signs of passage. Here and there, he
found a bent stalk amid the other weeds, a bit of bark
scraped from a trunk, but these things proved too elusive to
follow. They seemed to hold no pattern, reflecting natural
events caused by time, weather, or animals rather than the
steady tread of a man. Forced to guess, Sueldan pushed
through in a straight line. Suddenly confronted by weeds too
thick and tangled to part, he tried another way. This took
him only a few steps before two closely growing trunks stole
his path again.

Damn. Frustrated, Sueldan cast his gaze about the forest,
seeking the simplest route. Instead, he found a clear smear
through the green blanket of moss that coated a large rock.
Turning toward it, he went to study it. The shape and pattern convinced him he had found a boot track, and hope
sprang back to life. Surely the con man would want to sleep
on the flattest, clearest ground, so it only made sense to follow the path of least resistance. Sueldan shook his head. He
had no idea where that might be.

A cough shattered the otherwise soundless stillness, start-
ling Sueldan. He froze, every muscle tensed. Instinctively,
his head jerked in the direction of the noise, ahead and
slightly rightward. He moved toward it, torn between quiet
caution and announcing his presence. The first might allow
him to get closer but also might make his actions appear sus-

picious or even threatening. The second might send the con man running.

Memory glided into Sueldan's mind, dark eyes in a darker alley, filled with the icy glint of a killer. A shiver traversed him. His course seemed suddenly, obviously clear. "Hello. I just want to talk." He spoke only loud enough for his voice to carry as far as the cough.

No answer.

Sueldan continued forward, without attempting to cover the noise of his movement. "Hello?"

"Over here." The gruff voice barely reached Sueldan's hearing, now seeming more to his left.

Adjusting his course, Sueldan wove between several thick, viny trunks, avoiding a snarl of brambles. He wound through the brush for several paces without any confirmation or sound to further guide him. Boxed into a blind, he stopped, his own tone coarsening. "Where *is* here?"

"Here." The other sounded no closer, even farther leftward. It appeared as if the man were moving.

Sueldan backtracked, finding another route through the woods. Blanketed with moldering leaves, the ground yielded to his steps, then closed over without showing prints. Newer leaves clung to every branch, in shades of emerald and vivid green, dappling the shadows. Again, he paused at an impasse. "Where?"

"I'm over here." The other added sarcastically, "Would you like me to sing?"

"It would help," Sueldan grumbled to himself. He sought a landmark and settled on an oddly shaped tree. "Where are you in relation to the five big oaks growing from the same patch of ground?"

A brief pause followed, then the man spoke again, "Five paces in the direction away from the road." This time he said enough words for Sueldan to identify his voice as the same one he'd heard in Rannoh's tavern. "Turn left six more. Go around the briars and back into line. Four more steps."

The directions seemed impossibly precise. Sueldan wondered how the man managed to move more than a pace or two in any direction without running into something immovable. "Thank you." Gingerly he worked his way toward the five oaks growing so close together they resembled one massive, common trunk. From there, he counted paces deliberately. His foot mired in a twist of multiflora roses, and he fell. Brambles tore at his face and hands. Swearing, he scrambled to his feet, immediately jerked back by a vine still entangled around his boot. Clearing a bit of ground, he sat, delicately unwinding a vine furred with sharp spines from his ankle. Regaining his balance and his feet, he resumed counting. At five, he turned leftward, expecting to see the con man.

Sueldan found only more forest. Seeing a thick jumble of bramble bushes, he assumed the man stood behind it. *You could meet me halfway.* He kept the thought to himself. Memories of those assassin's eyes made him cautious. "Are you still there?"

This time, Sueldan got no answer.

Abrupt alarm surged through Sueldan. *He's playing with me.* The actions and intentions of the con man seemed absolutely inscrutable. The image of the man as a cold-blooded thief and as an upscale con man jibed enough. Addictive drugs and a few silvers as a reward for his life, revealing his presence but refusing company, following a group of near-total strangers—these things seemed every bit as unfathomable as leading an acquaintance nowhere. Sueldan shrugged. The con man's designs this time meant little. He could have killed Sueldan already and chose not to do so. The miner's son still had no money or valuables. He might not gain anything, but he truly had nothing to lose.

With a sigh of resignation, Sueldan took the designated

paces, stepping over or around tall patches of brush, bushes, and trunks. Mulch coated his boots, staining the leather; and the cold wetness seeped slowly into his toes. Four paces beyond the brambles, he stopped, folding his arms across his chest. "All right. Now what?"

Something slammed into Sueldan's back at the shoulder blades, driving him forward. His boot met empty air, and he tumbled into a well-hidden hole. He twisted, a shower of rotting leaves accompanying him as he fell. Then his left foot hit bottom, sending a shock of agony through his leg. His hand slammed against a rock, and his head hit earth hard enough to send a white bolt shooting through his vision. He sagged to the bottom of a crudely dug shaft, feeling dirt walls all around him. Panic scattered his wits. He surged to his feet, screaming and clawing, utterly blinded.

Pain and a calm, commanding voice brought Sueldan back to his senses. He sagged against the cavern, gasping in huge gulps of spring air. Spots and squiggles fled his sight, revealing a man looking down at him, with trees and sunlight in the background. Sueldan recognized the con man, and terror fled before angry accusation. "You pushed me!"

The other's sword cleared its sheath with a deadly rasp. "Why were you following me?"

Cowed by the steel, Sueldan found his rage fleeing and fear regaining ground. Afraid to look at the enclosing walls around and an arm's length above him, he focused on the open spaces beyond the other man. "Me? F–following you? You've been following . . . me." The last word emerged as an irritating squeak.

"Don't flatter yourself. Now, why did you leave your . . . um . . . friends to look for me?"

Sueldan blinked, suddenly realizing the con man had watched his every action since he'd left the camp. "I was following you to find out . . ." He could not help smiling. The situation seemed positively ludicrous. ". . . why you were following me. Could it be you were following me for the same reason?"

The dark man lowered himself to a crouch and grunted. He shook the sword. "Hilt end—ask questions." He made a short jab toward Sueldan. "Pointy end—answer."

Sueldan's heart raced fast as a galloping horse, and the walls seemed to be closing in on him. He allowed the shaft only a sideways glance, now certain an animal had created it. A hint of musk gave him the answer. Apparently, the con man had found an abandoned fox burrow, hidden it, and guided Sueldan to it. *But why?* "I'll answer any question you have. Just, please, let me out."

The con man seemed not to hear. "Tell me. Why would a fortune-teller, a family merchant's guild guard, and a nobody be traveling secretly together?"

"Wh–what?" Sueldan stammered. *A family merchant's guild guard? Dallan?*

The con man rocked backward on his heels, his shadow partially disappearing from over Sueldan. "You might be the least likely trio in existence. What are you up to?"

Sueldan shook his head, remembering his vow to Dallan. "I–I can't tell you that." He attempted to depersonalize the comment. "I can't tell *anyone* that."

"Ah." The sword glinted in the sunlight. "A secret worth dying for." He leaned forward again, giving Sueldan a full look at those assassin's eyes, impossibly sincere. This man would kill him without a compunction, might even enjoy it.

Nausea bubbled up Sueldan's throat, and he felt himself losing control again. "Please. If you kill me, you take the lives of innocent women and children, too."

Nothing registered on the con man's face for several moments, followed by a tooth-filled grin. "It's your silence that dooms those innocents."

In a warped way, yes. Another wave of panic struck Sueldan, and he fought it. With his wits scattered, he could not think. "Let me out. Please. Let me out. Let me—" He found himself incapable of other words. Suddenly heedless of the weapon, Sueldan clawed at the dirt. "Please. Please."

"Stop!"

"Please, please, please just—"

"Stop it!"

Sueldan whimpered, hating himself for the weakness but unable to help it. In another moment, the burrow would crush the life from him.

"You can't get out by yourself." The man set the sword down and disappeared beyond Sueldan's sight. Only his voice still carried. "I'll help you if you promise not to run. And to answer my question."

"I promise," Sueldan said, cringing. He would not betray Dallan's trust.

"Here." Something made of remarkably light wood slithered toward Sueldan. He stepped backward, spine touching an earthen wall, as a ladder sank into the pit.

Though surprised, Sueldan wasted no time clambering onto the rungs. It sank beneath him, barely strong enough to support his meager weight. He scrambled to the top, where the con man met him with a deft sword form.

"Don't move off the rungs."

Sueldan went still. Once out of the pit and into the mild breeze, the majority of his fear drained away, leaving only worried discomfort. "You carry a ladder with you?" The words emerged before he had a chance to think them through, incredulous.

"Everywhere. Never know when you might need one."

"Or any other tool," Sueldan agreed. "But isn't it awfully bulky to carry around?"

"Not after I fold it. Even fits on my belt." The con man

tapped his waist, the movement pressing his tunic against other shapes Sueldan could not identify. "Invention of mine."

"Clever." Sueldan allowed genuine admiration to seep into his tone. The murderous glimmer had left the other man's eyes, and he had no wish to rekindle it. "My name's Sueldan."

"Yes," the con man said, as if Sueldan had only guessed. "And also Tamison."

So much for a whole new identity. "Yes," he admitted. "But I prefer Sueldan for now."

The dark man shrugged.

"It's customary to tell me *your* name now." Sueldan followed the con man's attention to the sword. "Even when you're at the hilt end of a drawn blade."

The con man turned Sueldan an indulgent smile. "Don't have a name. Call me whatever you want." The smile broadened. "Make it as original as what you call your dog."

Obnoxious Irritating Bastard comes to mind. Sueldan pursed his lips. "How about . . . Con?"

"Whatever. Now, I believe you have a question to answer."

Sueldan took a deep breath, then let it out slowly. He wrapped his arms around the ladder, concerned about falling, or worse, getting pushed back into the enclosing pit. "I didn't tell anyone how you worked your scam in Rannoh's."

The off-kilter eyes narrowed. "Your point?"

"I don't betray my vows, especially when doing so could harm someone else."

"You're saying you promised not to tell what the three of you are doing together here?"

Sueldan nodded carefully.

Con's dark eyes slitted, snakelike, and the first hint of their deadly sparkle returned. "You'd die for someone else?"

"If I had to," Sueldan said, more bravely than he felt. "But I don't believe you're going to kill me."

Con's brows rose in increments. Though clearly affronted, he looked less threatening with those unnerving eyes wide open. "You think you could stop me?"

"No," Sueldan said. "I couldn't. But if you killed me, you'd never get the answer to your question. And I think that's why you're following us. In fact, I believe I didn't track you at all. You set the whole thing up, even the messed-up weeds, the boot track, the hidden burrow, just to trap me and get your question answered."

Con studied Sueldan for several moments, the breeze dragging long streamers of his silky, black hair. "You're not as stupid as most people."

Sueldan supposed Con meant that as a compliment. "Thanks. I think." Recalling Dallan's eagerness to keep Con among them, Sueldan added, "The best way to find out is to join us." The corners of his mouth twitched, but he managed to repress a smile. It might incite Con if he appeared to have won too large a victory.

Con sheathed his sword and gestured for Sueldan to climb off the ladder. "No."

The answer caught Sueldan off guard. "No?"

"I come and go as I please. For my own profit."

Sueldan eased from the ladder to solid ground, edging away from the pit. *Profit.* The word reminded Sueldan of the vast amount of money Con had won in the tavern, surely not for the first time.

As Sueldan moved aside, Con seized the shaft of the ladder, then carefully folded it to the size of a large pouch. He turned, still keeping an eye on Sueldan, and affixed the ladder to his pack.

"Your cleverness should have made you a wealthy man by now."

Con shrugged. "I could say the same for you."

"Me? You must be . . ." Sueldan trailed off, recalling Rifkah's admonishment that he learn to trust in his own determination.

Con continued, "I don't need the burden of worrying about anyone's life but my own. And I don't trust anyone to worry about mine."

"I saved your life once," Sueldan reminded.

Con turned Sueldan a stern look. "After you placed it in danger."

"What?" The word was startled from Sueldan.

"You're the one who figured out the scam. And tipped off that tavern owner who called the guards."

Sueldan swallowed hard. "I didn't—I mean I wasn't trying to—I didn't know he—" Sudden realization turned defensiveness to reproach. "Is that why you tried to make me an addict?"

"What?" It was Con's turn for clear surprise.

Finally obtaining the upper hand, Sueldan found it impossible not to press. "That drug you gave me. Don't tell me you didn't know it was expensive, illegal, and addictive."

Con's features formed concerned creases, and he did not seem to know what to do with his hands. The discomfort looked so out of place it alarmed Sueldan, though he had caused it. "I didn't tell you to use the stuff right away, you idiot! I told you it could get you out of a tight spot. Did you waste it?" He groaned. "You absolute simpleton. How—"

Sueldan pulled the pouch from his pocket, dangling it from his smallest finger.

The tirade stopped. "Oh." Con regained all of his daunting composure immediately.

Sueldan returned the drug to his pocket. "Now that I'm, once again, 'not as stupid as most people,' please explain how this could help me."

"Wait till you're at your most desperate."

"And it will help me how?"

Con shook his head.

Sueldan could not understand the reluctance. "You don't trust me with that information?"

"Don't take it personally." Con studied his fingernails. "I don't trust anyone."

"Not anyone?"

"Not anyone."

Sueldan thought of Linnry, of the bond they shared and how just raising it to the forefront of his memories caused his heart to ache. He missed her more than anything in the world. "Seems like an awfully lonely existence."

"Some of us like it that way."

"Some, maybe." Sueldan measured his words carefully. "But not you."

Con's dark eyes rolled in their sockets to meet Sueldan's gaze. "How do you figure that?"

Sueldan delivered his coup de grâce. "You've twice saved me from hunger, and you didn't kill me in that alley. Sorry to be the bearer of bad news, Con, but you like me."

Con's hand winched around his hilt, and a light flickered through his eyes.

Sueldan back stepped before he realized he had moved. His insight might well prove deadly. He had attacked the very essence of Con's character, and he might back the killer into the corner of needing to slaughter him to prove his theory wrong.

Con made no further aggressive moves, nor did he deny the accusation. Without another word, he turned on one heel and strode away. Within five steps, he had disappeared beyond the bramble bushes.

Sueldan chased after Con, but by the time he reached the brambles, the other had disappeared. Shaking his head at the strangeness of it all, he headed back toward his companions.

Chapter 6

DESPITE all that had happened, Sueldan's dreams seemed surprisingly sweet. He sat at the rickety wooden table he had built, stained with years of spilled foodstuffs. Linnry sat to his left, her cheeks radiant though the bones jutted sharply, her dark eyes soft with love. Still only three, Danara sang a familiar lullaby between bites of bread and fruit. The baby roundness of her face gave her a look of angelic sweetness, and the large brown eyes seemed determined to see everything at once. Ellith ate slowly, savoring every morsel, pausing frequently to describe their day in intricate detail. "An' then Mama tol' him these presimmons weren't as big as las' week's an' he should give us an extra for the same money an' . . ."

"Thank you, dear," Linnry interrupted. "Papa doesn't have to know everything." She smiled at Tamison. "He's tired. Maybe he'd like to talk about his day."

In his dream, Tamison grinned back, planning to save some good news for that evening in bed. "Go on, Ellith. I'm enjoying this." He studied the oldest of his girls, who closely resembled his wife. Long, black hair fell around her gentle features, small nose, and generous ears. Only a hint of green in her eyes and her thin upper lip betrayed his role in her lineage.

Ellith swallowed and continued, waving her fork for emphasis. "So, he tol' Mama his price was his price but Mama says she'd get her presimmons at the stand up the road and first he says all right but then he calls us back—"

Linnry broke in again. "Sutannis, dear. Don't eat with your hands. Animals eat with their hands. People eat with tablewear."

Tamison glanced at his son, who dropped the slice of persimmon to his plate. "What's the big deal?" he grumbled. "I'm eating the bread with my hands anyway."

"But, Mama," Danara added thoughtfully, "animals don't eat with their hands." She cocked her head, dark hair slithering over one ear. "They eats with their heads."

Tamison hid a smile behind his hand, so as not to belittle his daughter's insight nor his wife's correction of rude behavior. Danara had an undeniable point.

A man's shout roused Sueldan from his dream. Happy memory fled in an instant, allowing the dull reality of twilight to fill his vision. Dallan leaped to his feet, shaking a finger at the dog, then wiping it on his tunic. "That damned animal of yours!" His voice echoed between the trunks.

The dog studied Dallan, tail alternately wagging a few beats, then dropping. Its ears flicked forward and backward.

Rifkah sat, sorting food for the evening meal. "What happened?"

Dallan shook back curls that never seemed to need brushing. "He stuck his stupid eye on my finger."

"Huh?" Still half-asleep and wishing to return to his dream, Sueldan did not bother to sit up.

Dallan stood over the smaller, older man. "You heard me. He poked his stupid eye on my finger."

Rifkah made a noise of sympathy, and held her hand out to the animal. "Is he all right?"

"Is *he* all right?" Dallan whirled toward the fortune-teller. "I didn't touch him. He did it." He made a grotesque face, wiping his hand again.

"Poor boy." Rifkah ran her hands down both sides of the dog's face while it sat, tail stirring the leaves and tongue flicking across her face. "Poor widdle doggy."

"It's disgusting." Dallan clearly still saw himself as the wronged party. "One moment I'm sleeping. The next I've got a gooey dog eye on my finger. You know, that's the third time he's done that." He looked at Rifkah again and made a noise of revulsion. "The beast eats deer droppings, and you let him lick your mouth?"

"His mouth's cleaner than yours."

"You'll never know," Dallan grumbled back. Calmer, he turned his attention to Sueldan. "Why does he do that anyway?"

Resigned to waking, Sueldan pulled his legs under him and wished he had not spent half the day tracking and talking to Con. "Eat deer droppings?"

Dallan wrinkled his features. "Oh, no. I don't even want to know that. Why does he stick his eye on my finger? That has to hurt."

Sueldan shrugged. "Can't imagine he'd do it if it hurt him." The image of wife and children faded entirely from his consciousness, leaving only wistful memory. "He's trying to get your attention, I guess."

"Well, he got it." Dallan pulled a hunk of hard, brown bread from his pack, dropped to his haunches, and gnawed on it. "Next time, he's going to get my boot up his hind-quarters."

Tail waving, the dog sat at Dallan's side.

Dallan eyed the beast. "Go away. You're not getting my food."

Sueldan shifted his regard to his own share of the food as evening turned the trees and brush silver. From the corner of his vision, he saw Dallan break off a piece of bread and pass it to the dog. The guard ran a finger along its side. Hardly daring to believe what he had seen, Sueldan swiveled his head directly toward them.

Immediately, Dallan's scratch became a shove. "What's wrong with this stupid critter? I keep pushing it away and it stays here anyway."

Sueldan bit back a smile. "He wants you to like him."

Dallan made a dismissive noise and returned to his food. The dog lay down, sighing, its head on Dallan's boot. "Get away from me," he said, though he did not move his foot.

"So," Sueldan said between bites, deliberately reserved. "You're a *family guild* guard."

That got both companions' attention. Dallan also played cool. "Where'd you hear that?"

Sueldan refused to be sidetracked. "Doesn't matter. Why didn't you tell us?"

Dallan shrugged. "You didn't ask." He tossed the last of the bread into his mouth and brushed off the crumbs.

Rifkah continued to stare at the younger man. "Not directly. But I did base my entire judgment of you on the belief that you served the brotherhood. And you took all the insults personally, without bothering to correct me."

Dallan shrugged, returning to his food. "I have friends among those you dislike and bad-mouth. And a guard is a guard, right?"

"Wrong." Rifkah rose, walked to Dallan, and crouched at his side. "I'm sorry about how I behaved. I truly am. From this moment on, I promise to treat you better."

Dallan stared at his food, saying nothing. The dog crawled toward Rifkah without bothering to rise, dragging its chest and abdomen across Dallan's leg.

Rifkah reached forward, brushing black curls from Dallan's eyes. "All right?"

Finally, Dallan's attention flicked toward Rifkah. "All right," he fairly growled. His soft, dark eyes met her intense blue gaze, and he managed a slight smile. Sueldan watched some of the tenseness flee his body. "I don't really dislike you. I just don't like what you—"

Rifkah rolled her eyes and dropped back to her haunches. "—are?" she supplied.

Dallan pursed his lips. "Let's say what you *do*."

Rifkah's eyes gained ice in that moment. An edge returned to her tone. "And what exactly is it I do that you don't approve of?"

Dallan looked at Sueldan, who shook his head vigorously.

Dallan shrugged, a gesture clearly intended for Sueldan, then addressed Rifkah. "You know. That reading people thing. It's . . ." He made a noise of revulsion, like he might make after biting into an unexpectedly rancid bit of meat.

So close. Sueldan downed the last of his food, rose, and shouldered the ration sack.

Rifkah's reply contained the same rage the two had swapped since the trip began. "Well maybe if you dared to try it, you might find it more fascinating and less . . ." She repeated the sound Dallan had made.

Sueldan whistled, and the dog leaped to its feet. He started toward the road.

Dallan looked over his shoulder. "Where are *you* going?"

"Onward," Sueldan said, without turning or stopping. The dog trotted at his side, and he heard the rustling of the others preparing to follow.

"Look, I just don't like magic, all right?" Dallan spoke around a mouthful of food. "It's creepy."

"Creepy, is it?" Rifkah replied. "Well, maybe I find . . ."

The rest blurred into obscurity as Sueldan moved swiftly, and leaves rattled around him. Soon, another conversation, this time from the road, overshadowed his companions' bickering. He pushed forward, listening.

"Here's the deal." A gruff voice reached Sueldan in a Callosian accent. "We're requisitioning this mule and wagon. Refuse again, and we'll take it by force if we have to."

Another male voice joined the first, punctuated by the snort of a horse. "You wouldn't want that pretty little lady to get hurt, would you?"

A softer voice followed, quivering with poorly suppressed terror. "Please. This is all we have. Everything. My family and I—we'll die without it."

The words struck too close to home. Sueldan did not spare a moment for thought but galloped toward the exchange. His boots fell silently on the hard-packed earth, and the last edge of sun teetered on the horizon. He saw a dense blur ahead and charged toward it as the conversation continued.

"Callos' security takes precedence over any family." A different man spoke. "If I have to pull your brats out of that wagon, they'll pay the price."

A woman screamed, galvanizing Sueldan. He further quickened his pace. Within a half-dozen strides, details gained some clarity. A small wagon stood in the roadway, piled with dented copper pots, cloth, and other shapes he could not yet define. Half a dozen horses surrounded the wagon, three with riders mounted. Figures milled on the ground as well. The four-pointed, ruddy stars sewn to their dull-gray sleeves identified them as Callosian soldiers, though they did not wear the standard uniform nor display the banner or professional bearing of the ones he had very occasionally seen in Lathary.

Cursing the gathering darkness, Sueldan scanned the scene until his eyes ached. Air wheezed into his lungs, and a cramp ached through his side. His food sat like lead in his gut. Then, the last important images gained vicious definition. A chubby woman tumbled from the wagon, hair silver in the moonlight, arms pinned by a soldier nearly twice her size. A man plunged after her, small and thin, beating at the soldier with wildly flailing fists that seemed not to affect the larger man's actions at all.

The woman screamed again. A teenaged girl huddled against a stack of junk, whimpering. Unseen in the chaos, a child sobbed.

Still clutching the woman, the guard backhanded the man, sending him stumbling into the mule hitched to the wagon. The animal danced as its driver fell beneath its hooves. A moment later, Sueldan flew at the guard.

His momentum caused all three to sprawl. Still shrieking, the woman rolled free. The soldier crashed to the ground, swearing brutally. Sueldan's hands went straight to the man's throat, choking the curses to abrupt and desperate silence.

"Hey!" A soldier abandoned the children and raced toward Sueldan. His sword rattled from its sheath, the sound meaningless to the enraged man throttling his companion.

But Sueldan heard the steel whistling through the air. He rolled, strong arms jerking his victim sideways. The sword slashed his scalp, stinging. The soldier made a stifled sound of pain. His companion cursed. Without releasing his grip, Sueldan jerked his attention to the other soldier in time to see the sword whipping toward him a second time.

Finally letting go, Sueldan scrambled backward. This time, the blow missed cleanly. The man on the ground did not move, but the still-mounted irregulars sprang from their horses. The last man howled toward him, sword readied.

Only then did Sueldan realize his peril. Both swords swept toward him, and he dodged in the only direction he could, toward the three rushing into the fray. One blade sailed harmlessly by. The other nicked his side, tearing a superficial line of flesh and a hole in his tunic. Pain speared through him. Warm blood trickled down his collar and his britches. He dropped to one knee, anticipating worse agony before oblivion claimed him.

Metal rang against metal. A loud thump and crash filled Sueldan's hearing, followed by a harsh grunt. Roused by the sounds, Sueldan realized the three in front no longer menaced him. Behind him, the soldier who had first attacked aimed a blow at his neck. The last stumbled, arms protecting his face, amid shards of broken pottery. Another pot soared from the wagon, and the woman hammered at the Callos irregular with a copper pan.

Sueldan dropped flat. The sword hummed over his head. Blindly, he pitched sideways, bits of hardened clay stabbing his limbs and back. He lurched to his feet, slamming his head against the underside of the wagon. Consciousness swimming, he managed to stagger free. The world spun; pinpoints of light banished all other vision. Without effort, he kept his movements haphazard, desperately hoping to thwart the soldier's strikes as he fought a frustrating battle for clarity.

Sight and sound returned in a wild rush that proved nearly as disorienting. On the wagon, three children hurled handfuls of varying junk at a soldier grounded by the woman's crazed and brutal attacks with a lump of now-unrecognizable copper. The dog growled viciously, the man's ankle clamped between its teeth. Three soldiers sprawled on the ground, including the one Sueldan had strangled. Dallan exchanged swift sword strokes with one, and the last collapsed, Con's blade buried in his gut.

Rifkah held the mule's bridle, the only thing keeping the wagon upright and the children safe. Nearby lay the father, clutching a hand to his ribs and moaning softly.

Con ripped his sword free, spilling a putrid spray of blood and entrails. He headed toward Dallan, just as the guard cut down his opponent. Both hurried to assist the woman, only to find the soldier unmoving beneath her blows.

"Missy, let me handle this," Dallan said politely.

The woman stiffened, staring fiercely at the two men. She brandished her weapon.

Con went to assist Rifkah, leaving Dallan to handle the wild-eyed woman. The guard held up his empty hand in a gesture of surrender. The gore-covered blade hung limply. "Whoa, Missy. We're on your side."

The con man did not seem to notice Sueldan as he passed, but he did speak. "You're bleeding."

Startled, Sueldan pressed a hand to his side and ran the other through his hair. Both came away striped with scarlet. The sight brought a wave of pain, accompanied by dizziness. He slid to the ground. The world receded behind a buzzing curtain, then disappeared entirely.

Sueldan blinked awake, without any realization of having slept. A furry muzzle poked his cheek. Beyond the dog, a half-moon hung in a sky sprinkled with stars. The stench of blood, bowel, and death still fouled the air. A wide strip of cloth covered his head and ears like a woman's scarf, and more enwrapped his torso. He lay amid a spray of clay shards and shattered ceramics. Hoofbeats receded, accompanied by the creak of wagon wheels. He sat up.

"Careful," Rifkah cautioned, reaching to steady Sueldan. The dog whined, pawing him with nails that desperately needed trimming.

The pain fully roused Sueldan. He shivered in the cool night air. "The family. Are they all right?"

"Dallan sent them on their way," Rifkah assured. "The peddler broke a couple of ribs and gained some bruises. He'll live. The woman and children—shaken but unhurt."

"How many children?" Sueldan did not know why it mattered.

Rifkah gave him a curious look, then nodded as she figured it out. "Older girl. Two young boys. Brave darlings, all three."

Sueldan sighed.

"Like yours, I'm sure."

Sueldan closed his eyes. Nodded.

Dallan's voice cut through Sueldan's sorrow. "That was, without a doubt, the stupidest thing I've ever seen anyone do."

Sueldan's lids whipped open. "Huh?"

"Attacking a cold-blooded band of Callos irregulars unarmed. Are you suicidal? Or just witless?" Dallan glared down at Sueldan. "What in all-bladed hell were you thinking?"

"I wasn't." Sueldan admitted, lowering his head, too weak to argue. Lamely, he tried to change the subject. "Where's Con?"

Dallan blinked. "Who?"

For an instant, Sueldan wondered if he had hallucinated the con man's presence.

Then Dallan added, "Is that his name? He went to try to catch horses." His eyes narrowed, and he flexed muscles beneath sweat-dampened fabric. "If you ever do anything that stupid again—"

Rifkah interrupted, "Leave him alone, Dallan."

The rugged features swung toward Rifkah.

"Callos irregulars menacing women and children. Where do you think his thoughts were?"

Dallan made a noise deep in his throat. "If he acts this irresponsible when we're trying to help *his* family—"

"He won't."

"When things get personal, people get *more* irrational. How do you know he won't—"

"I *don't* know. I just trust that he won't."

"And if he does?"

Sueldan cleared his throat. "I *can* speak for myself." Though minor, his wounds throbbed, and their bickering intensified the pain.

Dallan ignored the other man, still fully focused on Rifkah. His lids lowered further, leaving only slits, and he glared at the fortune-teller. "You know because you're using witchcraft. Aren't you?"

Rifkah stomped her foot, stepping around Sueldan to meet Dallan face-to-face. She made a noise of frustrated rage. "You are so . . . irritating." She stomped her foot again. "Just because I can read people's pasts and futures doesn't mean I can't intuit and surmise the same as anyone else."

For several moments the two stared at one another, neither giving ground.

Sueldan rose with a sigh, resigned to the quibbling. At least, it distracted him from worrying about his family.

Finally, Dallan's eyes opened to reveal the soft brown rings that had gained Sueldan's trust three weeks ago. "You just seem so . . . sure of yourself to be guessing. And . . ." He tilted his head. ". . . right."

Rifkah actually smiled. "That's not because of magic. It's because I'm a woman."

Dallan managed a lopsided grin. "Really? Women are good at that sort of thing?"

The sound of breaking brush seized Sueldan's attention, and he left his two companions to identify the sound. Behind him, they continued talking.

"You're not going to convince me I'm the first woman in your life."

"Suit yourself," Dallan replied. "I was thirteen when the flu swept through Lathary and took my mother and sister."

At that, Sueldan turned. His companions still stood, eye to eye; but Dallan's gaze flitted past Rifkah to him. The guardsman amended, "Well, I thought it took them both. Actually, only my mother died. My sister disappeared in the middle of the night. I now know Callosian slavers kidnapped her."

Sueldan went back to scanning the woods. Evening had melted into night, and moonlight shone on the leaves. It lit the path well. Beneath the trees, however, the world condensed into a solid ball of gray-black that allowed little vision. He could tell only that a large shape headed toward them.

"Ahh." Rifkah's voice filled with understanding. "So that's why you've joined Sueldan."

"I–I thought you already knew."

Sueldan knew he had told Rifkah about Dallan's sister, but he had done so in strict confidence before the guardsman had joined them. He appreciated that the fortune-teller feigned ignorance to protect him.

"How would I know? You've told me nothing but how much you hate my talent since we left Lathary."

"You read Sueldan."

"I read Sueldan. Not you."

Gradually, the forms became visible through the gloom, two horses and a man between them. From the sounds of hooves through brush, Sueldan guessed at least one more horse followed. He suspected his companions heard their approach as well but found their own conversation more engrossing.

"But Sueldan knew about my sister."

"I'm not a mindreader," Rifkah responded. "I'm a fortune-teller."

Dallan's tone turned gruff. "Let's just pretend I don't know the difference."

An uncomfortable silence followed. Sueldan glanced at his companions again, to make certain they had not disappeared. They stood in the same position, Rifkah with hands on hips and Dallan with his head cocked to the left.

"I'm Latharyn," Dallan reminded, shifting his bulk. "Magic of any kind's rare."

"Rare in Lathary, perhaps. Merely uncommon in the rest of the world."

Sueldan looked back at the horses, now recognizing Con between a barrel-chested bay and a spirited chestnut. A gray and a second chestnut docilely followed the other two, pausing at intervals to graze. Sueldan headed toward the con man to help.

Rifkah's explanation wafted to Sueldan. "Mindreaders can tell people's direct thoughts, but not their emotions or intentions. Fortune-tellers focus on feelings. The stronger an event impressed the person, the more we can read about it. In my case, I can tell past and future, but not present. Most fortune-tellers can read one or another. Some read two or even all three. It's not an exact . . ."

Weeds crunched beneath Sueldan's boots, drowning his companions' conversation. A cold night wind rustled the greenery overhead and eased through the hole in his tunic, chilling. Welcoming the exertion, he claimed the bay's bridle from Con.

"Thank you." Con tethered the chestnut to a roadside tree, and it pranced to the limits of its restraint.

The dog raced over, barking sharply at the animal's antics. That further upset the horses. The bay jerked backward, nearly tearing the leathers from Sueldan's grip. Pain flashed through his injured side. Swearing, Sueldan ripped the horse's head back under control. The two unsecured horses wheeled and whinnied, one bolting back into the woods, the dog yapping at its heels.

Swiftly Sueldan tied the bay, while Con dove for the gray's dangling reins. Rifkah and Dallan dashed over to assist, and Sueldan turned his attention to the dog. "Dog, no! Get back here, Dog!"

The dog let out another series of shrill barks. The loose chestnut whirled back toward its herd mates and started running toward them. The dog barreled after it, still barking.

Con and Dallan wrestled the rearing gray as the chestnut thundered toward them.

Ignoring the horses, Sueldan shouted again. "Dog, no!" He waited until the animals drew nearer, then dove on the dog. His weight bore it to the ground, and it yelped in surprise. Twisting, it growled, teeth bared. Sueldan grabbed the narrow, black muzzle, holding it firmly closed. "No!" He met the animal's dark eyes, and his voice went deadly sincere. "No biting!"

The dog rolled its gaze away from Sueldan in submission. Still clutching the loose fur at the nape of its neck, he allowed the dog to stand. It looked at him, tail waving tentatively.

With the dog controlled, the horses calmed. Dallan and Rifkah tied them to trees.

Sueldan sat, releasing the dog's scruff but still keeping an arm around its thin torso. His head pounded. He stroked the dog with his other hand, softly explaining. "The horses are our friends, too. We need them to travel. You can't be chasing them all over creation."

Con turned on Sueldan. "Attacking six Callos irregulars unarmed and alone. That might just be the—"

Dallan, Rifkah, and Sueldan finished the thought in unison, "—stupidest thing I've ever seen."

Con stared.

Sueldan smiled, cautiously letting the dog free. "I already got the lecture."

"Yeah," Con said. "Well. It means more coming from me. I've seen some pretty stupid things."

The dog sniffed at the chestnut's hind hooves, earning a flat-eared glare and a raised hoof.

Rifkah hurried to rescue the dog, but Sueldan stopped her with a touch and a quotation from his own father. "Lessons learned the hard way last longest."

"Who are you talking about?" Dallan asked.

Sueldan looked at the guardsman. "The dog. He'll remember that when he chased horses he got knocked off his feet. It kicks him, he'll know to use caution around things bigger than him."

"Perhaps." Dallan pretended to consider, then gave Sueldan a searching regard. "But will his master?"

Sueldan clapped his hands to the throbbing head wound. "I won't forget this any time soon."

"Good."

Still sniffing, the dog moved toward the front of the horse. It made a shrieking sound of annoyance, lifted both front feet, and struck like a snake. Teeth and hooves closed down on the dog, who leaped out of harm's way. The barking resumed.

"No!" Sueldan commanded. "Come here."

The dog quieted, giving the horse one last look before returning to its master.

"Good boy." Sueldan scratched the dog's head approvingly, and the horse turned its attention to the leaves.

Rifkah glanced at the corpses. "We should get moving."

Dallan nodded agreement. "Choose your horses and mount up. I'll be right there." He headed toward the dead soldiers.

Con took the big bay, while Rifkah selected the gray. Believing it only fair for him to take the horse his dog had riled, Sueldan untied the chestnut's reins and mounted. He looked at Con. "Are you coming with us?"

The dark man shrugged. "Maybe. Where are you going?" The expression he turned on Sueldan sought more than just direction.

"Callos," Sueldan said.

"Rivertown, first." Carrying an armload of weapons and a single pouch, Dallan drew up beside Sueldan. He offered a sheathed sword and dagger, dangling from a leather belt. "You may need this."

Sueldan accepted the offering without admitting that he had never owned or used a weapon before. At the worst, it might keep highwaymen away, and he could always sell it for food.

Dallan handed up another sword and dagger set to Rifkah. "Just in case."

Rifkah took the sword without protest.

Con watched Dallan shove extra weapons and the pouch into his pack. "What's that?"

"Seven coppers. The sum total of their worth, apparently. And their sleeve patches. Never know if they might come in handy."

Sueldan had to wrap the belt twice around his waist. The sword proved heavier than he expected, dragging at his left hip and swinging against the horse's flank. He worried its touch might spook the horse; but it seemed to bother the animal less than it did Sueldan.

"Handy, sure," Con responded. "We, too, can look like bullies."

Dallan clambered onto the remaining chestnut and adjusted the leathers. "Off to Rivertown."

"Rivertown?" Con sent his bay into a walk toward the pathway. "I thought you were headed to Callos."

"Can't get there without supplies." Finished, Dallan sent his horse up beside Con's. "These bastards didn't have much. Probably why they were trying to steal from common folk."

Sueldan allowed his mount to follow the others, worried more about keeping his balance than steering. He kept his legs wrapped around its girth, and he clutched its mane as well as the reins. Humiliated by his many inexperiences, he preferred to keep them to himself. None of his companions seemed to be having any trouble at all.

"Callos has a much better market. And it's only a three-day trip to Rivertown's four."

Dallan gave Con a withering look. "What map are you following? The Bennorith River Bridge is another three-day ride beyond Rivertown. Five days from there to Callos. We don't have enough to get us that far."

Rifkah took the position beside Sueldan as they headed up the road, and the dog trotted behind and around them, following smells.

"If we hurry, we could reach the barges at Eirene just after daybreak," Con explained. "They can haul us straight to Callos. A three-day river ride."

Dallan considered the words in silence a moment. "If the barges sail tomorrow."

"This time of year, there's one leaving at least every other day. If I hadn't gotten tied up rescuing you, I'd have shoved off yesterday."

Dallan threw a glance over his shoulder. "You can blame Sueldan for that, not me."

Con made a gesture of dismissal. "Can't do that. I owed him."

"Yeah, you said that. What for anyway?"

"Ah, a question. I have a few of those, too. Maybe we could answer one another on the barge ride."

Dallan turned to the con man. "Maybe. Any ideas how we'll pay for this barge ride?"

Glad to finally enter the conversation, Sueldan suggested, "It seems to me we won't need the horses once we're on the barge. We could sell them."

Con swiveled his head and half his body to look at Sueldan behind him. "Exactly what I was going to suggest."

Sueldan smiled.

The con man added wickedly. "That should scare you." Facing forward again, he kicked his horse into a canter, and the others followed.

Chapter 7

SUELDAN and his companions snatched a few hours of sleep in a camp little more than a stone's throw outside of Eirene's limits. Well after daybreak, they rode into the partially constructed campcity, surrounded by the mixed aromas of fresh wood, water, sweat, and baking bread. Dark with river stains and splatters of previous cargo, log and plank dock works formed straight lines and edges. Two barges nestled between the piers. The nearest, painted white with red trim, sat quiet and empty, its sides scoured clean and its sails neatly folded and wrapped on its deck. The other sported two raised sails, the jib a faded cream with blue letters spelling EIRENE sewed crookedly across its face. The main sail formed a jaunty triangle of sapphire that fluttered intermittently in the light spring breeze. About a dozen men worked around it, placing crates on the decking while another man shouted orders around them.

A lengthy, one-story common building stretched through the center of the burgeoning town. Two private cottages sat just beyond it, surrounded by a haphazard spattering of tents. The makings of a third dwelling lay abandoned, the lowest logs gently intertwined and a pile of thatch peeking over the half-created walls. Sheep, pigs, and horses grazed in a shared pen; chickens wandered freely between the river and the buildings. Two women hung wet clothes on a line strung between a post on the dock and the common house window. Two others crouched just downstream of the docks, pounding cloth on the rocks. A group of young children chased one another between the structures.

The dog tensed.

"Stay!" Sueldan called, using the commanding tone that let the animal know he meant it.

The dog fidgeted. A chicken scurried toward the town, and the dog's ears flicked unevenly forward, then back. It looked up at Sueldan.

"Stay," he repeated.

The dog obeyed, though it moved stiffly, clearly suffering from energy that needed expending.

As they approached, men glanced over from the docks, in ragged pairs and trios before returning their attention to the crates. Finally, the dock-fore looked in their direction. Falling silent, he studied them for several moments. Apparently put off by their lack of wagons and goods, he returned to his job without another glance.

A boy of about four careened around the half-finished cottage, giggling, another at his heels.

The dog bounced, as if held by an invisible chain. It barked.

"Hush," Sueldan told it, then reminded, "Stay."

The dog went silent. It pranced sideways and back but continued to submit.

The scene blurred. Sueldan blinked to clear his vision, and the motion sent a tear trickling across his cheek. The air little resembled the salt reek of Lathary's docks, but the slam of wood against planking and the calls of the workers brought that day back to Sueldan's memory in vivid detail. The carefree antics of the children made him long for his own. He winched his hand over the doll in his pocket. It yielded to his touch, a soft unidentifiable lump through the cloth of his tunic.

At the edge of town, the four riders came to a polite stop. Con's horse lowered its head with a weary snort. Dallan's chestnut pawed the ground.

"May I?" Con asked, turning his head to Dallan.

The guard made a wide-fingered gesture for the other man to proceed. A day ago, he had not known this place existed.

Con sprang from his saddle, passing the reins to Dallan. He trotted toward the docks.

Again, the men looked up from their work, this time pausing to watch Con's approach. The dock-fore turned and headed toward one of the loading ramps, meeting Con at the bottom. With their leader occupied and his back turned, the dockworkers eased down their burdens to rest against them. Their break did not last long, however. Within moments, Con and the dock-fore parted. The con man headed back to the group, while the Eirenean waved his arms, sending the dockworkers scurrying.

Con accepted his reins from Dallan but did not mount. "Barge leaves tomorrow. He says he needs a better look at the horses, but he thinks we can work a deal. Said to wait for him by the first cottage." He led his bay toward the indicated dwelling.

Apparently taking his cue from Con, Dallan dismounted and followed. Sueldan and Rifkah did the same. The dog greeted its master with a whine, and Sueldan patted the silky, black head. "It's all right, boy. Stay close, and don't get in any trouble." Still holding his horse's reins, he headed after Con and Dallan, pausing only to make sure Rifkah accompanied him without too much difficulty. Her many-skirted dress complicated her dismount. The dog padded along between them.

The dock-fore conferred with one of his men, who took over his position. He picked his way back down the docks toward the cabin and the newcomers standing in front of it with their horses in tow.

Rifkah placed a hand sympathetically on Sueldan's shoulder. His wounds still stung on occasion, but he had removed the bandage from his head. His hair hid the healing injury well enough. He wiped his eyes with the back of his hand, forcing himself to concentrate on business. Then a movement at the corner of his vision seized his attention. A girl of about two or three years peeked around the cabin, eyeing them with shy curiosity. Wispy white-blonde hair dangled around pudgy features smeared with dirt. Her shift, though plain, lacked holes or patches; and her sandals looked new.

The dog's tail waved, and it whined a gentle greeting.

The girl held out a hand to the dog, and it glanced at Sueldan, tail waving.

Sueldan smiled. "Go ahead," he whispered.

The dog darted to the girl, licking her hands and face while she laughed.

Sueldan's heart soared as he watched the scene, imaging Danara in the little girl's place. His grin broadened. By the time he managed to look away, the dock-fore had reached them, holding out a work-hardened hand. He sported the broad nasal bridge of a Crestonian, and it made his widely set eyes seem not-quite straight. Blond hair, liberally sprinkled with gray, flopped, sweat-plastered, across his forehead.

Dallan touched the hand in the standard Crestonian greeting.

Only then did the dock-fore speak. "I understand you folks want barge passage."

"That's right," Dallan confirmed.

Sueldan blinked, saying nothing, trying to read some semblance of emotion in the dock-fore's coarse features.

But the man only grunted, examining each horse from hoof, to teeth, to tail. Finally, he stepped back, the same stolid expression on his face. "Nice horses. Where'd you get them?"

Sueldan thought he read a bare hint of accusation in the question. His heart rate quickened as realization struck. *What if this man knew those soldiers? What if they were friends? What if he knows?* Sueldan had no answers to his own questions. In Lathary, murder was punishable by decapitation. Roadway laws varied, however, depending on the nearest city's ruling brotherhood. Most allowed the killing of high-waymen, but he did not know if that extended to soldiers, even irregulars. In many regions, no rules governed the travel routes at all.

Terrified, Sueldan looked to his more worldly companions.

Con's attention flicked to his bay's rump. Nonchalantly, he strode toward it, looked, then covered the motion with a gentle pat. "Our share of war spoils."

Stunned, Sueldan lowered his head. The words were almost truth, if phrased in a deceptive way.

The dock-fore finally voiced his concern. "Two of these are branded military." He gave Con a searching look. "I could get in trouble for passing stolen military."

Sueldan bit his lip and swallowed hard. The dock-fore's gaze went directly to him, apparently finding him the weak link.

Arm still across Sueldan, Rifkah tightened her grip on his shoulder in warning.

Sueldan willed himself to calmness, turning his attention to the girl and the dog. She sat on the grass, the half of the dog that fit sprawled in her lap.

The dock-fore sucked in a deep breath, then loosed it slowly. He glanced toward the docks, then studied the horses again. He mopped his brow, shook his head. "Tell you what," he said thoughtfully, avoiding Con's direct gaze. "I'll get the truthseeker. He can sort this all out."

Sueldan's attention jerked back to the conversation. His abrupt movement sent his chestnut into nervous prancing.

Dallan also shifted restlessly, but his tone and words revealed only indignant irritation. "Is that your gallant way of calling us bald-faced liars?"

The dock-fore recoiled, looking more startled than affronted. "What?"

Rifkah abandoned Sueldan to take Dallan's arm with the gentleness of a lover. "You'll have to forgive him," she said with all the poise the two men lacked. "He doesn't like magic."

"A levitator accidentally dropped his mother." Con lied with astounding candor. "Injuries led to her death, poor thing. The hypnotist who tried to help only made things worse."

Sueldan steadied his horse, determined not to let anything his companions said visibly rattle him again.

Apparently shocked silent, Dallan did not address Con's ludicrous claims.

"Go." Con waved off the dock-fore. "Get your truthseeker. We have nothing to hide."

The Crestonian shrugged, then trotted around the common building.

Rifkah removed her hand from Dallan, who muttered, "Nothing to hide but six dead Callosian irregulars."

"It won't come up," Con assured him.

Ignoring Con, Rifkah added her whispered voice to the conversation. "Might be best to mount up and head for Rivertown. Avoid the whole mess." She moved toward her saddle.

"Oh, that won't look suspicious," Dallan rounded on the fortune-teller sarcastically, freezing her in her tracks. "Six dead Callosians, military brands on the horses, and sneaking away when a truth-magician's brought in."

"Truth*seeker*," Rifkah corrected.

Sueldan looked after his dog, who still struggled to fit fully into the girl's tiny lap.

Dallan gave the fortune-teller a hard stare. "I'm just saying, we can't stand up to a magician who can tell when we're lying. But, if we run, someone's going to search out why. Once they find those corpses, we'll be hunted down like animals. Probably killed before we can explain."

Sueldan shivered, fingers tightening around the bridle leathers. "But we didn't do anything wrong."

Dallan rolled his eyes, turning Sueldan an equally fierce look. "If we run, we might as well confess we did."

"It won't come up," Con repeated.

The dock-fore reappeared around the corner, a heavyset man in tow.

Sueldan's heart quickened, and he felt as if a terrible vigor filled his every part. He wanted to run until he spent it all, until he collapsed, until he left every problem behind him. Surely the truth would vindicate them . . . eventually, but they might spend days or longer under suspicion in a dingy cell. Worse, some out-of-touch lord from an unknown brotherhood might not see the incident from their side. He could choose to judge it murder and robbery, despite the details.

"Just let me handle the truthseeker." Con tugged his bay in front of his companions.

"You?" Dallan's regular voice sounded explosive in the wake of all the whispering. As the dock-fore and truthseeker drew closer, he lowered his volume, mimicking Con in a disrespectful singsong: "Get your truthseeker. We have nothing to hide. And by the way, Dallan's mother was killed by magi—"

As the dock-fore drew into hearing range, Rifkah kicked Dallan's shin.

Abruptly silenced, Dallan flinched with an angry hiss.

The girl dumped the dog from her lap, chasing it in happy circles. Sueldan wished himself almost anywhere else.

Still in front, Con took the opportunity to greet the dock-fore and the newcomer. "I'm called Con." He bowed his head in the truthseeker's direction, the greeting of the southern lands.

"Rennatta." The truthseeker returned the greeting. Sand-colored hair lay close-cropped against an olive-skinned scalp. Light brown eyes studied them with a nonchalance that approached boredom, and his jowly cheeks and chin softened otherwise sharp features.

"Ready?" the dock-fore asked.

Con smiled and nodded, without consulting Dallan. "Ready."

The guardsman's face purpled. To Sueldan, Dallan looked ready to commit the very murder they were about to deny.

The dock-fore wiped callused hands on his dirty britches. "Let's start with your name."

Con's eyes narrowed. "I just told you I'm called Con."

Rennatta nodded.

"Where'd you come from?"

"Porins."

Rifkah watched intently. The truthseeker also weathered Sueldan's scrutiny and, to the Latharyn's surprise, nodded again. "Truth."

The dock-fore seemed to take no notice, more focused on his queries. "And where are you going?"

"None of your business," Con replied with a composure his companions did not currently share.

The dock-fore's gaze flicked upward, directly into Con's

dark glare. "If you don't answer the questions, how will we know if you're telling the truth?"

"I did answer the question." Con raised his brows incrementally. "I thought this was to settle some concerns about our horses, not an interrogation about things I have a right to keep private."

The dock-fore's head bobbed, his thin gray-and-blond locks flopping with the movement. "I'm just trying to get some simple things out to give Rennatta a feel for how you answer."

The truthseeker intervened. "Don't need that. Just ask the stuff you want probed."

The dock-fore cleared his throat. His gaze went to the animals, waiting patiently in their riders' grips. "Are those your horses?"

Con did not hesitate. "Until you buy them, yes. They are ours."

"Where did you get them?"

"I told you." Con's attention followed the dock-fore's from animal to animal. "They were our share of war spoils."

Sueldan bit his lip hard to keep his entire body from tensing. Surely, this time, Rennatta would catch Con lying.

But Rennatta simply nodded again.

The dock-fore's eyes widened, then dropped to slits. "Are these horses stolen?"

Con shrugged. "Depends on what you mean by 'stolen.' "

Rifkah stiffened. Sueldan held his breath.

Con continued casually, "I personally don't believe that things recovered from enemies after a sanctioned war are stolen."

Sanctioned war? The words confused Sueldan, and he wondered how Con could possibly pass them by the truthseeker.

The dock-fore turned his attention to the truthseeker, his

right eye gliding toward his nose, his left seeming to disappear into its corner. "Anything?"

"No lies so far," Rennatta replied.

The dock-fore still seemed unconvinced. He studied the foursome. "Are you saying you're veterans?"

"Some of us." Con gestured at Dallan. "Show them."

"Show them?" Dallan repeated.

Con plucked at the stays of his own doublet.

Now following Con's lead, Dallan unlaced his leather jerkin and lifted his linen shirt to reveal a radiating sun beneath a pair of crossed spears tattooed over his heart. "Brotherhood Wars," he explained.

Rennatta nodded.

Sueldan stared. He had never seen Dallan bare-chested before, had never heard of the Brotherhood Wars.

Con gave Sueldan a warning look and a slight shake of his head. He drew the dock-fore's attention from their shocked companion by adding, "I'm a veteran, too."

Dallan jerked his head to Con also. For an instant, Sueldan got an echo of his own startled expression. Then, Dallan recovered, fumbling to restore his clothing as Con opened his. A dense tangle of chest hair covered small but well-defined muscles. He parted the hair to reveal a splotch of ink but released it before Sueldan got more than a momentary glimpse. Dallan shifted, clearly trying to see the tattoo as well.

Focused on his companions' revelations, Sueldan barely noticed the little girl creeping toward them.

"And you two?" The dock-fore studied Rifkah and Sueldan, dismissing her in an instant and him after a brief scrutiny of the awkward lay of his sword. "Never mind."

"Two military brands, two veterans," Con said. "Is it a crime for us to share our booty with friends?"

"Did you?"

Con considered. "You mean did we share these horses with our friends?"

"Yes."

"Yes."

Rennatta nodded.

Con fastened his clothing. "You've got what you need. Do we have a deal?"

The girl now stood in plain sight, one thumb stuffed in her mouth and the other arm wrapped around the dog.

The dock-fore's demeanor changed to one of nurturing sweetness. He stepped closer to the girl and turned her the loving smile of a father. "What do you have there, Trula?"

"Goggy," she answered around her thumb, tightening her grip on the animal.

The dog wiggled its entire body, then licked her cheek.

"Throw in the dog," the dock-fore said, "and you have a deal."

The dog. Sueldan's heart seemed to go from wild pounding to a sudden, absolute stop. He valued his family far more, yet he had discovered a tie to the animal as well. The dog had come to him in his darkest moment, had warmed him in Lathary's cold alleyways, and had helped him to survive hunger and brutal loneliness. He wanted Danara to squeeze and love the animal, to feel its fur soft against her face and its tongue lick tears and grime from her cheeks. He sought rationalization in practicality. Without barge passage, they would add a week to their travel, with meager money for food. Every moment they saved meant one less for Linnry and his children in bondage. Every copper spent would be one less for their hungry bellies, as well as those of his companions. The dog would become one extra mouth to feed.

Sueldan cleared his throat, delaying. Dallan and Con studied him, unwilling to bargain away a creature that did not belong to them. "How about . . ." he started, seeking the position of compromise. Even he knew reasonably healthy horses were worth far more than barge passage. He turned his gaze toward the girl and dog. She watched him, intent on every word. ". . . if you watch the dog for me until we come back this way?"

The girl smiled, pale eyes sparkling. "Can I, Papa? Please, Papa?"

"Deal," the dock-fore said, taking the gray's reins and leading it toward the pasture.

The girl hugged the dog more tightly.

Lost hours of sleep caught up to Sueldan that afternoon as they sat in the common house. A long narrow room took up the front half of the building, filled with makeshift tables made of barrels and crates. A series of doors in the back opened onto the private quarters of the workers, as well as those of merchants and passengers. Doors at either end of the building led to a kitchen and storage area in turn. The design seemed ludicrous to Sueldan, requiring someone to carry vats of foodstuffs from one end of the elongated structure to the other in order to prepare meals.

The four companions had pulled up barrels to a rickety table that still bore the flowery lettering of the crate panels that formed it. Rifkah sat to Sueldan's left, Dallan to his right, and Con across from him. The guard was determined to drag out information that the con man seemed equally determined to hide. Usually, the tedium would have irritated Sueldan, but now he saw it as a way to escape into his own exhausted sorrow. He let his arm dangle, missing the cold nose that normally thrust instantly into his palm. Needing something to stroke, he pulled the doll from the folds of his torn tunic and sat it on the tabletop beside him.

Sueldan's companions fell silent. It took him inordinately long to recognize himself as the object of every stare. He looked up. "What?"

Con snorted. Dallan's dark brows rose nearly to his hairline. "It's just that we've never seen you play with your . . . little dolly before."

Sueldan glanced at the weathered doll, at the scraps of brown linen, the cracked button nose, the thin thread of its smile. For a moment, it did not matter how ridiculous it made him look, or that his companions thought him insane. Danara had placed the doll beside her at the dinner table every evening, sharing the bits of food he managed to provide. Now, in a strange common room in a city he had never known existed, the doll brought his youngest daughter to him. He could imagine every detail: her favorite blue dress, so patched and faded he knew its color only from memory; her dark, soft eyes; her squeal of delight that seemed to define joy. He might have an even younger child now, but he dared not hope. If the rigors of slavery had not killed it, likely the slavers had.

Rifkah rose to Sueldan's defense. "Leave him alone. He's sad about his family. And his dog." She glared at Dallan. "Don't you ever miss your sister?"

Con smiled.

Dallan threw up his hands. "Thanks a lot. One more secret out, and I still don't know how he pulled off that veteran scam." He turned on Rifkah. "You know, that's exactly why I didn't want you along. You learn too much with that magic of yours; and you don't know when to keep your mouth shut."

"I'd have found out eventually," Con said, his eyes betraying the triumph his words and tone did not.

"Yeah." Dallan continued to glare at Rifkah. "But I'd have gotten some information in return."

Con shrugged, still grinning, surrendering nothing.

"I'm sorry," Rifkah said in true apology. "I didn't know it was supposed to be a secret. And I didn't use magic; you told me." Her voice hardened. "Remember? You haven't allowed me to read you."

Dallan looked away.

Sueldan stared at his hands, again fading from his companions' conversation. He did not bother to put away the doll.

Rifkah seized one of Sueldan's hands. "Tell us about your wife."

"My wife." An image of Linnry came instantly to Sueldan's mind, in graphic detail, accompanied by a bittersweet smile. "Linnry is beautiful. Perfectly beautiful." He reveled in the image, even as it blurred back to the obscurity of remembrance. "Perfect eyes. Perfect face. Perfect body."

"That should make her easy to recognize," Con quipped.

Dallan loosed a snorting laugh, earning him a vicious look from Rifkah.

Sueldan sighed, still lost in thought. He did have the presence of mind to describe her objectively. "She has fine, soft hair, worn short last time I saw it. Her eyes are large and closely set, her cheeks thin with the bones jutting here." He touched the forefinger of his free hand to each in turn. "Her ears—a little on the larger side. She has a nose a bit smaller than mine, with a slight upturn at the bottom. Her lips . . ." He looked around the group. "Like Rifkah's. Full, I guess. She has a long oval face. She was pregnant last I saw her, but that was years ago. When she's not, she's skinny, small-breasted, and . . . boyish, some have said."

Con tipped his head. "Interesting definition of perfect."

"Haven't you ever been in love?" Rifkah asked, loosing Sueldan's hand.

"Never," Con said emphatically. "It's a weakness."

"Actually," Dallan said with uncharacteristic insight. "It's a strength. Sharing your hopes and fears with one who never judges. Caring for someone more than you care for yourself. Trusting another with your deepest secrets, with your very life. It takes more courage than I've managed to gather . . ." He added carefully, "Yet."

Rifkah studied Dallan differently than she had in the past, with an admiration bordering on the very emotion they discussed.

Con rolled his eyes. "Not you, too, Dallan. And you seemed so—" He glanced at Rifkah and broke off. "I'd never have guessed you'd one day want to enslave yourself to a woman, to make yourself as vulnerable to enemies as he did." He indicated Sueldan with a jerk of his head.

Dallan shrugged. "My parents were very much in love. They achieved a level of happiness, a level of living I never would have believed possible. Just watching them together made me feel like I shared a piece of something . . . special. Someday, I want that, too."

Rifkah continued to look at Dallan, her expression soft. Sueldan could not help examining the guard, too. Now that he no longer baited Rifkah, Dallan seemed more like the kindly guard he had agreed to team with on this quest.

Quietly, Con shook his head. Likely, he would never understand.

Talking about what bothered him dispelled some of Sueldan's sorrow and awakened a curiosity that fatigue and grief had held at bay. "Con, how *did* you trick that truthseeker?"

Con swiveled his head to Sueldan, his inky, tangled mane swaying with the movement. Thus far, he had dodged all of Dallan's questions, which had centered on his veteran status and tattoo. Whether because he preferred Sueldan or his line of inquiry, this time, Con chose to answer. "Trick?" He glanced around, presumably to ascertain no one could overhear. "I didn't have to trick anyone. I simply told the truth."

Rifkah kept her tone delicate, apparently so as not to damn the flow of information again. "I was there, Con. Your truth and mine are not exactly . . . identical."

Sueldan bobbed his head in agreement. "You said we came from Porins, that those horses were war spoils." He recalled a detail even more egregious. "You said we took part in a 'sanctioned war.'"

"Did I?"

"You did," Sueldan insisted. "I heard you."

"I'll explain," Con promised. "But first, I have to let you in on a secret about truthseekers."

Dallan leaned forward, clearly interested in any information Con revealed.

"They don't actually seek truth," Con whispered urgently, as if he revealed one of the great mysteries of the universe. "They detect lies."

Dallan threw up his hands. "Oh. Well, that explains it."

Con further lowered his voice. "It does explain it. There's a chasm of difference between sensing truths and sensing lies." He turned his dark, haunting glance to Rifkah. "Isn't there . . . Magician?"

Rifkah shifted under the intensity of the con man's gaze. "Well, I–I never thought about it. I suppose there might be . . ."

"We did come from Porins," Con explained. "Not initially, but that wasn't the question."

Sueldan considered.

"And I didn't say those horses were our share of war spoils. What I said was—"

Sueldan remembered, "*I told you* they were our share of war spoils."

"Right." Con fairly beamed at Sueldan. "And I had told

him that. Before he brought the truthseeker. So I wasn't lying. And as to that sanctioned war, I think my actual words were something like: I don't believe things taken from enemies after a sanctioned war are stolen." Con sat back. "Since I truly *don't* believe such a thing, I wasn't lying then either."

Now, Rifkah mulled the words. "I don't know exactly how truthseekers work; but, if it's anything like fortune-tellers, you'd have to have unshakable faith in your own deception."

Con grinned. "Surely, believing in oneself is not a bad thing."

"No," Rifkah admitted. "But, apparently, it sure makes you an effective liar."

The barge cast off the next morning, carried by a north-eastern wind. They shared the huge ship with three merchants, a crew of twelve, and a young redheaded captain who dodged every stereotype of crusty old seamen with salt in their beards. No one stood on the docks to wave them off. Aside from the dock-fore and a few workers, the dockhands still slept, tired from an evening spent preparing the ship for travel. The dock-fore's daughter did come, twice stopping the dog from leaping onto the deck. As they pulled away, the dog ran back and forth along the planking, repeatedly gathering its legs for a jump into the water. Each time, it backed away, watching the boat draw farther from Eirene. Aching with guilt, Sueldan watched the white tip of its tail wave and stop in confusion. A bark, followed by a single, mournful howl, echoed over the river. Then, the town and the dog disappeared into an impenetrable smudge.

Dallan joined Sueldan on the gunwale. "Would I totally ruin my masculine image if I admitted I'll miss him, too?"

Sueldan forced a smile, seeking that quiet place he had found at the beginning of their trip. There, need usurped sorrow, allowing him the ability to focus on work instead of pining. "I think you destroyed that yesterday, when you gushed about love and marriage."

Dallan stared out over their wake in silence.

"Actually," Sueldan admitted. "I like you better this way. That swaggeringly manly act was starting to bother me as much as Rifkah."

"How do you know that was the act? And not this?"

Sueldan raised and lowered his shoulders. He did not know how he knew. He just did. "I saw you petting the dog. And feeding him, when you thought no one was looking."

Dallan made a deep-throated noise. "One thing I won't miss is the way he used to wake me up."

"The eye thing?"

"Yeah." Dallan shivered. "That was just creepy."

Sueldan turned his attention to the guard, suddenly glad for the distraction. He found it interesting that Dallan had twice used that same word, "creepy," to refer to Rifkah. Once again, he suspected that, like the dog, Rifkah occupied a more welcome place in Dallan's thoughts than he would admit.

"So, what are you thinking about?"

Sueldan watched the linear wake the square-hulled barge left in the water. "My family." He lowered his head. "I miss them so much, it's like . . . it's like . . ." He shook his head helplessly. "No pain I've known before. Like stab wounds, I suppose, but more permanent." He sighed deeply, finally speaking a concern that he had never voiced, even to himself. "They're my life, Dallan. They're all that makes my existence worthwhile . . . even just real. My children . . ." He sobbed, a wellspring of tears filling his eyes without warning. Speaking became an effort; he grew as breathless as if he had run the length of the deck. ". . . my children are my one positive contribution to the world. Without them . . . the world would be better off . . . had I never been born."

"Don't say that."

Sueldan continued to stare out over the river, listening to the rush of water beneath them, the stomp of footfalls on the deck, the flap of canvas in the wind. "I haven't worried about the trip back. Until now, I didn't realize why. If they're—" He forced out the words with even more effort. "—not alive. If we can't rescue them—I have no reason to go on."

"You're not talking about suicide."

Sueldan said nothing. A tear rolled to the aft rail. The water turned to a silvery blur, no longer worth watching.

Dallan's hand clapped to Sueldan's shoulder. "I said, you're not thinking of—"

Sueldan turned his gaze to the smeared image of the afterdeck. "No one would miss me."

"I would," Dallan said.

Sueldan shook his head, still looking down. Sorrow overtook him, a battering wave that stole his balance. The gentle rock of the ship suddenly seemed like a wild bucking, and he gripped the handrail to keep from falling.

"And I believe Rifkah and Con would miss you, too."

Sueldan could not help questioning. Finally, he looked toward Dallan. "Con?"

Dallan released Sueldan's shoulder. "He risked his life for you. He must have seen something in you worth saving. Are you going to piss on his sacrifice?" He added firmly, "And mine?"

Sueldan sucked in a deep breath and loosed it slowly. His thoughts felt sluggish, unimportant. Nothing seemed to matter.

Dallan chewed his lower lip, closed his eyes, then opened them with unhurried deliberateness. They seemed to gain a gleam of indisputable sincerity. "Sueldan, don't ask me how I know this. I couldn't tell you. But I believe with all my heart that your family is safe."

Irrational hope sprang to life. Sueldan knew logically that Dallan had no way to know the status of his family, that the guard had likely spoken from unreasoning hope and supportive kindness. Nevertheless, his certainty was soothing. The crying stopped, and Sueldan managed a shaky smile.

That night, stars sprinkled a black blanket of sky, with no moon or buildings to diminish the view. Tents sprang up across the deck, including the sheet of dull canvas that Dallan and Con cleated and clamped to the aft gunwale and deck. They placed the opening toward the wake, allowing the group privacy from the gruff curses and laughter of the off duty men as well as the discussions of the night crew. Rifkah was the only woman on board, and her presence apparently had no effect on the rowdiness or language of those sailors not currently responsible for lines, decks, cargo, and steerage. Unlike the somber ocean sailors, who had to contend with storms and swells, the rivermen had little danger to damper their spirits.

Filled with a dinner of fresh fish, fry-bread, and turnips, the four companions lounged mostly contentedly on their partially covered corner of the barge. Even Sueldan had found that comfortable place between ignorance and illogical trust that somehow, inexplicably, things would work out well.

The shrill of unfamiliar insects echoed strangely over the water, rhythmical background to the sailors' conversations. Sueldan sat propped against the gunwale, his legs straight in front of him. Con slouched inside the canvas walls, beyond view of anyone who might peek through the opening. Dallan lay on his back, his arms folded beneath his head. Rifkah sat cross-legged, eyes closed, lips moving ever so slightly.

"So," Dallan said clearly. "You're a veteran."

"So," Con said as clearly. "You're not going to let this go. Are you?"

"Brotherhood Wars?" Dallan persisted.

Con rolled his eyes. "Have there been any other wars in our lifetime?"

Sueldan looked at the other men, trying to guess Con's age. It proved difficult. Aside from having skin slightly darker than most Latharyns, and his killer's eyes, he seemed nondescript. His features contained a trace of the coarsening that came with age, and a few gray hairs marred the silky black of his hair. Sinewy limbs sprouted from a body nearly as thin as Sueldan's. The eyes seemed to change, at times ageless and deadly, at others wise and mysterious. Now, they looked tired, sunken into blue-black recesses. Only then, it occurred to Sueldan that, whatever Con's age, Dallan was definitely younger than himself. He knew of no wars at all in his own lifetime.

Rifkah questioned before Sueldan could, "Brotherhood Wars? When? What were they about?"

Dallan's head turned sluggishly toward Rifkah, as if he found her particularly dim-witted. Suddenly, Sueldan appreciated that she had asked ahead of him. "An entire war escaped your notice?"

Trying to forestall another argument, Sueldan interjected the truth. "Mine, too."

The tactic worked, too well. Dallan jerked to a sitting position, his attention abruptly on Sueldan.

Con glanced at Dallan. "It's not uncommon for people not embroiled in something to know nothing about it. I'd venture that you don't know much about diapering babies and wrangling children."

"I know *of* it," Dallan returned, still incredulous. "And we're talking about a *war,* by all the gods."

"As a soldier who fought in it," Con interjected. "Not as a regular citizen."

Rifkah cleared her throat. "You and Con apparently fought on the same side, same war. And you didn't even know it."

The fortune-teller's words redirected Dallan. "That's true. How can that be?" The guard's eyes narrowed suspiciously. "We *were* on the same side?"

"Lathary's?"

"Right."

"Yes."

The veterans stared at one another.

Sueldan watched the exchange, relieved to no longer bear the brunt of their regard. He knew separate, not always amicable, brotherhoods ruled each of the large cities, and that smaller towns answered to the laws and the brotherhood of their nearest city. The rest of what he understood about world politics could fit in his left shoe.

Finally, Dallan broke the stalemate. "Let me see that tattoo."

Con made no move to do so. "You won't recognize it."

Dallan grunted. "If it's legitimate, I should."

"Oh, it *is* legitimate. Just not . . . commonly . . . known."

Dallan's eyes went from slits to wide-eyed discomfort. "A secret unit?"

Con shrugged.

"So, you still work secretly for Lathary's brotherhood?" Dallan spoke through gritted teeth. "Are you spying for them now?"

Con maintained all the composure Dallan lost. "Would you believe me if I told you no?"

"Did I believe my mother was dropped by a levitator?"

His point made, Con threw up his hands.

Sueldan thought he understood Dallan's consternation. The guard had made it clear that, if Lord Byrran discovered their mission, it would mean serious trouble for Dallan.

"Prove it," Dallan demanded.

Con's brows also rose. "And how would you have me do that?"

"You can—" Dallan pursed his lips, considering. "You could—" He pointed at Rifkah. "Let her read you with magic."

Con followed the direction of Dallan's finger, stroking his chin. "I'll make you a deal," he finally said. "You let her read you first. Then I will."

It seemed like a reasonable request, yet Dallan frowned deeply. He considered for far longer than seemed necessary, looking from Rifkah to the deck repeatedly. Apparently, his distrust of magic was every bit as visceral as curiosity and self-preservation. "Fine. But only my future. Not my past." He gave Rifkah a warning look, surely realizing he could not stop her from doing as she pleased once he placed his mind in her care. "And you go first."

"You," Con insisted, without an instant of reflection.

"All right." Dallan finally gave ground. "But you'd better go through it when I'm done."

Con made a gesture of promise.

"And you have to give up past and future, if I go first."

Again, Con did not hesitate. "Fine."

That seemed to catch Dallan by surprise. His nostrils flared briefly, but he did not press. "Fine." He turned to Rifkah. "What do I have to do?"

Rifkah shook back her hair and moved closer. "First, it's

a good idea to ask me if I'm willing *before* you commit me to two readings."

She had an undeniable point. Dallan flinched. "Sorry. Will you please read only my future?"

"Glad to help," Rifkah replied with a genuine smile, as though the previous conversation had never occurred. She tossed the single blonde lock remaining on her shoulder to her back. Starlight glimmered through the pale strands. "Give me your hands."

Dallan complied.

Rifkah settled her palms beneath the guard's, and her fingers seemed to disappear, fully covered by his beefy hands. "Try to calm down."

"I am calm," Dallan grunted.

"Ah. Then this must be contented sweat."

Dallan pulled his hands away, wiped them on his jerkin, then settled them back on Rifkah's. "So, what's in store for me?"

Sueldan listened intently. His future lay integrally bound to the guard's.

Rifkah sat back on her haunches, and Dallan followed the movement, his hands still in place. "It's hard to tell without the context the past would give me."

"No!" Dallan's protest sounded too loud and sharp for the situation.

"Now who's hiding things?" Con asked.

Dallan swiveled his head toward the con man. "I'm not hiding anything. There are just things . . . things I'm not ready to share."

"Ah," Con said. "No secrets, just lack of sharing information. That clears it up completely."

"You agreed to the arrangement," Dallan reminded.

"I did."

Sueldan needed to hear the details. "Rifkah, what did you find?"

Rifkah looked at Dallan, who nodded cautiously. "Successes masquerading as great failures." Her fingers curled as much as they could around his huge hands. "I'm afraid I don't see your sister."

Dread clutched at Sueldan's heart, viselike. He had to interrupt. "Tell me the truth, Rifkah. When you read me, could you see my family?"

Rifkah's features went neutral, as if she worried that any emotion might make him believe she had kept back adverse news. "I saw some of them," she admitted. "But I couldn't make out specifics. I got strong sensations of something good, something bad. Danger."

The words struck Sueldan like blows. "Why didn't you tell me any of that?"

"I told you all of that," Rifkah said defensively. "Just not in so many words."

Sueldan tried to remember Rifkah's exact phrasing. It came back with surprising ease: *There'll be hardships. Some serious. But I believe your honest determination could carry you through them.* "What other details did you keep from me?" He tried to hold accusation from his voice. He needed to know.

"None," Rifkah said. "Honest. It's not for certain. The future never is. But I believe it is possible that you will reunite with at least some of your family."

"If you survive that long," Con added the piece that Rifkah would not.

The fortune-teller gave their newest companion a warning glare.

Sueldan clung to the best parts of Rifkah's words, refusing to contemplate the possibility that not all of his family members were safe.

"May I finish with what I was doing?" Rifkah asked.

"Please do," Con said, earning an equally stern look from Dallan.

"Dallan, you'll find that love you're looking for. In a close and unexpected place."

"If you survive that long," Con said again, this time drawing irritated glances from all three of his companions. He laughed. "Do go on."

"That's all I've got." Rifkah turned her glare into a wicked grin. "Your turn, Con."

Sueldan leaned forward eagerly. For reasons he could not explain, he wanted to know the man's real name as much as anything else.

Dallan rose and stepped aside.

Con also stood and stretched with bored nonchalance. The two men switched places.

Rifkah held out her hands, and Con settled his on top of hers. Dirt wound through the creases of each finger, the nails broken and grimy. The fortune-teller closed her eyes and lowered her head. A moment later, her lids whipped upward. She made a shocked, breathy noise, staring at Con with a look of sheer terror.

Sueldan had expected a seedy past but nothing so terrible it would shake Rifkah. "What do you see?"

"Nothing," Rifkah whispered. "Absolutely nothing. It's as if he isn't even here."

Chapter 8

DEAD silence followed Rifkah's proclamation. Then, gradually, sound returned. First, river breezes rattled the edges of their makeshift tent. A clamp rattled, and something thumped against the mast. A round of laughter rose from midship, followed by the barely audible buzz of conversation.

For once, Sueldan regained his composure first. "I assume reading nothing is . . . rare?"

Rifkah still stared at Con, her jaw sagging and her eyes wide. "Unheard of. Never . . . never. It's never happened that I know— How?"

Con rescued his hands from Rifkah and shrugged. "You're the diviner. Don't you know?"

Dallan rose, glancing from Rifkah to Con with an expression more distressed than any of the times he had referred to as "creepy." "What *are* you?"

Con rolled his gaze to Dallan, as if he found the question too far beneath his dignity to answer. He did reply, however, tone dripping with sarcasm. "A man. And you?"

Dallan ignored the question for another. "So how come she can't read you?"

"How should I know?"

Sueldan sighed. He wanted the answer also but felt certain that, even if he did know, Con would not reveal it. He tried to lighten the mood with humor. "Do you think we could all stop responding to questions with more questions?" He clapped a hand to his mouth in mock horror. "Did I just do it again?"

Rifkah joined the game. "And again, Sueldan?"

Sueldan laughed as the tension dropped a notch. Dallan still studied Con with stern discomfort. The ship rocked gently through a patch of rapid water.

"I believe," Rifkah continued, "that I actually asked the first unanswered question. About the Brotherhood Wars."

Still standing, Dallan threw up his hands. "How could you miss—"

Rifkah leaped to her feet, strode to Dallan, and pressed her palm to his lips. "Don't avoid the issue by belittling me again. Just answer."

Dallan went still until Rifkah removed her hand. "I'm not hiding anything." He gave Con an accusing look, dark eyes narrowed. "There was nothing remarkable about this war. One brotherhood trying to gain power over another. Got a bit out of hand."

Con wiped his palms on his britches, remarkably calm. "Callos decided to change the trade routes to bypass Lathary at the crossroads. Lathary was already hurting—to this day, it still hasn't recovered from losing the silver mine. Some of its best artisans had moved on, mostly to Callos. The brotherhood saw it as an attempt to shatter Lathary completely, perhaps to take it over. Callos recruited a few neighbors. Lathary retaliated and called some allies, too. The whole thing escalated to a war."

"Children." Rifkah folded her arms across her chest, her disapproving scowl returning.

"Much worse," Con said, with obvious agreement. "Children with deadly toys. A year and a few thousand of us . . . common expendables . . . dead, they called the whole thing off. The gains? A few fingers' breadths of forest and wild land here and there. Lathary even poorer."

Sueldan watched Dallan's face grow from pink to red to purple. "You bastard! I lost good friends, good men to that war. They fought bravely; they died with honor. We restored the trade routes, and we saved Lathary from utter ruin!"

Rifkah drew breath, and Sueldan cringed. Whatever disdain she held for the brotherhoods and their squabbles would only infuriate Dallan now. Apparently cued by Sueldan, she dropped her arms. The rage disappeared from her eyes. "After we closed the deal for passage, Dallan. When you were helping get the horses in the paddock, I heard you say you fought on the side of Rynthia, not Lathary."

The color gradually drained from Dallan's face as he considered the point longer than it could possibly have demanded. It seemed more as if he struggled for control. "I was lying to the dockman."

"Dock-fore," Sueldan corrected.

Dallan looked at Sueldan.

He explained, "Hey, I'd have joined the horse manure eater's guild to feed my family, if there were such a thing."

"I'm not scorning dock laborers . . ."

"Dockworkers," Sueldan amended again.

". . . I'd just expected you to pledge the miner's guild."

"I did." Sueldan stared at his boots, disliking the turn of the conversation. "Until I lost my nerve. After that, I couldn't even get an apprenticeship."

Rifkah shook her head, as confused about this as she was about the war. "Because you're afraid of mining, you couldn't get a job as a . . . a cooper?"

Con snorted. "Has nothing to do with fear. Latharyn skilled guilds are sewn up tighter than tourniquets, and you practically have to pledge them in the womb. Now, the un-skilled guilds wouldn't want—"

Dallan interrupted for a point more germane. "What exactly do you mean by 'lost your nerve?' "

"I was in that silver mine Con mentioned." Sueldan found himself surprisingly near tears. He had not directly considered the cave-in for many years. "The bare thought of tunnels makes me—" He broke off with a shiver.

Dallan clenched his fists. "But I'd heard—you know you're going to have to—" He whipped his head to Con, who returned a look of clear interest.

"He's going to have to what?"

"None of your business," Dallan growled.

Sueldan banished images of dark, enclosing places. "I'll do whatever I have to do for my family." He added emphatically, *"Whatever."*

Rifkah had stuck on a different part of the conversation. "Dallan, why did you lie to the dock-fore?"

Dallan regarded Con from the corner of his eye.

Taking the hint, Con yawned, stretched, and stood. "I'm going for a walk." He tossed up a corner of the canvas, ducked through, and headed across the deck.

Dallan lowered his voice to barely above a whisper. "Just in case there's still bad will between Callos and Lathary, I thought it best if we didn't let people know where we're from."

Sueldan considered. The valley peoples had spoken a common language since long before his birth, and dialects varied even within individual towns. His half-Carsean features would hide his origin well enough. Dallan appeared much more classically Latharyn, but he could have come from Rynthia as well. "All right," he wondered aloud, "now, why couldn't Con hear that?"

Dallan glanced around the flap, apparently to ascertain

that the con man was not spying. "Didn't you find Rifkah's inability to read him . . . um . . ."

"Creepy?" Sueldan supplied.

"Right." Dallan obviously fought a smile. "Creepy."

"Of course, I did." Rifkah seemed remarkably unconcerned despite her claim. "But it didn't seem like anything he was doing on purpose. I don't know how, but someone must have put some sort of magical aura on him that blocks other spells." Rifkah shrugged. "He admitted he used to scout for Lathary. In secret. If anyone would have access to such magic, it would be a brotherhood. They wouldn't let many people know about it, and they'd use it for men like him."

The description fit perfectly, far more likely than the weird scenarios taking shape in Sueldan's head: that the con man was a god or demon who had come to direct or destroy them. "Sounds right. Are you sure you didn't read him?"

Rifkah smiled at the compliment. "I'm really just assuming."

Dallan pursed his lips before speaking, "No wonder he tricked Rennatta so easily. He wasn't mincing words to bypass the magic; he could have claimed we personally gave birth to those horses and slipped it past any truthseeker. He put on that whole performance for . . . us." He punched his thigh. "Why didn't he just tell us?"

Rifkah resumed answering questions with questions. "Why won't you let me read your past?"

"Because it's none of your . . ." Dallan caught on. "Oh."

"Oh," Rifkah repeated.

Another thought made Sueldan stiffen. "Is it possible that Callos' brotherhood uses magic?"

"I don't believe—" Dallan started, immediately interrupted by Rifkah.

"You can count on it. Why do you think I suggested you get help?"

Physical hardships. That being self-evident, Sueldan did not speak it. "So, what kind of magic might they have?"

"They're not going to have magic," Dallan insisted.

Rifkah ignored the guard. "I know of seven disciplines." She counted them off on her fingers. "There's fortune-telling, mindreading, levitating, telekinesing, truthseeking, sixthsensing, and hypnotism, including mass hypnotics." She paused with the tip of one finger bending the same one on the other hand. "I don't believe there's anything I don't know about."

Dallan still looked skeptical. "And which of those would give someone a magical aura that's unreadable?"

"None," Rifkah admitted. "In the classic sense. But, as you know, there're variations. Like how I read pasts and futures, other fortune-tellers only one of those, and some only the present, the present and one other, or all three. Any combination is possible."

"What do the other types of magic allow?" Sueldan wanted to know what dangers he might face.

Rifkah turned Sueldan a look similar to Dallan's when they had asked about the wars. Suddenly, she smiled. "I forget you're Latharyn."

"Not anymore," Dallan reminded.

Sueldan blew air noisily through closed lips. "So where am I from?"

"Best," Dallan said, "to just dodge the question as much as possible."

"Fine. Now about that magic?"

Rifkah started to pace the small confines, the mild rock of the planking adding slight awkwardness to her otherwise remarkable grace. "Mindreaders read people's thoughts to various degrees. Most have very limited power, probably because the more potent are usually driven crazy or kill themselves."

"Gods," Sueldan said, finally fully understanding why Latharyns mistrusted magic. "Why's that?"

"Imagine knowing what others truly think about you. Or constantly getting bombarded by others' thoughts."

Sueldan barely dented the surface of the image before shivering in sympathy. At the least, it would make personal thought all but impossible.

Having made her point, Rifkah continued, "Levitators lift and telekinetics move or change small objects without touching them. Sixthsensers know where others are in relation to them, even if they're hidden. Hypnotists can make people sleep, change their behavior, or merely make individuals believe things they otherwise might not. Some can handle groups at a time."

"Wow," Sueldan said, particularly impressed by the hypnotists.

Rifkah dismissed the power with a wave. "It has limited use. Strong-minded people can be difficult or impossible to influence. Hypnotic suggestions must be at least somewhat reasonable, and they don't last forever." She went on, "As you know, truthseekers can distinguish truths from lies—to various degrees. Rennatta probably isn't particularly sensitive or he'd work somewhere more profitable. And a more acute reader might have called Con on his tactics, demanded declarative statements, at least, maybe even noticed he got no reading at all." She tossed a gesture toward her companions. "I'm not really sure about that, though."

Dallan stroked his chin. "I haven't heard you describe any kind of magic that would allow a man to avoid a reading."

"True." Rifkah shook her head. "I'd guess it was some sort of extension of sixthsensing. Sort of a reversal, a hiding of the presence." Her brow furrowed. "Of course, that would make him the sixthsenser, since wielders of magic can't give their powers to others."

It made as much sense to Sueldan. Someone with such an ability would prove at least as useful as a scout as someone who had the power placed upon him.

Now Dallan paced, head bent to rescue it from hitting the canvas partial ceiling. "So, how are we going to find out?"

Dallan's single-mindedness confused Sueldan. "Do we need to find out at all? Does it really matter?"

Dallan swung around. "Of course it matters. I . . . we . . . have the right to know who this man is. And why he's taken an interest in what we're doing. If he's a spy for Lathary, that's bad enough. But what if he's spying for Callos?"

Sueldan had not considered that. "But he's Latharyn."

"Are you sure?"

"He has Latharyn features. And I saw him in Lathary, long before I had any reason to go to Callos."

Dallan corrected, "Long before you *knew* you had any reason to go to Callos."

Sueldan shrugged. The difference seemed trivial.

"People can change their loyalties. And their appearances."

Rifkah moved to Sueldan's side. "Callosians are willowy, fair-skinned, and green-eyed, with small, birdlike features. Like those soldiers. If he's disguised, he's stunningly effective."

Dallan refused to release his point. "He hid his . . . his . . . whatever it is you people read from a magician, too."

Rifkah rolled her eyes. "I'll go talk to him, all right?"

"No," Dallan said. "I'll talk to him. Veteran to veteran."

Sueldan shook his head. He had already held two conversations with Con, learning enough to feel confident the con man was not a Callosian spy. He teased, "If he really *is* a veteran."

Dallan looked stricken.

Rifkah laughed. "Let me talk to him, please. I think he'll respond better to curiosity than suspicion."

"All right." Dallan dropped to the floor, reaching for his blanket. "I'm getting some sleep. The rest of you should, too." He looked pointedly at Sueldan.

Sueldan nodded, saying nothing. He curled up on the planking, listening to the sounds of Rifkah's departure, the indecipherable conversations, the rise and fall of the insect chorus. Drowsiness came easier than he expected, and sleep hovered tangibly close when Dallan spoke softly.

"Tomorrow, you and I need to go over the details of the catacombs."

Desperate not to lose the hypnogogic state so nearly sleep, Sueldan mumbled his reply. "Uhn-huhn."

A few moments of silence guided Sueldan even nearer to blessed oblivion. He had nearly reached it when Dallan spoke again. "Do you think she's safe?"

That fully awakened Sueldan. "What?"

"Rifkah. Do you think she's safe alone out there with . . . him?"

"Him?" Sueldan opened his eyes. "You mean Con?"

"Yes."

"Yes." Sueldan let his lids droop closed again. "I do."

"But he's so . . . and she's going to . . ."

Sueldan surrendered. "Confront him?" he finished.

"Yes."

Sueldan rolled to face Dallan. The guard lay on his blanket, his position tense and his expression alert. "You told me to get some sleep. But you're not going to let me, are you?"

Dallan grimaced. "Sorry. I'll be quiet."

"Thanks." Sueldan again shut his eyes, but this time sleep hovered, a distant abstraction. He sighed. "You like her, don't you?"

"What?"

"Rifkah." Sueldan studied his companion, who now lay with his eyes shut. "You like her."

"No, I don't." The denial sounded as lethargic as Sueldan's had moments ago. "Now who's not letting who sleep?"

"Dallan," Sueldan said, propping himself on one elbow, "You're a really lousy liar."

Without opening his eyes, Dallan gave the only reply he could. "Go to sleep, Sueldan. Go to sleep."

Rifkah found Con at the starboard gunwale, staring out over the broad, dark river. Starlight sparked red-and-blue highlights in the velvety sable of his hair. He kept one booted foot propped on the rail, the other flat on the deck. Despite the creak of timbers, the hubbub and occasional shouted commands of the sailors, and the flutter of sail, he apparently sensed her approach. And turned.

"So, you *are* a sixthsenser."

Con held up a stalling finger. He rolled something under his tongue for a few moments before swallowing it. "I heard you coming," he explained.

"Did you?" Rifkah allowed a hint of disbelief to enter her tone.

Con did not seem to notice. "I did. Sharp ears."

"Like daggers."

Con shrugged, returning his attention to the river. "Beautiful, isn't it?"

Rifkah stepped up beside him. The meager starshine striped tiny rolls of white water, minuscule disturbances in the surface. "Yes. But I prefer a bit more light."

"The new moon has beauty, too." Con picked his teeth with a finger. "So you're the one who got volunteered to question me. I figured it'd be Dallan. Soldiers form a sort of brotherhood in wartime."

It seemed useless to Rifkah to deny the obvious. "He wanted to come. I thought I could do better."

"You're certainly more fun to look at." Con lowered his foot from the rail. "What do you want to know?"

"How come I can't read you?"

Con sighed, looking past Rifkah. "I'll tell you anything but that."

That remains to be seen. Rifkah kept the thought to herself, not wanting to seem antagonistic when Con at least gave the appearance of cooperation. "Let's start with something easier. What's your name?"

"I told Sueldan the truth. I don't have one."

"You don't have a name?" It seemed blatantly impossible. "What do your friends call you?"

Con grinned again. "Con."

"Sueldan said he made up—"

The grin broadened.

Rifkah got the point, that she, Dallan, and Sueldan were his only friends. "Oh." She frowned. "What did your parents name you?"

"I wish I knew," Con said, almost wistfully.

Rifkah studied the con man, wondering when he would stop dodging her questions. "What did the people who raised you call you?"

"I raised me. I called me . . ." Con finally looked directly at Rifkah. "Me."

Rifkah loosed a gruff noise of frustration. "You want me to believe you nursed yourself?"

Con shook his head. "If you start my history at birth, we're likely to spend a few days here."

"Let's start at nursing," Rifkah prompted.

"My parents raised me my first year or so. Then I lost

them. The people who fed me after that didn't truly raise me. More like trained me."

Rifkah suddenly thought she understood Con's nature. And pitied it. She kept the latter emotion off her face and out of her voice. He would likely not tolerate it. "Were they relatives?"

Con shrugged. Though he did not say so, it was clearly another question he would not or could not answer. "Are we finished?"

"You promised Dallan you'd let me read your past."

"So?"

"So? Does your word mean nothing?"

"Should it mean something?"

Rifkah spoke before she could stop herself. "Oh, you poor thing."

Con looked at Rifkah, at the river, then swiftly back to her again. "That's a first."

"Sympathy?" Rifkah guessed.

"Pity," Con supplied. "Unless I'm purposely provoking it for the good of a scam. Most people find me vile."

"Do you?"

"Do I what?"

"Find yourself vile."

Con looked at his hands. "Usually," he admitted.

"I don't find you vile."

Con shuffled his feet. "That's because you couldn't read me."

"No." Rifkah empathized with the con man even more now. "I *am* reading you."

Con jerked his attention to her, his dark eyes filled with an expression of fierce terror. "You are? You can?"

Rifkah tried to put Con at ease with the truth. "Not with magic. With intuition and knowledge."

"Oh." Notably relieved, Con continued to meet her gaze. "Why do you pity me?"

"Because you deny, even denigrate, what you're missing. Love, trust, friendship." Rifkah studied him more closely. "Admit it, Con. You want them as much as anyone."

"I don't," Con replied with stony certainty. "Weaknesses, all three."

Rifkah refused to back down. "Then why did you rescue Sueldan?"

Con managed another smile. "He seems to think it's because I like him."

"Do you?"

Con's shoulders rose. "I can stand him. You, too. Dallan most of the time."

"People don't risk their lives in combat because they can stand someone."

"Maybe I had my own personal feud with those Callosians."

Rifkah would not let Con off with possibilities. "Did you?"

Con's shoulders fell back to their normal position. "No."

Rifkah took that as a confession that Con did like them and saw no reason to push further or to gloat. "And why are you still with us?"

"We happen to be going the same way."

Rifkah repeated the successful tactic. "Really?"

This time, Con stuck firmly to his claim. "Really."

"Are you watching us for some person, group, or place?"

"You mean spying?"

"All right."

"No." Con ran his gaze over Rifkah. "Do you believe me?"

Rifkah paused a moment, not wishing to belittle a legitimate question, though hesitation might seem equally offensive. She studied Con's face: the depthless askew eyes, the brows slightly raised in question, lips normal-sized for a Latharyn pursed to a pink line. "Yes. I believe you." She threw the challenge back to him. "Why wouldn't I?"

"Because," Con replied. "You know I'm a trained liar. And a damned good one."

"All right." Rifkah did not argue. "But you've got lots of other talents, real talents. Enough to derive your self-worth from those and drop the . . . the garbage."

Con rolled his eyes. "The 'garbage' is part of what I am."

"No." Rifkah refused to let him justify his worst faults with resignation. "The 'garbage' is simply part of what you allow yourself to be. You had a lousy past, Con. That's too bad. But it's not what I pity about you." Finding his direct gaze, she held it. "It's your willingness to sacrifice your future because of it. There's a lot of good in you struggling to get out. Try trusting us now and again. You might find that you like it."

Con's lids dropped, and his eyes turned steely. "Don't lecture me about morality, Fortune-teller. You're not entirely truthful yourself."

Now, Rifkah went on the defensive. "What do you mean?"

Con quoted, "There'll be hardships. Some serious. But I believe your honest determination could carry you through them."

Discomfited with the dangerous turn the conversation had taken, Rifkah dove on a smaller point. "You've got a remarkable memory. I believe those were my *exact* words."

"Garbage?" Con said. "Or one of my talents?"

"Depends on how you use it. Even lying can have ethics, used exceedingly sparingly and to help others." Rifkah ran a hand along the cool wood of the gunwale. "To *honestly* help others. Twisted logic can turn any action into a perceived kindness. Too many people justify lying, saying it's in the other person's best interests when it's truly only a way to avoid personal embarrassment."

"And some people use long lectures on morality as a way to avoid their own lapses from it."

Shocked nearly to anger, Rifkah glared at Con. "What's that supposed to mean?"

"You know how this mission will end. Hiding truth is the same as lying."

Rifkah said nothing. Con had an important point, one that had contributed to her near-arrest in Lathary. The brotherhood had not despised her simply for telling them what they didn't want to hear, but also for using her knowledge to goad them into doing things she believed they should do to fix the problems. "There truly is more than one likely outcome for Sueldan."

The corners of Con's mouth bowed ever so slightly upward. "You won't tell Sueldan. So tell *me* what his future holds."

"If I won't tell Sueldan, why should I tell *you?*"

Con lowered his gaze, then turned toward the water again. "Let's just say that if he's going to die, I want his dog."

"The truth," Rifkah huffed through gritted teeth.

"Trust me," Con said.

Rifkah bit back a sarcastic response. The simplicity of Con's words hid a deep significance that, she believed, he knew she would understand. If no one ever trusted Con, he could never learn to trust. Still, it was not her responsibility to rescue a savage con man from himself, nor to reveal information to one whom a companion who deserved her loyalty believed had come to spy.

When Rifkah remained silent, Con continued. "Dallan, you'll find that love you're looking for. In a close and unexpected place."

Rifkah's cheeks turned warm.

"And that lie wasn't to further your personal aims?"

The heat become feverish. "It wasn't a lie."

Con swiveled his head back to Rifkah. "Tell me those words weren't intended to start a romance between you two, and I'll believe you."

Rifkah found herself unable to meet Con's gaze. "It's one likely possibility—"

"—that you'll see to."

"Yeah. All right. So what?"

"So nothing." Con's expression framed a definite smile now. He looked back over the river. "What's in Sueldan's future?"

Rifkah sighed. She could feel more certain if she could only read the con man by magic. One skilled in subterfuge could surely hide his intentions from her, but she also saw advantage to Sueldan if Con knew. So far, he had helped, never hindered, her companion. "If he attempts this thing alone, he *will* die."

Con continued to look out over the river, but his fingers tightened on the rail. "And his family?"

"I don't know," Rifkah admitted. "I'd have to read them."

Con sucked in a long breath of damp air, releasing it slowly. "Who has to help him for him to succeed?"

"I don't know that either," Rifkah admitted. "I only know I'm not enough. And Dallan doesn't plan to assist."

"What?" Con jerked his head to Rifkah, who shrugged.

"That's what I read. He expects Sueldan to handle finding his family alone."

"I assume you're going to talk Dallan out of that notion."

Rifkah looked at the sky.

"Aren't you?"

Rifkah studied the stars, so bright in the moonless sky. "I don't feel I have the right to push him too hard."

"Why not?"

Rifkah felt tears sting her eyes. "He has nothing to gain, Con. I'm pretty sure . . ." she sniffled, ". . . pretty sure . . . his sister is already dead."

Chapter 9

TERROR ground down on Sueldan, and a sensation of imminent death exploded logic to a sudden, desperate panic. He ripped himself from the conjured thoughts that had brought him to this place. Timbers creaked. A crosshatch of riggings filled his vision, like a net cast to catch the brilliant blues of the sky. The tromp of footfalls and the cries of sailors returned to his hearing; the odors of grease, hemp, sweat, and damp wafted to his nose.

Sueldan remained in place for several moments while his heart rate returned to normal and his fingers gradually relaxed around the taffrail. Then, with a sigh, he lowered his head and cursed the weakness that would not even allow him to think about the task ahead. The mere idea of crashing through crude, unexplored tunnels created an unbridled hysteria he doubted he could ever learn to control, certainly not soon enough to rescue his family. Yet, in his heart, he knew he had no choice. It would clearly do no good to anticipate. When the time came, he would have to hope that need would overcome terror.

It's hopeless. Sueldan felt tears sting his eyes and forced them away with self-righteous anger. *It's never hopeless. I've done enough feeling sorry for myself. For Linnry. For the children, I have to stay strong. I can't fail them. I won't.* Sueldan summoned a resolve that left no room for doubt, but Rifkah's words hammered at his determination. He dared not contemplate which of his family he might lose.

Sueldan shook his head, brown locks flying. He could not afford to paralyze himself with thought. Dallan had detailed as much of his route as he knew, which turned out to be very little. The guardsman had also made it clear that he expected Sueldan to go alone, certain that only a smaller man with mining experience could negotiate the passages. The pronouncement had caught him off guard, though it seemed obvious when Dallan explained it. Once inside, the general layout mapped in his mind, Sueldan would open a way for his companion through a door or a window. They would kill Lord Mannkorus, the most senior member of the brotherhood, and anyone else who got in the way of freeing the slaves.

Earlier that morning, just discussing their families' hardships had kindled a scorching fervor that spurred in both men the desire to slaughter every lord in Callos. Since then, Sueldan's wrath had diminished. Contemplation of the catacombs consistently threw him over the edge of rationality. Not only would he have to break through dirt to create dark, enclosed tunnels, every ancient tomb would probably contain some skeletal remains.

Wood jabbed under Sueldan's nails, and his heart pounded in a frenzied cadence. Knowing he had once again entered the realm of panic, he forced his thoughts back to the ship. *I need a distraction.* Unclenching his grip from the rail, he turned toward the tent. A river bird shrieked, wheeling overhead, a splotch against the cloudless sky. Dallan's light tenor carried beneath the sound, raised in irritation. Sueldan paused. He did not wish to see the guardsman now, certain Dallan would only want to talk more about the mission. The volume of his conversation suggested that Rifkah was with him. Sueldan knew Con rested in another tent, ill to the point of missing meals for more than a day. *Maybe he could use some company.*

Veering toward the shipboard infirmary, Sueldan steered his focus to the mild roll and pitch of the deck, the warmth of the beaming sun, and the overarching blue-green of sky and water. Those details did not prove enough. Always, his mind raced to the impending rescue, the stark, dreary dread of tunnels and death, the desperate fear for his family. Almost before he realized he had moved, he reached the infirmary and peeked inside.

A beefy-handed Callosian with sandy hair graying at the temples, the physician bent over a sailor. The other man sat on a chair with his eyes closed, his expression pinched, and his hand held tentatively toward the doctor. Squinting through a magnifying monocle, the doctor studied the extended appendage. Sueldan glanced toward Con's bed, finding it empty, the blankets bunched and sweat-stained.

"Where's Con?"

The physician turned toward Sueldan, facial muscles wrinkled around the monocle. The green eye beyond it looked enormous. "Went walking."

Sueldan smiled. "So he's feeling better."

The doctor grunted noncommittally, then returned to his patient.

Withdrawing, Sueldan headed forward along the port rail. It seemed unlikely that Con would have gone midships, as this would have put him in the way of the working sailors. Besides, he would need a rail to lean against if the vomiting caught up to him again. Sueldan ran comments through his head, seeking a teasing greeting that might buoy Con's spirits as well as his own.

Sueldan had barely rounded the main cabin when he found Con, sprawled over the gunwale. His head hung toward the water, his arms flopped over the rail, and his weight lay precariously balanced. Alarmed, Sueldan ran to his companion. "Con? Con!" He grabbed shoulders that felt more powerful than they looked and jerked.

Con staggered backward, caught the rail with one hand, and dropped to an awkward crouch.

"Con, say something! Are you all right?" The question seemed stupid, but Sueldan could think of nothing else. "Con."

Dark eyes rolled to meet Sueldan's, the pupils like pinpoints. He opened cracked lips to emit a dry croak of acknowledgment.

"Stay here. I'll get the doctor." Sueldan started to turn.

"No." Con sank to the planking. "Can't . . . help. Dying."

Sueldan dropped to his knees beside Con. "Don't say that. You're not dying."

Con's lids drooped. "How soon . . . landfall?"

"Not long," Sueldan gripped Con's arms. They felt doughy and weak. "We should dock early tomorrow morning."

Con's eyes fell fully closed. "Not soon enough." His voice became nearly inaudible.

Sueldan loosed a soft moan, concerned he might miss his companion's last words. *He's just river-sick. No one dies from motion sickness.* Con's clear and terrible weakness belied that certainty. Sueldan wished he could leave, to run and fetch Rifkah. She would know what to do. But he was afraid Con might die in his absence. He leaned in close.

"Sueldan . . . do you still . . . have . . . what I gave . . . you?"

For a moment, Sueldan drew a total blank. He hesitated,

wading through a morass of fear and urgency. Then, the answer struck, and his hand went to his pocket. "The drug?"

Con said nothing, his breathing labored.

Sueldan pawed cloth from his pocket. Danara's doll tumbled to the deck, tangled in the pouch strings. "Yes, I have it."

Con's eyes pulled open, a thick gooey discharge forming in bands between the lids. He reached out a trembling hand and seized the pouch, the doll dangling from the strings. Shaking fingers fought with the snarl, then Con managed to open it without disengaging the doll. He stuffed a large pinch of the herb beneath his tongue, wadding leather and its remaining contents into his hand. His eyes slid closed again, but the pain seemed to melt from his face. An expression of utter peace replaced it.

Abruptly, Sueldan understood. "You're an addict," he accused.

Con said nothing. He remained in place, features calm, eyes closed, mouth pursed.

"This isn't river-sickness. It's . . . it's *need.*" Sympathy collapsed like piled straw in a storm. "You're a damned addict." He glanced at the doll, swinging between Con's fingers. Suddenly, he seemed unworthy to hold it, even to be in its presence. Sueldan lunged to free it.

"Water," Con said. "Please. Lots of it and soon."

Sueldan stopped in mid-movement.

Con opened his eyes. "Then, I'll explain."

Sueldan did not want an explanation. He wanted nothing from this man except his daughter's precious doll. "An addict."

Con repeated his words from their first meeting, "Every man has his demons."

"Yes," Sueldan agreed. "But some men's demons are self-inflicted." Nevertheless, he unclipped the waterskin from his belt and passed it to Con.

The con man clumsily uncorked the bladder and gulped down the contents. After several moments, he paused, water dribbling from the corner of his mouth. He placed a hand over his abdomen and smiled. "It's going to stay down this time." He looked at Sueldan, pupils restored to their normal size. "Thank you. You saved my life."

"We're even," Sueldan said gruffly, still staring at the doll.

"Not even close." Con followed Sueldan's attention. Carefully, he unwound the string from the doll and offered it.

Sueldan took the doll, clutching it lightly in his fist. "For a man who worries so much about weakness and vulnerability, you've sold yourself into bondage."

"Yes." Con took another long drink before answering. He seemed to grow stronger with every passing moment. "I'm going to share something with you that I've never told anyone, but only if you promise to keep it between us."

"That you're an addict?" Sueldan said accusingly, not certain why he felt so betrayed. He had looked up to Con's strength, had marveled at his sleight of hand, had wished for his stunning composure. Now, it all seemed like a cruel lie.

"No. Not *that* I'm an addict. *Why* I'm an addict." Con seized the rail and drew himself up. "Do you want to know?"

No. Curiosity proved stronger. "Yes." Sueldan added, "I suppose I owe you the chance to explain."

Con glanced around to make sure no one overheard. He lowered his voice. "I took it the first time before a dangerous assignment. The corpse I got it off once said it steeled his nerves. I figured I was dead anyway, so why not go calmly." He took another swallow.

"And you got hooked," Sueldan guessed.

"No." Con wiped his mouth on the back of his sleeve. "Not that first time. It did soothe me, but it was an unexpected side effect that got me to use it again."

Sueldan raised his brows to indicate interest.

"I realized that, while on it . . ." Con softened his voice still further, to a whisper so slight even Sueldan strained to hear. ". . . I became utterly undetectable to any form of magic."

Another realization dawned. "So that explains—"

"Right."

"Rifkah—" Sueldan fell silent. He stroked the doll, thoughts distant. Putting himself in Con's position, he could understand how the con man had come to place all his faith in an herb. And none in other people.

"I'm a guild of one. And this . . ." Con held up the pouch, still clutched against his palm. ". . . is my dues."

"And those dues are acceptable to you?"

Con took another drink. "It's no longer my decision."

"Those dues almost killed you."

"My mistake. I miscalculated the amount. I've developed what users call 'taming.' I've taken it so long, I need more for the same effect."

"I'm in a guild, too." Sueldan held up the doll. "These are my dues. It's a guild of thousands."

"Parents?" Con guessed.

"Friends," Sueldan clarified. "I'm hoping you'll quit your guild and join mine."

Con laughed, then shook his head with a sigh. "I wish, Sueldan, it were possible."

Sueldan proffered his hand. "It is."

That night, the harder Sueldan tried to convince himself he needed to sleep, the more it avoided him. Thoughts raced through his mind, swirling fragments of worry that seemed impossible to quell. He could not keep himself from contemplating the various fates that might have befallen his loved ones. Once, he caught himself hoping desperately that the casualty Rifkah had hinted at would turn out to be a miscarriage of the baby he had never met. He hated himself for an idea he could not banish. It would hurt him and Linnry, but the bare idea that he might lose one of his known children eclipsed it to a gentle, guilty pain. He agonized over the fear that panic might paralyze him into a failure his loved ones could not afford. He thought of Con, the victim of a self-injurious choice he could no longer escape. Even a nagging concern for the welfare of his dog remained to haunt Sueldan that night.

Sueldan rolled, drawing a soiled, woolen blanket more tightly around him. A river breeze twined through a gap in the tent structure, sending a shiver through his already tortured being. For the twentieth time, he begged his mind for respite, drove his thoughts toward benign repetition, this time slow counting. *One, two, three . . . Got to get some sleep. . . .*

Sueldan awakened to a bar of light across his eyelids and the clomp of Dallan's heavy footfalls. He groaned, assailed by the memory of startlingly real dreams that mostly consisted of him trying to run and his legs failing him. He opened his eyes, sweeping his gaze around the tent. A piled blanket marked the spot where Con had slept. Dallan stood at the tent flap, holding it open to admit the sunlight that had awakened Sueldan. Rifkah gave him a nod and a smile as she ran a comb through her dark blonde ringlets. "Good morning," she said.

Sueldan yawned. Unable to reply, he returned a wave.

Dallan turned. "Good morning, Sleepy. We're almost there."

Sueldan jumped to his feet before he realized he had moved, then immediately regretted his lack of caution. Dizziness crushed down on him, and he wobbled dangerously. He froze, waiting for the discomfort to pass.

Dallan turned back toward the opening in the tent.

As full awareness returned, Sueldan recognized sounds beyond the tent: the scrape of sandals on planking, the captain barking commands, the thump of heavy ropes. He hurried to join Dallan. *We're here. We're in Callos.* A chill pierced him. *Callos.* He looked outside.

Across a thinning stretch of translucent blue water, Sueldan caught his first glimpse of the city. Tow-haired dockworkers, sturdily muscled, stood on wooden planking, waiting for the ship in the brilliant sunlight. Callos seemed to scroll out in front of them. Centrally, a crenellated building towered over the others, the mansion of Callos' brotherhood by Dallan's description. A flag lay becalmed on its roof, a gold background graced by the red, four-pointed star that had come to symbolize evil in Sueldan's mind. Waves of shops and cottages radiated outward from that point, except toward the docks, where warehouses claimed most of the space. The farther the cottages got from the mansion, the smaller and sloppier the construction generally became, until it ended in an emerald plain of crops and pastures dotted with animals. From a distance, it resembled Lathary closely enough to seem familiar.

"What do you think?" Dallan stepped aside to give Sueldan some room.

Sueldan merely shrugged. It did not matter. He had a job to do, after which he would leave and gladly never see this place again. It might have consisted only of whitewashed palaces fresh with dew and it would still have seemed dark and ugly to him. "I think," he finally started, "my wife and children are slaves there."

Dallan made a noncommittal noise.

Sueldan glanced at the compact guard. "And your sister. I would think you would want to come with me. To free her."

Dallan frowned, running a meaty hand through his black curls. "We've gone over this. I'll get you there safely. That's all I promised. I'm too big for tunnels, and I'm not trained for them. I'd only get you caught and in trouble, put your family at risk. Once you're in, maybe dispatched a 'problem' or two, you can let me in the front."

Con glided to them, though Sueldan had neither seen nor heard him coming. "*We'll* let you in the front, Dallan."

The guardsman whirled, his curly mop falling back into disarray. "What?"

"I'm going with him," Con explained. His black cloak and tunic seemed to merge with his hair and eyes, making his dark skin look contrastingly ordinary in color. He showed none of the frailty of the previous day.

Shocked speechless, Sueldan opened his mouth; but nothing emerged.

Dallan shrugged. "As you wish. Sueldan could use the company, and I hardly think you'd give him away."

The ship rocked as sailors scrambled over the deck.

Con smoothed his tunic. "I'm not going to keep him company, Dallan." He gave the guardsman a direct and unwavering stare. "I'm going because he can't do this alone, and the companion he counted on has become too much of a coward to free his own sister."

"Con," Rifkah said warningly, heading toward the men. "Don't."

Dallan's nostrils flared. "This has nothing to do with cowardice. It has to do with practicality."

"Practicality, huh?" Con appeared stalwart, but Sueldan

· noticed a slight shift in his balance. The con man could flee in an instant. "So you're *practically* a coward."

Dallan's cheeks flushed, and his lips lost any semblance of color. He clipped his words but showed no other signs of anger. "I am going to help. Just not in the catacombs. I can't fit through small spaces. And I'll prove clumsy underground. I'll get you caught. Or worse."

A sudden realization narrowed Sueldan's eyes, and he wondered why he had not considered it before. "We're talking about areas that used to serve as storage rooms, not tunnels. Underground, yes; but there's no reason to believe they'll be small."

"So." Con's eyes flashed. "It *is* cowardice. Pure and simple."

"You bastard!" Dallan lunged at Con. "I'm going to rip your throat out."

Con danced lightly out of reach.

Sueldan also backed away, but Rifkah deliberately placed herself between the men.

"All I know," Con said, "is that you dragged him out here with the understanding that you had the same passion and stomach for this mission as he does. Now that he needs you, you're abandoning him. That doesn't seem like something friends do."

Dallan's reply turned venomous, but he did not try to get around Rifkah. "How would you know what friends do?" He glared between Sueldan and Rifkah. "And which one of my so-called friends can't keep his damn-fool mouth shut?"

Sueldan tried to defuse the situation. "I'll take whatever help I can get. Thank you, Con. I don't know why you're agreeing to this—I probably never will. But I appreciate it." He put aside the concern that the drug might impair the con man's ability to assist. He needed a companion, even if only for moral support. He dared not refuse such a generous offer.

Rifkah said, "I'm going, too."

Dallan stiffened. All of the anger drained from his demeanor. "What?"

Rifkah raised her brows but did not repeat herself. As softly as she had spoken, he had heard her.

"You can't—" Dallan amended swiftly. "I mean, I don't think you—you shouldn't—"

"Shouldn't what?" Rifkah smiled. "Shouldn't help a friend who needs me? That's the very reason I came."

Warmth made Sueldan flush, and he returned Rifkah's grin. Suddenly, nothing seemed impossible. "Thank you," he said, nearly choked by gratitude. "Thank you so much."

The ferocity slid from Dallan's face, leaving it creased with an expression that seemed meek, almost despairing. "Don't think I'm going to let you get your damn-fool selves killed."

Sueldan bit his lip, certain a smile would irritate Dallan. Although the guardsman had not stated so directly, Sueldan believed he had just agreed to accompany them underground.

Dallan did not give them the opportunity to make certain, instead immediately striding onto the deck to assist the sailors.

Sueldan watched him go, waiting only until he passed out of earshot to address Con. "You're amazing. How did you know that would get him to come along?"

Con wiped his nose on the back of his sleeve, a slight smile playing across otherwise unrevealing lips. "You give me too much credit. I didn't get him to come along." He jerked a thumb toward Rifkah. "She did." He added carefully, "And she got me to go as well."

Rifkah did not deny the credit. "It wasn't difficult. Surprisingly, for *either* of you." She turned a measuring stare on the con man. "What, exactly, do *you* get out of this?"

Con pursed his mouth, head shaking ever so slightly. "By all the gods, I wish I knew."

The damp, earthy aroma, the cool darkness dulled to gray by the light of a new lantern, the wooden pick shaft clenched between his fists and warmed by his body heat brought memories of Sueldan's day in the mines. His heart hammered, his breaths came in a pant, and he struggled to contain his thoughts. He forced his attention to the earlier events of the day, a trip to the market that had gained them the lantern, two picks, a shovel, and a scant amount of food. Con had also purchased two pouches of his drug, for more silver than Sueldan had seen in his lifetime. *His demon.* He shook his head, committing himself to returning the favor of Con's assistance by freeing him from this dangerous and expensive addiction. The self-assigned obligation dragged him back from the brink of panic, at least for the moment.

The tip of Dallan's pick struck the wall, and soil pattered to the crude basement floor. Con churned up the ground with the shovel. Rifkah moved between them, her grace marred by restless energy, bits of dislodged quartz shimmering in her sandy locks. So far, they had dug only downward, finally discovering this first of many cellars. They had found no corpses, but Sueldan steeled himself for that eventuality. After strangling a Callosian irregular, he believed he could handle that sight. The dank, enclosing blackness was a whole other matter.

Rifkah spoke, her voice a gentle echo that broke the crushing silence. "Dallan's way."

Con turned toward her, lifting his shovel. Dallan glanced over his shoulder. Sueldan forced himself toward the guard, his step awkward.

"It has the most . . . positive outcomes," Rifkah explained. A note of cheer in her tone seemed forced. Her clenching and unclenching fingers told a different story. Sueldan hoped her nervousness stemmed from the discomfort of being underground rather than any future knowledge of failure.

Jaw tight, determination high, Sueldan slammed his pick against the minuscule dent Dallan had made. Huge hunks of earth exploded from the attack.

Dallan back stepped with a snort of self-derision. "Still don't see what he needs us for." Everyone ignored the guard, who had become increasingly sullen since the first shovelful of dirt.

The pick thumped against the wall again, bringing distant memories of pounding against practice dirt piles. Uland's voice returned clearly to Sueldan's mind for the first time in years. "Straight on, Tamison! And put some muscle behind it. You're not peeling roots."

Con added his piece. "Should you fight a war alone because you're a more competent swordsman?"

"A *battle?*" Dallan corrected the analogy. "Maybe."

Rifkah ignored the discussion to place a hand on Sueldan's hip, a position that kept her clear of the pick falls. "You're amazingly good at this." She lowered her voice so only he could hear. "You make Dallan look like a little girl."

The image proved too much for Sueldan. He loosed a deep chuckle that dispelled some of his terror. Warmth spread through him at the compliment. A long time had passed since he had taken pride in anything. Ignoring Dallan's and Con's light bickering, he continued to strike the wall. Three more blows opened the way to another vault, nearly the size of the one they currently occupied.

Dallan scooped up the lantern with enough force to send the light swinging crazily. He thrust it through the new opening to reveal a rough rectangular room with a sagging roof. Three corpses lay peacefully on the floor, their skin mummified to leather stretched across jutting bones.

Sueldan's calm overturned. His mind conjured images of his father, brother, and uncle, their faces frozen in terror, their lips writhing into terrible screams. Pain jarred through his skull. He came back to himself suddenly, shivering in Rifkah's arms. The men studied him, Con with brows raised in curiosity, Dallan with eyes wide and mouth open.

"It's all right," Rifkah soothed, her tone flat and emotionless. "It's all right."

"I'm all right," Sueldan agreed uncertainly. He unfolded himself from Rifkah's embrace, still teetering on the edge of madness. "I can't do this."

"You can," Con said with finality. "And you will. Your family needs you."

Dallan looked suddenly stricken. Without offering a word of encouragement, he turned away and lowered himself through the freshly dug opening. The sound of his pick striking dirt raised a fresh wave of panic.

Sueldan clung to lucidity only by focusing on the truth of Con's words. His loss of control doomed Linnry and the children. He ran their names through his head in a chant that grew stronger with every repetition: *Sutannis, Ellith, Danara. Sutannis, Ellith, Danara. For them, I have to hold myself together. Sutannis, Ellith, Danara.* Buoyed, he hurried through the hole to join Dallan.

"Stop!" Rifkah nearly trampled Sueldan in a mad rush to Dallan's side. Knocked sprawling, Sueldan did not fight the momentum. He struck the ground and skidded, surprise eliminating any pain from the landing. By seizing an irregularity in the floor, he managed to keep himself from sliding into the corpses, though they hovered right in front of him. Furiously, he backpedaled.

Rifkah did not pause even for an apology. She launched herself on Dallan, slamming him aside. They collapsed in a tangle as a wall of earth crumbled around them. Faster than Sueldan could think to be afraid, it was over. An irregular pile of sandy soil and boulders filled one side of the cavern. Con stood in the opening between the basements. Dallan and Rifkah carefully separated, the guard's gaze fixed on the cave-in that would have buried him. Agony howled through Sueldan's body, all of it from muscles tensed to breaking.

Dallan spoke first, a soft expletive that seemed more awed than angry.

The names of Sueldan's children swirled through his head in a chant so rapid it blurred to his chosen alias. *Sueldan, Sueldan, Sueldan, Sueldan, Sueldan.* He squeezed his eyes shut, rocked himself, and gasped in ragged breaths.

"Is everyone all right?" Con asked.

Finally extricating himself, Dallan stood. "Thanks to Rifkah." He glanced at her. "Magic?"

"Yeah." Rifkah brushed dirt from her tattered dress with one hand and rubbed her eyes with the other. "Still hate it?"

"No," Dallan admitted. He gathered breath, as if to say something else, then shook his head instead. "Let's go."

Sueldan continued rocking himself, gathering the strength to face and overcome a horror that had plagued him since the accident.

Rifkah continued, "Fine. But from now on, I get to look to the future *before* anyone goes off digging rashly and alone."

Dallan accepted the admonishment without comment.

"Fine by me." Con dragged the shovel into the cellar.

Sueldan forced himself to his feet, gathering courage from his triumph over fear. Money had not proved a powerful enough motivator, even when it came to feeding his family; but the lives of wife and children had. "Let's go." He parroted Dallan, his voice shaky but his hands steady. He tapped a wall perpendicular to the one Dallan had chosen. "Is this one all right? It's more toward the mansion anyway."

"It is?" Dallan's finger stirred the air, and his eyes slitted as he considered direction from every angle.

Rifkah lowered her head, silent for several moments. At length, she nodded.

From that moment, the task became several orders easier. Sueldan took charge, handling all direction, picking, and shoveling while Rifkah reassured, and the other men simply followed. Dallan's moodiness returned. Occasionally, Sueldan recognized a snide tone in his voice, though the words slipped past him, unheard. The need to concentrate on his work, the excitement of coming ever closer to his family, made all else insignificant. Even the suffocating reality of being underground barely penetrated his understanding anymore. Fear became a meaningless abstraction, unable to breach the walls of determined need he had finally erected.

Sueldan lost track of time as his life became an endless landscape of dirt, mildew, ancient corpses, and lantern light. He ceased to measure time by distance or fear; those things became immaterial. Time passed only as a counterpart to growing fatigue. His arms ached from pounding through earth and rock. His legs cramped. His mouth grew dry as cotton. Still, he continued, oblivious to anything but his family's plight. Each crafted tunnel brought him that much closer to Linnry and the children.

Rifkah's firm touch on Sueldan's arm stopped him, drawing him from the trance that had kept him going past exhaustion, blind to his panic. "Something's wrong."

The companions gathered around the fortune-teller. Dallan seemed incapable of remaining still, pacing forward and backward. Sueldan dismissed his antics as pent-up energy; the guardsman had done little but watch the entire operation, difficult for a young, vital man. Con seemed much calmer, quietly rolling something, presumably his drug, around his mouth.

Rifkah shook her head, as if trying to remove an unwanted thought. She considered her words for a long time.

"The truth?" Con suggested.

Rifkah sucked in a long breath, loosing it slowly. "The truth." She sighed again. "I'm sorry. I just don't see anything good coming out of continuing this way."

Sudden nausea smacked Sueldan low in the gut. "You mean . . . you mean . . . my family won't . . ." He could not finish.

"Oh, no." Rifkah reassured. "Rescuing your family is still one of the possibilities."

Sueldan's mind discarded the doubt that tainted Rifkah's tone, that suggested it was one of the least likely possibilities. No matter the odds, he dared not quit.

"I sense magic. Probable . . . disaster." Rifkah gave her head a brutal shake. "I'm sorry, Sueldan. I can't lie. It doesn't look good."

Struck dumb by the confession, Sueldan only stared.

Con looked from Rifkah to Sueldan and back. "What exactly do you see?"

"I'd be more specific if I could." Rifkah watched Sueldan, features pinched. "The farther we go, the more his future becomes hopelessly entwined with mine and the more blurry things get. I just can't be sure."

"So." Sueldan lowered the pick and studied his hands. Until that moment, he had not noticed the blisters shrouded in layers of brown filth. His arms ached. His fingers straightened only with painful effort. Sweat and grit stung his eyes. He had come too far to surrender now. "This disaster. It's not . . . certain."

Dallan's pacing grew more agitated.

"We could try another way," Rifkah suggested.

Sueldan closed his eyes. The fortune-teller made it sound so simple, like the four of them could somehow blitz a brotherhood's mansion through the front doors, undetected. At least, this route seemed unlikely to have guards. "Would trying another way be . . . successful?"

"I don't know," Rifkah admitted.

Sueldan wrestled between his own intuition and Rifkah's magic, which had, so far, proved right. Though less accurate, his perceptions had brought him through the worst of times. *Or did they cause those bad times?* Sueldan brushed the thought aside. He had struggled too hard for self-respect to discard it now. He could practically taste success. Every moment he wasted meant another in bondage for Linnry, Sutannis, Ellith, Danara, and the baby. "I have to go on," he said.

"No." Rifkah seized his arm. Overworked muscles quivered beneath her touch. "Sueldan, it's dangerous."

Dallan finally stopped pacing. "Maybe he'll have better luck without us bumbling along with him."

Rifkah gave the guard a harsh stare.

"Look, I've always thought it best for the one who knows what he's doing to go underground alone. He can open the way for the rest of us."

Rifkah's tone turned as icy as her expression. "We've heard your opinion on the matter."

Dallan held out his hands. "And now we've established that, horrible as it might seem, I may have been right."

Once, Sueldan had fought it; now he pegged his hopes on Dallan's suggestion. "It's worth a try." He tightened his grip on the pick. "I always knew this might end in tragedy. The bigger tragedy would be to let fear keep me from trying." Icy terror seized him suddenly. "Unless the disaster you're seeing . . . is . . . for . . ." Sueldan slowed, not wishing to speak the words.

Rifkah soothed. "What I'm feeling is danger to us. I don't think it directly involves your family."

Con tapped his fingers against an outcropping. "Rifkah, why don't we plan on separating. Then, you read Sueldan's future."

Rifkah shook her head, releasing Sueldan's arm. "I tried. It's gotten distressingly muddled. I think it's because I know I'll change my plans depending on what I find."

A long silence followed.

Logic held little sway here. In his mind, Sueldan had no choice. "I'm going on. The rest of you can leave."

"Magic doesn't scare me," Con said. "I'm going with you."

Sueldan ignored the irony. The companion he trusted least had now become his staunchest ally. "Thank you," he said through gritted teeth. And headed toward his doom.

Chapter 10

SUELDAN and Con continued, dragging along only one pick, the lantern, and the shovel. Driven by his own desperation and stubbornness, Sueldan stifled the doubts reawakened by Rifkah's concern. They had known from the start the mission was dangerous. He would not fail because he could not. It was to him as simple as that.

Con waited only until they had gone two cellars past their companions. "Here." He offered a partially filled pouch.

Sueldan's hand come out naturally, then realization made him jerk it back with a flash of anger. "I don't want that garbage."

"There's magic," Con reminded. His dark clothing and swarthy coloring made him nearly invisible in the gloom. "Surely your family is worth just one dose."

"Far more, Con. More than you could ever imagine. That's why I can't take it."

Con continued to proffer the pouch. "What good are you to your family if you don't make it to them alive?"

Sueldan scowled, irritated by the delay. "Leave me alone." He tried to push past the con man.

Con refused to budge. "Sueldan. I'll let you go without

using it, but not without at least considering it. It'll hide you from their magic. You're unlikely to get hooked by the first dose."

The argument made sense. Sueldan hesitated, and that consideration alone fueled his rage. "You're just trying to make me into an addict, too!"

Con went rigid. "Is that what you think?"

Sueldan said nothing, his previous answer enough.

"Do you truly believe I would wish this curse on anyone else?"

"You've tried to push it on me twice, now." Sueldan trembled. "You want me addicted, too. Then you'll sell it to me to get money for your habit."

Con erupted in laughter that seemed genuine, if badly misplaced. "You think I'd count on *you* for *my* income?" He sobered swiftly. "Biting your fingernails is a habit. This . . ." he held up the pouch, ". . . is an addiction. A dangerous one that will, sooner or later, kill me." He lowered his arm. "Believe me. The last thing I need is competition for it. That only drives up the price, and it's already cost me what little life, dignity, and honor I may have had. I don't want to make you an addict. I just want you to survive whatever magic our fortune-teller detected."

Sueldan met Con's dark gaze, reading only sincerity and unwavering concern. As outrage dissipated, he considered the generosity of Con's offer. The drug had cost him a huge sum of money, and his very life rested on his ability to make it last as long as possible. To give up even a small amount was a sacrifice Sueldan could barely contemplate. He would do whatever it took to rescue his family. *Yet,* he wondered, *what good would it do to glide past magic if I enslave myself to a drug I can't afford? Which would be worse for my children, a lifetime of bondage in Callos or watching their father turn criminal for an addiction, then die in slow agony?*

Sueldan closed his eyes. He would gladly sacrifice his freedom for that of his family; but the choice was not that simple. He had no proof that taking the drug would definitely
rescue him from detection. It worked for Con, but perhaps
uniquely for him. Maybe he carried a hint of magic or something in his makeup that allowed it to function. It seemed
unlikely that a side effect so useful would go unnoticed so
long. Even if it did exactly as Con claimed, it could not hide
them from natural senses, and Sueldan had no training in
moving without sight, smell, or sound. More importantly,
caution might bring him through this, regardless of whether
or not the drug even existed.

Con waited in silence. He had made the proposal. The
decision was wholly Sueldan's own.

"Thank you," Sueldan said, and meant it. "I want my
family back, but my life is worth something, too."

"You're declining?"

"Yes."

Con flipped the pouch back into his pocket.

"And, Con?"

"Yes."

"Someday, we're going to get your life back, too."

Con chuckled softly. "Rifkah's right about one thing. You
truly are determined." He rolled his eyes a moment before
he turned. "Let's go."

Only then, Sueldan realized the choice was not as entirely
his as he had first assumed. Alone, Con was virtually safe
from magic. Saddled with a less wary companion, he might
die for Sueldan's incompetence. *No wonder he dodged friend-
ships for so long.* Sueldan only hoped his judgment would not
betray Con's newfound trust.

If Con had thoughts along the same lines, he did not
voice them. Shovel in one hand, lantern in the other, he
waited near an earthen wall for Sueldan and the pick.

Sueldan raised the tool. It seemed heavier for the delay, his rhythm lost, replaced by the burdens of exhaustion and making decisions that contradicted the wisdom of companions he considered more intelligent and more experienced. Trusting his own abilities, his own insight, had brought him little good in his life; but it had won him Linnry once. And, he promised himself, it would do so again. Clinging to a mental image of her for strength, he slammed the pick against the wall. Dark dirt erupted into a spray, then tumbled to the ground. Blitzed with grit, Con sprang backward and glanced questioningly at Sueldan.

Dallan tried to engage Rifkah in conversation, with little success. Lost in her own arduous considerations, she spared no notice for her remaining companion. They hurried through the irregularly hewn passageways and ancient cellars, mostly in silence, trudging over piled earth and chipped stone. Weighted by guilty secrets of his own, Dallan studied Rifkah's pale hair, now smeared with filth, her willowy features, and the multiskirted dress, its festive colors now blunted by dirt, rips, and darkness. Despite her scruffy appearance and desperate need for a bath, he found her disarmingly beautiful. The realization made him smile, and he had to choke off a laugh. *What a time for thoughts like that.*

Apparently misreading Dallan's motive, Rifkah whirled on him. "Are you happy?"

The anger in her tone chased the grin from Dallan's lips. "Do I look happy?" He gestured at his own grimy features and clothing. "Why would I be happy?"

"You got your way."

"My way?" Dallan stomped his foot, sick of lying, tired of being misunderstood. "You mean I got to hack through

corpse-filled basements, weathering cave-ins and nasty jabs
from people I consider friends, nearly make it to our goal,
only to have to turn around and handle things the way I told
everyone was best in the first place?" He widened his eyes,
giving Rifkah the benefit of his full stare. "Do I look like I'm
dancing around singing 'I told you so'?"

"Then why were you smiling?"

"The absurdity of truthfully answering Rifkah's question
at that moment nearly prompted another smile. Dallan
grunted instead. "You don't want to know."

"More secrets." Rifkah whirled with a flash of skirts and
stormed toward the exit.

Dallan trotted after her. "Wait."

Rifkah ignored him.

"Wait!" Dallan quickened his pace, catching her
shoulder.

Rifkah whirled fiercely, as if she found his touch an unfor-
givable affront.

"You want to know why I was smiling, I'll tell you."

Rifkah nodded curtly.

"I was just thinking . . ." Dallan gave her a soft, lopsided
grin, ". . . how very attractive you are."

Rifkah jerked her shoulder free. "Very funny." She
turned away, taking another heavy-footed step.

Dallan did not follow, but he did call after her. "Damn it,
I'm not kidding."

Rifkah stopped, paused, then turned slowly.

It was what Dallan wanted, yet he suddenly found speaking a formidable challenge. "I'm not kidding," he repeated,
delaying. "You are beautiful." To lighten the mood, he
added, "Well, not at this precise moment when you look like
you'd rather castrate me than hug me. But usually . . ."

Rifkah stared, features still taut.

"I mean, I admit I didn't like you much when we started.

But over time, I—" Dallan swallowed hard, wishing he had never started. If nothing else, the timing was very wrong. "I—" He tried to take a cue from Rifkah, but she seemed abruptly, unremittingly distracted. "What's wrong?"

"Sueldan," Rifkah whispered.

Dallan whirled, expecting to find their other companions. Instead he saw only the passageway they had just vacated.

"He's in terrible danger."

Dallan swiveled toward Rifkah. "What do you mean?"

"I've got some distance now."

"Magic?" Dallan did not understand. "I thought you had to touch someone to read them."

"Not necessarily." Rifkah shook her head, as if to clear it. "I've always needed to be close before, though. I think, maybe, I've just been so focused on him. So intent." She clamped her hands to her temples, wincing. "We have to go back."

Dallan obeyed without question, heading toward the opening.

A stranger's voice echoed through the exit to the next cellar. "You move, you're both dead."

Despite the threat, Dallan could not stop himself from spinning toward the speaker. A quarrel targeted his chest from across a cocked crossbow. The sinewy man holding it wore the standard gold uniform of Callos' military, with the red four-pronged stars on the sleeves. Another emerged from behind him, clutching a sword, and scurried toward Rifkah and Dallan.

Dallan's hand dropped to his hilt, and the tip of the quarrel dipped slightly. "Draw it and die."

Without warning, Rifkah made a break for the deeper tunnel.

"No!" Dallan yelled.

The Callosian swordsman charged Rifkah. Steel slammed

the side of her head with a sickening thud. Thrown sideways, she crashed into the cellar wall and sank limply to the ground.

"No!" Dallan shouted again, in desperate anguish. The crossbow forgotten, he launched himself at the Callosian, sword rasping free.

The bowstring sang.

Pain seared Dallan's left palm, and his attack fell suddenly short. The quarrel had pierced his hand, pinning it to the dirt wall.

For an instant, no one moved.

Dallan jerked his hand free, shaft and leather vanes gliding through the wound. Agony overpowered him. He grunted, senses fleeing. Then, need took over. He heard the click of the crossbowman rearming, felt the warmth of the closing swordsman. He wrenched his own blade upward and met the Callosian's more by luck or instinct than skill. Parrying, he returned a power stroke that sent the other man staggering toward his companion. Too late to redirect, the second quarrel impaled the Callosian swordsman. He stiffened, gasping, bloody froth bubbling from his mouth. Dallan shoved the dying man at his fellow. The crossbowman skipped aside, desperately clutching at his belt.

Now, all of Dallan's training returned. He bore in, kicking the crossbow, and it flew from its wielder's hand. Fumbling his dagger, the crossbowman recoiled, but not far enough. Dallan's blade sliced open his throat. Blood splashed Dallan's face and clothing. Then, the second Callosian slumped to the ground.

Dallan retreated, sword raised, looking wildly for other opponents. The abrupt silence seemed deafening. Finding no one, Dallan sheathed his weapon and forced himself to return to Rifkah's body. She lay utterly still, like a broken doll, on the cavern floor. *Dead.* Tears flooded Dallan's eyes. "No," he whispered, a soft parody of his earlier screams. "Not Rifkah. Not now." He slumped to his knees beside her, sobbing, and clamped both hands to his face. "No."

Blood stung Dallan's eyes, and his fingers throbbed. Only then, he looked at his own wound. A ragged hole marred his palm, leaking a steady crimson stream. His hand felt on fire.

Dallan rose and stumbled blindly toward the Callosians. Ripping a chunk of fabric from one of the uniforms, he wadded it into the cavity. The pain sent brilliant flashes through his vision, and he swore viciously at himself as he worked. Using another golden strip, he wound a crude bandage around his hand.

A soft moan wafted beneath his curses. Dallan jerked his head toward his enemies, wondering which one needed a final mercy blow. Both lay, wholly still, in sticky pools of their own blood. Dallan's heart quickened. Hardly daring to believe, he looked toward Rifkah.

The fortune-teller stirred dizzily.

Alive. Dallan rushed to Rifkah's side. "Rifkah." He shook her. "Rifkah."

She said something he could not hear.

Dallan lowered his ear to Rifkah's mouth.

"Don't do that," Rifkah hissed. "It hurts my head."

A lump bulged just above her left ear, and blood matted a clump of dark blonde hair. Dallan saw no gaping wounds and realized the guard must have hit her with the flat of his blade. He crouched beside her. "Rifkah, I'm going to carry you out of here, all right? I'll get you help." He steeled himself for her command to assist Sueldan instead. He would have to decline. He could not abandon a needy companion for one whose peril and location remained uncertain.

"All right," Rifkah rasped to his surprise.

Relieved, Dallan hefted her, one arm beneath her bent knees, the other supporting her torso. He knew head injuries could affect memory and appreciated that this one seemed to have made her forget Sueldan's plight, at least for the moment. As he carried her through the cellar exit, a worse thought invaded his mind. *What else has she forgotten?* "Rifkah, do you know who I am?"

"Dallan," she huffed out. "I'm hurt, not stupid."

Dallan managed a smile. She might never know that, moments before, he had assumed her dead.

Rifkah's lids glided closed. "What happened?"

"We got attacked," Dallan explained, carrying Rifkah toward the outside. "Remember?"

"No."

"You're going to be all right. I'm getting you some help."

Rifkah paused. "What happened?"

Dallan studied Rifkah, her fine features contrasting starkly with broad lips, ringlets forming a wild halo around her long face. His injured hand ached, making concentration nearly impossible. "Callosian guards. We got attacked. Remember?" He maneuvered her carefully through another cellar.

"No." Rifkah's eyes opened, dull blue and haggard.

Worried for his companion, Dallan quickened his pace.

"Dallan?"

"Hmm?"

"Your face. It's bloody."

Hands full, Dallan rubbed a cheek against his shoulder in a futile gesture. "I'm fine."

"What happened?" Rifkah asked.

Dallan patiently explained again, "We got attacked." He tried not to let her lapses worry him. He had seen soldiers with concussions who acted similarly and recovered fully. "Do you remember what I said happened?"

"We got attacked," Rifkah returned, correctly this time.

"That's right." Dallan turned the first sharp corner.

Moonlight funneled through the last opening, and he heaved a sigh of relief. "We're almost there." He sprang toward freedom, nearly onto the swords of five Callosian guardsmen.

"Hey," one shouted. "Get him."

Dallan swung the only weapon he had ready. Rifkah's legs caught the leading man a blow that sent him sprawling. Another lunged toward them. Dallan reversed direction, driving Rifkah's feet into his gut. Dirt sprayed the back of Dallan's neck, and Rifkah let out a smothered yelp. Only then, Dallan realized he had driven her face into the cavern wall. "Sorry," he mumbled.

The Callosians realigned.

Dallan seized the moment to lay Rifkah gently on the ground. As he reached for his hilt, three guardsmen attacked simultaneously. The ferocity of their charge drove Dallan backward. His foot mired in Rifkah's skirts, and he tumbled down on top of her.

Rifkah screamed. A sword jabbed at Dallan. Supine, he skittered backward, still pawing for his sword. The Callosian's blade rang against stone, then another cut for his head. Dallan rolled, drawing simultaneously. He made a crazed sweep that sent two of the men scrambling. Rifkah half-crawled, half-staggered toward the wall, cringing behind raised hands. Fearing for her safety, Dallan rushed the guard nearest her. Another caught him a pounding blow across the shoulder blades. Breath dashed from his lungs, and his sword spun from his grip. He collapsed against Rifkah, gasping, driving her to the ground. A powerful hand clamped his wrist. Dallan whirled to confront this new attacker. Another grasped his injured hand, driving a wave of agony through his entire arm. Still struggling for breath, he froze.

"Next time," Rifkah croaked beneath him, "leave me lying where you found me."

Eyes squeezed shut against the anguish, Dallan surrendered to his captors.

As the wall crumbled beneath Sueldan's assault, he fell back into the cadence of pounding, pulling, and sweat that had carried him this far. Caught up in the determination that Rifkah had celebrated and Con had cursed, he found no need to contemplate the possibility of failure. The meek and hopeless Tamison, self-reviled, no longer existed, replaced by a man hell-bent on finishing a mission. He could taste success, an overwhelming sweetness that swept aside the discomfort of a mouthful of sand. Sweat glued his hair to his forehead and trickled in a hot line down his back. The screaming pain of his overtaxed arms gradually settled to a dull, pounding ache.

Then Sueldan struck a wall that sent his pick bouncing backward. Angered by his weakness, he threw his strength into another blow. Again, the pick struck a solid that felt more like packed stone than earth, rebounding with a sudden ferocity that sent him flying. He landed on his bottom, only a tiny shock of pain gliding up his spine. The pick dropped awkwardly. Dirt slid from the wall in a small, straight avalanche, revealing stone fitted and mortared in all directions.

Con lunged toward it. "It's a man-made wall."

Sueldan made no comment about the self-evident observation, only rose and reclaimed his pick.

Con swiveled his head. "So what's beyond it?"

Sueldan shook dirt from his hair. "You're mistaking me for Rifkah."

Con examined the stonework more closely. "No, I'm just assuming you came prepared."

Sueldan clutched the haft tighter, feeling more comfortable and safe with it than the sword and knife at his hip. "I am prepared."

Con's eyes narrowed. "Prepared for what?"

"Prepared," Sueldan explained, "to face whatever comes. To open the way for Dallan and Rifkah. To question or kill Callosian lords. To do whatever it takes to find and free my family."

"Ah." Con returned his attention to the stones. "Then you surely know what's beyond this wall."

Becoming irritated, Sueldan pressed with a single word, stretched out for effect, "Because . . ."

"Because," Con said calmly, attention still on the wall. "That's what preparation is. It's scouting an area. Knowing what and who is likely to be where. Their strengths and weaknesses. Forming a strategy." He regarded Sueldan again. "You didn't do any of that, did you?"

"Yes, we did." Sueldan glared at a companion who, apparently, considered him a fool. "We have a strategy."

"All right," Con challenged. "Then tell me what and who are beyond this wall."

"I . . . can't." Sueldan admitted.

"So you don't have a detailed diagram of the mansion?"

Dumbly, Sueldan shook his head. "That . . . wasn't an option."

Con's eyes regained their hard, deadly gleam. "That . . . is always an option. A necessity even." He dropped to his haunches. "No wonder Rifkah saw only disaster. If you charge in there blindly, you may create some chaos. You may even kill a few enemies, but you're not going to rescue anyone alive."

Acid crawled up Sueldan's throat. The idea of abandoning his mission now, so close, seemed a bitter madness beyond contemplation. "I—thought I—we could—"

Con's lids dropped further, then gradually rose. "Dallan's a soldier. He should have prepared better than this." The words emerged with wary acceptance. "Didn't he tell you anything about the layout of the mansion? About the guards? The brotherhood?"

"Well, yes." It had never occurred to Sueldan that such information could be had by commoners. "But not in the kind of detail you seem to think is necessary." He paused, separated from ultimate happiness by a physical wall that he could break and a substanceless realization that it might just as well be a solid construct of iron. "Dallan mostly talked about breaking in. Once there, I'd get him in, too." He added flatly, "I do know where all the doors and windows are. Then, I'm to kill as many lords as possible."

"Kill them?" Con studied Sueldan, head cocked. "Did Dallan ever explain how wanton murder would free your family?"

Sueldan returned Con's stare, scarcely daring to believe he might receive a morality lesson from a trained liar, a cut-throat con man who was also a drug addict. "He said the brotherhood would never give up their . . . slaves willingly." Sueldan bit his lip as the plan unraveled. He had tunneled his thoughts on the goal, shielding himself from all but the most obvious pitfalls. He had overcome a stark terror that had hounded him for half a lifetime, had traveled further than ever in his life, had worn himself to exhaustion; all for naught. "We'd look for Linnry and the children at the same time. Once the brotherhood . . . died, no one would stop us from taking them."

Con sighed, looking back the way they had come. "This isn't worth it." He shook his head. "Let's go." Turning, he started toward the most recent opening.

Sueldan glanced from his companion, to the wall, and back. Desperation welled up in him, an agony he could not control. Driven beyond rational thought, he struck the stones with the pick and all of his strength.

"Sueldan!" Con shouted.

Chips of granite stung Sueldan's cheeks. Pain howled through his arms. Buzzing filled his head, deafening him to Con's warning. In the deepest portion of his mind, he knew he was doing something stupid, but he could no longer stop himself. He had given everything to this mission, had convinced himself it all had meaning. He could never rally such heroic effort again, and the thought of his family spending months longer in bondage while he slowly gained information, studied minutiae, sought openings and weaknesses became unbearable. Likely, in that time, the brotherhood would discover and guard their tunnels; and he would not get a second chance.

Again and again, the pick rang against stone. Sueldan lost track of Con. His universe became the movement of his arms, the flying fragments of rock and dried mortar, and the clang of metal solidly striking. Suddenly, resistance gave way to nothingness. Sueldan staggered forward one step. Then, water spewed through the opening, crashing into his chest. The force hurled him to the ground, robbing him of breath. Pain jarred through his back, and his head rang against hard ground. Water surged over him, filling his mouth and nose. Only his spasming throat spared his lungs. Hurled legs over head, he worried more about suffocating than drowning.

Strong hands clutched Sueldan, jerking him to his feet. His head broke the surface. At that moment, his throat gasped open, admitting blessed air. Immediately, he tried to run for safety and slammed right into Con.

"Whoa." The con man's hands tightened on Sueldan's arms. "Be still."

Sueldan wondered how the other man could remain so calm. "We have to run! Water's going to fill this cavern." A worse thought seized him. *All the caverns. Rifkah and Dallan may not have made it out yet.* "What have I done?"

Still clutching Sueldan, Con answered a question meant to be rhetorical. "You broke through a cistern. Look."

Sueldan made himself turn. The small hole he had created had widened to a gaping maw. He could now make out the vertical shaftlike shape of the cistern. Water gushed like blood from an open wound.

Water rose to Sueldan's thighs, but he managed some composure. "Con, we've got to get out of here."

Con made no move to obey. "The levels will equalize before it reaches your waist. Then, we're going to have to go in."

"In?" Sueldan felt dizzy. "I thought—"

"They're going to notice this." Con waved a hand around the damage. "We have to act before they do."

Sueldan nodded, glad he did not have to make a career out of subterfuge. The rules made no sense to him. "All right. What do we do now?"

As the water slowed to a trickle, Con shuffled to the opening in the wall and peered inside. He jabbed a finger upward.

Sueldan splashed to Con's side and glanced through the opening. The shaft continued up to at least three times his height. A bucket lay sideways on the lip, tied to a rope that looped over a towering wooden contraption. Below, Sueldan saw only water and could not guess how deeply the cistern descended. "And how do you propose we get up there?" His words echoed, and Con pulled him sharply and suddenly backward.

Con made a gesture for silence, then suggested in a whisper. "Climb?"

Climb. Sure. Sueldan shrugged, willing to try.

Con sat at the opening, then gracefully lowered himself into the water. Treading with broad strokes, he worked his way to intact stone. His fingers settled into crevices in the mortar, and his legs rose from the water. Painstakingly, he clambered up the side.

Sueldan waited only until Con had ascended a man's length before lowering himself into the water. It felt warm against his soaked breeks and tunic. The sword dragged at his hip, dead sinking weight. He stuffed his fingers into clefts in the rockwork and wedged his toes into others beneath the water. Secured, he released one hand and raised it above the other, seeking more chinks. His fingers caught a ledge slick with algae. He clamped them tightly against it, reaching for a higher hold with his other hand. His first grip slipped, and he felt his balance fail. He scrabbled for a hold, cracking his fingernails against stone. He swore, tumbling back into the water.

A moment later, something huge and hard slammed against Sueldan, driving him deep beneath the surface. Consciousness reeling, he churned wildly through the water, surging toward the light. The sword hampered him. It felt like an eternity before his head broke through, and he found Con beside him in the water.

"Sorry," Con said sheepishly.

Sueldan stared, finally discovering the dangerous part of having a companion. He waited for the world to still, for his headache to subside.

Con hissed a confession. "I'm not the best climber."

The words shocked Sueldan. He would have believed Con infallible at anything sneaky. "Didn't you have to climb as part of your . . . um . . . work?"

Con returned Sueldan's stare, brows rising in slow increments.

Gradually, it dawned on Sueldan that his own job had required operating underground, at which he had mostly failed miserably. "Are you afraid—" He wondered if the drug caused Con to fear heights, if it damaged his steadiness or equilibrium, or if he developed tremors as his levels diminished. He had seemed ruinously shaky on the ship when withdrawal had nearly killed him.

Con cut Sueldan off with a rapid shake of his wet locks. "Not afraid of anything. Better talk as little as possible."

Sueldan glanced up the shaft again. Their low conversation did not reverberate as his first words had, but it still made sense to keep as quiet as possible. Swiftly, the pains of Con's fall on top of him merged with the gentle throb of his overtaxed muscles, indistinguishable. He nodded.

Con looked thoughtfully at the top of the cistern. He stroked his chin a moment, then smiled. He worked his way around Sueldan, back to the opening they had created. Still treading water with his legs, he gathered handfuls of the smaller stones.

Uncertain what his companion intended, Sueldan supported him in the water as well as he could without losing his own buoyancy. He did not question; he would know soon enough.

Con remained focused on the lip of the cistern, still the length of three men above them. He drew back his right arm and hurled a rock. It sailed up the shaft, ricocheted from the wooden construct, then plunged back toward them. Suddenly menaced, Sueldan paddled backward. The stone slammed down in front of him, splashing his cheek with cold pinpoints, then sank.

"You could have warned me," Sueldan whispered accusingly.

Con threw another rock. This one thumped against the bucket, driving it sideways.

Sueldan had to ask. "What are you doing?"

Con did not reply, apparently worried about losing his focus. He pitched several more stones, his target now clearly the bucket. Finally, one large rock caught it a heavy blow to the side that sent it hurtling down the shaft.

Sueldan flattened against the wall and shielded his head with an arm. Con whirled and leaped into a sitting position on the edge of the jagged opening. The bucket missed them both, splashing to a stop on the surface of the water, then slowly starting to sink. Sueldan lunged to rescue it.

"Let it go," Con whispered, hopping back into the water. He grasped the rope affixed to its handle, yanking hard downward.

With his gaze, Sueldan followed its course up to the wooden device. It seemed secure. "What are you going to do?"

Con did not answer directly. "Watch me." Catching the rope in both hands, he swung his legs to the shaft. Fist over fist, step by step, he used wall and rope to work his way upward.

Sueldan watched the con man climb, the rope jerking like a live thing in his wake. Despite Con's disparagement of his climbing ability, Sueldan suspected it would not prove nearly as easy as the other man made it look. Then, remembering how Con had fallen on him before, Sueldan moved to the opposite side of the shaft.

The precaution proved unnecessary. With the rope to assist, Con had no trouble reaching the top of the cistern. Once there, he crouched on the lip and surveyed the room. Apparently finding it safe, he waved Sueldan up.

Sueldan swam to the rope, seizing it in both hands. The strength he had gained from his years on the road crew allowed him to easily lift his disproportionately short legs to the mortared-stone wall. Mimicking Con, he shuffled up the wall stones, seizing ever higher on the rope. Attention entirely focused on the wall, he lost track of time and his companion. Soon, his legs cramped from the unnatural position.

The rope tore calluses from his hands, and the ache of his muscles began a fresh round of agony. Eventually, he reached the top. With Con's assistance, he clambered from the shaft and perched on the lip, panting. Each breath brought the taste of apples and salt. A chilling draft penetrated his sodden clothes.

Con hunkered down beside Sueldan, saying nothing, waiting for him to recover.

Gradually, Sueldan's breathing returned to normal. His muscles did not, but they did quiet to a bearable level of pain. "All right," he whispered.

Con rose.

Sueldan also stood, finally glancing around the room. Dusty barrels and kegs stood in random positions around a room otherwise empty. From the smells of fruit and jerky beneath the more powerful odors of mildew and mustiness, he guessed they had entered a food storage area. He saw a single, wooden door.

"Ready?" Con said.

Sueldan shrugged. He did not feel particularly prepared for anything, yet he doubted he ever would.

"Now that we're back on ground level, I do know the layout of this mansion," Con informed his shocked companion. "So follow my lead."

"How?"

Con silenced Sueldan with a wave, then headed for the door. Gesturing for Sueldan to remain well back, he pressed his ear against the panels. Apparently hearing nothing worrisome, he tripped the latch and peered through the widening crack. The hinges creaked. Sueldan held his breath and crept toward Con.

The door burst open. A half dozen fair-skinned men charged Con, who scrabbled to close a door he had already lost control of. He reached for his water-logged sword, and three Callosians dove on him.

"Con!" Sueldan rushed to assist, barely catching Con's words, muffled beneath the guards' heavy bodies.

"Run, you fool!"

"There's another!" one of the guards shouted in a heavy Callosian accent. "Get him."

Sueldan scrambled into retreat, dodging a pawlike hand. He sped toward the cistern, two men in hot pursuit. In four running steps, Sueldan reached the lip. The image of a long fall into apparently depthless water brought him up short. He tried to judge whether the impact might incapacitate or kill him.

That moment of indecision proved Sueldan's downfall. A foot thrust between his stole his balance. He fell, elbow crashing painfully against the stone lip. The world spun in frenzied circles. Then, he found himself on the ground, head dangling down the long shaft. The rocks and water looked even more menacing. He rolled.

Two swords, at throat and chest, froze Sueldan. He lay still as another guard pinioned his arms and legs. One sheathed his weapon. The other continued to threaten as the first two hefted him, stripped him of weapons, and carried him through the doorway.

Trapped against leather jerkins that smelled of grease and sweat, Sueldan found himself roughly bounced through torchlit corridors and a series of rooms. Occasionally, he glimpsed a simply crafted desk or table. Mostly, he saw only swirls of light, a blur of walls, floors, ceilings, and legs. He missed most of what the guards said to one another, but one exchange came clearly to him.

"Aswan's talent's failing."

"Only sensed one intruder."

"Yeah. What's all about that?"

Sueldan found himself awash in guilty contemplation. It had happened just as Rifkah and Con had warned. Magic had defeated them, and his own refusal to take Con's drug had undone them both. *I got him caught. I'm going to get him free.* The promise rang hollow. At the moment, Sueldan could not even help himself.

The Callosians stopped in front of an iron-bound wooden door. Suddenly, they spun Sueldan to the floor. Dizzied by the obviously practiced maneuver, he struck the stone floor before he thought to tense. Pain jarred through him, reawakening the dull chorus of aches. One guardsman held him still with a well-placed foot, while another menaced him with a sword, and the third unlocked the door. It swung open, hitting the wall with a solid thud that echoed. Hauled abruptly to his feet, Sueldan shuffled forward, a massive hand on his arm and a sword poking his spine. The door slammed shut on his heels. Then the guardsmen hefted him again.

Rows of iron bars replaced the furnishings and hallways. The guards holding Sueldan paused again, granting him a sideways view of cells and Con disappearing around the corner with his captors. Another door squealed open and he found himself airborne. This time he managed to brace himself before slamming onto a stone floor with enough force to jar the breath from his lungs. Agony shot through his shoulder, and stone abraded a line of skin from his cheek. Dazed, he heard the door bang shut behind him and the stomp of retreating footfalls.

Sueldan overpowered pain with short sharp breaths. "Damn it!" he yelled, furious with himself. "Damn it! Damn it! *Damn it,* I'm an idiot!"

Dallan's soft voice answered, "No argument here."

Shocked, Sueldan whirled, the sudden movement inciting the aches he had nearly vanquished. "Dallan?" His gaze swept the ragged line of bars, and he found the guardsman several cells down on the opposite side. "They got you, too?"

Dallan moved stiffly toward the bars, as if in pain. The mottled, inconsistent light made it difficult for Sueldan to distinguish bruises, but he doubted they had caught the Latharyn guardsman without a fight. "Ambushed us at the exit. Both of us."

Rifkah, too? Terror swept through Sueldan, and he scanned the prison desperately. The idea of Rifkah suffering for him became too much to bear.

"Around there." Dallan jerked a thumb in the same direction the Callosians had taken Con. "Walled off her cell. Knew she was magic." Dallan started to pace. "Worried about her powers, I guess." He stopped, one hand wrapped around the bars, the other resting against them, clumsily bandaged. He gave Sueldan a serious look. "Tell them *nothing*," he warned. "Do you hear me?"

"Nothing," Sueldan repeated.

"Remember that."

Irritated by his companion's concern over information when friends' lives lay at stake, Sueldan grew sarcastic. " 'Nothing' is not difficult to remember."

"It can be, under . . . duress."

"Duress," Sueldan repeated, the full impact of the word taking inordinately long to register. *He thinks they'll torture us.* He shivered. Already in pain, he felt infinitely vulnerable, but he tried to sound strong. "There isn't anything they can do to me worse than what they've already done."

Dallan resumed pacing, disappearing into the dappled shadows.

Sueldan lowered his head to the stone floor and tried to ignore the cold seeping through his wet clothing. Exhaustion warred with worry and won. Before he even contemplated doing so, he was asleep.

Chapter 11

A CLANG slammed through Sueldan's hearing, awakening him instantly. Four men shared his cell. He closed and opened his eyes repeatedly, surprised to find them there, expecting them to disappear with the blurriness he blinked away. They remained, clearer now and undeniably real. Two closely resembled the dainty, birdlike Callosian merchants who came to Lathary to trade. One wore red and gold, the other was dressed in unmarked silks. Though equally fair, a third man towered over his companions, arms thick as tree trunks and furred like an animal. He wore a spiked belt from which several objects hung, including a whip, shackles, and angular items of leather and metal that Sueldan could not identify. The fourth sported the standard Callosian uniform, a sword at one hip and a massive ring of keys at the other.

Sueldan stiffened, beyond action. His thoughts were fragmented, useless. He tried to swallow, but his mouth had gone excruciatingly dry.

The man in colors shook his head. His coiffed hair did not move, but a trickle of perfume covered the reek of mold momentarily. "Let's start with your name."

Sueldan opened his mouth, but only a croak emerged. He

glanced toward Dallan. The guard stood at the bars, watching everything. The "nothing" he had demanded surely excluded names, since the guards had likely heard them calling back and forth.

Dallan gave Sueldan no signal.

The speaker inclined his head toward the giant, who drew the whip from his belt and coiled it menacingly.

Sueldan gathered saliva and tried again. "Sueldan." He found himself adding, "Who are you?" He could have slapped himself for asking. Antagonizing someone with so much power over him seemed painfully, dangerously foolish.

But the man only smiled. "You can call me Lord Hiroise." He pointed to the other man in silks. "Palius."

Sueldan glanced at the largest man, who continued to play with the whip, his grin gap-toothed. He seemed to enjoy his work, an asset for a torturer—a meaningless point, at best. Even if a torturer despised what he did, he surely functioned more competently if he at least appeared eager.

"I'm going to make this easy," Hiroise continued. "I'll tell you in advance which questions I want answered. If you're honest, you won't get hurt. You may even leave here alive. All right?"

In no position to argue, Sueldan nodded. A shiver traveled the length of his spine, then strengthened and spread until his whole body trembled.

The only one who seemed to notice Sueldan's distress was the torturer, whose grin went toothy, predatory.

The lord continued, "I need to know for whom you're working, your orders, and how you got into my storage room. That, and nothing more." He gave Sueldan a patient look. "Go."

Sueldan huddled into himself. His clothes had dried while he slept, but they now felt crunchy and stiff. *Nothing,* he reminded himself, thoughts racing.

"Answer!" Hiroise demanded.

Sueldan balled tighter.

The whistle of thin leather through air was Sueldan's only warning. Bitter pain cut across the back of his neck, his shoulder blades, and his left arm. A scream tore from his throat before he could think to stop it. The agony of the whip strike captured all of his attention for several moments. He panted, groping for orientation, for other sensation, for the simplest thought. Gradually, reality muddled back into his awareness, though the sting diminished only slightly. He wiped a tear from his eye. *Nothing. Tell them nothing.* He focused his thoughts solidly on Dallan's words, an anchor for his strength.

Lord Hiroise cleared his throat. "You may think yourself brave, but you're merely foolish. My questions are simple and will be answered. How much pain you endure is wholly up to you."

Sueldan braced himself and waited. An idea straggled into his mind. *Did Linnry suffer this?* He had heard masters battered slaves if they disobeyed, if they dallied, sometimes for no reason at all. *Do my children . . . suffer . . . this?* Grief became nearly all-consuming, tinged only with the earliest stirrings of anger.

The second lash caught Sueldan unprepared, lost as he was in his thoughts. Agony slashed his back, and the blow dropped him, prone. He tasted dirt, felt blood trickle along his side in a warm stream. His vision blurred. Again, he heard the thong's whistle. Then another line of anguish tore into his back. He screamed again. The sound echoed in his own ears, distant and strange.

"Linnry," Sueldan sobbed. "Oh, Linnry." The thought of her sustaining this brought a bitter taste to his mouth. He vomited, right hand clamping the only wound he could reach, the one on his opposite arm. His fingers came away sticky and scarlet.

Only then was Lord Hiroise's voice no longer obscured by buzzing. "Listen to your friend."

Sueldan glanced toward Dallan. The guard still stood at the bars, his expression anxious and pitying. "Sueldan, tell."

Tell. The word refused to register. *Tell.* Sueldan cleared his throat, attempted to wet his lips. It was all delay. *Tell?* Apparently, Dallan wanted him to answer the Callosian brother's questions. Even through a fog of pain, Sueldan realized the guard was giving him a hint by speaking the briefest, simplest instruction possible. *Answer the questions,* he finally managed to interpret. *But keep those answers as short as possible.* He sat up and looked toward the torturer.

The huge man had stepped back, whip still in his hand. Blood beaded at the end of the thong. His face was unreadable.

"I'll tell," Sueldan managed to croak out, hoping he had not misinterpreted Dallan's signal. He inched away from his stomach contents. The odor, mixed with grease, sweat, and mildew, became nearly overpowering. "Please. Repeat the questions."

Lord Hiroise motioned at the torturer. As the largest man back stepped, the guardsman moved slightly forward with a jingle of keys. "Who sent you? What were your orders? How did you get in?"

Sueldan suspected they would not like his answers. "I sent me. I have no orders. And I got in through the cistern." From the corner of his eye, he glanced at Dallan, who nodded approvingly.

Lord Hiroise turned his attention to the silk-clad man he had named Palius with a gesture that seemed more resigned than hopeful. Palius studied Sueldan in close silence for several moments before glancing back at the lord. "Truth."

Hiroise pursed his lips, scowling. "Really."

Palius made a broad nod that served more like a bow. "Yes, my lord."

A truthseeker, Sueldan realized dully. Just as Rifkah had said, the Callosians relied on the magic Lathary despised. First, a sixthsenser had located them; and now a truthseeker would unravel any lie he dared to speak. He struggled to remember how Con had slipped deceptions and half-truths past the truthseeker in Eirene but found his mind too muddled to focus on details. It seemed more likely that the drug, not twisted explanations, had rescued Con then. *I blundered again. If I'd heeded Rifkah, if I'd taken that accursed drug, we wouldn't have gotten caught.*

Hiroise sighed. "All right, then." He made a dismissive gesture. "Perhaps one of his companions knows more."

"Wait!" Sueldan scrambled after the lord and nearly bashed into the guard who placed himself firmly between them. "I'm the one who insisted on coming here. The others are—" He choked off the word "innocent," afraid his feelings about Con might make it appear a lie. "—just helping me."

"Sueldan!" Dallan's warning reached them all clearly, with the judgmental snap his father's tone had so often held. "Hush."

As the pain faded to a dull ache, Sueldan considered his strategy more carefully.

Near the door, the Callosian lord glanced from Dallan to the torturer. "I think we've found our next volunteer."

"No!" Sueldan craned to see Hiroise around the guard. He softened his words. "I mean, 'no, lord, please.' I–I came to free some slaves. Family members. If—" He tried not to think about the words too carefully. If he did, he might not speak them. "I'm a hard worker. At least, if I could be with them—?"

All four Callosians stared at Sueldan.

Apparently believing the onus to break the silence had fallen to him, Palius said, "He seems to believe he's telling the truth."

Dallan slapped a hand to his forehead in obvious disdain. He turned away from Sueldan, pacing to the back of his cell.

Lord Hiroise continued to examine Sueldan. "Are you offering to be my—servant?"

"Slave." Sueldan cringed, the word a curse as horrible as blasphemy. "I'd rather be in bondage with my family than free without them."

Hiroise's brows knitted. He turned his head toward Palius, who nodded once, then shrugged. Hiroise faced Sueldan again, his expression still bewildered. "I'll . . . um . . . consider your . . . um . . . offer." Shaking his head, he gestured for his companions to leave. The guard edged toward the door, pulling the huge ring of keys from his belt.

Sueldan crouched, his wounds throbbing, his head pounding. He closed his eyes.

The door swung open. He heard the four men shuffle out, then the door clanged shut again. The lock clicked. Footsteps receded down the corridor. More distantly, the huge ironbound door thudded open, then crashed closed. Finally, silence returned to Callos' prison. Nursing his wounds, Sueldan lowered himself to the floor and sought solace in the quiet darkness. He escaped into memories of Lathary's prison, where no one but his own hard labor had harmed him physically.

Dallan's voice shattered the image. "Sueldan?"

Sueldan opened his eyes. "Yes."

"Are you . . . bad?"

"Not too bad." Sueldan downplayed his injuries. "I'll be all right."

"Good," Dallan said. "Then I feel much better telling you this: You, Sueldan, are a complete and utter idiot!"

"Dallan." Sueldan sucked in a deep breath, forcing himself to a disheartened calm. "I'm inclined to agree."

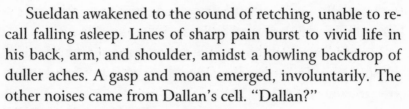

Sueldan awakened to the sound of retching, unable to recall falling asleep. Lines of sharp pain burst to vivid life in his back, arm, and shoulder, amidst a howling backdrop of duller aches. A gasp and moan emerged, involuntarily. The other noises came from Dallan's cell. "Dallan?"

The only response was more heaving.

"Dallan?" Sueldan rose stiffly, hurting. "Are you . . . ?" He panted through pain. "Are you all right?"

Dallan made a strangled noise. A thud followed.

"Dallan?" Sueldan crowded to the nearest corner of his cage, gaining a slightly larger view of his companion's cell. A puddle of scarlet-streaked goo trickled toward the front of the cell. Dallan sprawled partially in it, his eyes closed, his fingers limp.

"Dallan!" Sueldan could not believe he had slept through whatever had harmed the guard. "Dallan!" Realizing he would get no answer, he shouted wildly. "Help! Someone come help! We need help!" For several moments, Sueldan continued screaming while Dallan lay frighteningly still. The futility of his action gradually dawned on him. He lowered himself to the floor, his own aches catching up to him again. His back throbbing, he clutched the bars. The rusty metal bit into his cheek, its cold a welcome distraction from the pain of heart and body. *Please don't be dead. Please don't be dead.* The words became a mantra.

It seemed like hours before the distant door creaked open and unintelligible voices reached Sueldan. Releasing metal that had warmed to his touch, he stood. "Help, please. Help my friend."

The door banged shut. The click of its locking echoed. Then, footsteps thumped toward Sueldan, seeming shufflingly slow. The four familiar Callosians finally appeared, dressed nearly the same as the day before.

Too worried about Dallan to fear his captors, Sueldan thrust a wild gesture toward his companion's cell. "He's hurt. Or sick." *Maybe dead.* "Please, help him. Please."

Lord Hiroise, Palius, and the guard hurried past Sueldan to peer into Dallan's cell. Only the torturer tarried long enough to turn Sueldan a dark and chilling sneer.

Sueldan retreated, suddenly cold to the marrow. "Please," he whispered. The pain of his wounds deepened.

With a visceral chuckle, the torturer joined his fellows. All four stared at Dallan. The lord spoke first. "What do you think happened?"

Palius shook his head.

The torturer spoke in a rumbling bass. "Vomiting blood? Poisoned himself. Keep us from finding out something."

Hiroise stroked his chin, frown deepening incrementally. "Working for someone." He slammed a hand against the bars. "Damn. Should have started with this one."

Sueldan rubbed his hands together, dislodging jagged crumbs of rust. His thoughts raced amid the background chorus of his wounds. Pieces fell together: Dallan's secretiveness, his incomplete planning, his silence about his sister, his insistence that no one know their country of origin. Clearly, he did have an agenda he had refused to discuss with his companions. *Gods. What if he is dead?* The thought knifed ice through Sueldan's spine.

"Did his chest move?" Hiroise said suddenly. "I think I saw his chest move. If we can get to him before he dies—"

The Callosians' scrutiny grew more intense. The guardsman shifted position. Clutching the ring, he stabbed a key into the lock. It clicked open.

Sueldan heard a scrape. Suddenly, the door exploded open, slamming Hiroise and the torturer backward. Abruptly pinned between door and bars, the guardsman dropped to his knees. Hair plastered with blood and vomit, Dallan sprang into the corridor. He and the other guardsman reached for the Callosian's sword simultaneously. Hand caught in his own key ring, the guard moved slower. Sueldan saw white bone jutting from the man's wrist, his fingers and arm striped red.

As awareness of his injury reached the Callosian guardsman's awareness, he crumbled. Dallan jerked the sword from its sheath and through the bars of the door. Palius ran, screaming, down the corridor. Hiroise and the torturer staggered to their feet. Ignoring the lord, Dallan lunged for the giant. The torturer scrambled, too slow. The sword pierced his neck, its tip appearing in the back. For an instant, he stared in horror. Then, his lids glided closed, and he collapsed to the floor. Planting a foot on the larger man's chest, Dallan wrenched the blade free.

Too concerned about Dallan's safety to pay attention to his lurching stomach, Sueldan jabbed a finger toward the distant door. "Dallan! Those two!"

Despite the battle, Dallan remained calm. Pushing the cell door back toward its closed position, he freed the pinned guardsman, who sank to the ground. Dallan seized the bloody key ring and raised it in triumph. "They won't get far without these." He tossed the ring toward Sueldan. It struck the floor an arm's length outside the cell, then skidded through the bars. "Get yourself out. And the others." He followed the path Palius and Hiroise had taken.

Wishing he had paid more attention to the proper key, Sueldan chose one at random and tried it in the lock. It failed, and he selected the next.

On the floor, the guardsman groaned.

Sueldan's heart pounded. He glanced toward the guard, concerned he might interfere. The Callosian dizzily struggled to sit, mangled wrist clutched in his other hand.

Come on. Sueldan tried the next key, then the next. Each failure fueled his desperation. He glanced at the guardsman again.

The Callosian still had not risen. His breaths came in ragged pants.

Sueldan winced as he poked another key into the lock. That injury put all of his to shame.

Dallan reappeared, a quaking Lord Hiroise pressed against him, the bloodied sword at his throat. Dallan glanced at Sueldan, still in his cell, then at the guardsman. "Get in." He inclined his head toward the cage he had vacated.

Eyes slitted with agony, the guard stumbled to obey. Without a fight, he entered the cell.

Sueldan frantically tried more keys.

Dallan slammed the door shut, then pulled to make certain it was secured. Still holding Hiroise, he turned toward Sueldan. "Don't you ever pay attention?" he said impatiently.

In no mood for belittling, Sueldan hissed. "Yes. Just not to the same things you do." He twisted savagely. This time, the lock gave. He shoved his door open.

"Hang onto that key," Dallan cautioned. All the cells use the same one, I think."

Sueldan clutched the metal so tightly, it bit into his palm. He rushed around the corner where he had seen the guardsmen take Con. He ran past several empty cells and one blocked by two sheets of wood nailed over the door. *Walled off her cell. Knew she was magic.* Recalling Dallan's words, Sueldan stopped suddenly and backpedaled to the boarded-over area. He slammed a fist on the wood three times.

A moment of silence followed, then frantic pounding from the opposite side answered him.

Rifkah. Sueldan glanced briefly toward the other cells for Con but saw no other occupants yet. Several of the cages remained beyond his direct sight. He jabbed the iron ring beneath one edge of the board that hid the keyhole and pried. The board yielded only slightly. Again Sueldan tugged, throwing his weight behind the effort. Wood cracked, then splintered. An irregular hole appeared, through which he could glimpse half of the keyhole. Seizing the spikes of wood, he peeled away a few more pieces. Bits of wood slivered into his fingers, but he managed to make way for the key. Opening the lock, he tugged open the heavy door to reveal Rifkah.

Matted with dirt, her ringlets appeared brown and flat. Sunken and dull, her blue eyes met his, and a light flickered through them. She dumped herself into his arms.

Though Rifkah's fingers dug into his wounds, Sueldan wrapped his arms around her. "It's all right. You're free now."

"Dallan," Rifkah whispered through broad, dry lips.

The guardsman responded from closer than Sueldan expected. "I'm here. Let's go."

"We need to find Con," Sueldan reminded.

Dallan looked askance at his prisoner.

Lord Hiroise licked his lips. "Second to the last cell on the left. You'll never get out of here."

Sueldan charged forward, ring clenched. He realized suddenly he had lost the right key again and cursed himself. If he hoped to save his family, he would have to become as wary as Con and as careful as Dallan. As he reached the indicated cell, he glanced inside it. A naked male body lay in the center, neck awkwardly askew, skin conspicuously pale. It was not Con. A filthy pile of cut raven locks lay beside the corpse.

The others arrived while Sueldan contemplated the scene. Dallan grunted, shaking his head. "Let's go."

Rifkah looked away, addressing Sueldan. "Where's the opening to the tunnels?"

"No." Dallan adjusted his grip on the lord. "They'll expect that and catch us as we leave. Or bury us to starve."

Sueldan shivered at the image.

Dallan started back the way they had come, nudging Hiroise along with his bandaged hand. "We're going right out the front. They won't expect that."

Sueldan followed, shocked. "They won't have to expect it. They'll see it."

Dallan did not bother to look behind him. "If this man wants to live, he'll assist us." He eased around Palius' corpse in the hallway.

Hiroise studied the truthseeker as they passed. "Just tell me what you need." He swiveled his head toward Rifkah, green eyes pleading. "And promise me my life for my cooperation."

Dallan came to a halt at the thick oak door that separated the dungeon from the mansion. "Sueldan, I believe you have the keys."

Sueldan darted forward, around Dallan and the Callosian prisoner.

"I promise," Rifkah said with sincerity. "So long as you get us out safely, I won't let him harm you."

Sueldan looked up in time to see Dallan scowl, clearly unhappy with Rifkah's words, though he did not contradict them. Even Hiroise had to realize that Rifkah could not likely stop Dallan should he choose to betray that vow.

Worried Dallan's motives and intentions might elude even his companions, Sueldan hunted for the proper key.

Escape from the mansion of Callos' brotherhood proved as easy as Dallan seemed to believe it would. At Hiroise's orders, the guards stepped aside and let them leave without challenge. The lord proved more resilient than Sueldan expected, calmly cooperative, soft-voiced yet commanding, and knowledgeable about the city. Apparently testing the Callosian, Dallan asked him to lead them to the docks, a destination they all knew. Hiroise did so without any attempt to delay or subterfuge.

Once outside the mansion, Dallan kept the sword sheathed; and Hiroise accompanied them with apparent willingness. He gave over his coin pouch without complaint, and Rifkah used some of the money to purchase food and waterskins. Camped away from the docks, at the river's edge, the companions bathed in turn and then settled for the night amid the drone of insects and the shrilling of frogs.

Only then, did Hiroise dare to ask, "Will you free me now? My wife and children . . . will worry." He glanced pointedly at Sueldan.

Sueldan winced at the sudden reminder of his own critical failure. Cool night air soothed wounds still wet from his bath, but his heart could not be comforted so easily.

"Not till we're on the boat," Dallan said gruffly.

Sueldan saw the wisdom of the guard's words. Otherwise, they would become trapped at the river's edge, at the mercy of Callos' forces. He steeled himself for the inevitable battle. "I'm not getting on that boat."

Dallan glared.

"I haven't accomplished what I came to do. My family is still trapped here. Slaves."

"Hush!" Dallan snapped, eyes dark with warning. "This isn't the time."

Sueldan struggled against the instinct to fight. He knew he should not reveal such plans in front of an enemy, yet he secretly hoped that Hiroise would empathize and assist. So far, he had proved a reasonable prisoner. "I'm not leaving without my wife and children. I can't let them spend another day in bondage."

"Sueldan!" Dallan drew his sword and whipped the blade through the air. Hiroise and Sueldan both recoiled. "Keep your mouth shut! You're acting more stupid than usual."

"I disagree." Rifkah finally spoke. "I think Callos might be willing to trade one of its lords for a few slaves."

Hiroise stiffened and opened his mouth to speak.

Before he could, a gravelly voice replied from nowhere. "Except for one little problem."

Dallan crouched. They all whirled toward the sound. A shadowy figure stood beyond the edge of the camp, partially outlined by the moon.

"Callos has no slavery."

Sueldan recognized the voice. "Con?"

The man glided closer, becoming more visible. Though dressed in his standard black, he little resembled the man who had accompanied them to Callos. His ebony locks barely reached his chin, streaked with runnels of gold he had not quite managed to fully wash away. His face looked inextricably different, and he moved without his usual fluid grace. "No slavery at all."

Lord Hiroise edged away from the newcomer. "I was about to say the same."

Dallan snorted, still studying Con. "Do you think they would brag about such a thing to the peasants?"

"There is no slavery in Callos," Con repeated emphatically.

Hiroise nodded.

Sueldan stared, frozen in place. He trusted Con's ability

to obtain information, yet he found himself impossibly mired in disbelief. If Callos had no slavery, his hope became meaningless. Everything he had done, every gathering of determination, every moment of courage and suffering became a desperate lie. "Gods," he whispered, trapped in that dark moment of nothingness before fortitude collapses into doomed helplessness.

Rifkah's arms encircled Sueldan, warm and comforting. She helped him to sit.

Apparently convinced of Con's identity, Dallan turned his attention back to the lord of Callos. "I don't believe it."

Sueldan's throat squeezed shut. "Linnry?" he forced out. "My children?"

"They're not here," Con said.

"Shut up!" Dallan seized Lord Hiroise by the hair, and his blade went to the Callosian's throat.

Con stepped toward the pair. "He didn't say it. I did." His hand went to his hilt. "Are you going to threaten *me*?"

Sueldan looked up to see Dallan glaring, red-cheeked, at the con man, still gripping the Callosian brother. The fist around his hilt blanched. In contrast, Con seemed a solid pillar of self-righteous calm.

Rifkah released Sueldan. "Dallan. Compose yourself."

Dallan's lips went as white as his hand. He turned his gaze to the fortune-teller. "You stay out of this," he growled.

An idea wiggled through the fog of despair hovering over Sueldan's thoughts. Not quite ready to give up, he said, "Rifkah, check him. Is he lying?"

Rifkah jerked her attention back to Sueldan. She opened her mouth, as if to reflexively deny having the ability to detect such a thing.

Sueldan gave his head a short sharp shake, disguising it as a toss of his hair.

Apparently cued by the expectation in Sueldan's look,

Rifkah smiled. "Of course." She placed her hands on Con. "Say it again."

Now Dallan's brow furrowed, though he did not ruin the deception. Con knew Rifkah's abilities, but Hiroise would not. Since he had had a truthseeker in his cabinet and knew Rifkah used magic, it seemed unlikely he would challenge the assertion.

Dutifully, Con said, "There's no slavery in Callos."

Rifkah nodded, acting satisfied. She turned to face Hiroise now. "Will you submit to a reading, too?"

The lord rolled his eyes to Dallan. Rifkah copied the gesture.

The sword retreated from Hiroise's throat, and Dallan released his hold. He did not move, however, as Rifkah came over to touch the lord. She closed her eyes.

"There's no slavery in Callos," Hiroise said.

Rifkah did not move. Certain she was reading him, Sueldan spoke to buy her more time. "None whatsoever? Lord Mannkorus?"

Hiroise swallowed. "Mannkorus has no slaves. To my knowledge, there's no slavery whatsoever anywhere in Callos." He qualified. "If there's an underground trade to countries that do allow it, I know nothing of it." He stared at Rifkah, awaiting confirmation she did not give him.

Instead, Rifkah glanced up at her subject. "Describe that wife and those children of yours." She stepped back.

"They're—" Hiroise started and stopped. "I—" He swallowed harder. "I'm not married. I made them up hoping you'd let me go. For them."

Rifkah smiled. "Truth," she said. "Lord Hiroise?"

"Yes," he replied carefully.

"You now realize this was an unfortunate . . . misunderstanding."

Sueldan held his breath.

"Yes." Hiroise did not hesitate.

"If I were to convince my companions to release you right now, would you assure us you won't . . . compound the mistake."

"Rifkah," Dallan warned. He lowered the sword but still did not sheath it.

This time, Hiroise took Rifkah's hands. He met her eyes. "If you let me go now, without hurting me, I'll see to it you're not pursued."

"Truth," Rifkah said. "And thank you."

"Rifkah," Dallan said again, in clear reminder. Surely, he believed she had taken the farce too far.

Sueldan trusted Rifkah's judgment implicitly. "Let him go," he said, as if he held the authority to command Dallan.

Con remained silent. His input might well have the opposite of its intended effect on Dallan in his current mood.

Dallan slammed his sword into his sheath. "Go," he said. "Go, before I change my mind."

Without a word, Lord Hiroise scrambled into the darkness and ran toward the mansion.

Sueldan expected Con to follow, but the dark man simply addressed Rifkah. "You did read his future, I presume."

"There'll be no pursuit," Rifkah confirmed. "But if we had held him, his guardsmen would have come after us. We did the right thing."

Sueldan suspected they were already being sought. Assuming Hiroise kept his word, he would end that hunt. "Thank you." He did not know where to go from there. If Callos did not hold his family, anyone might. "Rifkah, would you read my future again?"

"Tomorrow," Rifkah promised.

The thought of waiting any longer than necessary pained, but Sueldan knew she had to rest. They all needed sleep. "Thank you," he repeated.

"We're going to have to move the camp," Dallan announced.

"Not necessary," Rifkah said with a yawn. She curled up on the ground.

"I'll take first watch," Con said, his features lapsing back into their familiar formation, his stance returning to normal.

"Great," Dallan said with obvious sarcasm. "That'll reassure me."

Sueldan found a position near Rifkah, seeking solace in her presence and her future words. Despite the pain in body and soul, he managed to find sleep.

Chapter 12

A SHAKE of her shoulder awakened Rifkah. She opened her eyes to a dark blanket of sky interrupted by a wash of moon and stars. Insects shrilled a constant song, pierced by a chaotic harmony of frogs. Dallan crouched at her side.

Rifkah sat up. "My watch?" she mouthed silently.

Dallan shook his head and jerked a thumb away from the river. He rose.

Rifkah looked at their quietly sleeping companions, then at Dallan's retreating back. She followed him carefully through a broad patch of enclosing water weeds. There, he stopped and motioned for her to sit on a log.

Confused, Rifkah obeyed, and the guardsman sat beside her.

Despite exhaustion, desire stirred through Rifkah. She wanted to lay her head against his firm chest, to use his warmth as a barrier against the night chill, to feel his fingers caress her hair. Instead, she yawned and stared expectantly.

"Rifkah," Dallan said with a softness that had not characterized his voice since their capture. Alone in the tunnels, she now remembered, he had called her beautiful, had gazed over her with the thoroughly biased tenderness of a lover. He had seemed close to admitting he shared her feelings for him. "Are we really safe?"

Rifkah studied the brown and flaxen highlights the moon struck in Dallan's otherwise coal-black hair. "You of all people should know: there's no such thing as 'safe.' "

Dallan looked stricken.

"But Callos won't pursue us."

Some of the discomfort drained from Dallan's features. "You're certain?"

"I'm certain." Rifkah yawned again. "I read him completely, future and past. Apparently, he believed I'm a truth-seeker." She added forcefully, exhaustion receding. "Clever idea Sueldan had. *You should tell him that.*"

Dallan's brow furrowed. "Tell who what?"

"Sueldan. You should compliment his quick thinking. It would mean a lot to him."

"You think so?"

It seemed obvious to Rifkah. "He looks up to you. And you've been pretty hard on him lately. Exactly how many times did you call him an idiot?"

"But," Dallan stared, wrinkles seeming permanently stamped on his forehead. "But he's old enough to be my—"

"Older brother?" Rifkah inserted.

Dallan considered. "Yeah. But almost to be my father."

Rifkah gave Dallan a pursed lip look.

Dallan surrendered. "All right. Maybe not that much older. But definitely older than me. What's he looking up to me for?"

In no mood to catalog Dallan's virtues or Sueldan's faults, Rifkah shrugged. "He does, Dallan. The reason is immaterial. A little appreciation won't kill you."

Dallan winced. "No. Appreciation won't . . ."

Rifkah waited.

Dallan said nothing more. The buzz of water insects grew louder to fill the hush.

"Is that all you brought me here to ask?" Rifkah finally pressed.

Dallan sighed. "No." He caught one of Rifkah's hands between both of his, the fresh bandage smooth and cold compared to his uncovered, callused palm. "Rifkah, when we get back, do you think it's possible you might . . ." He trailed off again.

"I might what?"

Dallan studied their hands. "You might . . . stay. With me, I mean. Somewhere."

Oh, yes. Gods, please tell me this is a proposal. Rifkah squelched the thought, yielding to logic. "No," she forced herself to say.

Dallan dropped her hand and his gaze.

Rifkah returned her hand to her lap. It felt awkward there, as if she had never noticed she had hands before that moment.

"No?" Dallan repeated. "Oh."

Several more moments passed in silence.

Abruptly, the guard spoke again. "I just thought . . . I mean it seemed like you wanted . . ." He sighed deeply. "I really believed you felt the same way I do." He raised his head, his dark eyes soulful as they met hers. "I love you, Rifkah."

Rifkah wanted to cry, joy mixed desperately with sorrow. "I love you, too," she admitted.

Dallan sat still, stunned. "Then why . . . ? Then why . . . ?" He could not continue.

"Because you're hiding something from me."

Dallan blinked. "Huh?"

"You won't let me read your past. And Con is convinced you knew Callos had no slavery."

Dallan plucked bits of leaf from his britches. "How do you know what Con thinks? You can't read him." A hint of excitement tainted his sorrow. "Can you?"

"I can read him the same way you can." Rifkah blinked back moisture that filled her eyes, desperate not to reveal how difficult her refusal was on her as well as on him. Her weakness might give him an escape.

"So, because I want to keep my past to myself, you won't give me a chance?"

Dallan's choice to cling to his lie broke the last vestiges of his spell. Suddenly, Rifkah wanted nothing to do with him. "Good-bye, Dallan." She rose.

"Wait!" he said.

Rifkah started back toward the camp.

Dallan caught up to her in a stride. "Please, wait. What do you want from me?"

Rifkah stopped. "If you really loved me, you wouldn't hide things from me."

"I fought a war. What if I just want to shield you from the violence?"

Rifkah turned her head toward Dallan, not bothering to remind him he had once used her as a sword. "Is that what it is?"

Dallan hesitated. "What if . . ." He measured her reaction to every word. ". . . I did . . . something . . . horrible?"

Dallan had a point. Rifkah knew war could turn otherwise ordinary men shockingly vicious. She pondered the words. "If I really love you, nothing from your past can change that."

"What if it does?" Dallan looked genuinely worried.

It won't. Rifkah could not speak the platitude aloud. She could not know for certain. "Then we weren't meant to be together."

Dallan closed his eyes. "Can you at least promise not to tell anyone else?"

"No." The response surprised even Rifkah.

"No?"

"If keeping the secret might harm someone innocent, I don't want to have to choose between my honor and someone's life." Rifkah rubbed her hands together. "I'm sorry."

Dallan took Rifkah's arm and gently led her back to the log. He gestured for her to sit. As she did so, he joined her, wrapping strong arms around her.

Rifkah felt as if she melted against him, reveling in his warm solidness. She wondered if, after she heard him out, she would ever let him touch her again.

Apparently, Dallan wondered the same thing, because he held her for a long time before speaking. "Rifkah, Callos didn't take Sueldan's family."

That now being evident, Rifkah thought little of the revelation. Then realization dawned, and she asked the all-important question, "How long have you known?"

"From the beginning," Dallan admitted, releasing Rifkah. "And my sister died many years ago. Of illness."

Rifkah went rigid. "That's what you've been hiding?"

Dallan nodded, his expression filled with pain.

"So you've been lying to us all along."

Dallan shielded his eyes and nodded again. "I'm sorry."

Rifkah battled outrage, wanting to hit him, to scream. But she just sat in calm indignation. "Your lies nearly got us killed."

"I know," Dallan's voice became nearly inaudible. "Don't you think I know?"

Rifkah bit her lip, still struggling. "Why?"

"Why?" Dallan's head moved almost imperceptibly back and forth. "I did it for my country, at the behest of its own brotherhood. They charged me with inciting Tamison . . .

Sueldan . . . against Callos, seeing to it he arrived there safely, and killing as many lords as possible." Dallan stared into Rifkah's eyes, still reading her. "I'm a veteran. Callos was the enemy. I thought I was doing something . . . patriotic. Something noble."

"Go on," Rifkah said coldly.

"You and Con weren't supposed to be with him. I–I . . ."

"You what?" Rifkah had anticipated something wholly different, a murder or deception against someone of stature. Picking on a small and helpless man seemed beyond cruelty and, certainly, beyond the interests of a city with the size and power of Lathary.

"That's . . . all," Dallan said. "Do you hate me?"

Rifkah dodged the question. "Oh, there's more. Why did Lathary's brotherhood want Sueldan to kill Callosian lords? And where is his family?"

Dallan's fingers winched on the log, and bits of bark crumbled to the ground. "Rifkah, please. I've already said too much. My life—" He met her gaze again.

Is forfeit. Rifkah realized Lathary's brotherhood would kill Dallan for the lapse. She could not morally force him to continue.

Dallan examined Rifkah for a long time. Suddenly, his features set placidly. He closed his eyes, opened them slowly, then forced a lopsided grin. "I know it sounds bad. I don't deserve your forgiveness, let alone Sueldan's. But—"

Rifkah interrupted, not yet ready to consider exoneration. "What was the purpose of this . . . this stupid game?"

Dallan's shoulders rose, then fell heavily. "They didn't tell me. All I knew was he was a thief, caught in the very act of stealing. The brotherhood reprieved him from losing a hand only because they discovered he had certain qualities that made him just right for this mission." He shrugged again. "It seemed a small price to pay—perform an act for the good of Lathary in exchange for escaping deserved mutilation."

"And those qualities were?"

"I don't know for sure. I can guess: competence with and knowledge of underground work, an appearance that doesn't clearly tie him to Lathary—"

Con finished the sentence for Dallan. "—and a family to hold as hostages."

Startled, Rifkah let out a short shriek.

Dallan sprang to his feet. "Damn you to all-bladed hell! Con, this is a private conversation!"

Con pressed through the water weeds. "Best kind. Learn the most from those." He stopped a safe distance from the enraged guardsman.

"How much did you hear?" Dallan fairly growled, hands balled to fists at his side.

"Enough," Con replied, "to finally fully understand what's going on."

Dallan's breathing became fast and deep.

"I'm not going to report you, Dallan," Con assured him. "You wanted a detail from my past, I'll give you this much." He lowered his voice, as if revealing the world's darkest secret. "There's no love lost between me and Lathary's brotherhood."

Though Dallan had often groused about not trusting Con, the words did seem to pacify him. His fists unclenched, and his demeanor softened ever so slightly.

Rifkah zeroed in on the pertinent. "So Sueldan's family has been in Lathary all the time?"

Dallan continued to watch Con. "I don't know."

"You can count on it." Con rested a booted foot on the log where Rifkah still sat.

Relief flooded Rifkah, and she smiled. "So they're safe."

Con snorted. "Anything but."

The coldness of Con's tone made Rifkah's chest tighten. She and Dallan stared simultaneously. "What do you mean?" she asked.

Con rubbed his hands and glanced at the moon. "Let's put together the information we have." He lowered his gaze to Dallan, then Rifkah, in turn. "The brotherhood catches Sueldan stealing. Most likely food for his family."

Surprised by the accuracy of Con's guess, Rifkah rewarded it. "That's right! How did you know?"

Con pressed his hands to his lips. "Reading people. Like you, it's my strength."

It seemed an odd ability for one who displayed so little of his own motivations and emotions. Yet, Rifkah realized, it made sense. Con would tend to assume others could divine him as easily as he could them, so he would hide his thoughts and feelings.

Con continued, "They've probably known about the tombs for a long time, and we all know they have a long-standing feud with Callos. One day, a man who can negotiate tunnels, who can't be traced directly to them, who doesn't even know he's working for them, falls fully into their power. They show him 'mercy,' make him blitheringly angry with Callos' brotherhood, and loose him into the catacombs with instructions to kill."

The details finally came together for Rifkah as well. "So they just wanted to kill Callosian lords?"

Con shrugged. "Giving Sueldan more detailed instructions might have tied him to Lathary. And started another war that Lathary couldn't win."

"So Dallan's role . . ." Rifkah started.

". . . was mostly to get Sueldan here safely. I'm guessing he would help kill lords if the opportunity arose. They picked a family guild guard to throw Callos off track if Dallan got caught. He's clearly Latharyn, but they could deny a direct connection to the brotherhood."

Rifkah looked at Dallan, who shrugged sheepishly. "That's more, even, than I knew; but it sounds right."

One thing still did not fit for Rifkah. "So why did they keep Sueldan imprisoned for two years? What was the purpose?"

Con had an answer for that, too. "Let enough time pass to throw Callos off the scent? Training? They may have learned Sueldan was afraid of enclosed places and figured two years in confinement would overcome that. Or, they may have put him to work, honing his muscles, toughening his spirit. Maybe it was just a way to make him even more desperate for his family."

Rifkah felt her cheeks grow hot. The tactics of Lathary's brotherhood enraged her. "Or maybe all of those things."

Dallan stood helplessly silent. Clearly, he had not realized the vicious methods of those he had willingly served. "I . . . didn't know."

Rifkah rose, driven to action. "Sueldan's family? What's likely happened to them?"

Con's blistering and deadly composure slipped. He slouched to the log beside Rifkah. "My dear, it depends wholly on their use to the brotherhood. Once Sueldan has served his purpose, they'll likely kill the wife. The children, they may find . . . use . . . for."

Rifkah studied Con, understanding. She now believed she knew who had raised him.

Dallan lowered himself to one knee in front of Rifkah and took her hand. "Rifkah, what do I have to do to make this right?"

Rifkah stared into dark eyes desperate for forgiveness and haunted by guilt. The wind caught black strands of hair, pulling the lightest curls straight. His rugged features seemed lost. "We need to free Sueldan's family."

Though capture meant death for Dallan, he did not hesitate. "I'll do everything I can to assist him."

Con drew up his sinewy form and spoke the words that shocked Rifkah beyond anything she had ever heard. "I will, too."

The sun rose on a day thick with birdsong and blackflies. Sueldan stared at a blotch of light streaming through a gap in the foliage until his vision glazed. The conversation had started with Dallan explaining his cleverness in Callos' prison: forcing himself to vomit, then mixing it with blood from a deliberate reopening of his wound. Next had come praise for Sueldan's deception against Lord Hiroise. Dallan's subsequent early morning confession wiped the joy of the latter away, sitting like lead in Sueldan's mind, uncontemplated. The one man he had believed in, who had seemed motivated by a need as great as his own, whose trust he had so fully embraced, had betrayed him. The apology had seemed earnest, yet so once had the need to rescue his sister.

Beside Sueldan, Rifkah placed a small hand on his shoulder. The others had left them alone in the clearing to think. "I'm sorry."

Sueldan lowered his head. "Why? Are you going to sell me out, too?"

Rifkah made a quick movement Sueldan could not see. "I don't think so." She crouched in front of him. "But if I was planning to, do you think I would tell you?"

Startled, Sueldan looked at Rifkah. The dark blonde ringlets fell wildly around her soft, young face; and she grinned in obvious jest.

"The whole world's not against you, Sueldan, if that's what you think."

"No. Just my friends. And the lords of my country." Sueldan thought back on his life. "Oh, and chance. And my sister and brother-in-law."

Rifkah sighed, rocking backward. "I don't know if it'll make you feel any better, but I found nothing else worrisome in Dallan's past."

It didn't. "He let you read it?"

"Yes. And I found only honor and kindness. Even during the war. He's a good friend, Sueldan. And a strong ally."

The words had the opposite of their intended effect. "So, I'm the only one beneath his . . . honor and kindness."

"What can I say?" Rifkah shook her head, loosing another sigh. "He likes you, and he's genuinely sorry. He made a bad decision."

Irritation rose in Sueldan, a hot counterpoint to his despair. "We could have died for his bad decision. We still might. He lengthened my family's suffering. He—" Sueldan sputtered, blood warming. "Are you dismissing that as unimportant? Are you defending what he did? Are you belittling my misery, my children's anguish?"

Rifkah's smile grew.

Caught off guard by her apparent insensitivity, Sueldan lost his outrage. He sucked in a deep breath and turned away. Tears stung his eyes, then ran down his cheeks. He made no attempt to stop them.

Grass rustled, then Rifkah stood in front of him again. "Damn it, Sueldan. Chance doesn't know you love your family."

The words made no sense to Sueldan, but Rifkah's tone snapped him to attention. "Huh?"

"Circumstances aren't aware. They just happen. The

world doesn't know it's treating one person worse than another."

Rifkah's point denied every tenet of religion. "What
about the gods?"

"What about them?"

"They're aware."

Rifkah crouched to Sueldan's level. "A bit vain of you to
think the gods themselves have nothing better to do than
spend their time ruining your life."

Vain? There was a word Sueldan had never heard ascribed
to him before. He responded defensively, "I don't think I'm
worthy of any god's attention."

Rifkah threw up her hands. "Then we're back to chance.
And there's only one person capable of affecting your luck."

Sueldan managed a sheepish smile. "Me?"

"Sueldan, there's no reason for me to recheck your future.
I told you before that your determination can get you
through this. Excusing yourself as a victim of fate; feeling
sorry for yourself—those things will get you nowhere."

"You're right." Sueldan wallowed through self-pity, seeking the spark of fire that had brought him through Callos'
catacombs. "But won't a reading help us decide what to do
next?"

Rifkah's grin seemed more genuine now, no longer offensive. "Readings rarely change. They just give me a general
idea of what a person can expect."

Sueldan's brow furrowed as her explanation seemed to
contradict his experience. "But you were telling us whether
specific actions would likely go well. You saved Dallan from
a cave-in. You knew Callos would have magic and our mission there would end in disaster."

"Ah. So you were paying attention." Rifkah joined Sueldan on the log. "I get general long-term information for
everyone else. I told you I can't read myself, but that's not

wholly true." She added hastily, "I didn't lie; I just didn't see the need to wade through every detail of how my magic works. Basically, I can get near-future, short-term stuff on me. Inconsistently. Once you add me to the picture, things get terribly muddled. So long as you throw your lot with me . . ." She shrugged, then took his hand. "Sueldan, you're a good man. Competent at many things. Your real enemy isn't bad friends. It isn't chance. It's you."

Sueldan closed his eyes, thinking of all the mistakes he had made in his thirty-one years. "I know."

"But not for the reasons you think."

Sueldan opened one lid, brow raised. "Oh?"

"You think you're weak, luckless, and incompetent." Rifkah met the one available eye. "And you are."

Sueldan's other eye popped open. "And this is supposed to make me feel better?"

"Oh, I'm not trying to appease you," Rifkah admitted. "I'm trying to educate you. You're all of those things because that's what you believe. If you believed yourself strong and competent, like I do, you'd accomplish a lot more. Try going into something believing you'll succeed. If you fail, you're no worse off. But if you do succeed . . ." She left the point open to Sueldan's imagination.

"I went into the tunnels believing I *had* to succeed."

"And it was the most fulfilling failure you've ever lived," Rifkah said. "Wasn't it?"

"You mean aside from the whip wounds," Sueldan said facetiously.

"Yeah, aside from those."

Sueldan gave Rifkah's question serious consideration. "You might be right." He thought about his past and the things he had attempted. "Do you really think a person's mind-set makes that much difference?"

"I know it," Rifkah said firmly.

Sueldan did not feel so certain that he did, but he saw no reason not to try it. For the upcoming trials, he would need every advantage he could find or muster. "Please, get the others. By tonight, we'll have a plan that could . . ." He grinned. ". . . that *will* succeed."

Rifkah patted Sueldan's hand and rose. "Now that's the determination I want to hear." She hurried to get the others.

Less certain than he sounded, Sueldan stood and paced. And started thinking.

By the time Con and Dallan returned to the clearing, Sueldan had an idea. He waited only until they stepped within hearing range before blurting, "Dallan, if you succeeded at the mission the brotherhood gave you—"

Dallan cringed. "I didn't." He added abashedly, "Thank the gods."

Not wishing to deal with Dallan's shame any more than with his own, Sueldan shook off the comment. "But what if you had. If a few of Callos' lords died, along with their truthseeker and torturer. And me, too. And you didn't get caught."

Con stood in his usual thoughtful silence. Dallan's dark eyes held a gleam of distress, and he fidgeted. Beside him, Rifkah smiled encouragingly.

"Wouldn't Lathary's brotherhood owe you? I mean, wouldn't they be willing to give you a job at the mansion? Maybe one of trust?"

"Well," Dallan said. "I suppose. But I didn't—"

Sueldan interrupted when he'd heard enough. He looked at Con. "Do you think you could arrange it so word got back to Lathary?"

Con looked affronted. "You mean . . . a lie?"

Uncertain if Con were joking, Sueldan replied carefully, "I definitely don't mean for you to hurt anyone else. I just thought maybe you could play up the importance of the ones you and Dallan already killed and ascribe their deaths to me. Maybe Lathary's brotherhood could receive, um, evidence that Callos lost a lord or two. In a way they'd believe it." He added emphatically, "Even though it wouldn't be . . . exactly correct."

"So you want me to lie," Con asserted.

Sueldan could hardly deny it. "Yes."

Con shrugged. "I can handle that."

Rifkah continued to smile.

Clouds striped the sky like spilled ink, tainting the docks in a pall of gray. Dockhands scuttled over the planking, tossing crates and barrels to the deck. Dallan quibbled over the price of passage with the willowy captain, limited by the remaining coinage in Lord Hiroise's purse. Rifkah kept her attention toward the city, clearly worried about Con returning in time to join them. Cheered by the knowledge of a workable plan and his companions' easy acceptance of his leadership, Sueldan did not waste a thought on their competent and well-informed companion. Con would know the barge had arrived and when it would depart. He would come in time to join them.

Finally, Dallan rejoined his two friends, his expression as dire as the weather. Fear that the guardsman might have failed to buy them passage shook Sueldan's composure. They could walk, of course, but it would lose them an intolerable amount of time.

Dallan did not keep them in suspense. "Well, we've got

passage, but it cost us everything. And we're going to have to pitch in this time."

Relieved, Sueldan did not care. In fact, he hoped honest labor might keep his mind occupied enough to snuff the impatience that would make every moment drag. He sprang to the lower decking, near a pile of precariously stacked crates and a pair of young dockworkers. Without hesitation, he began tossing crates to the sailors.

For a moment, the workers stared at Sueldan. Then, they leaped to attention, quickening their pace to nearly match his. On the barge, the sailors scuttled, suddenly faced with a larger backlog on the deck than the dock.

Filled with confidence and purpose, the labor comfortably familiar, Sueldan wanted to dance. Instead, he broke into song, working to the tempo of its beat. The crates on the deck shrank to nothing. The dockworkers retreated for a rest and a drink. Not wanting to lose his rhythm, Sueldan sprang to the barge and helped the sailors haul the newly placed cargo to the hold.

Reveling in the exertion, Sueldan did not notice the dock-fore until the stranger stepped directly into his path. Sueldan looked up, sudden dread sapping his excitement. Panting and sweating, he looked into a fair-skinned face with delicate features and eyes like emeralds. "I–I'm sorry," he stammered out, uncertain what he had done wrong.

The dock-fore ignored the apology, his accent heavily Callosian. "Name's Athfin. You ever need a job, you look me up, hear?"

For a moment, Sueldan found himself utterly speechless.

Athfin continued to study Sueldan. "I asked if you hear me."

"Yes," Sueldan said quickly. "I hear. I'll let you know . . . if . . ." The words that followed seemed more like a perma-

nent and defining state of being, ". . . I find myself in need
of a job. Thank you."

Athfin nodded once. "Please see that you do. I need hard
workers." He glanced toward the docks, and staring laborers
suddenly hustled back to work. He stepped aside.

Unable to suppress a broad grin, Sueldan seized another
crate and fairly skipped toward the hold. The captain of the
river barge caught him there. A tall man, he towered over
Sueldan, his blond hair tangled by river winds. "Whatever
he offered you, I'll match it. Plus, you'd get a percentage of
the haul."

Sueldan set down the package, stunned. "Thank you," he
forced out. "I'll think about it."

"See that you do." Then the captain disappeared to handle preparations for launch.

Sueldan trotted up the gangway in a daze. For years, he
had doggedly pursued every occupation in Lathary. Now,
when he gave employment no thought at all, it seemed he
had become the object of desire for every unskilled labor
foreman in Callos. Apparently, guilds held less sway here
than back home. Or, perhaps, Rifkah was right. Whether or
not circumstances noticed a change in his attitude, potential
employers had.

Con arrived just in time for castoff, announcing the success of his mission but refusing to delineate details. Satisfied
with Sueldan's assistance with loading, the captain re-
quested no more work from them. They spent the river days
in their tent, discussing and refining strategy for the coming
confrontation. Con believed he could infiltrate the mansion,
too, separately from and in a different capacity than Dallan.
He distributed weapons, fresh clothing, and supplies that he
had procured in Callos. Sueldan and Rifkah would lay low
until contacted by Con. Based on what the guard and the
con man found, they would decide the specifics of the plan.

That night, Sueldan lay on a blanket for the first time since his arrest. Fresh and smelling of soap, it softened the deck like down, floating him toward sleep. Tired and stiff from more stalwart labor, his whip wounds calmed to a dull ache, he embraced the darkness that drifted tantalizingly close.

A thought intruded. *Tomorrow is Sutannis' birthday.* Suddenly wide awake, Sueldan realized his son would turn thirteen years old, an important date they could not celebrate together. He had now missed three of his eldest child's birthdays; the first had occurred shortly after his arrest. *I'll make it up to him. I'll make it up to all of them.* It seemed like a hopeless dream, but he clung to it. His mind shifted to his other charge. He wondered if the dog would remember him and how attached it had become to the dock-fore's daughter in Eirene. The animal had brought him through some of his worst times, snuggling and caring unconditionally when the rest of the world seemed to have abandoned him. The thought of losing it forever pained, yet the idea of snatching it from the arms of a child hurt at least as much.

Sueldan pulled Danara's doll from his pocket. Though tainted with his sweat, with even more dirt, it still retained a hint of her baby scent, real or imagined. His family felt closer than they had in years, and Sueldan found sleep.

Chapter 13

THREE days later, a score of workers met the barge at Eirene's dock, including the tow-headed, Crestonian dock-fore from whom they had bought their passage to Callos. True to Dallan's promise, Sueldan set to work hefting cargo. This time, despite his injured hand, the guardsman joined him, matching him crate for crate. Their friendly competition grew contagious, and soon the sailors and dockworkers nearly stumbled over one another to see who could haul the most.

Now that they had arrived, impatience became the stronger motivation for Sueldan. The quicker they finished, the faster they could be on their way to Lathary. He heaved another barrel to the planking and turned for more.

A blur of black and white caught the corner of Sueldan's vision. He barely managed to whirl back in time to catch the full force of a flying dog. It slammed into his chest, sprawling him to the deck. Its tail fluttered like a fan, and a hoary tongue filled Sueldan's face. It whined, backside swinging with its tail.

"Dog!" Sueldan laughed, clutching the soggy, furry body to him. It wriggled free immediately, prancing circles around him. It made a deep noise, part-whine and part-growl, a warning not to abandon it again, then surrendered to obvious joy once more.

Dallan paused to watch, still clutching a crate. "I think he remembers you."

The dog threw itself at Sueldan again, stealing his tenuous balance. Thrown flat on his back, Sueldan found himself smothered in dog kisses. "Help!" he sputtered.

Laughing, Dallan tossed his crate and headed for another. "What, and risk a gooey eye on my finger? You're on your own."

Sueldan managed to shove the dog off of him long enough to gain his feet. The animal continued to dance around him. Giving it one last pat, Sueldan hurried toward the hold to keep Dallan from getting too far ahead of him. The dog trotted eagerly at his side.

Sueldan kept pace with his muscular friend, leaving the dockworkers to clear up the cargo piled on the dock. "Tie," he declared as they both dropped their last package to the dock.

Dallan smiled. "Naw. Anyone who can keep up with me with a critter constantly underfoot deserves the win."

Sueldan did not argue. He had spent more than his share of time on his hands and knees, regathering dropped crates. "I just hope we weren't transporting crockery."

The two men sat on the planking, panting. Sweat trickled over every part of Sueldan, stinging his eyes and the last of the healing cuts from his beating. Finally calm, the dog lay beside him, its head on Sueldan's thigh. Dallan tied back his damp black curls with a rag. "Look, Sueldan. I really am sorry."

"I know," Sueldan replied, without thinking. A moment later, he realized that the bitterness he had harbored had disappeared. Without all they had suffered, he would not have stalwart and trustworthy companions now. He would have lacked the necessary assistance, the needed mind-set that would allow him to free his family. He would have been a different man: crushed, broken, utterly defeated. More likely, dead.

The dock-fore approached, handing each of them a mug of water.

Sueldan and Dallan gratefully accepted the offering. Each took a long draught of fresh, cool water before the dock-fore spoke, "If you ever need a job—"

Sueldan nearly spit out his water. He forced himself to swallow, though it stretched his throat like a solid ball. "Thank you, we'll consider it."

The dock-fore nodded. "My daughter looked real cute with that beast of yours, but she lost all interest after the first couple days. I'd charge you his upkeep, but it was worth the seven coppers to find out I shouldn't waste my money buying her a dog of her own."

Sueldan smiled, glad to have his companion back without having to drag it from the arms of a sobbing child. He patted its sodden head. It remained in place, tail thumping like a rope against the planking.

The dock-fore headed off, leaving Dallan and Sueldan alone once again. Suddenly, Sueldan realized he did not want his companion to speak. He had forgiven the guardsman for his mistake, and he no longer wished to discuss it. It would only make things more awkward between them.

Dallan drew breath.

Sueldan winced.

"There's Con." Dallan pointed.

Sueldan glanced in the indicated direction. Past the chaotic movements of the scurrying dockworkers and sailors dragging toward the common, he saw Con approaching.

Dallan stood.

Dumping the dog's head from his lap, Sueldan did the

same. He had barely lost the ache of his last wild spate of work and now had compounded it with another. Together, they headed toward the con man.

Con stopped in front of the docks, waiting for them to descend to him. Dallan spoke first. "You could have helped us, you know. Last I checked, your arms weren't broken." His tone suggested he could remedy that situation if Con did not give a sufficiently apologetic reply.

Con shrugged. "I was buying horses. Rifkah's with them." He flung a gesture toward Eirene's common. "I thought you'd want to get to Lathary as soon as possible."

Sueldan nodded vigorously, a thrill winding through his chest. Horses would shorten the trip from two and a half weeks to one.

Dallan scowled. "Why didn't you tell us you had money? We could have bought our way out of that labor."

Con's eyes widened slightly. "But you were having so much fun. I didn't want to intrude."

Dallan took a threatening step closer.

Instead of retreating, Con held out a hand with two coins balanced on the palm. "Here. Will this make it up to you?"

Dallan looked at the money, his scowl deepening. "You think you can buy my—" He broke off suddenly, and the corners of his mouth curled to neutral.

On tiptoe, Sueldan looked over his companion's broad shoulder. The coins seemed of standard size and shape, but they gleamed deep amber in the sunlight. *Gold?* Stepping around Dallan, Sueldan plucked one from Con's hand and studied it closer. "This . . . is . . . gold?" He now held more money between his thumb and first finger than he had handled in his lifetime. "Where? How?"

Con dumped the other coin into Dallan's hand. "Let's just say Callos' brotherhood wanted our new mission to go . . . well."

Dallan's brow knitted. "We don't have to—"

"No," Con interrupted. "You don't have to anything."

"Gold?" Dallan seemed unconvinced. He did not close his fingers around the coin, as if he worried it might taint him. "They expect us to kill someone."

"They claim they don't, and I didn't promise anything like that." Con glanced around cautiously. "Although people will likely die. If a lord gets in my way . . ." He shrugged. "Let's just say I believe my life the more valuable."

Emboldened, Sueldan nodded agreement. "Any member of my family is, too."

"All Callos hopes for is my interference with the program that produced me. Anything more is a bonus."

Dallan added nothing, but he did accept the coin.

Just knowing Callos held Lathary's brotherhood, not them personally, responsible for the break-in and killings was enough for Sueldan. The coin seemed like a frivolous dream.

"Let's go," Dallan said evenly.

The dog shoved Sueldan's hand with its nose, bringing back memories of frigid nights huddled against it, of hopelessness, hunger, and desperation. With a shiver, he wondered how long his luck would hold out.

Dallan broke from the rest of the party to make the journey to Lathary alone. Believing it possible that Lathary's forces would watch for Callosians trailing the guardsman, Con led Rifkah and Sueldan ahead. They would arrive first, find a hiding place in the city, and wait until Con contacted them. Dallan and Con would approach the brotherhood individually, with at least a few days separating their arrivals at the mansion.

Con took Rifkah and Sueldan through quiet woodlands and along muddy deer and livestock trails, avoiding the main roads. Rifkah remained mostly silent, pouncing on Con for information whenever he returned from one of his forays to check on Dallan. Sueldan brooded over details. Neither he nor Rifkah could risk being seen by any citizen of Lathary, yet he did not know the streets well enough to completely hide. They would need sustenance, baths, a place to keep their gear. Clearly, they needed an accomplice. Con would have to spend his time infiltrating the mansion, gaining the brotherhood's confidence, and locating Linnry and the children. Someone else would have to serve that purpose, and Sueldan did not like what seemed to be his only option.

Six days of riding and two on foot brought the three companions to Callos several hours past nightfall. Cloistered behind a copse of squat bushes with his dog and companions, Sueldan studied the sleeping city. A half-moon revealed the ragged outlines of cottages and shops. Occasional bright points of lantern light interrupted the gloom, lone workers finishing repairs or projects that could not wait until morning. Plumes of smoke from scattered hearth fires smeared the stars into streaky bars of light against blue-black sky. The weather had warmed in the month since they had left Lathary, and the active chimneys marked the homes of the very young, old, or sickly.

Sueldan located Rannoh's tavern amid the familiar dark shapes that defined the city of his birth. His time away seemed more like years. He was a different person, though still madly in love with his family; in his mind, the town had changed as well. *Sheldora is family, too.* Sueldan clenched his jaw. He pictured her as a child skipping around their parents' cottage, her dark hair floating in carefree streamers.

Sueldan remembered the day his family had slaughtered the small flock of chickens they had raised from hatchlings. He had helped hold the birds in place while his brother and father severed their necks. One had escaped his grip, charging headlessly around the yard just as four-year-old Sheldora frisked toward the nearest corner of the cottage. She had run, screaming in terror. Sueldan flinched in guilt at the memory. He had caught and calmed her, amid Uland's and Sutannis' gentle laughter. The blood on his hands and clothing only frightened her worse, and it took his mother most of the afternoon to soothe her.

Sueldan shook free of the memory, haunted by Sheldora's distress but warmed by his father's and brother's amusement. Few things had broken Uland's somber facade; but, he now realized, nearly all of those had come from Sutannis. At the time, Sueldan had found nothing funny about the incident, believing he had traumatized his sister for life. Now, he managed a lopsided smile. He could never remember his father laughing with him as he had with Sutannis, but at least Sueldan had given Uland something to laugh about.

With a sigh, Sueldan turned his thoughts back to the present. Sheldora would likely refuse him again, but at least she would not turn him in to the brotherhood. Maybe she would take pity on Rifkah's plight. He looked at Con, crouched beside him. "Can you handle a lock?"

Con's head swiveled to Sueldan. "You mean, can I make one?"

Sueldan blinked. Though Con betrayed no particular expression, he knew the con man was teasing him. "Yeah, that's right. I want to lock myself *out* of somewhere."

Con smiled, revealing herb-stained teeth. "Where you trying to get into?"

"Rannoh's."

"Ah. *Our* place. You think we're welcome there?"

I'm not welcome anywhere. Sueldan put aside the self-deprecating thought. It no longer suited him, especially since two
separate towns had vied for his employment.

Rifkah broke in before Sueldan could answer. "Of course
he's welcome there. It's his sister's place."

Con snorted.

Sueldan sighed. "If you read that from my past, then you
also know about our last . . . disagreement. Con's right. I'm
not welcome there."

"You'll never know unless you try." Rifkah's soft reason-
ing seemed irresistible.

Sueldan had already decided to do just that, so he took
little convincing. "That's why I need Con to handle a lock.
If we walk right in the front, people will see us. Possibly
guards. We need to sneak in the back, but it's kept locked."

Con rose to a crouch. "You know what's there?"

Sueldan nodded, the gesture lost in the darkness. "Storage room. I know my way around basically. Can you handle
it?"

"Of course." Con placed a hand on the dog's head, and it
sighed contentedly. "What do you plan to do with this?"

Sueldan followed Con's movement. "He's going with us."

Con shrugged. "It's your life." He disappeared into the
night.

Hurriedly, Sueldan followed, Rifkah and the dog trailing.
He did not find Con, so he headed directly for Rannoh's,
certain the con man had not gone far. Insects hummed
and shrilled in chaotic patterns, much softer than in the
woods or near the river. Small dark shapes with serrated
wings passed in front of the moon and stars at intervals, bats
swooping for insects. Otherwise, Sueldan and Rifkah met no
one on the short walk to the back of Rannoh's tavern. There,

Sueldan expected to meet Con, but the dark man never arrived.

The dog whined.

Sueldan hushed it with a warning touch. As the seconds stretched, anticipation turned to irritation, then worry. *Did Con get caught?* He started to pace.

Face lined with worry, Rifkah stepped up to the small wooden door, took the lock in her hand, and pulled. It opened easily in her grip. "It's not locked," she whispered.

Sueldan turned in mid-stride, shaking his head in amazement. *Con was already here and gone.* He marveled at the other man's efficiency. *Can't think of anyone I'd rather have on my side.* Aware they could not replace the padlock from the inside, he put it in his pocket. He gestured Rifkah to stand aside.

Rifkah obeyed, herding the dog in front of her.

Sueldan eased open the panel, eyes scanning the widening crack, listening intently. The hinges creaked only slightly, the sound just enough to stiffen every muscle. Lantern light seeped over crates, barrels, utensils, and foodstuffs, leaving many areas deeply shadowed. Sueldan saw no movement. Carefully, he eased inside, breath held. A breeze funneled in, cooling sweat he had not noticed until that moment. The tops of beets and celery swirled in the draft.

Now more concerned for someone outside seeing the open door, Sueldan waved Rifkah in. She scrambled through the opening, the dog trotting after her. Sueldan closed the door. He turned to find Rifkah huddled behind a crate and the dog headed down the storage room corridor toward the common room.

Unable to call the animal, Sueldan glided behind the crates and snapped his fingers. The dog stopped, looked back. In the corridor, something moved. Sueldan ducked down beside Rifkah.

For a few moments, Sueldan heard only the shuffle of footsteps on the planking. Then, Sheldora's voice reached him. "Oh, hello. Where did you come from?"

The dog sneezed and snuffled. His tail thumped against a wooden box or barrel, and his toenails clicked.

"This isn't a good place for a doggy." Sheldora's voice grew closer. "How did you get back here?" Her tone turned suspicious. "Did the children . . . ?" Her voice grew distant; apparently, she had turned.

Afraid to face Sheldora and Rannoh together, Sueldan crept out from behind the crate before she could call in her husband. As his sister started back down the corridor, Sueldan quickened his pace. The murmur of sound from the common room filled his ears, forcing him to move even faster. He vaulted over a small crate, dodged around a keg, and seized Sheldora's arm just above the elbow. His other hand gagged a scream. He pulled his sister against him, dragging her back into the shadows.

"I'm not going to hurt you. It's only me."

Sheldora whirled toward Sueldan. The sudden movement broke his hold. He scrambled for another, but she hurled herself into his arms.

Awkwardly, Sueldan turned his flailing into an embrace.

"Tamison." Muffled by his tunic, Sheldora's voice sounded breathy. "You're alive. You're here."

Stunned by his sister's welcome, Sueldan could only nod in mute agreement.

"They said you were dead. I thought—" Abruptly, Sheldora pulled free and studied Sueldan, a tear streaking her cheek. "It *is* you. It really is."

Self-consciously, Sueldan rubbed the damp spot Sheldora had left on his tunic. The dog whimpered, sitting beside Sueldan, looking from man to woman expectantly.

Uncertain what else to say, Sueldan patted the dog.

"Sheldora, I'd like you to meet my dog." He gestured toward the crates. "And my friend."

Rifkah stood carefully, inching from the darkness. "I'm Rifkah."

Sheldora looked from Sueldan to Rifkah and back. She plucked free a few errant curls clinging to her forehead. "So . . . Linnry . . . ?"

Sueldan took his sister's hand. "We think she's alive, Sheldora. We're going to rescue her. And the children. But we need your help."

The door between the storage corridor and the common room clicked closed. Rannoh's voice, though soft, sounded threatening. "What do you need this time, Tamison? More of my hard-earned money? My food?" He fairly hissed. "Why don't you just *steal* it?"

Sueldan swallowed, his newfound confidence stripped away in an instant. Suddenly, he wished he had gone anywhere else. Red-faced, he waited for one of the women to help him, but neither one spoke, leaving him to reply.

Rannoh stood with his back against the door, arms folded across his chest. He did not wait for an answer. "Just get out of here, you miserable scoundrel! Get out before I call the guards."

Lame horse. Flightless falcon. Time ran backward, and Sueldan succumbed to the familiar self-loathing. He turned and ran simultaneously, slamming into a crate full of onions. The edge battered his knees, jarring pain up his legs. He tumbled over the crate and slammed, shoulder first, into a barrel. Liquid sloshed. The barrel teetered, then crashed to the floor. A trickle of golden froth seeped through a crack. Sueldan found himself sprawled on the floor in a puddle. Bruised more in pride than body, he sat, splay-legged.

Rannoh made a wordless noise of irritation and headed

toward the mess. "One more thing you owe me for, you worthless, little—"

"Stop it, Rannoh," Sheldora said softly but with authority. "He's still my brother."

Sheldora's defense, though meager, was enough. Sueldan stood, head high, teeth gritted. He emphasized each word. "Don't . . . hurt . . . my . . . sister."

Rannoh stopped, blinking. Sheldora whirled toward Sueldan.

Too angry to consider the consequences, Sueldan glared directly into Rannoh's eyes. "If you ever *ever* threaten my sister again. If you ever lay a violent hand on her . . ." This time, he managed to complete the threat, not only to himself. ". . . I'll kill you."

Rannoh's face crinkled in clear confusion. "What in all-bladed hell are you talking about?"

"The last time I came to see her, Sheldora was *afraid* to talk to me. *Afraid,* Rannoh."

Rannoh rolled his eyes, tossing his hands in the air. "Of course she was afraid. The guards . . ." He placed a protective arm around Sheldora's shoulders.

Sheldora's eyes turned moist. "They said . . . they said . . . they'd ruin us if I treated you as anything more than another customer. They said they'd hurt us. I . . . wasn't supposed to tell Rannoh. Or you." She sobbed.

Rannoh wrapped Sheldora in his arms. "I love my wife. I would never do anything to hurt her."

Sueldan believed him. He grappled with the understanding of what he had just learned, and it infuriated him. He thrust his hands into his pockets. The left sank into the dirty bundle of rags that comprised Danara's doll. The other closed around Con's gold piece. Its cold touch revived his courage. "I didn't come for favors, Rannoh." It was not true, but Sueldan knew his brother-in-law would respond better to a request when he no longer felt owed. "I came to pay you."

Rannoh stroked Sheldora's hair and gently kissed her head. "Forget it, Tamison," he said, his tone weary, beaten. For the first time, Sueldan empathized with the frustration of a hardworking husband and father burdened with a destitute brother-in-law. "Use your handful of coppers to feed your—" He broke off, but not soon enough to keep from triggering aching memories of Linnry and the children. "—self." His gaze rolled to the dog. "And your pet." He glanced next at Rifkah, who stood in polite silence while the family worked out its problems.

"No," Sueldan said. He rolled the coin between his fingers and into his palm. "I'm a different man now. A man who pays all his debts." He hefted the barrel back into place, stepped around the crate that had tripped him, and offered the coin to Rannoh. "In full."

The barkeeper glanced at the coin around Sheldora. He gave it a second, longer look, then stared. "That's gold."

Sueldan swiveled his head toward Rifkah, who gave him an encouraging smile and a wink.

Rannoh continued to study the coin. "Where did a . . ." He caught himself. ". . . you get gold?" He shook his head, barely moving the coarse, wavy locks. "Never mind. I'm sure I don't want to know."

Sueldan said what he had to, "I earned it, Rannoh." It was not wholly true and, yet, in a way, it was. "I earned it."

Sheldora slipped free of her husband's grasp to look as well. She wiped tears from her eyes and smiled.

Cautiously, Rannoh plucked the coin from Sueldan's hand. "I owe you some change." He continued to study the coin. "Fifty silvers all right?"

"No," Sueldan said.

Rannoh closed his hand around the gold and jerked his

attention to Sueldan. It was a reasonable offer, and it surely seemed ungracious for Sueldan to refuse it.

He explained, "Keep it all. With whatever's extra, I'd like to buy lodgings for me and Rifkah."

Rannoh placed the coin in his pocket without other answer.

Sheldora cleared her throat. "Tamison, this isn't an inn. We really have no place . . ."

Sueldan forestalled with a hand. "Shel, I'm not asking for anything fancy. Just a place to hide until we free my family." He added hurriedly, "We can help you out. Rifkah could tend customers. She's excellent at reading people." He avoided mentioning her magic, uncertain how Rannoh would feel about it. "She could probably catch brawls *before* they started." He glanced at Rifkah. He should have asked prior to volunteering her.

Rifkah nodded encouragingly.

Sueldan continued, "I could clean after hours and organize back here while there's customers." He made a sweeping gesture to indicate the jumbled storeroom.

Sheldora focused on his more important words. "Free your family?"

"It's a very long story. I'll explain it in full after your customers leave."

Rannoh pursed his lips and ran a hand through his hair. "What about the guards?"

Sueldan looked more pointedly at Rifkah. The time had come for the person who could read the future to enter the discussion.

Rifkah obliged. "Any moment now, the brotherhood should be convinced he's dead. They won't be searching for him. So long as we're reasonably careful, they shouldn't cause any trouble."

All eyes went to Rannoh who lowered himself thoughtfully to a box. After a long, silent consideration, he spoke. "Let me hear your story, first. And your plans."

For the first time since childhood, Sueldan looked forward to detailing his vision of tomorrow.

Rannoh's and Sheldora's living quarters above the kitchen seemed palatial to a man who had gone from a crowded, broken-down hovel to prison to homelessness. Though they lacked the finery of the brotherhood's mansion, the furnishings demonstrated sturdy practicality. Doors separated sleeping quarters from the main room where Sueldan now stood, staring out the window at the bustling city below. A girl herded geese through the broad road directly beneath him. They seemed in no hurry, honking noisily and pausing to root beneath every scrap or pile of earth. Women wandered in and out of the shops, and men scrambled with burdens or tools. Sueldan envied them, longing to become a simple part of Lathary's daytime routine.

Three-year-old Latvah grabbed his uncle's foot, growling and pretending to bite.

Sueldan skittered aside, feigning terror. "Help! Help! I'm being devoured by a hungry bear!"

"I'm a lion," Latvah corrected in a rumbling animal voice. He threw back his head to reveal features strikingly similar to Sueldan's own. Hazel eyes lighter than either of his parents revealed the Carsean grandmother he had never met. His round cheeks and narrow nose most resembled his uncle's. He snarled loudly.

"Help!" Sueldan leaped to the tabletop. "I'm being eaten by a hungry *lion!*"

Twin sister Lira sprang to her uncle's rescue. "Back lion!

Back." She shoved Latvah, who turned his attention to her. He roared.

Lira ran, screaming and laughing simultaneously.

The dog barked.

Latvah lunged at the animal with another voice-straining roar.

Clearly confused, the dog held its ground. As the boy's face came suddenly into its space, the dog licked him twice.

"Ugh." Latvah sat on the floor, the fearless lion undone by dog slobber. He wiped his cheeks with the back of his hand, then turned his attention back to uncle and sister. Snarling viciously, he crawled onto the table and toward his uncle.

No longer menaced, Lira became the guardsman. "Uncle Harlowe, Mama and Papa don't let us play on the furniture."

Cowering at the edge of the table, Sueldan barely remembered to respond to his newest alias. Rannoh had insisted on it in case the twins mentioned him to anyone else, and it seemed a logical plan. For a few seconds he dodged this way and that to avoid the lion. Finally, in a grand display, he pretended to fall from the tabletop into a deep pit. Curled beneath the lip of the table, he remained silent for several moments.

"Uncle Harlowe?" Lira's pretty little voice sounded worried. "I said Mama and—"

Sueldan sprang up suddenly, and Lira retreated with a shriek. Latvah reared backward. On hands and knees, Sueldan approached Lira. "Then," he suggested, "we won't tell Mama and Papa." Snagging the girl, who closely resembled Rannoh, he tickled her.

Lira laughed, squirming.

Latvah jumped on Sueldan's back, growling and snarling.

Sueldan whirled, abandoning Lira to wrestle her brother to the ground.

Lira continued to giggle. "You're fun, Uncle Harlowe. Can you stay forever?"

The question struck something deep and painful. Sueldan rued the time he had missed with his own children, wished he could promise them and their cousins that he would never, ever go. But it would be a lie. If he survived challenging the brotherhood, he would surely have to leave Lathary. "Forever is a long time. Let's just enjoy the time we have."

Latvah shoved Sueldan's arm. The man flung himself over the boy's head, rolling. "Oh! You threw me." He lay on the ground while the twins scampered onto his chest and abdomen. Apparently, taking care of the children and the business simultaneously strained Sheldora's ability to do either. She had suggested that, once freed, Linnry might wish to watch the twins along with their own children, for pay. The idea thrilled Sueldan despite its impracticality. It seemed unfair that he would finally draw the families together, only to separate them. After just a week, he had fallen madly in love with his niece and nephew.

The door opened suddenly.

The twins looked up from their uncle, then abandoned him on the floor.

Sueldan propped himself on an elbow and twisted toward the door. He watched the children run to Rannoh, surprised to find himself slightly jealous, wishing himself the man whom his children preferred over anyone. He wondered if he would ever have that again.

Even the dog ran to Rannoh, swept in by the children's exuberance.

Rannoh hefted Latvah, placed him back on the floor, then lifted Lira and held her. He addressed Sueldan. "There's a man in the kitchen says he needs to talk to you. Rifkah claims he's all right." Rannoh's narrowed eyes suggested he disagreed, then they widened slowly in realization. "You know, I think he's that same damned con man who took my money." He pinned Sueldan with his gaze.

Sueldan neither denied nor confirmed the possibility. If Con had returned, it could only mean information about his family. Raising old antagonisms seemed pointless.

"Who took your money, Papa?" Latvah demanded.

Sueldan headed for the door, patting his nephew on the head as he passed. "Easy, Latvah. I don't think your papa needs any lions attacking his customers." Sueldan pushed past Rannoh and through the doorway. He charged down the stairs, desperately eager. The dog ran after him.

When he reached the door that opened onto the kitchen, Sueldan finally paused. It occurred to him that Con might have brought the worst of all possible news. For several moments, he stood, torn between excitement and stark terror. The dog stared at the door, as if it expected it to open of its own accord.

Rannoh joined Sueldan at the door, without the twins. He gave his brother-in-law a questioning look.

Sueldan drew in a deep breath and pushed open the panel. Rifkah perched on the hearth stones. On a nearby stool, Con sat with one foot resting on a dowel and the other on the floor. Scrubbed clean, dressed in a fresh, tailored shirt and britches, he looked barely recognizable. The ragged cut he had inflicted upon his hair in Callos' dungeon had grown just past his ears, now hacked meticulously straight. As always, his expression gave away nothing. A slight smile creased his lips, though whether a welcome for Sueldan or a tease for the barkeeper, he did not bother to guess. "What's the news?" Sueldan begged without greeting.

The dog squeezed past him to shove its nose in Rifkah's lap.

Con paused only an instant, but it seemed like hours to

Sueldan. "They're all alive. Your wife. Two daughters. Two sons."

Two sons. I have another son. Joy thrilled through Sueldan's chest, and he smiled stupidly. "Praise the gods." He drifted into the kitchen. Rannoh followed, closing the door.

Con gave pointed attention to the barkeep.

Lost in thoughts of his family, Sueldan took inordinately long to understand Con's concern. He followed the con man's gaze. "You can speak freely." Rannoh already knew his side of the story. He hoped the information Con added would help Rannoh to understand the brother-in-law he had seen only as a hopeless panhandler.

Con pursed his lips and fidgeted. Surely, he realized that Sueldan had the most to lose if he had chosen to trust wrongly. "As far as I can tell, they kept your wife alive to get the children to cooperate."

Sueldan listened with pounding heart, shaking his head slightly to indicate he did not understand.

Con's gaze slithered back to Rannoh. "If they do what their trainers want, they get to spend the night with her. If not, they go without."

Sueldan's cheeks flushed. The image of little Danara crying for her mother at night proved too much. He snuffed it, forcing himself to listen. "Trainers?"

But Con said nothing more. He rose and paced a step, caught himself, and shoved his hands in his pockets. Sueldan had never before seen him nervous. Apparently, the dog also noticed the strangeness. It whined.

Rannoh took the hint. He strode for the door to the common room. "Let me know if you're not going to get back to the twins tonight."

Barely managing to spare the attention, Sueldan waved agreement. Accustomed to spending time alone together, Latvah and Lira would do fine without an adult for a while.

When the barkeep passed out of earshot, Con relaxed visibly. "They're training your children as elite combat forces. Spies, as Dallan would say. Like they trained me."

Sueldan's heart hammered a slow cadence of consummate terror.

Apparently oblivious, Con continued, "I don't know how much longer Linnry's got. The main trainer's been arguing for years that your children will train better as orphans. My . . . actions . . . over the last few years may have turned the brotherhood against the idea, but my return's going to get them seriously thinking about it."

Sueldan swallowed hard.

"Look, you might as well know. Dallan wasn't the only one hired by the brotherhood to get you into Callos' mansion."

Focused on Linnry's danger, Sueldan accepted the confession easily.

"I didn't get detailed orders," Con explained. "Obtaining seemingly impossible facts is an integral part of my training. They just told me to make sure you accomplished your mission." He smiled wickedly. "Little do they know, that's exactly what I'm doing."

Sueldan understood that Con had attacked him in the alley for drug money. Their second meeting suddenly made less sense. "Wait a moment. When you cheated Rannoh and the others, when I rescued you from the guards." His eyes narrowed in suspicion. "You were never in any danger, were you?"

Con loosed a wordless sound deep in his throat. "The fewer people who know what I am, the better for the brotherhood. The guards wouldn't have pegged me for a minion, and the lords wouldn't have told them." He shook his head. "The guards may or may not have brutalized me. But once the brotherhood learned what I was doing and why, they'd have executed me for certain."

Discovering the heartlessness of the lords toward their own creation only made Sueldan more certain they would have to act swiftly. "My children. Do they . . . remember . . . me?"

Con leaned against the stool again. Rifkah's hands absently stroked the dog, dislodging fur, her attention fully captured by the con man. "I didn't talk to your family directly. Too risky. Don't want to broadcast what's coming and can't cast suspicion on me or Dallan. You may need us for later attempts if we have to abort the first. Even if you get your family out, it won't hurt to have friends working amidst enemies."

Rifkah stared, shook her head, then stared again. "You mean you might continue working for the brotherhood after this?"

A slight smile twisted Con's lips. "Like I said, there's advantages. Maybe to me, too. At least, I'll know what vicious little schemes they're planning, and maybe I can spare someone's else's child."

Rifkah's grin lit her entire face, a spectacular contrast to Con's spare expression. "Con. You're turning into a regular hero."

Con's smile wilted. "I'm no hero." His tone implied offense. "This is personal."

Sueldan steered the conversation back to his family. "But all my children are fine, right?"

Con's head swiveled toward Sueldan. "Yeah, I guess. I've met the oldest, the boy."

"Sutannis?"

"Right. He's getting pretty serious about his training. Seems to like it, though he's not built for becoming great at it."

A chill spiraled through Sueldan. "Sutannis *likes* it."

Con shook back his hair. "It's exciting stuff for a young man who hasn't yet figured out he can die."

Eager for more, Sueldan pressed. "What about the girls?"

Con tapped his foot against the rung. "Haven't worked directly with them. From what I've heard, the older one—"

"Ellith," Sueldan said.

"Yeah, right. That one. They've worked at convincing her you abandoned them, worrying at her sense of trust. The younger one . . ." Con paused, this time anticipating Sueldan's interruption.

Flushing, Sueldan obliged. "Danara."

"They've been having her call all men 'Papa.' The little boy, too." Con looked at Sueldan expectantly.

Sueldan shrugged. "What's his name?"

"Piss." Con stood up, stretched. "I don't know. You want to add it to your alias?"

Sueldan stiffened, then stared as intently at Con as Rifkah had done. "How'd you know?"

Con waved Sueldan off with a wordless noise. "You're an easy read." He added, too casually, "We're going in tonight."

The words refused to register. Sueldan blinked. "What?" he finally said.

"You're rescuing your family. Tonight."

"Tonight?" Sueldan's breathing quickened to a wild pant. Dread mingled inextricably with excitement. He could scarcely wait to free them, but now that the moment had actually come, he felt weak and ill-prepared.

Con seemed to take no notice of Sueldan's discomfort. "Here's how it's going to work . . ."

Chapter 14

DIZZY from overbreathing, Sueldan forced himself to slow, even as his heart hammered faster than he could count against his ribs. Clouds obscured the moon and stars, smearing the night into an inky gray darkness that made the meager light seem ghostlike. The mansion of Lathary's brotherhood pressed a black shadow against the gloom, and the brick walls and wrought-iron gates appeared insurmountable. Beneath a pulsating chorus of shrieking insects rose the occasional voice or clink of mail, reminding Sueldan of the human obstacles he would need to surmount, dodge, or outwit. Even with Con's scouting and Dallan's assistance, the task seemed impossible.

As if reading Sueldan's thoughts, Rifkah leaned toward him and hissed in his ear, "Success."

"Success," Sueldan repeated in a spare whisper. He tried to direct his thoughts as she advised, but reality intruded. Positive ideas and need alone could not get him through this trial. He glanced about for Con, knowing he would not find the con man. As previously directed, Sueldan headed for the south entrance.

A massive, armored shape passed in front of the gates.

Sueldan froze, studying the figure in the darkness.

"Go," Rifkah murmured. "It's him."

Sueldan worried for his vision, wishing he could experience the intense heightening of senses he had heard others developed in urgent situations. Hesitantly, he approached the gate. The guardsman on the other side moved toward it simultaneously, racheting the leftmost panel open a crack. The sound merged rhythmically with the insect song, but the guardsman still cringed visibly.

Concerned about getting Dallan caught, Sueldan hurried to the opening. Only then, he recognized his friend, dressed in Latharyn colors dulled by the gloom. Sueldan slipped into the courtyard. Without a word, Dallan gently shut the gate and retreated. Somewhere nearby, Sueldan knew, Dallan's companion guard lay bound and gagged. At some point, Con would tie Dallan beside that man, making it appear as if someone had ambushed both sentries. A stray idea eased his tension for a moment; he wondered if Con might not enjoy bashing their burly, young friend over the head and binding him.

Sueldan moved swiftly toward the three-story mansion, oblivious to its multiple rooftop widow's walks and gables. Every time his foot made a noise against grass and stone, he cringed, certain guards could hear it in the town square. He wondered why it seemed the more he forced himself to remain quiet, the louder everything he did became. He quickened his pace. His skin crawled, feeling a million unseen eyes upon him. He anticipated the deadly sting of sword or arrow.

Con met Sueldan at the base of the mansion, shaking his head at the obvious clumsiness. Sueldan ignored the silent ridicule. He doubted he could have moved through piled pillows quietly enough for his companion's approval. Without a sound, Con unclipped his lightweight folding ladder from his belt, extended it, and placed it against the building. With minimal triangulating, it barely reached the roof. He gestured for Sueldan to climb.

Sueldan did so, every muscle feeling like a coiled spring. His skin twitched, still expecting death to come without warning. Yet he reached the rooftop without challenge, and Con touched down a few moments later. The con man slid his ladder carefully up behind them, folded it, and returned it to his belt. He crept toward a widow's walk.

Con had determined that the brotherhood gave Linnry essentially free run of the main mansion, keeping her from escaping with threats against the children and Sueldan. Con had explained where her room was and the place where Sutannis trained. The remaining layout of the mansion, he kept to himself for the moment.

Sueldan lowered himself gently to his hands and knees. Carefully, he crawled toward Con, glad that his companion chose to continue assisting. At some point, Sueldan knew, the con man would consider the gamble too risky and leave Sueldan to his own devices. Con had made that clear, and Sueldan had never argued about it. He did not expect his friends to die for his family.

Designed for women to watch for returning ships carrying their husbands and sons, the short widow's walks had sturdy rails at front and back. Crouched between those, Con hefted the central trapdoor that led into the mansion, his body blocking any muted starlight that might slip into the crack and warn anyone below. He returned the hatch and rocked thoughtfully back on his heels. Rising, he met Sueldan halfway to the walk. "Guards. Several awake."

Sueldan opened his mouth to reply, but Con shushed him with a raised finger and a warning look. For a long moment, the con man hunched in consideration. He shook his head. "Another day."

Sueldan slid to the rooftop, stunned silent. He could not

believe Con would surrender so easily. "Surely, there's a different way in."

"Surely. I'll scout it for another try."

Sueldan knew he should trust his companions. If Con believed they should wait, they should wait. Even Rifkah had seemed uncomfortable. Though she refused to admit it, Sueldan felt certain she had divined a tragedy that she hid behind a facade of confident desire. She had stated only that the outcome of this night seemed as good as any other. The last time Sueldan had continued against his companions' warnings, he had nearly gotten all of them killed. "All right," he finally managed. "But how did you miss that?"

Con remained silent too long. "Changed the setup. And different during the day," he explained briefly. "Miscalculated." He tapped his lip. "It happens."

"What about D?" Sueldan shortened the guardsman's name, still worried that countless eyes and ears scanned him from the darkness. The brotherhood would likely forgive the sentries for getting caught unaware when nothing got stolen or damaged, but he doubted those two would draw night gate duty for a long time.

"I know," Con whispered back. "I'm worried about that, too." Looking entirely unworried, he rose and peeked over the side of the roof. "Damn, so close. She's just right there." He pointed to a third-story window one floor directly beneath him.

Sueldan moved beside his companion and looked. Linen curtains fluttered in the night breeze. Beyond them, he imagined his wife curled on a pallet, his daughters snuggled beside her. Longing sparked, then flared into a bonfire of desire. He had come too close to give up now. "Could we climb down, then back up to her window?"

Con pulled Sueldan back. "Sure. How well do you tread water?"

"Huh?" This time, Sueldan lowered his gaze all the way to the ground. An algae-coated pond filled the area just below the window. "I can swim all right. You saw me in the cistern."

"Yeah," Con acknowledged. "But the cistern wasn't filled with critters."

Critters. Sueldan shivered. As a child, he had heard stories of the monsters who filled the brotherhood's moats and ponds. His hand slipped to the long knife at the belt he had constructed from folded strands of heavy rope.

Con stared, responding to Sueldan's gesture. "You're kidding."

Sueldan lowered himself to his bottom. "There aren't really monsters in there? Are there?"

"Depends on what you consider monsters. I saw a cat fall in a pond once. Fish chewed it up pretty bad." Con forced Sueldan to meet his eyes. "Anyway, my ladder won't reach that high mired in water or slanted beyond it."

Sueldan continued to study the area. "What about a straight climb down to the window from here?"

"Climbing's not my strength," Con reminded.

Sueldan huffed out a frustrated sigh. Born of desperation, an idea wriggled into his mind. "What if we used the ladder?"

Con's eyes narrowed, then returned gradually to normal. "If I tied it and steadied it, you might make it to the window." He did not sound confident. "You willing to take that risk?"

Sueldan did not hesitate. "Yes."

Con studied the area once more.

Sueldan joined him. He might survive a fall. If he landed in the pond, he might not even break a bone, but if the impact stole consciousness, he would likely drown. In either case, he would have to fend off the biting fish.

"It's your life." Con skittered up the rooftop, removing his rope belt as he moved. Within moments, he had the top of the ladder anchored to a gable. Flattening himself to the tiles, he clutched the ladder at the highest rung, pressing it flush to the wall. "Whenever you're ready."

Sueldan sucked in a deep breath. Edging cautiously around his companion, he placed weight on the second rung. It shifted slightly, and he rushed to place his other foot to balance the load.

Con grunted. "Hurry."

Wind slammed Sueldan's face. The ladder shifted more. Equilibrium lost, he felt himself falling. His hands winched instinctively tighter around the wood, clinging.

"Hurry," Con repeated between gritted teeth.

Sueldan obeyed, scurrying down the rungs as quickly as he could. The ladder lurched, twisting on itself.

Con made a soft but urgent noise. Sueldan leaped for the sill. His feet made contact as the ladder flopped over, dumping him. Feet braced on the ledge, momentum thrown backward, Sueldan scrabbled madly for a grip. His fingers brushed the gauzy fabric of the curtains, and he wound his hands desperately through them. Clinging, dangling over the water, he edged toward the window, praying for whatever held the curtains in place. As soon as possible, he switched his hold to the upper sill and rolled through the opening.

The curtains wrapped around Sueldan, blinding him but breaking his fall. He landed on something soft. A startled hiss of breath brushed his cheek. Realizing he had fallen partially on top of someone, he clawed for the other's face. If he or she screamed, it would destroy the last remnants of secrecy.

The curtains moved with Sueldan. Awkwardly, they dragged around the person's face, muffling sound but also making identification impossible. He glanced around the room, relieved to find the door barred. Aside from the sleeping pallet, he saw only a storage chest.

Sueldan's captive struggled wildly beneath him. A smaller figure wriggled between his left knee and abdomen. A sleepy child's voice emerged from the tangle of curtains, "Mama?"

Sueldan jerked his head toward a girl he barely recognized. Hacked short, her black locks feathered unevenly around a long face with delicate features and generous ears. "Ellith?" he asked hopefully, freezing.

The moment his attention was distracted, the person beneath him heaved. Balance lost, Sueldan tumbled to the floor, banging his shin painfully against the pallet, his elbow on the planks, and accompanied by a wash of straw ticking. He looked up to find the girl's face peering into his own. "Papa?" She jerked back. "Mama! Mama! Look! It's Papa. *Real* Papa."

The thump of his landing, the shouts of his daughter, every sound made Sueldan cringe. He hissed out a desperate shushing sound as the curtains fluttered to the floor beside him. Linnry crouched, staring at him from over the side of the pallet. Her eyes were recessed deeper than he remembered, and a few lines creased her face; she looked stunningly beautiful. "Linnry," he whispered, struggling to rise. His leg struck something on the floor.

Ellith pounced on the object. "Ulie! Ulie, wake up." She shook it wildly. "It's Papa. *Real* Papa."

A small figure sat up, yawning. Sparse, mousy locks lay, sleep-plastered, around a plump, red-cheeked face. "Papa?"

Still on the floor, Sueldan studied the young stranger who returned his stare through dark eyes. His face was toddler round with a thin upper lip and a straight, fine nose.

Ellith knelt beside the boy and placed an arm around him. She spoke slowly, carefully, as if to an infant. "Remember, Ulie, I told you about real Papa? I said he'd come get us and take us away from this place."

Linnry jerked her head toward the children, obviously surprised by the words. Sueldan tried to concentrate, putting all his understanding together. Surely "Ulie" was a shortened form of "Uland." Linnry clearly had no idea that Ellith had chosen to educate her brother about their father. Likely, the mother had never corrected the brotherhood's lies about him, afraid it might force them to go harder on the children or to kill her to keep her from interfering. "Tamison?" she asked with clear caution.

Sueldan grinned, joy thrilling through every part of him, even as he worried over losing everything he had just found. "It *is* me, honeymoth." He used a personal nickname, hoping to convince her. He could only guess what the brotherhood had told her about him, how many tricks and deceptions they had used against her and the children. She might well have believed him dead, or she might see this as a trap, a test of her trustworthiness or loyalty. He launched into a litany of personal facts then, things others might have discovered but likely not in such scope and volume.

Linnry let Sueldan speak only a few words before hurling herself into his arms. She felt good against him, healthier and heavier than he had managed to keep her. He reveled in the closeness of her.

A knock echoed against the thick door, followed by a gruff male voice. "Is everything all right in there?"

Sueldan's heart clutched. He gestured urgently for the children to remain silent.

Linnry hesitated a moment. "Huh?" she finally murmured loudly.

"Heard some noises in there," the same voice called through the panel. He knocked again. "Can I come in?"

Sueldan scrambled beneath the pallet.

"Come in?" Linnry said tiredly. "Oh. No. I don't think so. Not proper."

"The person below you said he heard a thump. I'd like to check it out."

Linnry yawned. "Oh. Little Uland's on the floor. Must have fallen off the bed again."

Silence fell. Sueldan held his breath.

Finally, the man spoke again. "All right. Let me know if you need anything."

"Good night," Linnry called back.

Uland wriggled under the pallet with Sueldan, who smiled. It would take time to win over his youngest child, which he could not spare now. He crawled out, careful not to bump the floor in the process. "Time to go," he whispered. Rising, he untied the rope belt. "Children, you must stay quiet. Not another word until you're safely beyond the mansion, all right?"

"Awright," Uland said, voice muffled by the pallet. Ellith simply nodded.

Sueldan tied the rope around Linnry's waist. "Where're Sutannis and Danara?"

Linnry watched her husband work. "I haven't seen Sutannis in months. They say he's not interested in seeing me. I think it's part of their horrible training." She turned Sueldan a pleading look that said far more. She worried for her eldest son's life.

Sueldan finished tying and tested the knot. "He's alive," he reassured her, based on information Con had gathered. "Spends his time on the second level. Not far from here, actually." He reached for Uland.

Linnry's expression softened. "They always have some excuse for keeping one of the younger ones from me at night. I think it's their way of making sure we don't escape, of keeping us under their full control."

Ellith tugged on Sueldan's tunic as he hefted Uland. He looked at his daughter.

Ellith stared back.

Sueldan handed the boy to his mother. "Do you have something to say, Ellith?"

The girl nodded broadly.

Only then, Sueldan remembered he had sworn her to silence. "Go ahead. You can speak."

"Danna's in the dark room. That's where we stay at night if we don't work hard enough at our lessons."

Sueldan glanced at Linnry, who shook her head, looking frantic. "We can't leave her."

A perfect image of Danara as a three year old filled Sueldan's mind, her soft black curls, her warm eyes, her baby giggles. "I won't leave her," he promised, taking Linnry by the hand. He sprang to the pallet. "I'm going to lower you out the window." He glanced outside. Starlight shimmered from the pond where night breezes riffled the surface. "I'll have to swing you past the water." He clambered down lightly, careful not to make a loud noise against the floorboards, and wound the rope around the wooden pallet for support. He kept the end in his hands. "I've got friends down there to help you." Finally, he looked at Linnry. "Can you hold on to Uland?"

"I–I think so," Linnry said, looking over Sueldan's setup. "Are you sure . . . ?"

A sense of déjà vu invaded Sueldan. The last time he had seen Linnry, she had expected him to bring home the dock pay they had so desperately needed. He had betrayed her trust. It would not happen again. Not ever. "I'm sure," he said, not needing to hear the rest of the question.

Linnry stepped onto the pallet, clutching Uland, with Sueldan's assistance. She leaned forward, studying the layout below.

"Ready?" Sueldan said.

Linnry nodded, though she looked anything but. Her body tensed, and she supported Uland with white-knuckled hands.

Sueldan helped wife and son to the sill, then retreated to the floor. He checked his supports and prepared for their weight. "Step out," he whispered.

After a moment's hesitation, Linnry obeyed.

The sudden change jerked Sueldan's arms. Teeth clenched, he held the two in place for several moments, dangling just outside the window. Slowly, he eased woman and boy downward. He gestured Ellith to climb onto the straw mattress, and she obeyed.

"Tell me," Sueldan gasped out, "when they're about a body's length above the water."

Ellith stuck her head through the opening. She gestured for Sueldan to go lower. He let more rope through his fingers as Ellith continued to gesture. Finally, she made a jerky motion.

Sueldan stopped. "There?"

Ellith mumbled an affirmative sound.

"All right. I want you to swing them, now. Side to side along the building. Can you do that?"

Ellith leaned out the window, grasped the rope in both hands, and moved. Sueldan could not see the result, but he could feel the racheting scrape of the rope against the sill.

After a few moments, Ellith's head poked back in the window. "There's two men out there, Papa. One's a guard, I think."

Better be Con and Dallan. To assume otherwise meant delivering his wife and child into danger. "Do what you can to help them," Sueldan instructed, gradually giving more rope.

"They've got them," Ellith announced. An instant later, the stress left the rope. Suddenly unopposed, Sueldan's momentum hurled him backward. He seized the pallet, steadying himself, then sprang to the straw and thrust his head out the window. He caught a vague image of two people the right size hurriedly ushering Linnry and Uland into the shadows.

Hand over hand, Sueldan hauled the rope back inside. "Now, where's this dark room?" He wound the rope around Ellith, shocked at how tall she had gotten, the first slight hint of a woman's curves beneath her sleeping gown.

The girl watched him work. "Go out the door. Turn right." She gazed thoughtfully at the ceiling. "Fifteen steps, turn left, ten steps, then down eleven steps . . ."

Sueldan interrupted. "Whoa. What's all this 'steps' this way and that? Can't you just describe the way?"

Ellith tested the knots with a surprisingly expert hand. "No, Papa. I've only come from it blindfolded."

Sueldan sighed at this new challenge. He had come so far. He would not leave without all of his children, could not let the brotherhood retaliate for the escape against Sutannis and Danara. "Right out the door," he repeated. "Ten steps—"

"Fifteen," Ellith corrected. "Turn left, then ten steps, down eleven stairs, left, through the room that smells like spices. Right and five paces. Another right through the door."

Sueldan groaned. He unwound his pulley/pallet system, certain he could support Ellith's weight without it. He would need to swing her and watch that she safely reached the ground. "Fifteen steps right, ten left, down eleven, through the room that smells like spices. Then . . ." His mind blanked, too worried for Ellith to continue. "Damn."

Ellith perched on the sill. "Right fifteen, left ten, down eleven, left, through the spice room, right five, right."

It seemed hopeless, but Sueldan showed none of his concern to Ellith. "I got it," he said. "What can you see from the dark room window?" He needed a target for his friends.

"Window?" Ellith put her hands on her hips. "Why do you think we call it the *dark* room?"

Sueldan considered a moment. Con might be able to figure out the safest escape from whatever location Ellith's directions took him. He had no hope of doing so himself. "When you get down there, tell the men I'll get back here with Danara as soon as I can."

"I will."

"Ready?"

"Ready." Without further warning, Ellith jumped.

Caught partially off guard, Sueldan tightened his grip on the rope. It burned through his hands, raw agony, but he dared not let go. He looked through the window. Ellith swung slightly, halfway to the water. More cautiously now, Sueldan lowered and swayed his daughter. Two shapes appeared as she drew closer, and he recognized them for certain now. *Thank the gods.* He swung her into Dallan's arms.

The guardsman swiftly untied the girl, and Sueldan reclaimed the rope. He reveled in his success only a moment, then paused at the door. Night would keep most of the mansion's occupants in bed, but guards would surely wander the corridors. With only a blind description to guide him and no knowledge of layout or dangers, Sueldan knew he would not have as easy a time rescuing Danara. He pressed an ear to the panel, listening. He heard only the pounding of his own heart, magnified by the thick wood of the door.

Any time's as good as another when you're totally ignorant. Sueldan realized he controlled nothing but the speed of the operation. He desperately wished he had Con with him, then more fervently appreciated that the squirrely con man was assisting his family instead. Raising the bar, Sueldan opened the door a crack, prepared to close it in an instant. Hearing nothing, he edged it open more. So far, his luck was holding.

He lowered the bar, slid into the corridor, and closed the door behind him.

The corridor stretched in both directions. Sueldan turned right and slunk without counting. Shortly, the area opened to rooms on left and right. Voices wafted from both. Sueldan froze. *Left ten steps. Can't go in there.* He pressed against the wall, throat filled with fear, heart wild. *Wait, not there. I haven't gone even fifteen little girl steps yet.* Steeling his courage, he sprinted past the openings.

A voice chased him. "Hey! Who was that?"

Several replies followed, all jumbled into indecipherable noise. Sueldan ran, hurling himself blindly around the next left. Cringing, prepared to dodge anything, he found himself in a room clearly designed for pottery. Intricately painted vases sat on stands and shelves. A wheel took up most of the center, with dried bits of gray clay clinging to its every part. He saw nothing living, but footsteps pounded at his back.

Dodging the wheel, Sueldan flew through the room and out the opposite door. A staircase opened ahead of him. *Down eleven.* Saving every second, Sueldan hurled himself over the left banister. He fell farther than he expected, landing hard. Dropping the weight from his ankles, he rolled.

"Intruder!" A man yelled from the top of the stairs. Boots pounded the steps. "Intruder!" A dozen voices took up the cry.

Regaining his feet, Sueldan skidded into a broad entertaining room. Pillowed couches lined both walls, with rose petals scattered across them. Between the couches, several doors interrupted the walls. Desperate, Sueldan grabbed a latch at random, jerked the door open, and hurled himself inside. He pulled the door closed behind him.

Sueldan found himself in a cramped storage room directly

facing a middle-aged Latharyn dressed in the uniform of the brotherhood's guard. For an instant, Sueldan stood, frozen with terror. *It's over.*

Gradually, other details registered. The man's eyes seemed glazed, he reeked of alcohol, and he lurched to unsteady legs.

Unsteady himself, his ankles throbbing, Sueldan drew his knife. He held no chance against the horde outside, but he might manage to handle this one man.

The guardsman mumbled something amid a blast of foul-smelling breath. Without a weapon, he lunged at Sueldan.

Sueldan retreated, jerking his blade back to rescue the guard from impaling himself. The irony shocked even Sueldan. *Am I attacking him or defending him?* In the end, it didn't matter. On his own, the guard collapsed into drunken oblivion. Worried for the thump of his landing, Sueldan caught him, lowering him to the floor.

The hinges squealed.

Sueldan dove beneath a shelf covered with spice bottles and flasks. A rush of air accompanied the opening of the door, and he could hear others slamming around them.

"Get up, Jorthan. There's an intruder."

"Napping on duty? Again? Lord Byrran—"

Jorthan moaned.

Sueldan pressed deeper into the recesses of the shelf, making himself as small as possible.

"No time for this," another said. "This way!"

The guard who had confronted Jorthan closed the door, and footsteps drummed through the entertaining room.

Sueldan sprang from his hiding place. He looked first at the senseless guardsman, knowing exactly what Con would do from their experience in Callos. Sueldan struggled to undress the guard, the body like dead weight, the limbs flopping forever into his way. Finally, the man lay naked. Unable to drag the heavy body, Sueldan covered it with a drop cloth, then pulled on the uniform. It fit reasonably well over his own clothing, and he tucked his hair under the cap. In a hallway lit only by torches, it should hide him well enough.

Sueldan pushed open the door to the empty couch room. Rose petals lay strewn around the room, and some of the doors stood ajar. He imagined either the maids perfumed the couches differently at other times or Ellith mistook the aroma of roses for spices; but he felt certain he had found the spice room. Quietly, he stalked to the door through which the guards had exited, across the room and to the right of the entry. *What's next?* Rhythm lost, Sueldan could not remember. Forcing himself calm, he listened to his memory, in Ellith's voice: *Five steps, then right.* Though still rapid, his heart rate felt more exhilarated than panicked. *Five steps to my baby girl.*

Now, nothing could hold Sueldan back. He glided through the exit into a bulbous corridor broken by many doors. Five of his own paces would bring him past the second door on the right. A child's steps might lead only to the first. As worried for opening a guard's or lady's bedroom door as confronting the returning sentries, he tripped the first latch. The door eased open soundlessly to reveal an empty bed, the covers thrown back, clothes scattered over simple furnishings. He pulled it shut and moved on to the next.

This door also came open quietly, revealing a tiny, dark interior. Torchlight from the corridor trickled over a bed where a small figure slept beneath a piled blanket.

Footsteps thumped toward Sueldan. Snatching a torch, he ducked into the room, hauling the door shut behind him. Then, worried for the sound of it slamming, he thrust his hand between door and lintel. The edge hammered his palm, and he loosed an involuntary hiss of pain. Carefully, he edged it shut with barely a click of the latch. He threw the bolt.

Only then, Sueldan dared to turn. Black hair tumbled over the blankets, the only visible feature of the child slumbering beneath. The bundle rose and fell in a regular cadence.

Anticipation banished all fear. Sueldan smiled as he knelt at the child's head, wedging the torch into a crack between the wooden pallet and the wall. The light played over a finely woven cover, sparking highlights through the silky hair. Sueldan brushed back the blanket. Danara's face had matured from its pudgy roundness to a short oval. Otherwise, it looked the same: large dark eyes, heart-shaped lips, and fine cheekbones. Love filled him at the image, and the urge to hold her became nearly irresistible. Instead, he shook her shoulder and whispered. "Danara."

The girl continued to sleep.

"Danara." Sueldan shook harder.

One sleepy eye fell open. Her breathing went erratic. She rolled to the other side, snuggling back into the pallet.

"Danara, it's Papa."

"Papa," Danara repeated tiredly. "Go away, please, Papa."

"Danara." Though still soft, Sueldan's voice turned urgent. "You have to get up."

Danara sat up, eyes bare slits. "Papa, please. Let me sleep."

Sueldan stared, shocked by the matter-of-fact manner in which she accepted his presence, how easily she believed his identity. *Does she even remember having a Papa?* Then, he recalled Con's explanation, that the brotherhood had trained his youngest two to call all men Papa. "No, Danara. It's me, your father. Your one and *only* Papa." He used Ellith's term. "*Real* Papa. Remember?"

Danara yawned. Dutifully, she held her eyes as wide as possible to examine him. "What do you want, Papa?"

I want you to remember. Sueldan wondered if it were even possible. She was only three when he went to prison. She had known him scarcely half her life. He glanced at the door. He would have plenty of time to reestablish their relationship once he got her safely from the mansion. "Come with me, Danara."

"Oh, no." Danara shook her head until the tangles flew. "I can't leave. I'm supposed to stay here."

Sueldan looked toward the door. "The plan's changed, sweetie. We have to leave now."

"No." Danara gripped the sides of the pallet. "I'm not allowed to go."

Sueldan fidgeted. He could throw her over his shoulders and run, but she would surely scream. They would never make it to the proper window. He wiped sweating palms on woolen pants that felt strange to his touch. Every second gave the mansion more time to mobilize, but it was time well-spent gaining cooperation from his daughter. *This can't be rushed.*

Sueldan removed the guardsman's cap, shaking his hair free. He reached through the uniform to his tunic, finding the doll crushed deep into his pocket. He worked it free, withdrew it, and dropped it beside Danara.

The girl looked at the floppy patchwork of dirt that barely resembled a doll. One of the scraps of brown linen that served as an eye had fallen off. The cracked button nose hung loose, but the thread smile remained. Danara studied it without a hint of recognition.

Sueldan sat on the edge of the pallet. Gently, he sang one of the lullabies he had used to get all three of the children to sleep while Linnry sewed ever more patches onto disintegrating clothing:

No crying, little baby;
Papa is here
To guard you from dangers,
And hold you so dear.

Hush, hush, my baby;
Sleep is your friend.
Soft on your pillow,
Where day and dreams blend.

Danara stared, brow furrowed. She clutched the doll, studying her father.

Sleep, little baby;
Safe through the night.
Your Papa will watch you
Until the first light.

Danara ended with Sueldan's last words of every night. "Good night, Sutannis. Sleep well, Ellith. See you in the morning, Danara." She smiled broadly. "Papa." Still holding the doll, she wrapped her arms around him. "Papa. I remember."

Sueldan returned the embrace, her small form comfortably warm against him. His mind told him he hugged his eldest daughter, but he did not care. He loved them all. Had them back—all except one. "We have to go," he whispered. "Quietly. We've gotten your mother out safely, along with Ellith and Uland. It's your turn."

This time, Danara hopped out of bed. "Let's go." She headed for the door.

Danara made it sound so simple. Sueldan raced her to the door, replacing his uniform cap as he moved. "Danara, I may have to lie to get us out. Can you play along?"

Danara nodded, reaching for the bar.

"Wait." Sueldan touched Danara's arm, then headed back to the bed. He arranged the covers into a rumpled heap that vaguely resembled a sleeping child and took the torch. Returning to Danara, he doused the flame, plunging them into utter darkness.

"Ready?" Sueldan whispered.

"Ready," Danara replied bravely.

Though Sueldan hated the so-called training she had endured, at least it seemed to have prepared her for escape. She did not question, and he doubted she would panic or reveal him either. Unbarring the door, he peeked into the corridor. Seeing no one, he inched out, catching Danara's arm and drawing her behind him.

"Wait," Danara said softly, reaching into his uniform pocket.

Sueldan watched his daughter, a frown spreading and concern driving him to action. "We don't have time—"

Danara hauled out a scrap of linen and held it over her eyes. "You won't look like a real guard without this."

Smart girl. Sueldan tied the blindfold in place. Despite the dangers they still had to maneuver, he enjoyed a warm flush of pride at his daughter's cleverness. "Come on."

Fighting the urge to flit through puddled shadows between the torches, Sueldan and Danara walked openly between the couches. They met no one else until the staircase. Sueldan stepped aside for a group of three guardsmen to pass.

As they reached the bottom, the one in the lead studied them. "Where're you going with her?" He inclined his head toward Danara.

Terror clutched Sueldan, but he forced himself to speak, trying to sound irritated and in control. "I'm following Lord Byrran's orders. Were your orders to interfere?"

Placed on the defensive, the other guard stammered. "I–I, no. No need to get snippy. We're hunting for the intruder."

Sueldan wished to make the encounter as short as possible without causing suspicions. "His lordship wanted the family watched together. In case that's what he's here for." Without further explanation, Sueldan headed up the stairs, certain the guards watched him from behind. He only hoped he had fooled them, at least for the next few moments.

Retracing his path proved easy for Sueldan, though the walk seemed endless. They did not run into any more guards. Carefully, Sueldan opened the door, shoved Danara through, and barred it. He ripped off the blindfold, and she pulled the doll from her pocket.

Throwing off the guard uniform, Sueldan unraveled the rope from his waist and tied it around Danara. As with El-lith, he lowered the girl from the window, swinging her alongside the building and above the water, praying the increased security would not hamper his companions. As Danara reached the ground, a lone figure appeared briefly, then disappeared as swiftly. The rope pulled, then went slack. Sueldan hauled it in, trying to decipher what he had seen. Gradually, his mind sorted Con from the dark shapes and shadows, though he did not feel certain whether he relied on real vision or wishful thought. Fully ready to send himself into the same danger as his family, he wrapped the rope around his waist, tied it tightly to the pallet, and dropped.

Air sang around Sueldan's ears. For a moment, his body could not reconcile the rope. He felt himself speeding toward the ground, then, abruptly, he jarred nearly to a stop. He swung over the moat, throwing his legs forward and back for momentum.

Con caught him. "Hurry. Guards everywhere. It's just you and me."

"Sutannis," Sueldan hissed.

"Leave him. We'll try another time."

Con worked at the knot. Sueldan's mind stuck on his eldest son, so like his sweet-tempered uncle. Sueldan had failed his brother; he would not lose his like-named son. He could not let the brotherhood take its revenge on the only remaining member of his family. Security seemed bad now, but it would only get worse in the future, once they realized his target. Rifkah had said he might not get every member of his family free, but she had also told him to think success; it would get him through things he would otherwise abandon or fail.

"Second floor, right?"

Con looked around, his eyes as flat and dark as always. "Two windows over." He pointed. "But you're not—"

"Get the others safe," Sueldan instructed. "And yourself." He wondered whether the increased security in the courtyard had forced Con to already club and tie Dallan, or if the guardsman was assisting Rifkah. "If I don't make it, take care of my family."

Clinging to the rope, Sueldan got it swaying wildly again.

Con's soft voice chased him. "You'd damn well better make it."

Ten times, Sueldan flew past the indicated window without managing to catch the sill. Focused, he did not know whether or not anyone saw him. In a strange, childishly magical way, he allowed himself to believe that, if he could not see the guards, they could not see him either. Though delusion, it soothed, and he caught the sill on the eleventh try.

One leg thrown over the ledge, the other dangling wildly, Sueldan hurled himself inside. He thumped to the floor and rolled, trying to muffle the sound. He came up in a crouch, only then allowing himself to assess the layout. Fully dressed, Sutannis stood in the room's center, his resemblance to his uncle the only thing that allowed his father to recognize him. He had grown taller than father or uncle, his ruddy cheeks still hairless and spotted with pimples. Remarkably short, his hair stood on end, pointy stubble. He stared.

Sueldan grinned. "Sutannis, it's me. Papa. Hurry. I'll get you out of here." He worked at the remaining knot.

Sutannis took several steps closer, saying nothing.

Sueldan finally got the last loop untied. He looked up, only to find Sutannis nearly on top of him. The boy's fist crashed into his face. "Intruder! Help! Help! He's in here."

Pain ground through Sueldan's nose, incapacitating him. He clamped his hands over it, unable to move, to speak.

Sutannis' booted foot slammed into Sueldan's stomach. Tossed backward, he staggered, banging his head against the wall. Half senseless with shock and pain, Sueldan slumped to the floor.

"Intruder!"

"Sutannis, stop yelling," Sueldan ordered. He clambered to his feet, fingers striped with blood, his nose raw agony. "It's your father. Tamison."

"I know who you are." The tone contained venom, and Sutannis snatched up a sword from a nightstand. It rasped from its sheath. "You're the hopeless bastard who damned us to poverty, then abandoned us with nothing."

The words hurt nearly as much as the blows. "That's not true. I—"

Sutannis swung. The sword whooshed through air, a powerful stroke that Sueldan partially dodged. He threw up an arm in defense. The deflection cost him a stinging slash across the forearm but saved him from much worse.

"Sutannis, please."

The door banged open, admitting several guardsmen who charged in with drawn swords.

Sueldan whirled and swore, backing toward the window

as the men closed the distance swiftly. Two swords hammered toward him at once. Sueldan retreated. His foot came down on something hard, and he stumbled over an object far larger than he expected. As he fell, the blades sailed over his head. The erratic motion of his fall rescued him from a third attack. Then he found himself tangled with Sutannis. Hissing, too close for sword work, the boy punched his father again.

Agony lanced through Sueldan's nose. He clutched it, staggering into a guardsman, who tumbled. A sea of swords swept toward Sueldan.

I'm going to die. Sueldan dove beneath one blade, ducked through two more, and hurled himself out the window.

Sueldan struck ground before he realized he was falling, pain shocking through his entire body. Without bothering to assess the damage, he ran, stumbling within two steps. A hand caught his arm, half-carrying, half-dragging him through the courtyard. Fighting oblivion, Sueldan trusted the other to lead him, passively following through a twisty route that brought them to an open gate. There, the first person handed him off to a second, who guided him into a horse-drawn wagon and buried him in hay.

Only then, did Sueldan surrender to unconsciousness.

Epilogue

SUELDAN awakened to a rush of pain that made him groan. Full sunlight poured into his eyes, blinding him. He rolled to his side, sparking agony through his left arm, his chest, his right leg, and his face. He whimpered. Even breathing hurt.

A gentle hand stroked Sueldan's cheek, and a damp cloth passed over his face.

"Rifkah," he croaked.

"Linnry," his wife corrected.

Linnry. The name, the voice, sounded like music.

Sueldan caught her hand, embracing it, wishing he had the strength to hold all of her. "I love you," he said. "I never ever stopped thinking of you."

Lightly, as if afraid of breaking him, Linnry kissed Sueldan's cheek. "I know. Your friends have been enlightening us. Me and the children, we're lucky to have you."

Sueldan rolled to face Linnry, bullying his way through the pain. The sun blazed into his eyes, brilliantly haloing Linnry's china doll cheeks, her fine black hair, and her huge dark eyes, features that would forever define beauty for him. "Do you really believe that?" He could not reconcile the desperately poor job he had done providing for his family with Linnry's words.

"I always have."

For the moment, Sueldan remained content to lose himself in Linnry's radiance, to bask in love and the triumph of her return. The many questions that assailed him retreated into a distant corner of his mind.

A bark cut through the quiet world Sueldan built around himself, based solely on the presence of his wife. A child's shout followed. Suddenly, Sueldan found his face full of tongue and fur. The pain in his nose increased fourfold. "Oww. Oww. Dog, back off."

"Goggy! Goggy! Goggy!" Uland shouted, hugging onto the animal's waggling rear end. "You goggy, Papa? *Like* goggy."

The dog whirled to engulf the child in kisses, knocking Uland into a giggling heap. A horse whinnied. Beyond it, Sueldan heard voices: Dallan's, Rifkah's, and Ellith's. He asked the necessary, "Are we safe?"

Con approached, then crouched at Sueldan's side. "Safe enough for the moment." He glanced at Linnry, who took the hint immediately.

"I'm going to go check on the girls. Anything you need?"

Sueldan shook his head. His stomach growled, but he felt awkward asking his wife to fetch him food after he had provided so miserably. There might be none available anyway.

The spell broken with Linnry's departure, Sueldan started in on his litany of questions. "Is everyone else all right?" He shielded his eyes with a hand, every movement painful.

Con shifted, blocking the sun. "You're the only one hurt, if that's what you mean."

"I'm . . . in a lot of pain," Sueldan admitted.

"You could have some of my—"

"No."

Con shrugged. "It's your suffering." He opened his pouch, placing a pinch of his herb beneath his tongue, and settled back to savor it. "As far as we can tell, you busted a couple ribs and your nose. We think your arms and legs are just bruised and cut up."

Sueldan suspected his left arm had broken, too. Either way, it would heal. The physical pain bothered him far less than the agony his heart had suffered over the last two years. And last night. He plied Con as he had not Linnry. "Is there . . . food?"

"Good food. Thanks to your brother-in-law."

Sueldan blinked in disbelief. "*My* brother-in-law?"

"Supplied the horse and wagon, too. Said it was 'change' for an overpayment. Know anything about that?"

Sueldan shook his head but answered in the affirmative. "Sure. And you do, too, Con."

"Yeah." Con rolled his tongue around his mouth, then swallowed. "Just so you know, he did a lot more than that. Turns out he was a veteran, too."

"Really?"

"Handled those guards like one."

One surprise after another. Sueldan winced. "So he's not safe in Lathary anymore either." The idea that Rannoh had surrendered his livelihood for him seemed ludicrous. His brother-in-law had loved that tavern.

"Still is." Con cinched his pouch. "I made sure no one who could have recognized him made it back to the brother-hood."

Sueldan did not request details, hating the idea that innocent men may have lost their lives for him, even if they were brotherhood loyals. "Help comes from the most unlikely places."

Con chuckled. "You said it right."

Sueldan sighed, closing his eyes. "So where do we go from here?"

Con stared off toward the camp noises. "Wherever you want. I'd suggest Callos. They owe you the same debt Lathary thought they owed Dallan."

"I've got a job there," Sueldan remembered.

"At least one. And you'll have company."

"You mean my family?"

"I mean Dallan and Rifkah. There's not the bias against magic in Callos. And Dallan could serve a brotherhood he trusts. Or a shopkeeper. Or he could work with you."

The words shocked Sueldan. "Go unskilled?"

"Skilled. Unskilled." Con threw up his hands. "There're no guilds in Callos."

"No guilds," Sueldan repeated. He looked up at the dog, a bead of saliva drooling off its tongue, its breathing joyful pants of dog breath. He suddenly realized the job he really wanted, that would truly make him happy: training dogs. He felt suddenly free. *Callos and freedom. Who'd have thought I'd wind up putting those two together.* He knew it would take a long time to fully win back the trust of his children, but he would enjoy every moment of the effort. Well-provided for, well-loved, they would surely come around. And thrive. A thought intervened, a terrible contrast to the happy future he could finally visualize for himself and his family. "Sutannis—"

"Attacked you. I know. Heard the guards. I'm sorry, Sueldan." Con hesitated, "Or is it Tamison again?"

The dog ran off to chase the children.

Sueldan considered. "Are all my children safe?"

"Depends on what you consider 'safe.'" Con smiled. "Three of them are with us."

Sueldan managed a joke of his own. "Well, *you*'re with *me*, so I guess they're safe enough." He could not help adding, "And Sutannis?"

"He's safe enough, too, I guess." Con ran a hand through his hair, its blackness complete. The sun sparked red, green, and blue but not a hint of brown in the strands. "If you can handle him turning out like . . ." He trailed off.

"You?"

"Yeah. Maybe."

"I guess I can . . ." Sueldan's thought collapsed into memory: a dark alley near the carriage house, a grimy hand across his mouth, the eyes of a killer. ". . . rescue him."

Con jerked his head to confront Sueldan directly. "You're kidding, right?"

Sueldan gave no reply.

Con dropped to his haunches. "Let me understand this. You're going to risk your life to rescue a young adult who doesn't want to be rescued?"

"Right."

"Alone."

"If . . . necessary." Sueldan gave Con a longing look.

Con's brows rose in increments. "You think I'm insane?"

Yes. Sueldan remained cool. "I think . . . you're up to the challenge."

"But you're missing the main point. Sutannis wants to be where he is, doing what he's doing."

Sueldan could not accept that. "No, he doesn't. He's just like me as a young teen. Just like his grandfather." *A minstrel.* Even after all those years, the image of the elder Uland singing still amused him. "The only thing he truly wants to do is aggravate his father."

"Why?"

For the first time in his life, Sueldan believed he understood. "He doesn't know it yet, but it's one way of proving I love him."

"And smashing your face in? Is that his way of proving he loves you?"

"Apparently."

Con shook his head. "I'll never understand families." He drummed his fingers on his leg. "All right. Let's say I decide to help. What do I get out of it?"

Sueldan smiled. "The same thing you've gotten out of all of this. The satisfaction of knowing you helped prevent more of you."

Con grunted.

"And, when we're finished with that, we'll get you free of your addiction."

Con's hands sank naturally to the pouch. "One success, and you think you're capable of miracles."

Sueldan eased himself to a sitting position, ignoring the aches that shot through so many parts of his body. The horse grazed near a cartful of hay and unburied foodstuffs. Rifkah, Dallan, Linnry, and Ellith chatted, while Danara and Uland played a wild game of fetch and chase with the dog. "Apparently, with the right friends, I am."